Additional Praise for Howard Norman's *The Haunting of L.*

"A tantalizing story of intrigue and adultery, made powerful by the subtle, vicious manipulations of husband and wife and the passive wariness of the narrator."

—*Portsmouth Herald*

"In a sense, *The Haunting of L.* offers a protracted debate about the existence of the soul. But here, too, Norman refuses to play by simple rules. . . . There is considerable suspense here, and great depth of feeling, but it's the sheer, melancholic oddity of the book that will haunt most readers to the very end."

—*The Atlantic Monthly*

"It is a parable writ with a delicate hand."

—*Los Angeles Times Book Review*

"Howard Norman's *The Haunting of L.* has the makings of pure, thrilling melodrama. But the book proves more nuanced than that, thanks to Norman's controlled use of language and his insight into personal obsession. . . . Throughout the book, Norman conveys a sense of impending dread. . . . The author brings the same sense of emotional and erotic complexity to his treatment of photography."

—*Art & Auction*

"This Gothic spellbinder . . . part thriller, part meditation on appearance and reality, fakery and art, the book is a very strange, entertaining read."

—*Book* magazine

"On the surface, *The Haunting of L.* is quick and light, pulling the reader into passages that are comic and erotic and emotionally moving at the same time."

—*The Boston Globe*

"Norman, author of *The Bird Artist* and *The Museum Guard*, both impeccable novels, returns to Nova Scotia . . . [*The Haunting of L.*] is indeed a page-turner."

—*Entertainment Weekly*

"A potent mix of eccentric characters, mixed moral motives, and love story . . . The progressive intrusion of the alien and repressed into the familiar—what Freud calls the 'uncanny'—provides the rich base of Norman's art, in which he is becoming a practitioner of uncommon subtlety."

—Publishers Weekly

"Elegant, brilliantly spare . . . Both utterly human and fantastic, Norman's thoughtful, nuanced closing chapters make The Haunting of L. the haunting of us. The shudders they send through us keep resonating. This final installment of his Halifax-based trilogy, which includes The Bird Artist (1994) and The Museum Guard (1998) confirms Norman the poet laureate of the Canadian Maritimes."

—St. Louis Post-Dispatch

"An engagingly original novel whose strange images, bleak settings, and quirky dialogue may bring E. Annie Proulx's The Shipping News to mind. But ultimately, The Haunting of L. is pure Howard Norman, whose fertile, offbeat imagination makes readers eager to see just what he'll think of next."

—The Virginian-Pilot

"[Howard] Norman's novels are mysterious, evocative, and utterly original in both their ability to transport the reader somewhere new and in the profound shared humanity."

—Pittsburgh Post-Gazette

# THE HAUNTING OF L.

## Also by Howard Norman

*The Northern Lights* (1987)

*Kiss in the Hotel Joseph Conrad* (1989)

*The Bird Artist* (1994)

*The Museum Guard* (1998)

# THE
# HAUNTING
# OF L.

*Howard Norman*

PICADOR

FARRAR, STRAUS AND GIROUX

NEW YORK

www.picadorusa.com

Picador ® is a U.S. registered trademark and is used by Farrar, Straus and Giroux under license from Pan Books Limited.

For information on Picador Reading Group Guides, as well as ordering, please contact the Trade Marketing department at St. Martin's Press.
Phone: 1-800-221-7945 extension 763
Fax: 212-677-7456
E-mail: trademarketing@stmartins.com

Parts of the book *Chronicles of the Photographs of Spiritual Beings* by Georgiana Houghton (Univ. of London Library, 1882), referred to as *The Unclad Spirit*, are directly quoted, while in other places the author's idiosyncratic language inspired invented ideas.

Library of Congress Cataloging-in-Publication Data

Norman, Howard A.
    The haunting of L. / Howard Norman.
        p. cm.
    ISBN 0-312-42166-4
    1. Triangles (Interpersonal relations)—Fiction. 2. Photographic assistants—Fiction. 3. Spirit photography—Fiction. 4. Photographers—Fiction. 5. Young men—Fiction. 6. Accidents—Fiction. 7. Manitoba—Fiction. I. Title.

PR9199.3.N564 H38 2002
813'.54—dc21                                    2001051120

First published in the United States by Farrar, Straus and Giroux

First Picador Edition: February 2003

10  9  8  7  6  5  4  3  2  1

*For Jane and Emma*
*For Stuart Dybek*

*This act of madness and despair.*
Still, it is a planned thing.
　　　　　　　—Joseph Conrad

# CONTENTS

View of My Employer's Wife   3

View of Kala Murie Stepping Out of Her Black Dress   24

View of Kala Murie Eating Wedding Cake   55

View of Kala Murie and Me Asleep Together   80

View of Kala Murie Cutting In on Ghosts   111

Esquimaux Souls Risen from Aeroplane Wreck   129

People, Aghast, Watching a Resuscitation   164

Portrait of a Dangerous Man   188

View of Kala Murie Drinking Chinese Coffee   201

The Verificationist David Harp   224

View of Kala Murie Advising Endless Prayer   246

View of Mrs. Sorrel Crying Out, "Merciful Lord—Mr.
    Harp's Been Killed!"   267

The Haunting of L.   298

View of Kala Murie Taking the Sea Air   321

# VIEW OF
# MY EMPLOYER'S WIFE

In the four-poster bed, my employer's wife, Kala Murie, lying beside me, the world seemed in perfect order. It was four o'clock in the morning, March 13, 1927. I almost drifted off to sleep. But then I felt a jolt of unease. This was natural to my character. It occurred to me that hidden deep inside my sense of the world in perfect order was the fear that the worst was on its way.

It was snowing. The room had light only from the coals in the fireplace and the streetlamp outside the window.

The world in perfect order. My room at least. I was living in room 28 of the Haliburton House Inn on Morris Street, Halifax, Nova Scotia. The *Herald* for March 12 carried the headline: TEMP. DROPS TO COLDEST IN 50 YEARS. There was a photograph of a man wearing a thick overcoat, face invisible under a knit cap, leaning into the terrible blizzard that took the city nearly a week to dig out from under. The caption of that particular photograph was *Postal Em-*

*ployee Dirk Macomb heads home—the right direction?* A little humor in the bleakness.

Also on page 1: the British ambassador to Canada would stay in Halifax until the weather cleared. The Shipping Page announced that a Danish steamer, the *Lifland*, after delivering sugar for the Woodside Refinery and lying in harbor for a week, was locked in ice and couldn't set out for Glasgow via London. Also on the Shipping Page: "The schooner *Annabel Cameron* was at first waterlogged but within a day icelogged, and the entire crew finally rescued by heroic dorymen navigating a barrage of needle ice and fog." I remember thinking that that sentence had a nice ring to it.

More important to my immediate situation, though, was the brief article on page 11: *Expert to Lecture on Spirit Photographs.* That expert was Kala Murie.

Kala and her husband—my employer, Vienna Linn—and I had arrived at the Haliburton House Inn on January 8. Our train journey had originated in Churchill, Manitoba, and had taken a total of nine days, the last leg of which, Winnipeg-Halifax, was all fits and starts. The blizzard hit mercilessly hard on that stretch. Half a dozen times the engineers had to stop the train and with the help of porters hack away at ice. "You get a thousand miles of snow on a roof," a porter said—he was clutching a cup of hot tea, his boots caked with frozen slush—"I've witnessed it cave that roof in."

Vienna and Kala at first occupied room 5 together in the main building. My room was number 28 in the annex, a building with a separate entrance next door. But by early March Kala had moved to room 20. As Kala put it, their marriage was "a loveless sham—always had been, I suppose." She could be quite blunt. To describe it in the simplest of terms, Vienna was a photographer and I was his assistant. He had persuaded the proprietor of the Haliburton House Inn, Mrs. Bettina Sorrel, to rent him use of one of the pantries directly off the kitchen as a darkroom. Ten dollars a month.

I had been away from Halifax since September 1926. When I returned, I never once walked past the house where my mother, aunt, and I lived together, at 127 Robie Street. It was as if the past would judge me. The house would judge me. That merely looking at it would somehow cause me to calibrate my life, and in all aspects of usefulness I would come up short.

Next to the bed in my room was a square oak table. On the table was a round doily, a heavy iron candleholder, a white candle in it. The housekeeper always put a new candle in, if need be. Otherwise, there were oil lamps set about. The armoire was nearly six feet in height, a few inches taller than I am. It was situated across from the bed in the left-hand corner of the room, next to a window overlooking Morris Street. For Halifax, Morris Street was steeply inclined. One late afternoon I looked out and saw a daredevil boy ice-skate down. The street was glazed in ice. The boy disappeared into the fog extending up from the harbor.

Also in room 28 was a thickly braided, oval rug stretched partly under the bed. And a writing desk, with a blotter, inkwell, drawer full of Haliburton House stationery.

On the evening of March 12 it had taken me half an hour to get the room's temperature at a comfortable level. That is, pleasing to Kala. We were talking all along. I finally took the

Bible from its drawer, propped the window open using the
upright Bible, and that did the trick. "Just enough cold air let
in," Kala said. "Thank you. Now the bedcovers have a purpose."

I was not a photographer. I didn't have much talent for
that, or ambition. But all the time I was inventing captions
and thinking hard about captions. On any given day—long
before I ever met Kala and Vienna—I might be, how to put
it, *preoccupied* by captions. The habit could some days nearly
wear me out; it was pitiable, like talking to myself in captions. So that, for instance, if I left my raincoat inside on a
rainy day, I would immediately think, *Man Who Forgot Raincoat Standing on Street*. Now and then I would startle myself.
One time I stepped up to the counter in an apothecary and
said, "Man with Headache Asking for Help." Stepping back a
few cautious paces, the pharmacist said, "Are you asking for
headache powder, son?" He looked as if he might call the
police at any moment. "Yes—yes," I finally said. "That's exactly what I meant."

After we'd made love on the night of March 12, I slipped
from the bed and stood by the window and watched Kala
sleep. At one point deep in the night, I held my arms outstretched, pointed my thumbs upward as if framing a scene
that I was about to photograph, and thought: *View of My
Employer's Wife*. Why I didn't think something more intimate, such as *View of Kala Murie Sleeping*, I don't know. She
slept on her stomach, her dark red hair fanned out on the
pillow, her face all but hidden. She had turned the bedclothes down to her knees. More than once she'd told me
that the only part of her that ever got cold was her feet and

legs up to her knees, and that it had been that way since childhood. "I always thought—when I was six or seven—that my knees were full of ice or something like that. Strange what a child will think. That my knees kept everything below them cold. I may have dreamt it, I don't remember." Though she kept a nightshirt close at hand, Kala slept with nothing on except for woolen fisherman's socks, sometimes two pairs. In fact, just before dinner on March 12 I'd accompanied her through the blizzard to Springs All-Purpose, a store at the bottom of Morris Street, where Kala purchased three new pairs of socks. I often took a walk with her. During one, she asked to see the house I'd lived in, and I quickly said, "It burnt down. It burnt to the ground." It was a lie that caused me such remorse that the following week I visited my mother's snow-covered grave in the Robie Street cemetery and apologized out loud.

The evening of March 12 had gone like this: Kala and I had returned from Springs All-Purpose at about five o'clock. It was already dark. We each set our boots by the fireplace in the sitting room, to the left of the front door, directly across the foyer from the dining room. Kala then went upstairs to her room. Then, at seven o'clock, I met Kala and Vienna for dinner. I don't know, really, how we managed to remain so civil, this little ritual of ours. Having dinner together, I mean. Yet we did maintain a certain civility—for a time. One night, while I was working side by side with Vienna in the darkroom, he said, "Despite what's happened between us three, I do hope you and Kala continue to join me for dinner. It's not so much to ask, is it, to let a man, for an hour or so, be absolutely certain of his wife's whereabouts?"

When Vienna asked that, I felt he was being so civil he was about to explode. He was capable of instilling such tension in a single sentence, I often felt that the first word of that sentence was a match lighting a fuse. That as long as he kept talking, we'd be all right. His silences, however, made me want to dive under the table.

Anyway, Mrs. Sorrel showed us to our usual windowside table. She was a tall, slightly stooped woman about sixty years of age, I would guess, with gray hair pinned up in circular braids. Always acting the gentleman, Vienna pulled Kala's chair out for her, waited until she sat down, then sat down himself. He always sat next to Kala. I sat directly across from Vienna. Odd how, even in the face of tremendous betrayal and under insidious restraint, his little rituals kept going. Holding out a chair, asking, "And how was your walk, dear?"

Once we were all seated, Mrs. Sorrel said, "I hope you enjoy your dinner, you three. Excellent lamb stew tonight. And, special treat, we have pearl onions. Mr. Linn, there was developing fluid on the kitchen floor again. Merely a footprint's worth, but still— I don't mind you working through the night most every night, it's just—" She cleared her throat. "Well then, *bon appétit*. My son Freddy's waiting tables as usual." She returned to the kitchen.

"She always surrounds her complaints with niceties," Kala said. "I admire Mrs. Sorrel's talent with people. I don't have that talent."

"It's an innkeep's talent," Vienna said. "The position requires it."

"Still, it seems to come naturally to her," Kala said. "Her chattiness. The way she looks you in the eye."

"Perhaps the way to put it," Vienna said, "is that your talent lies with more than one person at a time."

"What do you mean?" Kala said.

"Your lectures. Your ability to stand up and speak in front of an audience. Your *public* talent. I'm sure Mrs. Sorrel couldn't manage that."

We each of us ordered the stew. After Freddy, a sullen man about thirty years old, half dropped, half set our plates down, he went outside for a cigarette. In plain view of our table, he leaned against the wall, flicking ashes, staring at the snow. "According to the newspaper, these are some of the coldest nights of the century," Kala said. "And yet look at Freddy. He's out there with no hat or scarf or gloves. Glutton for punishment—that's his type, isn't it. That's the type Freddy is. Poor Mrs. Sorrel."

Kala took a bite of stew, looked at me, and said, "Peter, has Vienna told you his promising news?"

"What promising news?" I said.

"Quite promising," she said. "My husband's finally received a reply from his benefactor, Mr. Radin Heur, in London. Actually, it's from a man who works for Mr. Heur. A miracle any letter's gotten through in this weather. I simply can't believe the stinginess of it, Vienna, your not telling Peter the promising news." She looked directly at me again. "You see, Peter, Mr. Heur is quite interested in determining—yes or no—the *authenticity* of the photograph Vienna took of the airplane wreck up in Churchill. The one that by the grace of God I survived. The photograph of the *aftermath* of that plane wreck, I mean. I'm sure in your letter you sent Mr. Heur that you described the photograph beautifully, dear."

"Kala, I think that's quite enough," Vienna said.

"Mr. Heur intimated a large sum—*if* the photograph's verified as authentic," Kala said. "Isn't that how it was put in the letter?"

"Verified as authentic," Vienna said. "That's precisely how it was put."

"If there isn't some—*manipulation*," Kala said. "Some *technique* responsible for showing visible souls rising from those poor shattered Eskimo bodies." She lifted a piece of lamb with her fork, then let it drop again onto her plate. "And to think how narrowly I escaped. To think it might have been *my* soul rising, Vienna. How dreadful to think it. Really, I'm losing my appetite. Peter, I would bet Vienna has the letter in his pocket. Do you have it in your pocket, dear?"

"I happen to, yes," Vienna said.

"And since so much money is at stake—" Kala said.

"How much?" I said.

"My assistant here doesn't need to know business details," Vienna said.

"Oh, that's where you're mistaken," Kala said. "Because you risk Peter feeling left out." She looked at Vienna while speaking to me. "Peter, the letter mentioned the sum of twenty thousand dollars Canadian." She now reached across and took hold of Vienna's wrist, which she often did when about to defy him. "In the least, enough to get us out of debt to Mr. Heur, and then some."

"Better if we discuss this later," Vienna said, almost wistfully, as if it were already a lost cause. Then, guaranteeing to rile him even more, Kala said, "Peter, be a dear and rub my feet. They're killing me." She arranged herself slantwise, still close to the table, but with her legs now set across my lap. "Don't think anything of this, Vienna. It's only that Peter's at a more convenient angle."

I was massaging her foot with my left hand. "I thought you were left-handed," Vienna said in a measured voice. "Can you manage with my wife's feet and still use your fork properly?"

I picked up my fork with my right hand and took a bite, carrot in broth. "Actually, I'm ambidextrous," I said. "I thought you'd noticed."

"Well, I notice some things and don't others, apparently."

"Look there," Kala said. "Freddy's on to his next cigarette." But neither Vienna nor I looked at Freddy.

"Perhaps my wife's feet are aching less now, do you suppose?" Vienna said.

I had my hand along Kala's thigh, and she said, "And since it is a fake. Since *Esquimaux Souls Risen from Aeroplane Wreck* is a complete fraud. An excellent title, by the way, Peter. Brilliant. Vienna, you should be grateful. Especially nice touch, the antiquated use of the French *Esquimaux*." This turn in the conversation seemed to pique Kala's appetite; she took three quick bites of stew. "Anyway, since the photograph's a complete sham, it's all the more interesting— No. No, that's not the word. Perhaps *nerve-racking* better fits the situation. Nerve-racking is more to the point. It's all the more nerve-racking that Mr. Radin Heur is suggesting that he send his very own personal photographic expert—

what's his name again, dear, the man who actually wrote the letter?"

Vienna shifted in his chair, took a sip of wine; his entire countenance relaxed when he now saw me press the loaf of bread to the breadboard with one hand, pick up a knife and cut a slice of bread with the other. "Bread, anyone?" I said.

"Not for me, thank you," Kala said. She turned, sat stiffly facing Vienna. I glanced down and saw her slip her shoes on.

Vienna didn't reply about the bread. He reached into his woolen suit coat's pocket. He always dressed formally for dinner—at all times, really. He took out the letter, unfolded it, scanned down the page, and said, "David Harp."

"David Harp. David Harp," Kala said. "Harp's a world-renowned verifier. Verificationist. That's the word he used to describe himself, a *verificationist*." She reached her knife over to a separate plate containing slices of tomato, cut a slice into three parts, then impaled all three parts on her fork and ate them. "He works for the British Museum, Mr. Harp does. He verifies photographs all day long, isn't that so, dear?" Kala hovered her fork over the remaining tomatoes but denied herself any more. "Oh, just read the thing, Vienna."

So Vienna read the one-page letter:

Dear Mr. Vienna Linn,

Your letter was offered for my expert opinion, under circumstances separate from my work at the British Museum. I read it with great interest.

I could even imagine a benefactor offering as much as £20,000, should circumstances warrant.

In my capacity as independent verificationist, then,

I shall arrive in Halifax on the liner *Winifredian*, March 18. I shall, as per your suggestion, register under my name at the Haliburton House Inn. I hope to then begin my work as soon as possible.

With all professional interest,
David Harp

"Notice he doesn't actually mention the name Radin Heur," Kala said. "But he works for Mr. Heur. This David Harp is the one Mr. Heur relies on. To determine the truth of things. To say fake or not fake."

"He'll see it's a fake right away," I said.

"The question is, what purpose might it serve David Harp to say it isn't," Vienna said. "Twenty thousand dollars split two ways, for example. If Mr. Heur relies on David Harp to the extent I believe he does, then he won't ask for a second opinion."

"What do you have to lose, except, eventually, your life?" Kala said.

We ate the rest of the meal in silence. Through the window Freddy saw that we were done eating. He came back inside and cleared away our plates. He smelled as if cigarette smoke had frozen on his clothes.

"Well then," Vienna said. He wiped his mouth with his cloth napkin, set the napkin down, pushed back from the table, and stood. "I'm off for a drink with my newfound friend, Sergeant Maitlin, of the esteemed Halifax Police Department. Where else would I be off to? And later there's work to be done in the darkroom. Sleep well, dearest." He altogether avoided looking at me. Yet he addressed me:

"I won't absolutely require your assistance tonight, Peter, but as you know, work has piled up. It's up to you, naturally. I'd understand if you chose to retire for the rest of the evening."

As if to fend off the slurring effects of the wine, he said all of this slowly. It all but made my skin crawl, the civility. He leaned over and kissed Kala on her forehead, took a sip of wine, then took along the half-filled glass as he headed toward the stairs.

Kala and I sat until we saw Vienna leave the Haliburton House Inn. "Shall we have some Goldwasser?" she said. It was a Polish liqueur. I'd never heard of Goldwasser until Kala introduced me to it. "This stuff is very useful on cold nights," she'd said. We were in my room in the Churchill Hotel. "And so many nights in Canada are cold, aren't they, in one way or another. Except now, here, with us together." Goldwasser was slightly bitter, cool to the tongue. A sediment of gold flakes slid about the bottom of its squarish bottle. When we arrived at the Haliburton House Inn, Kala had bought a dozen bottles and asked Mrs. Sorrel to secure them in her office.

"I'll go in and get a bottle," Kala said. "I'll bring it to your room."

By ten o'clock the candle was guttered, the fireplace logs burnt down to cinders. Snow had begun to fall heavily. Kala had three shot glasses of Goldwasser in quick succession. Once I'd gotten the room at a comfortable temperature, she slipped out of her clothes. She sometimes allowed me to undress her, but in either case, she let me know her preference. When making love, Kala insisted I look into her eyes, and in the midst of it, I felt I had little choice. Kala was *direct* in her appetites, is how I thought of it. Direct in what she wanted and in saying it without words. Afterward, right away almost, Kala would lean over, press an absentminded kiss onto either of my hands, pick up her leatherbound copy of *The Unclad Spirit: Chronicles of Spirit Photography*, and begin to page through it with great concentration. She'd study the photographs, muttering favorite passages under her breath.

For over five months now I'd seen this was a book Kala returned to the way others might the Bible.

*The Unclad Spirit* was published in 1882. The book's author was Georgiana Houghton. She was Kala's mentor and model of intelligence and strength of character. Kala called her "Miss Houghton." Over the months I came to know Miss Houghton's passions for spirit photography—her *beliefs*. Kala would read long passages—sometimes entire chapters— to me in bed. *The Unclad Spirit* consisted of Miss Houghton's journals, letters, anecdotes, other assorted entries based on years of investigation into the phenomenon of spirit photography. I'd never heard of a spirit photograph until I'd met Kala.

A spirit photograph is one in which someone whom Miss Houghton called the "uninvited guest" was present.

On the occasion, say, of a wedding, funeral, birthday, family reunion, baptism, no one actually *sees* or speaks to this person—the person isn't even vaguely recalled. Yet when the official photograph of the event is developed, there *he* is, or there *she* is—the uninvited guest.

In her well-traveled researches, Miss Houghton discovered that the uninvited guest was seldom a complete stranger. In fact, most often it was an estranged wife or husband, a cousin, an aunt or uncle, any of whom had done something so unforgivable they'd been forbidden all contact with family. However, it wasn't always a relative. When describing the appearance of a wife's secret lover in her wedding-day photograph—she was photographed standing alone under an elm tree—Miss Houghton wrote: "The illicit paramour now attended the wedding in perpetuity."

Eventually Kala read what she called the human interest stories in *The Unclad Spirit* to me so often that I practically had them memorized, which would've pleased her no end. I once commented that people back in the 1880s could be pretty merciless, kicking a brother or cousin or sister out of a family like that.

"Only back then?" she replied.

I have Kala's copy of *The Unclad Spirit* in front of me. I quote from page 47:

> Alas, even if the photograph is burned, its ashes scattered to the wind, still, the memory of actually seeing the uninvited guest often long persists and can drive a person quite or near to madness. I myself have interviewed people broken by this experience and therefore in hospital.

At the end of *The Unclad Spirit* is a glossary. Miss Houghton had invented a vocabulary to define all kind of situations relating to spirit photographs. For example, the agony caused by seeing an uninvited guest—the sheer torment of it—she called "a haunting." The complete definition

THE HAUNTING OF L.

read: "**Haunting**. *Wherein a mental image never leaves the person alone with peace-of-mind.*"

Halfway down page 33—let me find it—a woman named Martha Ritner offers her own testimony, which Miss Houghton calls an *epitome* of a haunting:

My sad yet unspeakably loathsome cousin, Franklin Ritner, appeared in a photograph taken on the occasion of my fifty-fifth birthday. There he was, just to the right of my beloved husband. However, Franklin had died two years earlier. I tore to shreds the photograph the moment I saw it. Now, ever since, when I wake up in the morning, deplorable cousin Franklin wakes, as it were, with me. When I sit down for dinner, he sits with me. When I say my evening prayers, godless Franklin listens in; I often pray he'll disappear. Franklin is a constant—should I read aloud a letter to a friend in order to hear if it sounds as sincere as I meant it, I have, therefore, against my will, read it aloud to Franklin. I very much love writing letters, but now feel I must refrain—at my desk, Franklin looks over my shoulder. The letter becomes an indiscretion.

Kala's eyes always teared up when she read this passage. "I suppose Martha's life could've turned out worse, though," she said. "Because finally she did come back to her senses. She carried on bravely. She finally got cousin Franklin out of her mind."

Already for five or six years by the time I first met Kala

on September 11, 1926, in Churchill, she had earned a living—annually a pittance, with the occasional windfall—
composing what she called "dramatic presentations" based
on the writings of Georgiana Houghton. She usually performed these in private homes for small gatherings of spiritualists, groups like the Progressive Club of Toronto, whose
membership also held séances.

Kala herself was direct about her chosen profession. "I'm
part proselytizer, part actress, part scholar," she said to me as
we lay in bed in my room in the Churchill Hotel, the second
or third time we slept together. Kala had already educated
me on who Miss Houghton was and what *The Unclad Spirit*
contained. "I suppose I'm split in thirds that way. But I'm
good at it, though it's an odd calling. It's as if it chose me, in
a way, and I chose it right back. When I first ran across Miss
Houghton's writings, I didn't know what to think, really. But
slowly I embraced her. That's how it feels, like I'm embrac-
ing what she believed."

"And you actually think these photographs are real?" I'd
said.

Looking back on the moment, I realize how precarious
it was. We were entwined on the bed, and I questioned
her belief. How could I doubt her? Everything might've
ended then and there. But Kala held me even more
tightly.

"The thing is," she said, "I don't really care if spirit photographs are, in the technical sense, real or not. Though I
think some are. No, what's important is that I subscribe to
how Miss Houghton thinks about the world. It's her philosophy about the 'uninvited guest' that most endears me to

her. She says that these people appear not so much out of revenge as out of devastating loneliness. She understands why these people have to come back."

I didn't understand it at all. But after she told me these things, we made love more unremittingly than ever before or since. Later, sitting up in bed in nearly pitch blackness, Kala said, "All in all, it's a manageable calling, I suppose. I go out and do my lectures. I study the faces in the audience. Sometimes only a few people show up. Other times—well, once it was close to a hundred. That was a surprise. I study the looks on their faces. They judge me, and why shouldn't they? And you can't ever say it's one reason or another, why somebody comes to listen. Some are people who lost loved ones in the war—"

"What's that have to do with spirit photographs?"

"They long to see loved ones again. Spirit photographs hold out the possibility."

"Now that sounds desperate to me."

"Perhaps sadly so. One man said to me, 'One of these photographs—it would be as if a prayer were answered.' By the way, that was a man whose son had choked on mustard gas. He told me all about it. He had lost a son and wanted some kind of message from him. Simple as that."

"This is a bit over my head, Kala."

"Stick with me. It won't be." She laughed slightly. We held each other awhile longer. "They invite me, they pay money to hear me, they get to judge me. I can see some think I'm a crackpot. Others think I'm a visionary—I mean, they think Miss Houghton was. Now and then a letter reaches me— Vienna and I have moved so often. I've had to secretly leave a forwarding address, which angers my husband. He absolutely forbids me to leave a forwarding address. I've defied that. So a letter might reach me. I always write back a sympathetic response. I wish whomever good luck. I think it's fair to say that I have a small following."

That night Kala fell asleep around 12:30, possibly as late as 1:00 a.m. As I mentioned, I almost drifted off, but finally didn't. Staying awake while Kala slept felt like some kind of psychological *incident*—yes, that's the word I want. Because I reacted badly. I was susceptible to giddiness, nervousness, remorse, or other unnamable, wretched confusions, sometimes without letup, for hours on end. I was given to pacing the room. I'd make up captions in rapid order—basically, these captions described what I saw out the window. *A Street, A Snow-Covered Automobile*—simple things anyone might notice. Flattened-out language. The sort of caption I wouldn't be proud to have under a photograph in the newspaper is what I mean.

Usually what I did with the rest of the time was simply to watch Kala sleep. In fact, I'd persuaded myself that doing so was a kind of expertise. That I should consider my own sleeplessness not only (to take a phrase from Miss Houghton) as a "spiritual condition" but as a philosophical opportunity. Why? Because by watching Kala sleep, I might gain knowledge, feel certain emotions, or construct memories I would not otherwise have.

However, after midnight—on into the first hours of March 13—things were different. Because at first I could scarcely look at Kala. Because each time I did, I felt, sharply, the foretaste of regret. That phrase also comes from Miss Houghton—it was one of Kala's favorites. Eventually, I applied it to my watching Kala sleep. Because when I watched her sleep, I memorized her. Or tried to. Memorized her face, hair, shoulders, hands. Her face had features just shy of sculpted: strong nose, mouth, brow. She often talked in her sleep, if only in broken sentences or single words which, if written, would require an exclamation point to follow them. If I said, "You talked in your sleep," she'd immediately reply, "What did I reveal?" She always put it like that, looking both curious and embarrassed.

The foretaste of regret. I was convinced that I was building up such an archive of memories—all these various views of Kala sleeping—that I could never get them out of my mind. And where would that leave me, should it happen that we didn't stay together? I'd suffer one of Miss Houghton's *hauntings*, except without any photographs involved.

In the bathroom I splashed cold water on my face. I then stood by the window. I thought up ten, twenty, thirty captions. I watched Kala sleep awhile. When I finished captioning what I saw out the window, I resorted to captioning what was in the room: furniture, bathtub seen through the open washroom door, towels, fireplace—all the familiar objects that, once you articulated them in a caption, became a touch unfamiliar. Finally, I sat on the edge of the bed, looked in the bureau mirror, and said out loud, "*Man Not in His Marriage Bed.*"

I slid under the bedclothes next to Kala. Looking at her, it seemed that in spite of all the broken-ribbed, bruised pain she had suffered in the airplane wreck in Churchill five months before, her beauty was undiminished.

The draft from the window didn't disturb the candle. *The Unclad Spirit* was squared nicely on the night table. The weight of the bedclothes felt good. My bare feet were touching the fisherman's socks Kala wore.

The world seemed in perfect order, then I experienced a jolt of unease. I got out of bed, took the few steps to the marble-top stand, lifted the pitcher of water, and poured a glass. At the slightest nick of the pitcher against the glass, Kala sat bolt upright. "Oh, Peter, I'm happy it's you," she said.

I stood near the window. Snow was falling so thickly I imagined that to Kala, just coming into full consciousness, it might appear as if a white quilt had been hung over the pane.

"May I have some water?" she said.

I handed Kala the glass of water, then returned to the window. She took a long drink. Moving the candle aside, she set the glass on the doily. "I had the most disturbing dream possible," she said.

"Tell me."

"I was alone, sitting among all the wreckage."

"The wreckage of the plane."

"Yes."

"And—"

"And the bodies were— The three bodies, the three Eskimo lay around me, just as they really had. They were dead, Peter. In the dream they were dead. But I still spoke to them. I said, 'I'm sorry. My husband did this.' "

I turned toward the window. "Peter, don't turn away from me, please. Please don't." We said nothing for a few moments. "Peter, could it possibly be true?"

Still facing the window, I said, "That Vienna did what, exactly?"

"That he—somehow *arranged*— He's capable of such a thing, Peter. As you well know, he's indeed capable of such a thing."

"Of trying to—"

"—murder his own wife, but make it *seem* an accident."

"You're right, he is capable of such a thing," I said. I looked at Kala. She'd shawled the bed quilt around her shoulders. "But I don't believe that's what happened."

Kala picked up *The Unclad Spirit* and pressed it to her chest. She took another drink of water. Again she placed the glass on the night table. Looking past me out the window, she said, "Well, I'm afraid you're wrong."

# VIEW OF KALA MURIE
## STEPPING OUT
## OF HER BLACK DRESS

I had arrived in Churchill, Manitoba, on September 11, 1926. I would soon discover that it was Kala's wedding night.

About this new life I had no expectations. That kept manageable my fear of disappointment. It sufficed that I was no longer in Halifax. For the time being, that was enough. What happened was, I'd simply answered an advertisement in the Halifax newspaper, the *Herald*:

GENERAL ASSISTANT. Knowledge of the art of photography. Darkroom experience required. Contact: Vienna Linn, Churchill, Manitoba

I qualified, especially the "darkroom experience," since by that time I'd worked in the *Herald*'s darkroom for nearly five years. I immediately posted a letter. Just short of five weeks later came the reply:

Dear Peter Duvett,

    You have the position secured, if you still want it. Write travel plans—to same address.

Vienna Linn

No "Sincerely yours" or "Best wishes"; a man of some directness, I thought. Keep your expectations reasonable.

Wanting to put things in motion right away, I then wired Vienna Linn. His return message was prompt and encouraging. Its only note of concern was put as a question: *Have you located Churchill on the map? It's no walk in the park up here. Your services, however, will be most welcome.* I happily gave notice at the *Herald*, put what few pieces of furniture I owned in the basement of my apartment house on Water Street, paid my last month's rent as was owed, purchased a train ticket to Winnipeg. I was on my way.

I sat up in coach and hardly slept the entire journey, scrimped on meals, navigated the swaying aisle of the train, keeping to myself. Mostly I read my book, *The Strange Life of Mrs. J. Doyle.* It was about a real-life woman, Mrs. John Doyle, who'd lived her entire life in Dublin. One day, at age eighty-five, she fell down a flight of stairs in a neighbor's house. When she woke in hospital, she had what the doctors called "selective amnesia." She could now remember things only from the year 1895. All other years had been erased from her memory. The Dublin paper ran the headline: KNOCK ON HEAD SENDS MRS. DOYLE BACK TO 1895. Somehow, tumbling down the stairs had given Mrs. Doyle a "photographic memory," but only for 1895. A kind of fame then pursued Mrs. Doyle. Historians, journalists, scholars of every sort—plus the occasional psychic—appeared at her door, wanting Mrs. Doyle to verify certain rumors, help decipher unsolved mysteries, look at photographs and talk about what was in them, "as if," the author, Walter Manning, wrote, "it was a chance for humanity to fully recapture Time itself." There Mrs. Doyle sat, day after day in her shabby room in Dublin, as visitors came and went and Mrs. Doyle told what she remembered. And in fact, no one disputed a single detail she offered. At the same time, Mrs. Doyle couldn't for the life of her remember any number of her family, certain nieces, nephews, grandchildren, that is, because they hadn't been alive in 1895. I read the book pretty much straight through. Every page, I wanted to know what happened next. To feel some nervousness, excitement, agitation, even fear about *what happened next*, was how I judged a book as good or not. In terms of *The Strange Life of Mrs. J. Doyle*, I thought the author had a lot of skill, to keep a reader paying close attention for 409 pages chronicling poor Mrs. Doyle's fate, quite an accomplishment. The author was sympathetic to Mrs. Doyle. I could tell that from page 1. I myself would have liked to have spoken with her. With a day's travel to Winnipeg yet to go, my nerves a bit frayed from lack of sleep, I set down the book for a while and thought, *Too bad you don't get a choice in the matter—which years to forget. I'd throw myself down the stairs, if I could pick and choose.* I laughed quietly to myself in the darkened train car. Passengers all around were snoring, mumbling in their sleep, staring out windows, curled up in as many shapes as an alphabet. I couldn't sleep. I thought up about thirty captions describing my fellow passengers. I might have slept a little.

By arrangement, the pilot Driscoll Petchey met me at the train. He accompanied me by taxi to the small airport—a landing strip and one building. We boarded his single prop plane. On its side, more or less scrawled in big black cursive writing, it read, *D. Petchey knoweth clouds*, which struck me as comical and religious. Around 11:00 a.m., we set out north. Petchey was about fifty, give or take, with a weather-beaten, handsome face, thin lips that disappeared into deep clefts on either side of his mouth, a protruding Adam's apple, uncomfortable to look at, because it was like watching a gear fitting inside a human body. The entire journey, Petchey talked a blue streak. Actually, we both had to shout over the sounds of the wind and the engine. "My life" and "the godforsaken beauty of the north," Petchey went on, about this, that, or the other subject. It was distracting entertainment. I was grateful, since I was such a jittery passenger. Did not like flying at all. He said he lived in Churchill but also rented a room in Winnipeg. I asked why he chose to live in Churchill. He thought for a moment. "The real truth is," he said, "all Tourist Bureau 'summer bird-watching' nonsense aside. Hey, reach in that metal box at your feet, get out the government brochure, will you?"

I unfolded the brochure. "Read the first part," Petchey said.

"Okay, sure," I said, glancing first at a photograph of a bunch of children, Eskimo and otherwise, standing in front of the Hudson's Bay Co. store. I read: "The town of Churchill is located on the western shore of Hudson's Bay at the mouth of the Churchill River. In summer, white Beluga whales abound. Churchill's residents maintain a frontier spirit, in a town where Eskimos and Cree Indians thrive at the outskirts, and best understand the beautiful starkness of the surrounding tundra and sea. The occasional polar bear saunters past the Post Office, surely a sight to behold! Yet each spring the 20th century arrives in full regalia, when European grain ships arrive to load grain sent up from Canada's western provinces."

"Enough—goddamnit!" Petchey spoke and laughed at the same time. "Language like that cracks the eardrums, eh? As I was saying, rarely do persons travel up to Churchill, look around, and say, 'Home sweet home.' People live there because there's more *oxygen*. Or to flee some demon or other. Of course, there's families, a church, I don't contest that."

"Well, I just answered an advertisement in the newspaper," I said. "I wanted a new job. No more, no less."

"There's always more or less—but no matter, you've got yourself a new job, eh? And you're now employed by Mr. Vienna Linn. You're employed by quite an unusual man."

"Is he civil? That's what I care most about. Is he a civil man, because my last employer—"

"He's always been civil to me. But my opinion? He's on the lam from something. Some *deed*. I don't know this as a fact, mind you. But I've seen fugitives from justice—I'm not saying he's that. I've seen escapees from their own past lives—I'm not saying Vienna Linn's that, either. It's just that I've got a nose for such individuals, eh? Yet in diction and how he carries himself, he's somewhat the opposite of a lowlife. And here's something else. See, I was the one who flew Vienna Linn and his fiancée into Churchill. From that day on, it's struck me he's a type of genius, or expert at affecting as much successfully. Fiancée in tow, he settled right down in Churchill and stayed the godforsaken winter, which is the real test. Staying the winter, that does speak for the man. For her, too—Kala Murie is the fiancée's name. I don't know what nationality that is. Vienna right away set up shop. His camera work is top flight—at least to my eyes, his tripod camera work is. And here's something. Thomas Swain, who owns and runs the Churchill Hotel, your new home—Swain told me, Vienna paid his and, separately, his fiancée's room a year—that's twelve full months—in *advance*. Now, mind you, that phenomenon, Peter Duvett, made a prominent item in *The Hudson's Bay News.*"

"Seems like nobody's business," I said. "It was in the newspaper?"

"Funny thing, isn't it. Small towns. You'd think, if the smallest most insignificant item of someone's life was written up for all to see, it'd eliminate rumor. But rumors fly around Churchill, too, just like any other northern town, I suppose."

"I'll remember that."

Vienna Linn did not meet my plane. I was surprised by that. The rutted landing strip was two hundred or so meters from the hotel. From the air, circling on approach, the configuration of Churchill had begged the question: Where's the center of town? As Petchey calibrated the wind for landing, he pointed out the post office, the school, the Hudson's Bay Co. store, and I also noticed a road of sorts lined with small houses, a group of squalor shacks along the river. I saw no people out and about.

I stood next to my suitcase as the propeller ratcheted down. I thought, *Man Standing Next to Leather Rectangle*, a caption no doubt born of the fact that I sensed my life had been reduced to its most basic properties and proportions. Without fully realizing it, I lifted the suitcase and clutched it to my chest.

"That's how a little boy holds his suitcase, waiting for Mum and Dad," Petchey said. I set the suitcase down. He walked past, lugging a sack of letters and packages. Then he stopped, turned toward me. "I recognize the look," he said. His face exaggerated a wild-eyed disbelief, which made me laugh a little. "City boy wonders, Will there be slippers by the bed?"

"That's not how I lived in Halifax," I said. "Not even close to that."

"My point is, Churchill's a place where you've got to get truly acquainted with yourself. Be your own best friend. See how deep your well runs. Are you resourceful, I'm talking about."

"I think I'm resourceful."

"Time will tell, eh?"

"Thanks for the advice."

"It's free advice. And you're welcome."

He walked on ahead to the Hudson's Bay Co. store, and I went to the hotel. I noticed it was three stories high. I stepped inside; nobody was behind the check-in counter. I set down my suitcase for the second time. The staircase had scrolled banisters. There was a fire blazing, the fireplace looked like a small cave. The lobby had two sofas opposite each other, both facing a low, wooden table. There was a rocking chair in each corner. The table had a few newspapers and magazines on it. And an oil lamp. Standing ashtrays next to each sofa. Along the wall, to the right if you faced the fireplace, was a writing desk and a chair. There were two electric floor lamps, but also a candle on each surface, two iron candelabras on the mantel. I studied the fireplace again. It didn't strike me as being intelligently built. I thought most of the heat would get swallowed up. The draw was good, though. I went over and stood by it. It threw off heat, but didn't heat the entire lobby. There was a coal stove in a corner nearest the entranceway. It wasn't burning a fire.

The lobby seemed cozy enough, but there was nobody in it. I walked back to the counter and tapped the bellhop's bell—nobody. So I wrote my name in the leather-bound registry, crossing each *t* in Duvett individually, the way my first-form teacher, Mrs. Bromie, had bent over me and insisted.

I looked across and read a placard set on a tripod at the doorway to the dining room:

KALA MURIE
*will lecture on*
THE UNCLAD SPIRIT
The life and philosophy of Georgiana Houghton
—*learn the truth about spirit photographs*—

I had never heard of a spirit photograph. I walked past the placard and into the dining room. The half dozen or so tables had been placed at the back of the room. Chairs were set in neat rows in front of a lectern.

For some reason—I can't account for it—I took small notice of Kala Murie at the lectern, but instead studied the audience. That was easy, because it consisted of only four people. One elderly Eskimo man and two elderly Eskimo women sat side by side in the front row, directly opposite the lectern. In the back row was a man who, at first glimpse, seemed about Driscoll Petchey's age. He was leaning forward in rapt attentiveness, the lecture already being in progress. I sat in a chair at the far left end of the last row. He hadn't noticed me yet. He was wearing a herringbone jacket, white shirt buttoned at the collar, black shoes. His short beard was neatly trimmed, his hair combed back tightly to his head in what appeared to be slick black triangles on either side of a part down the middle. I thought right away that it was Vienna Linn. I attempted a caption, but the words *drawn forward* were all that came to mind. As he listened to Kala Murie, his expression was somewhat childlike in its excitement: *Go on, what happened next?* Yes, of course, that's what you most want to know in any good story. He shifted in his chair, leaned forward again, slowly nodding encouragement. He in turn looked somber, amazed, distraught, drinking in every word spoken by his fiancée.

The Eskimo man and women handed something along their row. Each took a bite; whatever it was, it stretched like taffy.

This tableau (I took two years of French in school)—the near-empty room, the woman speaking passionately—struck me as both pitiable and strange; you can't help how feelings suddenly combine, and besides, this was my new employer and his fiancée, I had best pay attention. Though I didn't know, of course, exactly what I'd just walked in on. I moved to the center of the row. Kala noticed, narrowed her eyes, scowled as if reprimanding me for being late and drawing attention to it, all the while never breaking stride in her lecture.

Then I truly looked at Kala. And could not look away. Simply put, she was the most exquisite woman I'd ever seen. *Exquisite* was not a word I had ever needed before, a word in waiting. It was as if seeing Kala had suddenly given me the ability to describe her, if only to myself. She wore a formal black dress—it could have served as a mourning dress, I thought. It had a high collar held by a cameo pin. As she spoke she absentmindedly fidgeted with this cameo, touched it lightly like a talisman. She had dark red hair that, on either side, swirled up in a wave, held by embroidered combs. I had seen women's hair done up like this in magazines. Kala had a slightly upward tilt to her chin as she spoke, a strong, alert face, though even from my first station at the back of the room and then in the last row, I noticed deep circles under her eyes. "World-weary," my mother might well have said. As I later discovered, my private estimation that Kala was thirty-two or thirty-three years of age fell short. She was thirty-eight.

Kala leaned slightly forward, resting her elbows on the lectern. Her voice seemed now to push past a natural shyness—this might've been a theatrical trick, I didn't know. The placard had said "lecture," but what I saw and heard seemed both lecture and performance. As I listened, I thought that there was a restrained tone to her voice, even a flatness, which allowed any rise in pitch to seem a small excitement. It was a voice not without fervor, yet not preacherly—it was striving. I had attended two stage dramas in my life. Kala Murie, I thought, could hold her own with both featured actresses. Now and then she glanced down at a notebook or loose pages, it was difficult to see which, yet it appeared that for the most part she'd memorized her lecture.

Kala now stopped talking. She composed herself, rubbed the sides of her head as if trying to erase a headache, closed her eyes, opened them again. Taking a deep breath, she said, "As if speaking in the voice of Georgiana Houghton, I shall now relate a letter from Mr. Anthony Slater of London, England, sent to *The Spiritualist*—it is dated May 8, 1872."

I have the book in front of me now. Let me turn to the passage she read. Here it is, on page 114:

I visited Mr. Hudson, told him my object in calling, and after a few preliminary remarks on both sides, he proceeded to take a negative of me. It turned out to be a very good, clear, sharp negative—nothing more. I requested him to try another, which he did, selecting indiscriminately from some *previously* used and dirty glasses one for this occasion, and after going through the usual routine of cleaning, done in my presence, he poured on the collodion, and placed it in the bath. I remained in the darkroom all the time the plate was in the bath. I saw it put into the camera frame and then into the camera, which had been previously focused on me, and all that Mr. Hudson had to do was uncover the lens. I saw the slide drawn up, and when sitting saw the cap or cover of the camera removed, and after the usual exposure replaced on the lens. I then accompanied him into the darkroom and saw the developing solution poured on the plate, but not the vestige of anything appeared, neither myself nor background, but a semi-opaque film all over the plate, as if it had been somewhat overexposed. I then asked for another attempt, which was carried out under precisely the same circumstances, namely, that I witnessed the whole proceedings from beginning to end. I must now, in justice to the "psychic force," gentlemen, tell them what I asked mentally, and *felt what I asked*—that if it were possible for the spirit of my mother to come and stand by my side, and with me to portray her presence, to please do so. The result you may or may not have seen is a fine female figure draped in white, standing before me with her hand resting on my head. I need not say I was as pleased as I was astonished, and felt determined to further investigate the matter, as I felt certain Mr. Hudson had played no trick on this occasion. Having read in *The British Journal of Photography* that the editor thought it very unlikely that he would get any spirit pictures if he took his own instrument and plates, I took the hint and did as he suggested, not that I doubted the artist or the spirits in the least. I accordingly made a new combination of lenses, and took also a new camera and several glass plates. I did, in Mr.

Hudson's room, all the looking on, and obtained, in the same manner as before, a fine spirit picture.

It was again repeated with another sitter, and with like success; *collusion or trickery was altogether out of the question.*

Having completed her reading of this letter, Kala lapsed into silence a moment, near to the edge of a swoon, but seemed to recover quickly, and caught her balance by clutching the lectern. Now she looked directly at the three Eskimo people and said, "Mostly—*mostly*, it should be said, Georgiana Houghton wrote about the 'uninvited guest,' which I've defined for you"—she cast me a glance of disappointment—"at the beginning of my lecture. But Miss Houghton was also aware of a blessed and astonishing phenomenon, spirit pictures as a kind of séance, evidenced by the letter I have just read to you, the testimony of Mr. Slater, *documented* testimony."

The Eskimo people, it seemed to me, appreciated Kala's attentions, but looked puzzled and spoke in low tones amongst themselves a moment. Kala took a drink of water, set down the glass, and said, "I know. I know. It's remarkable, isn't it? But it all happened. It's all the truth."

"Mr. Slater felt sad about his mother being dead, eh?" one of the Eskimo women said.

"Yes," Kala said, "and, emboldened by grief, he physically and mentally"—Kala pointed to the side of her head—"he *willed* a 'return crossing,' over the bridge from one station in the afterlife to another. That is, from Heaven to a spirit photograph. And her journey to permanent residence in the photograph—she now lived in the photograph—the photo-

graph was now her home, you see. She survived all difficult
tests put forth by natural human skepticism. Therefore, ladies
and gentlemen, let me say again, *clearly*, that Mr. Slater's letter
proves an example of spirit photography as successful séance.
Mr. Slater's mother was called back."

"When I was a little girl," the same woman said, "I saw a
group of ghosts out in a kayak."

Kala held a direct gaze on the Eskimo people for a moment, which made them look, to my mind, uncomfortable.
"Thank you for your kind attention," she said, bowed
slightly, and waited for applause.

Wild applause from Vienna Linn; and when she heard
only his clapping, she gestured for him to stop. He immediately stopped clapping. "Perhaps there are questions?" she
said. "Are there any questions at all?" Kala said.

Vienna stood up. "It was splendid, dear," he said. "End-
lessly fascinating. Bravo! Shall we have tea?"

The Eskimo people had gathered at the end of their row,
waiting to see what happened next.

Kala stepped from behind the lectern, walked directly up
to Vienna. He kissed both her hands; she said, "Thank you,
Vienna dear," so then I knew for certain that he was my new
employer. It seemed to me that Vienna's affections buoyed
Kala up with happiness. Her face was flushed and beaming.
They held hands. It didn't appear to be for show. I now noticed another man standing at the back of the room. He did
not seem interested in the proceedings, really; he was glaring
at me.

Vienna caught my attention. "Ah," he said, "you must be
Peter Duvett. I know most everyone else in Churchill—you
must be Peter."

We met halfway down an aisle and shook hands. Viewing him close up, I saw that he had a rather long face, a sardonic smile, and that his sideburns were flecked with gray. He was about six feet tall, with the narrow shoulders of a child never really quite grown out of gawkiness. Yet what was unusually striking was his eyeglasses. His eyes seemed to waver like stones beneath the surface of two tiny ponds, the lenses were so thick; I imagined Vienna Linn could merely see into the glass, not through it.

"Taken aback, no doubt," he said. "It's the eyeglasses, isn't it?"

"My apologies. I didn't mean to—"

"I'm quite used to the reaction, Mr. Duvett."

"Peter."

"Peter—quite used to it. I've had poor eyesight since I was a boy, which might be why I stubbornly chose photography. I've had good lenses all along. But these latest ones are a miracle. Utterly changed my life. Obtained them in Budapest. Ten years ago, was it? I had three pairs made. They fairly work magic with glass in Budapest. These lenses afforded me a new life. A photographer with feeble eyesight, quite a cross to bear. My new spectacles are quite a spectacle, I like to say. One has to have some humor about one's natural flaws, don't you think?"

"Well, I'm glad they came up with such good lenses."

"Not inexpensive, mind you. When I wear them, I see almost perfectly. But when I don't wear them, my fiancée, Kala Murie, well—she has to lead me around breakfast to bed to bath, in whatever order the day may bring. But otherwise— for instance, looking out the window just now, I see the snow's picked up."

"Summer's just ended down in Halifax."

"Think of that! Our Reverend Painter—H. Dawson Painter. You'll meet. He said, 'Weather goes from angelic to annoying to deadly on any given day up here.' Painter's sickeningly quaint, but his weather report is accurate."

"I think I saw his church from the air."

"It so happens—did Petchey tell you?—it's a mere few hours away from my and Kala's wedding. I'd bet Petchey told you."

"He mentioned your fiancée but not a wedding."

"Well, the wedding's tonight, and that's why I'm nervous as a schoolboy, and there's still—what?—two hours, almost three, before church bells. Except the wedding's here, in the hotel. No bells, in fact. Painter will officiate because someone legally has to."

I glanced over at Kala.

"Oh, of course Kala will change into her wedding dress," Vienna said. "And I'll get dressed to the nines. She always wears that black dress for her lectures."

"This is an important night, then."

"*Important* hardly suffices, young man."

"Of course not. I said it awkwardly—just to say something."

"No offense meant, none taken."

"Sorry—thanks. Thank you."

"We'll have a small amount of get-acquainted time before I take my leave of you, Peter. Join Kala and me for tea in the lobby, why don't you?"

"Maybe for a few minutes. I'm a bit worn out from my flight up here."

"The weather coming in?"

"Rough, I'd say."

"Nothing new in that."

"I hadn't flown before."

"Good to be on solid ground, then."

"Yes."

"Good."

"What are those shacks along the river?"

Over Vienna's shoulder I saw Kala greet the Eskimo man and women, each with a kind of smiling forbearance.

"Basically," Vienna said, "it's the Eskimo part of town. There's Cree Indians, too. They've lived here forever, of course. From before any wooden structure. You might say it's their abode—not Churchill per se, but the surroundings. Even somebody as unenlightened as me knows that much. Europeans are just interlopers, though they might be interlopers for ten centuries to come, the way history works, you see."

"Nobody was around the shacks. I didn't see a single person from the air."

"Well, most Eskimo families are downriver just now, hunting, fishing; to return shortly, I'm told. Reverend Painter keeps track of such comings and goings. The freeze-up isn't that long off—two months, give or take. After December 15, Driscoll Petchey doesn't fly out until around May, with certain exceptions. Emergencies. So get your letters to loved ones written and sent out by December 15, Mr. Duvett."

"I won't be sending any letters."

"I see," Vienna said. He studied my face a moment. "Well then. The hotel's got a room waiting. Two nights paid in advance, as my return letter to you promised."

"That helps, thanks."

"Allow me to ask, while Kala Murie's occupied, there, with admirers: Considering the remoteness of the place, why would a handsome young man like yourself, Peter, come to Churchill?"

"Plain and simple, I was sick to death of my job. At the newspaper. As I wrote you, Mr. Linn."

"Vienna, please."

"Vienna—"

"And rest assured, I read your letter carefully, and I'm pleased that you've traveled all this way. Rest assured."

"I'm relieved to know that."

"However, you might find one similarity between your old job and your new one not to your liking."

"What's that?"

"The hours. In one of your communications to me, you mentioned upward of ten hours a day in the newspaper darkroom, didn't you?"

"Yes, I did."

"Some days—not all, but some—and possibly on into the night, ten hours in a row might be required. But with no café to unwind in afterward, no beautiful young ladies promenading by and such. I've lived in cities, Peter. London. Paris. Budapest. Amsterdam. Copenhagen, for a short while. In fact, we came here, Kala and I—living in sin—directly from Montreal, about a year ago."

"Mr. Petchey said you'd been here through the winter."

"Ah, Mr. Petchey. He once told me that he knew—by intuition—just *knew* that my face was on a WANTED poster somewhere in Canada."

"And wanted for what?"

"Mr. Petchey did not divulge."

"He talked a lot in the plane."

"He talks a lot; what he divulges is quite another matter."

"Anyway, Mr. Linn—Vienna. It wasn't the hours. At the newspaper, I mean. It was the sameness. Of subject. Local dignitaries. Weddings. Tourists walking down the gangplanks of steamers in from Europe, all of that. Besides which, Halifax doesn't have cafés like in Paris."

"Again, my concern is, you'll mainly be developing portraits. In the main, nothing but."

"That's fine. I feel different about things already. Thanks for hiring me."

"See if you thank me in a few months."

"Half of being somewhere new is that I'm not in Halifax, is how I see it. The rest I'll take day by day."

"The only choice in life, eh?"

"I guess so."

"Sameness—but wasn't there the occasional murder, for instance? There, in your city, a murder photograph to develop, some incident that spiced things up a little."

"Well, of course I didn't hope for that."

"Of course not. What sort of person would?"

"I did develop a photograph of a drowned person once. They even used my caption: *People Watching a Resuscitation.*"

On the bottom of the front page of the Halifax *Herald* had been a photograph of people standing in a circle, observing a doctor trying to resuscitate a woman. But she had already died by the time the doctor arrived.

"Could you say that again?" Vienna said.

"*People Watching a Resuscitation.* But my first suggestion was *People Aghast, Watching a Resuscitation,* but the editor took out *Aghast.*"

"A pity," Vienna said.

"I offered up captions most every day, but that was the only one they ever used. Maybe because the regular caption writer was out sick that day."

Driscoll Petchey came into the dining room, walked up to us, and said, "Vienna, when're you going to take my picture, eh? I could secure your future with one of those rich gentleman patrons of yours over in England you're always hinting at. My mug in their drawing room would put the fear of God into those lords 'n' ladies, eh? Look at me, I'm an authentic type. Roustabout grizzled pilot daring bad weather, dive-bombing the occasional white bear, catapulting high amongst the Christian and pagan gods fighting it out over the godforsaken Arctic wastes—"

"I'd have to make up lies about you, just in order to counteract all the lies you tell about yourself, Mr. Petchey," Vienna said. To me it was friendly banter. "However, yes, you would seem to be photogenic. I work by commission only, as you know."

"How about I'll trade you a free escape in my plane to anywhere you choose, in exchange for the chance to photograph me? Plus you keep 50 percent of whatever you're paid from London for my portrait."

"I'll think it over."

Driscoll Petchey then started toward the lobby, turned, and said, "Don't let Vienna Linn, there, tire himself out telling lies about me, Peter. It's his wedding night. A man needs his strength." Then Petchey walked out into the lobby.

Now each member of the audience came up to have a look at me. "Peter Duvett," Vienna said, "meet Mr. Moses Nuqac." I shook hands with the elderly Eskimo man. "On his right is Mrs. Nuqac, Mary. And on his left, here, Mrs. Naniaqueeit—also Mary." I shook hands with the two women.

"I'm baptized," Mr. Nuqac said. His roundish face, red-brown, was friendly in a solemn way, and when he grinned, I saw that many of his front teeth were missing. Intelligent hard-set eyes. His face struck me as somewhat Oriental in structure. His wife's and friend's faces struck me similarly. They were stout in their tattered dresses, leggings, sweaters, patched woolen coats. "My wife, Mary, here, is also baptized. Mary Naniaqueeit is not."

"I'm pleased to meet you," I said. The three laughed and shook my hand again, and Mr. Nuqac, in thick-tongued yet more than competent English, said, "Vienna, I know that in Kala Murie's talking I missed a lot, eh? But tell me, why is she so surprised by what happens in them photographs, because down at our house, there's spirits coming by for visits all the time, eh? One way or another they visit. They're gone awhile, then they come back." He then spoke his language to the women, obviously translating what he'd just asked Vienna. The women each gave me a quizzical look: *Yes, what is so surprising?*

Vienna did not know how to answer.

Now another man entered the room. He was about five feet eight inches tall, stocky, with thinning pale blond hair and an unkempt thick beard.

"And here we have Thomas Swain, owner of the hotel," Vienna said. "Thomas—Peter Duvett, recently of Halifax."

Swain offered me a smile that was actually a downturned mouth, accompanied by a sharply exhaled "Yes, yes, hello" and a stiff handshake, not at all unfriendly.

Vienna turned to the man I'd seen at the back of the room. "Peter Duvett—meet Samuel Brant," Swain said. Brant remained leaning against the wall. He looked to be about my age, that is, twenty-nine, maybe a year or two older. Finally, he stepped up to me. I reached out to shake his hand, but he ignored the gesture.

"I'm the bellhop," Brant said. "But you won't see me wearing that clown outfit bellhops down in the city wear. You're from Halifax, I hear. By the way, I applied for the job as Vienna Linn's assistant, once I heard it was up for grabs. I was willing to keep working the bellhop position, too. But I didn't get the job, now, did I?"

"No, you did not," I said.

"Samuel, here, is an all-around handyman," Vienna said. "He can fix anything. As a bellhop, he's—understated. He prefers to go upstairs unencumbered whenever possible."

This remark made Swain smile and nod. "Nonetheless," Swain said, "we get one or two or three new customers on average per month. Often somebody who's been thrown out of their house by a wife or husband—no luggage to speak of. Maybe a sack of laundry. Bird-watchers in summer. I wouldn't want to forget those nice people, would I?"

"You can manage to carry your own suitcase up, though, right?" Brant said to me.

"I think I'll let you earn your keep," I said.

I walked to the front desk, picked up my suitcase, walked back into the dining room, and handed the suitcase to Brant. He held it out like a tray, jiggled it, then said, "You're traveling light here, Duvett. What's inside, nothing but lady's un-derwear? I hear some men have a nasty little secret down in the city."

"What secret is that?"

But Brant didn't know where to take his insinuation from there; he was just testing my mettle. He dropped the suitcase, catching it by the handle just before it hit the floor. He swung it around, missing my face by inches, then carried it into the lobby and up the stairs.

"You've lucked out and caught Sam Brant at his most hospitable," Swain said.

"I've already signed the register," I said to Swain.

"You're in room 22," Swain said. "Up the stairs to your left. Just reach around behind the counter, get your key."

"All right, then."

"You have two nights already paid for."

"That helps."

"My hotel's not serving dinner tonight," Swain said. "I'm sure Vienna Linn mentioned that he and Kala are getting married. On these very premises. But otherwise, dinner is served from 5:00 p.m. to 8:00 p.m. After cleaning up the kitchen, our chef, Mr. Berthot, sets out for his house promptly at 8:55. You can set your watch by it."

"What should I do for dinner tonight, then?"

"Mr. Berthot's no doubt finishing up the wedding cake just about now," Swain said. "But he'll prepare your dinner ahead of time. We'll have it sent up to your room, how about that?"

"If Samuel Brant's going to bring it up, I'd rather come down and get it myself."

"I'll bring it up personally," Swain said. "At 7:30, if that suits you. That'll give me half an hour to spruce up for the festivities."

"I appreciate it."

"This one time only," Swain said.

Swain walked into the lobby. Vienna Linn then noticed that Kala had slipped out, no chance to introduce us. He appeared to be genuinely baffled. "I don't know why Kala disappeared like that," he said. "Perhaps—well, often she avoids a group of men talking. Yet she said she looked forward to meeting you, Peter."

"No harm done," I said. "She must have a lot on her mind. That lecture and getting married the same day."

"Yes, it's probably that it's so close to the wedding. Emotional enough on its own. Then there's her bath to take, wedding dress to get just right, some privacy before the event. By the way, Peter, please don't consider it ill mannered, our not inviting you. Kala wishes to keep it—"

"It never crossed my mind."

"Let's sit in the lobby, then."

In the lobby we sat on opposite sofas. Then Vienna Linn said, "What was I thinking—forgot the tea!" He went into the kitchen, returning with a tray on which was a teapot, two cups and saucers, a bowl of sugar cubes, a small pitcher of milk. He poured each of us a serving and we sipped our tea.

"I apologize for not meeting your plane," he said.

"No bother at all."

"Quite a small turnout, at the lecture."

"It was interesting. I might've caught more—spirit photographs and such. But I came in late."

"New subject to you, I imagine."

"That's right."

"You'll be spending time with us, Peter. You'll hear all about Kala's work."

"Anyway, she looked pleased. Everyone in the audience—"

"Every one, plus one, plus one—"

"—a small turnout, but they all seemed to say nice things to her afterward."

"So few people. You might imagine Kala—truly—to be humiliated, especially with the sullen Brant in attendance. How could he understand an intellectual life?"

"But the Eskimo woman—Mrs. Nuqac—she had a response."

"One thing to know straightaway, Peter. What you heard was *not* Kala rehearsing for the larger world. She brings to each and every lecture the utmost preparation. The utmost dedication. Even if, finally, she manages to preach to the converted. Or further convince only herself of Miss Houghton's—worth."

"I envy your dedication to Kala Murie," I said.

"Diplomatic fellow, aren't you?"

"Sounds like damning with faint praise."

Vienna laughed and said, "Well, she only searches for the one face in the audience, really. The possible like-minded person. Or perhaps she can more or less pick out the person who *desires* to be like-minded and just needs a little encouragement."

After more tea I said, "Can you tell me a little more of what work I'll be doing for you? You said portraits."

"What I do here in Churchill?" Vienna set down his cup,

leaned back on the sofa. "My present employment is quite
sedentary, truth be told. I'm hired by the local church, Jesuits, of course. Reverend Painter's flock— He has a group
of missionaries all over the territory, you see. They call him
'Father.' Jesuits do that. I call him Reverend— Each time he
corrects me. Missionaries of course have been around up
here for a long, long time. Painter for about three or four
years. A very, very busy man, Painter. His immediate predecessor had some luck in converting Eskimo people to the
faith. Not a lot of luck, however. So I was told. Painter's first
year here was spent more or less settling in. Going through
church records, meetings with townsfolk every week, that
sort of thing. He let people get acquainted with him. Then
he cranked up his efforts considerably. Now he brings in
people from Padlei, Eskimo Point, other villages north along
the Bay, and so forth. I'm—myself—not God-fearing. In
fact, I'm a wretched unbeliever, so therefore consider myself
in one sense a mere hireling of the Jesuits. I'm building up a
collection of portraits of Eskimo Painter baptizes, you see.
Should I have told you precisely this in my letter?"

"I wanted to get out of Halifax."

"—as I see it, Painter's *lackeys*, who come and go, while
by no means stupid people, strike me as quite desperate."

"How so?"

"Well, to *convert* the primitive savage—that's the basic
idea, isn't it. Painter reports to his superiors, I suppose you'd
call them. The important thing for him is his annual report.
So, by *desperate* I mean he gets a five-year-old to memorize
the Lord's Prayer—whatever prayer—some such thing. Some
such thing, and that apparently qualifies them for member-

ship. Plus the numbers, if you will. My portraits provide the evidence of his good works here in the hinterlands. Mostly—to my mind—it's employment. Don't judge me too harshly, please. Otherwise, I do enjoy my conversations with the native people, when they choose to converse. Keep it close to the vest, most of them. Not all have been or ever will be baptized, by the way. You met Mrs. Naniaqueeit—she doesn't submit to Painter's charms. She'll go down fighting. No matter to her that Painter offers a sum of money. She won't submit, even as a kind of social etiquette, just to get along."

"I read somewhere that Eskimos shun getting their photographs taken. The camera steals their souls."

"Historical rumor, call that. Camera stealing the soul. I'd heard that, too. But after a month or so here in Churchill, it struck me as the worst sort of condescension. Because—look: if whatever can be called the Eskimo idea of the *soul*—and they'd no doubt have some private word for it, if they bother with such a notion in the first place—a *soul* couldn't be so easily captured as by a camera. A camera couldn't reach that deeply. You know what might capture a soul up here? Some sort of spirit folk—they've got hundreds. You hear a lot about spirits up here. So, yes, a revengeful spirit folk might nab a soul, but not a goddamn camera, Duvett. Never a camera. Never a European contraption.

"Cameras stealing souls. That's a good example of how stupid you can feel after learning certain things firsthand, things that utterly contradict everything you'd thought was true."

"What's Painter think about all this?"

"Oh, Painter and I haven't actually had any long discussions. But my feeling in general about him is, if he believed a camera could actually capture an Eskimo soul, he'd pay me, or someone else— Who? Well, Samuel Brant would be a likely candidate. Pay someone a fortune to burst in at night on Eskimo families sleeping and get some photographs. He'd go to any length."

"And would *you* do that for money?"

"Ah, an ethical inquiry— Are you a philosophical man, Duvett?"

"I had a little university. I read a lot of my mother's library. She had a big library. But when it comes to philosophizing, I'd most likely disappoint you."

I don't know why I lied about having some university.

"But do you have a life of the mind? Do you still read books, for instance?"

"In fact, I read one on the train, Halifax to Winnipeg."

"I ask, because if books are of interest, my wife-to-be has a number of them. In the hotel she's a veritable lending library, one might say. I think, in fact, she's left a book in your room. Her favorite book. A kind of welcoming gesture. And I've placed an album of portraits in there, too. Hope you don't mind."

"Not at all."

"I'll finish my tea, then it's upstairs."

"Same for me."

"I enjoyed our conversation, Peter. It bodes well. Not too many things bode well, do they?"

"I haven't thought about it."

"Funny thing, I don't consider myself a talkative man, despite all my chatter just now. Kala says I'm half mute all the time. Or is it mute half the time? I suppose she's right. I often don't relish conversation. In the darkroom I might not say all of ten words. Don't be offended."

"Now that I know what to expect—"

Yet when he finished his tea, Vienna still chose not to go upstairs. "Speaking of philosophizing, Peter," he said. "I don't suppose you have any opinions about hotel lobbies."

"Beg your pardon?"

"We're sitting in a hotel lobby, aren't we, modest as it is. Have any opinion about it?"

"Nothing comes to mind. I'm tired, though."

"I think I've mentioned London, Paris, Copenhagen— I've sat in any number of hotel lobbies. I've even done a series of photographs of hotel lobbies. Did not sell a one. Back when I saw myself as an artist."

"I'd like to see them."

"To me, a lobby's an in-between place, emotionally speaking, and I tried to catch that in my photographs. And in a way, personally, I prefer the lobby. One is not upstairs in the room yet—how to say it?—where joys or disappointments you might never forget take place. And yet, one isn't back out on the street, either. Not back out on the street, where memories immediately start up."

Vienna was staring into thin air. "You've thought it through, haven't you?" I said.

"Sorry—sorry. Hours spent alone in the darkroom, I often mull things over. It comes out sounding neatly packaged, these statements of mine. Bores Kala to tears."

"I'm tired, but I was thinking just now, maybe philosophy

won't matter as much, since it's your wedding night, if that's not too personal a thing to say."

Vienna ignored my comment. "You'll likely not see Kala and me at breakfast," he said. "You and I can start in the darkroom, let's say 3:00 p.m. tomorrow. Between about midnight and 3:00 p.m. will have to suffice as our honeymoon—"

"Three p.m. is fine with me."

"The darkroom's really a large storage room; third floor, turn right, and go to the end of the hallway. You'll see a door marked STORAGE. It works well enough. Swain lets me use it gratis. He's a churchgoer, it turns out. He likes that I work for Painter."

We both stood and shook hands.

"All great good fortunes to you and Mrs. Linn," I said.

I picked up my key from the wooden mail-and-key hive behind the counter. As I reached the second-floor landing, weariness set in hard. I stopped and looked across the lobby to the opposite side of the second floor. There was a small high-ceilinged room, a kind of sitting room or library, with a wall of bookshelves holding only a scattering of books. The books leaned at odd angles. Some were stacked up. There was a table, three chairs, a reading lamp, candles in candle-holders. Just to further acquaint myself with the hotel, I started down the hallway to the right of the landing, toward the sitting room. It was completely dark outside now. As I turned the corner, I glanced to my left. The room at the end of a separate brief hallway had its door wide open. Without thinking I stepped closer and saw that the living room led to the bedroom; the rooms were roughly the size of my apartment in Halifax.

Kala Murie stood in front of the three-sided bedroom mirror. I viewed her in profile. She lowered the black dress to her waist. Now, her breasts fully exposed, she held up her hair with both hands. I hadn't noticed that she wore earrings at the lecture. And when she turned to set an embroidered comb in a small wooden box on the left side of her bureau, she saw me. Her face was all candor; the fullness of her composure was, I felt, well met with the fullness of her body; looking at her, I had to consider the wholeness, because to consider any part, the curve of her breasts or hips—she simply now let the dress fall to the floor and stepped out of it—would have got me halfway to madness. The loftiest or most exaggerated caption of shocking romance and possibility would merely have been a crude understatement. I was smitten by my employer's wife-to-be, with whom I had not exchanged a word. Mere hours after arriving in Churchill. Smitten by what the moment contained. The drift of her dress to the floor was of such heart-stopping clarity that not only was I bereft of all familiar balance and emotion but she was so singular a presence, I was blind even to Kala's reflection in the mirror. It had to be there, but I didn't notice. She slowly walked from her bedroom to the main doorway. She grasped the doorknob.

"There's no way to be properly introduced now, is there?" she said.

"I'm Peter Duvett," I said, but by then she'd closed the door.

## VIEW OF KALA MURIE

## EATING WEDDING CAKE

Samuel Brant had left my suitcase just outside room 22. Once in my room, I put it on the two-poster bed, lit the two oil lamps, one on the bedside table, the other on the bureau. On the writing desk I saw *The Unclad Spirit*, the book Kala Murie had celebrated in her lecture, the one Vienna had said was her favorite. It was a thick book bound in dark brown leather. The wording on the cover, including the author's name, Georgiana Houghton, was in black. I lifted it, felt its weight, admired the binding, but didn't open it.

Next to *The Unclad Spirit* was an album of Vienna's portraits.

I unpacked my clothes into the bureau. It had five drawers. I used only the top three. I set my empty suitcase (it had belonged to my father) and my extra pair of shoes under the bed. The room had one window. Though night had fallen, I could see the moonlit Churchill River meandering off into the distance, a few shacks, bleak tundra all around. The river held a kind of sheen; it looked to be iced over, but I knew it wasn't.

A few ravens, far bigger than Halifax crows, were close to the hotel. Ravens out at night. That was strange enough, though I'd never bothered to think if crows were or weren't flying around the parks in Halifax at night. Plumes of smoke— maybe peat or coal—came up from each shack's stovepipe chimney, the wind immediately flattened the smoke against the roofs, then the smoke was gone. I watched a child in what looked like winter bundling—I couldn't tell at that distance whether it was a girl or a boy—step from one shack and begin walking toward another. About halfway the child did a somersault. I sat on the bed. It was the only place to sit. Now enough's happened for one day, I thought. An unsettling sense of desolation connected me to the outside world, or at least what I'd just seen out the window. I had a small panic. Take five deep breaths, I said to myself, and did that. It was the instruction my mother always gave me, "so you don't choke on anxiousness." My mother and I made a word game out of such moments. You'd take a deep breath, let it out, and say, "What am I doing here?" Then, with each subsequent deep breath, you'd subtract a word, *What*, followed by *am*, followed by *I*, followed by *doing*, followed by *here*, until the question disappeared and the anxiousness along with it. This usually worked.

The quilt folded at the end of the bed was a bit frayed. But the bedclothes and pillowcases smelled freshly laundered, no small fortune in that.

I took up *The Unclad Spirit* again, opened it to the title page, and a note fell to the floor:

Mr. Duvett,

    You may study this remarkable book for a night or two, then kindly return it to me. In fact, I am to lecture on it at 5:00 p.m. today. Should you arrive on time to attend, please know that you are most welcome.

Kala Murie

Setting the book on the bed, I poured some water from its pitcher into the flowered bowl, splashed water on my face, drying with a towel folded neatly over its dowel. I took off my shoes, set them next to the other pair, lay back on the bed. I was aware that, other than looking at the book and album, trying to stay calm and getting my thoughts in order, setting up my room in a methodical way was all I had to occupy my time until dinner. I got up, hung my coat on the silent butler near the door. I sat on the bed again.

I opened the book. Centered on the first page was a photograph of Georgiana Houghton. She appeared matronly, about age sixty, and wore a high-collared blouse fixed with a cameo pin. Right away I saw the influence on Kala's way of dressing for her lecture. Miss Houghton, too, had on what looked to me like a black mourning dress. In the photograph she was glancing slightly to her right. She had a pleasant, drowsy face, "overfed, yet not without cheer," as my mother once said of a neighbor. Underneath the photograph it read:

Georgiana Houghton
*spiritualist*

*"Dreaming with eyes open about
the ones who walk here."*

Across from the title page was a spirit photograph, the first I'd ever seen. Its caption read:

### The Darling and Hobbes Families
### September 17, 1884

It was a wedding photograph: bride, groom, mother of the bride, father of the bride, mother of the groom. The first sentence of the entire book was in italics: *There is another world, but it is in this one.* Reading along, I learned that the mother of the bride, Emmeline Darling, had been widowed two years before. However, in the photograph—I kept flipping the page back to the spirit photograph, studying it—standing just behind her and seen most fully over her left shoulder, was the slightly hazy countenance of her husband, Edward Darling! Edward Darling was obviously the "uninvited guest." His right arm was curiously outstretched and slightly bowed; his right hand cupped air, as if he was performing some kind of benediction, or a swimming stroke while standing up. At least this was my impression.

Georgiana Houghton wrote at length about Edward Darling, "not the most upstanding of men." Let me read:

In his lifetime, Edward had brought his family to near ruin, financially, morally, in every possible way. Before his death, his whereabouts had been unknown to his family for nearly a year. During his married life he had been no stranger to philandering. His gambling debts at the time of his disappearance from the family home amounted to £1,350. To pawnshops in nearby London he had sold a number of his wife's heirlooms. The police report verified that, at the moment of his death, he had been "collaborating with a prostitute" in London; said prostitute herself testified that Edward Darling's last words were of a practical nature.

The description of all the distress and humiliation that Edward Darling caused his family continued for a dozen or so pages in *The Unclad Spirit*. To me, it was excellent reading, because it caused me outrage and laughter in equal measure, because it listed activities that traced a wild and dramatic downfall. And yet all along I felt sorry for his family—and finally he dies, but then shows up in his daughter's wedding photograph. He still wouldn't leave them alone.

I read on. Now came a description of the wedding itself. "Nothing out of the ordinary happened," said Emmeline Darling, "except perhaps for the palpable absence of unhappiness." Twenty-three people, family, friends, gave Georgiana Houghton their testimonies of the wedding. None, of course, had seen Edward Darling in attendance.

Last came the testimony of the "immigrant photographer," whose name was Frederik Levy. He had done portraits of the entire faculty at Oxford and other dignitaries as well. Emmeline Darling had taken Levy in as a tenant after Edward had left his wife and three children without so much as a note pinned to the bedclothes. "There was no romantic attraction between Emmeline Darling and myself," says Frederik Levy. Miss Houghton spoke with Levy in London. "I believe she thought I had Old World manners. We did have what might be considered a delicate evening. Mrs. Darling had come down with near-pneumonia. I prepared soup— mostly a broth, a family recipe—and fed it to her. It was

quite medicinal and also proved to be a soporific; she slept
and by morning felt much improved."

I'll skip ahead a few pages, to where Frederik Levy speaks
about the wedding photograph he developed. "About the
photograph in question," he says, "circumstances beyond my
control and having nothing at all to do with my technical
abilities forced an astonishment. I developed the wedding
photograph as I would have any of thousands of others. Still,
Mr. Darling appeared."

Things got stranger and stranger. Later that same September, both of Emmeline Darling's sons—Jonathan, age nineteen, and Sebastian, age seventeen—were so distraught at the
spirit photograph (they despised their father) that one night
they roused Frederik Levy from his bed and held a revolver
to his head as he developed a second photograph from the
original negative. They watched his every move, saying,
"What are you doing now? What are you doing now? Explain it to us." Levy completely obliged. And when, as Levy
reported, "once again Edward Darling imposed his presence," the sons immediately apologized to Levy. The Darling
family was now so impoverished that the sons had to pawn
the revolver. The small amount they received for the revolver
they gave to Levy, "a remuneration for discomforts suffered
by their desperate actions," Houghton writes.

Meanwhile, their sister—the bride, Victoria, on her honeymoon in Scotland—had not yet been told of the spirit
photograph. Two days after she returned home, it was shown
to her. She fainted. She came around quickly, and her new
husband, Stephen, destroyed both copies of the photograph
and the negative. Frederik Levy remained a tenant for an-

other six months, during which he took individual portraits
of Jonathan, Sebastian, Victoria, and Stephen, but no group
portraits. According to Miss Houghton, Levy "left Emmeline's home on cordial and sympathetic terms." Emmeline
and Frederik exchanged letters for a year between London,
where Levy set up shop, and Canterbury, where Emmeline
continued to live. Finally, Levy moved to Holland and they
lost touch.

It was a good story, whatever my opinion about spirit
photography. A good story; I had from the start wanted
to know how it would end. I looked at my pocket watch:
7:05 p.m. I was hungry but didn't want to bother Swain almost half an hour before my dinner was to be delivered, especially after he'd gone to such trouble with Mr. Berthot. So
I took up the album of portraits to kill time.

The album consisted of forty-two portraits. I counted
them before I studied them. Now I paged through slowly,
looking at each face of the Eskimo men, women, and children. Absolutely no imagination had gone into the captions.
*Mr. Mark Nuqac, age approx. 50, baptized Aug. 6, 1926*, was
standard fare. Each subject looked equally stiff and uncomfortable as the next, staring straight at the camera. Each sat in
front of a black cloth backdrop—you could see the wooden
frame. The photographs were shoulder-up, and their expres-
sions struck me as fixed without happiness or sadness or anything, really—the term *poker-faced* came to mind. As if each
person was thinking, This is just something I must get
through. But I was putting words in their mouths, because
their faces didn't suggest any. I started through from the first
portrait again, looking more carefully this time, as if truly be-

ing introduced to my new neighbors, though as it turned
out, I actually met only a few Eskimo people during my
time in Churchill. I mouthed all the forty-two names, as Vienna Linn had written them, *Nuqac, Sipiaq, Tiukitooip*, and so
on, of course not sure I was pronouncing them correctly.

Looking up from the album, I noticed that the window
had etched on it what reminded me of an ostrich plume of
frost. (I'd seen ostrich plumes once, held by a mannequin in
a storefront window in London.) I doused the oil lamps, in-
tending only to close my eyes for a few minutes. When I
woke, the album was on the floor. I had no idea what time it
was. Then I remembered the wedding downstairs. I lit the
bedside candle, carried it in its holder to the door.

Under my door had been slipped a note: *I knocked—you
were dead to the world. Did not wish to disturb.* Swain had signed
the note.

I carried the candle downstairs to the lobby, then blew it
out, setting the holder on the check-in counter. I saw by the
grandfather clock in the lobby that it was 3:30 a.m. In the
lobby I switched on an electric lamp. I went into the dining
room. It was obvious that this was where the wedding dinner
had taken place. Maybe the wedding had been held there,
too. The room was shadowy, just enough light from the
lamp, and the lobby fireplace still had a small blaze.

Much of the bottom layer of the wedding cake was still
on its platter, a few curlicues of frosting, the little wooden
replica of a bride and groom toppled on their sides; they
looked to be resting their heads against pillows of frosting.
Empty bottles of champagne—maybe delivered by Petchey—
littered table and floor. Candles were burnt down to stubs. I

saw a fiddle bow, with some cake frosting congealed to it, but there was no fiddle in sight. The hotel was not that big, I thought—I must've been really knocked out not to have heard music. I sat in a chair in front of the cake. I reached over, took up the carving knife, cut a slice of cake, and stuffed it into my mouth. The lemon frosting had hardened a little, but the vanilla cake itself was delicious. I took a second piece.

"Help yourself—" I turned toward the voice.

There stood Kala Murie in the doorway. Her hair fell loosely about her shoulders. She was wearing a kind of nightshirt, white, with an embroidered hem, which reached down to her ankles. She had on thick socks. "It's the middle of the night and I'm famished," she said, her voice slightly hoarse compared to what I'd heard in her lecture. "Absolutely starved." She cast me an appraising look. "My Lord, Mr. Duvett, didn't your mother teach you any manners?" She shook her head ever so slightly back and forth, smiling faintly. "Not invited to the wedding, you *don't* get wedding cake."

I set the piece of cake down on the table. "I didn't get any dinner," I said.

She walked over to the table, moved along it until she stood opposite me.

"And whose fault is that?" She took hold of the back of a chair. "At least invite me to sit down, Mr. Duvett. On my wedding night. There's such a thing as etiquette, even here in this uncivilized place."

"Well, you had a wedding. That's civilized. Please sit down, Mrs. Linn."

"Kala Murie," she said, sitting in the chair she was holding on to. "I still intend to go by that."

"I should go upstairs."

"Well, you could. Then again, you could sit and talk with me."

"As you said, it's your wedding night. It's late. I shouldn't be here with you."

"An upstanding citizen, are we, Mr. Duvett? I was so hoping my husband would hire the opposite type. Oh, I didn't mean that, forgive me. I'm just entertaining myself—"

"—on your wedding night."

"Would you cut a small piece for me?"

I did so immediately, and she ate it in a few bites. "You see—*famished*," she said.

"Since I was a child, I always heard a bride never gets the chance to eat during her own wedding."

"A child where?"

"London."

"But I detect only the slightest accent, Mr. Duvett, and I was led to understand you'd come up from Halifax."

"The last four years living in Halifax flattened it out, I think. And that's my biography."

"All the other years just a blur, then, is that it, Mr. Duvett? I see. But for such a young man, what? Thirty, perhaps."

"Almost, yes."

"For such a young man. And am I to understand that you have only the most routine of memories? Not much for a conversation—"

"Nobody's ever asked me my life's story, Mrs. Linn— Kala. I've no practice in telling it."

"A pity."

"I should go back upstairs. You came down here for some privacy, I bet."

A surprising touch of anger in her voice, Kala said, "I came downstairs to bide my time going back upstairs."

There was a silence now, during which Kala seemed to wince at some private thought, then get embarrassed that I'd noticed. "Did you ever get"—she seemed to search the dark air for the right word—"*ambushed*. Ambushed, Mr. Duvett, by something from childhood. It just appears in your thoughts? Well, that just now happened. I'm sorry. It was rude of me. I wasn't furrowing my brow at you. It was the other thing."

"My whole childhood made me wince," I said, immediately regretting it. "I don't know what I meant by that. I'm not complaining—I hate that complaint. You hear it often enough, 'Oh, my childhood was terrible.' I hate that."

"Even if it's true?"

"Even then."

"I'm foisting, aren't I? I'm foisting my innermost thoughts on a total stranger. My, my. A bad habit I picked up from my husband."

"No—no, it's generous of you, actually. Thank you. I think I should go upstairs now, though."

"Oh, I suppose Vienna already browbeat you with big questions, didn't he? Give him a little breathing room, if he's in a talkative mood, rare as that is—*whoosh*, off he goes with big questions."

"My employer seems like a civil man."

"Yes. He was civil just hours ago—he fell asleep."

Kala reached out and swirled some frosting and ate it from her fingers.

"I only meant, he spoke his mind with me. A little."

"How nice."

I stood up. "Congratulations, then, and I wish you all great good fortune and happiness."

"Let's go into the lobby, shall we? There's the fireplace. I'm not dressed properly, as you might have noticed. Properly for this cold dining room, I mean."

I simply followed Kala into the lobby. Her nightshirt clung, she smoothed it while walking. I sat down across the low wooden table from her, both of us at the sofa end closest to the fireplace. "Lord, it's empty here," she said. "It's as if we're the only two in the hotel."

I got up and added three logs to the fireplace, almost added a fourth. Sitting down again, I said, "I owe you an apology. I didn't mean to see—"

"—see me practice disrobing for my husband?"

"If that's what you were doing, yes."

"Maybe I was just practicing *disrobing* in general." Kala laughed, nodded encouragement for me to laugh, a kind of permission, I guess, but I didn't laugh. She looked away a moment. "Well, mindless of me to leave the door open."

"I apologize."

"At the time, Mr. Duvett, you didn't look—not exactly— *sorry*."

"I can't imagine how I looked."

"Not sorry, I can tell you that."

Silence again, but then I said, "I enjoyed your lecture. What little I heard. And thanks for leaving a copy of—

The copy of the book. I read a chapter. I read other parts, too."

"Which chapter?"

"About the Darling family. The wedding."

Kala stood up, walked to the floor lamp, and switched it off. She sat back down on the sofa. "Oh, I was just thinking that since my husband's the only photographer here, we didn't get a wedding portrait taken. I was just now thinking that. Distracted me—sorry."

"I should go upstairs now."

"So, you read about the Darlings."

"Chapter One. I tend to read a book in the order presented."

"Such a cad, Edward Darling, don't you think?"

"Anyway, please, if you'd tell Mr. Linn I enjoyed his album. The album he left me to look at."

"All right. I will."

"He's a very fine photographer, Mr. Linn is. I have a feeling I'll learn a lot from him, even just being his assistant."

"Really, you think so?"

"Yes, I think he's a fine photographer."

"How fine do you have to be, taking those portraits? How artistic?"

"Has he done many other sorts? He told me about the hotel lobbies."

"He's taken other sorts, yes."

"I hope to see them someday."

"I'm sure that you will." She shivered, actually said, "*Brrrr.*"

"Should we sit closer to the fire?"

"No—but just inside my door, you remember which room, of course. Just inside the door to the left, there's a sweater on the chair. Would you be a dear and get it for me? Despite the fire, I'm feeling a chill."

"I don't think—"

"What was I *thinking*? Of course, you don't want to go into our room. How thoughtless of me."

"You said Mr. Linn's asleep."

"No, actually, he's gone to the darkroom. To work. He often works all night. You'll learn *that*. As we speak, he's in the darkroom working."

"He woke up, then."

"Yes, I was there. I saw him fall asleep. I witnessed my husband—on his wedding night—leave the room. Words were exchanged. Husband and wife."

"I only meant, if he's for some reason come back to your room—"

"He hasn't."

"Sweater, just to the left of the door."

"Yes. Thank you."

When I returned with the sweater, Kala was standing close to the fireplace. She had added a log, I noticed, and was just setting the poker against the cobblestone sidewall. She took the sweater from me and slipped it on, then sat down again on the sofa. "My husband—" I was sitting opposite her again. She looked away, then back to me. "You may well think Vienna is civil. But I guarantee you, he is not a *principled* man. Nor was he especially principled when I first met him, one who later broke with principle. Became corrupted by greed, say, or necessity, or even wanting to please me, to give me fine things. It was nothing of the sort."

"Maybe I'm about to learn too much. I'm going up-stairs."

"You *asked!*" She sighed deeply. "You asked, didn't you, what kind of photographs my husband took, and now I'm trying to answer you."

"I just meant, what subjects he preferred. What he took photographs of."

"Well, he has a specialty, really."

"Specialty?"

"I don't mean portraiture. Lord, no. He's deathly bored by that, though, for now, it's a living. No, you see, Mr. Duvett, my husband's specialty is— He photographs catastrophes. Train wrecks and the like. Accidents, so to speak. Most often, the wreckage of trains."

"Oh well, at the *Herald*, the newspaper where I worked, we had a man named Orrin Ward, and Orrin was sent out to things like that. He had the stomach for it, I guess you'd say. One time, there was a Birney Car that went right up into a storefront window. Somehow slid off the tracks and kept go-ing. Orrin went out there. That was a front-page photo-graph."

"I see," Kala said. She now sat next to me. She looked at the grandfather clock in the lobby. "It's near to 4:30," she said. "My husband's in the darkroom. He'll be in there at least until 9:00 a.m., I have little doubt."

"I'm thinking," I said, "since I'm awake now, it might make a good first impression if I volunteered to work right away. That'd make an impression, I think."

"Is a good first impression important to you?"

"Only that it's better than a bad one."

"Good and bad, Peter. Those are things I do think about."

"You and Mr. Linn are a match, then. Both being philosophical."

"Actually, Vienna and I are different as night and day." She moved quite close to me. "Possibly, he'll be in the darkroom as late as noon," she said. She took my hands in hers. She held them firmly.

"What you say about Mr. Linn, they aren't exactly endearments. I think I should go upstairs."

Still holding my hands, Kala pressed herself against me. "Your new employer," she said, "has a certain timidity, most often brought on by drink."

"I don't want to hear this."

"My husband couldn't consummate our marriage."

"Or else, I'll go to the darkroom. That'd be better."

"And I didn't actually wish him to."

Kala leaned closer yet, put her mouth to my ear, and simply breathed, "Would you like to consummate our marriage?"

"On behalf of whom?"

I did not pull away.

"On behalf of me," she said.

I tried to think myself out of the situation—*Man Seeing the Pulse in a Woman's Neck, Smelling Her Perfume, Feeling a Closer Heat than from the Fireplace, Heart Filled with a Woman's Breath, Heart Racing*—tried to imagine myself just stepping back from all this, standing by the check-in counter, observing me with Kala on the sofa, tried making a judgment.

"Look, if you're not interested—" Kala said. She moved away only the slightest bit—"not interested in my sudden hopes and dreams, well, that's one thing. Just say so. But if you simply can't make up your mind, how insulting. Considering what I have to lose."

"It's your wedding night."

"A fact, and it can either make you more interested or put you off. There's no in between."

She kissed along my ear to my chin, then along my chin, touched my ear lightly with her tongue, breathed a touch more quickly, and let out an almost imperceptible moan. "You go on up to your room first," she said. "I'll just happen by." And then it was decided.

Already I felt educated in how much could happen in any given hour.

It was only the second time I'd stepped into my hotel room and now there was to be adultery. A few moments later Kala opened the door without knocking. I was searching for a box of matches. "There's enough light to see by," she said, when I'd picked the matches up from the bedside table. I set the box down. "Look what I've got."

I turned and saw that Kala was holding a small, squarish bottle. "I brought it all the way from Montreal," she said. "It's less than half filled. But it'll be pleasant to finish it."

"What is it?"

"Goldwasser, it's called. It's good for a lot of things."

"Oh."

"Want a taste?"

"Not just yet."

"You might like a taste later."

Kala opened the bottle and took a quick drink. She set the bottle down next to the matches. "Would you undress me—what little there is to take off," she said. I got down on

my knees, then rose up, slipping the nightshirt along the
length of her body up over her head. Taking the nightshirt
from me, dropping it to the floor, Kala said, "That took just
the right amount of time." I quickly got out of my clothes.
When we were under the bedcovers, Kala asked, "Would you
mind?" and then helped me put a few drops of Goldwasser
on each of her nipples, and drew my face near and, in every
way other than with words, firmly suggested that I lick and
then gently suck her nipples. I admit that I liked the taste of
Goldwasser very much. It was an acquired taste, acquired
with such consuming vividness, I had the odd feeling it
would be the last sensation I'd have before I died, no matter
how or when I died. From this request, or instruction, or
generosity, or astonishment forward, I didn't think, *What will
happen* now? (if I thought at all), because the next thing was
already here. Then the next. We used all the Goldwasser that
was left, drinking some.

When we finished for the first time, we both slept. I don't
know how much time passed. Kala woke me up. We made
love again. Then she reached for *The Unclad Spirit*, said, "I'm
going to light a candle, Peter. You sleep."

But I took the book from her and set it back on the table.
"Kala," I said, "what did you mean, that Vienna wasn't principled?"

"Must we talk about him? Here. Now. Given the moment."

"I only meant, how *principled* must you think I am? Lying
here with you. Here with you in the first place."

"What we just did—twice—were the two most principled things I can imagine." She was teasing, reached over and

poked me in the ribs. When I fell silent, she said, "Oh, we're quite serious now, are we?" I'd turned toward the wall. She held me from behind, our feet touching. "I generally keep my socks on," she said. "In case you wondered."

"I was asking something seriously, I guess. Maybe I shouldn't."

"Well, it's already asked, isn't it?" She kissed me on the shoulder. "All right, then, serious it shall be. A serious moment while we think up what to do next, all right?"

"All right."

Kala sighed deeply. "You mentioned the man at your newspaper who went out to the accidents."

"Orrin Ward."

"Well, this Mr. Ward didn't *cause* such accidents, now, did he?"

"He went out to the accidents. Of course he didn't cause them."

Kala moved away from me. She sat up, reached over, and again took up *The Unclad Spirit.* Clutching the book to her chest, she sat on the opposite end of the bed, facing the door. "Well," she said, "Vienna caused train accidents in order to photograph them."

"What are you saying?"

"—or at least helped plan the catastrophes. He made the *arrangements.*"

I sat up against the bedboard. When I reached over and touched Kala's hand, she pulled it away. "You wanted serious, Peter. Here it is."

"Yes, but I didn't expect—"

"Poor, poor boy. A woman speaking frankly about her

husband makes you quite uneasy, doesn't it? I can sense that it does."

"What you're saying is that Vienna Linn—"

"—has hurt people. A few have died as a result of his— photographic specialty."

"Why on earth would he do such a thing? Things."

"Largely, he fell in with a man named Radin Heur. You'll hear his name soon enough, I'm sure. Of that I'm certain. Radin Heur looms large in my husband's—*responsibilities*."

"And who is this Radin Heur?"

"He's a man whose special interests are perfectly well-met with my husband's. Or I might say, Vienna's photographs of accidents attend to Mr. Heur's obsessions."

"That all sounds neat and clean."

"A perfect fit, yes. Radin Heur requests a photograph. Of, say—and this is a fairly recent example, less than two years ago—of the milk train that was derailed just outside Winnipeg, Manitoba, you see. He advanced a considerable amount of money to my now-husband. My now-husband then hired people. He calls them intermediaries. Also special- ists in their own right. And then the so-called accident occurs. And then Vienna—miraculously armed with fore- knowledge of the incident—has been waiting at the scene. And photographs are taken. Then the photographs are devel- oped and sent to London. Never sent directly to Mr. Heur. That wouldn't do. Too incriminating or something. They're sent to another sort of intermediary. A secretary, usually. But eventually Mr. Heur lays hands on the photographs. He has a private gallery in his home, one hears. Vienna knows a lot about Mr. Heur, but tells me very little, actually. When we were in London, he visited Mr. Heur several times. I wasn't invited along, you see. He lives in a very elite part of London, I do know that much. He's a very wealthy man. A political personage. He's apparently—though I think it's loosely defined—quite a *religious* man as well. On a first-name basis with God, perhaps something of an evangelical." Kala cleared her throat, said, "Miss Houghton's book has a term that I think pretty much applies to Mr. Heur: he's a *radical spiritualist*. Of a particularly nasty sort, I believe."

"What's photographs of a train wreck got to do with him being a spiritualist?"

"It's a rather perverted twist on things, I think. Mr. Heur obviously thinks he can act like God, doesn't he, hiring people to do such deeds and such. But don't ask me to explain it further, Peter. It's not good."

"I can see that much."

"Anyway, the photographs are then packed up securely and sent to London, usually along with the negatives—part of the bargain—an important detail—and usually quite soon after, the rest of the money arrives. Deposited in a bank account, and we are suddenly flush. And then we move to a new place. And that, Mr. Duvett, is who your new employer is and how he's made a living. And how he's kept me, five years now, in a manner to which I've grown accustomed. Which is *modestly* kept."

"Why are you here? In Churchill."

"Churchill's an out-of-the-way place, isn't it."

"I won't be involved in this sort of thing."

"Naturally, after hearing what you've just heard, why wouldn't you pack your suitcase and leave?"

"Your husband said I'd be developing portraits, and that's all he said."

"I think that's all he expects of you."

"Out-of-the-way, meaning Mr. Heur can't find you? That you're in some kind of trouble?"

"You're not a slow learner, are you, Peter? Yes, there was trouble. Things went wrong. My husband had taken a large sum of money in advance and then the most recent train wreck just last year was botched. We were living in Montreal at the time. In a good hotel. Vienna sat for hours in the lobby. After this fiasco, Vienna put out word amongst his contacts. A situation presented itself, and here we are. Where I couldn't possibly have imagined I'd ever be. Much of Mr. Heur's money is already spent. Much—certainly not all. And this, it turns out, is my wedding night."

"So, when Vienna earns enough to pay his debt—"

"Oh, he'd have to work here for twenty years. Perhaps that's a bit of an exaggeration, but almost not. He told you, I imagine, what the work at hand is. He'd have to arrange for every Eskimo man, woman, and child for a thousand miles around to be baptized, then take their portraits, and even then might come up short. No, no, Peter, Vienna owes a far grander amount than what can so easily be called just a debt."

"What would you call it, then?"

"Let me put it this way. I told Vienna that he had to marry me because if Mr. Heur had him murdered, I'd at least get what he owned." Her face tensed up, she squinted twice, her eyes seemed suddenly tired. "Which is small bank accounts in three different provinces across Canada. There's a

small amount in Copenhagen, too. There's his camera. That's
it. But it's 100 percent more than if there was nothing. You
must think me an opportunist."

"So, all right, then. All right, then," I said. "You married
for a *practical* reason. I can understand that. But you did have
a wedding. You didn't have to do that. You must love Vienna
Linn. You knew his past. What he'd done. You were there.
You're now Mrs. Linn and—" I think I was babbling, more
or less, undignified at best.

"Fact is, we both wanted a wedding. Before we died,
wanted a wedding, and who else was there? The ceremony
itself was quite nice. In my mind, during it I imagined someone just stepping into the hotel: 'Oh, look, a wedding!' That
was a nice feeling."

"My mind's suddenly made up. I'll get Driscoll Petchey
to fly me out of here tomorrow."

"I see what kind of man you are. You're the kind of man
who has fixed ideas of what's plausible, aren't you? That's
dull-witted of you. You have to improve on that. You see, I'm
afraid I'm drawn to the implausible, Peter. The implausible
makes life interesting. Sometimes intensely so—sometimes.
Take marriage, for example. The idea of it, let alone the
actual thing. It's quite implausible. Toward marriage I never
harbored any optimism—not a splinter's worth. Yet, just
hours ago, I married Vienna. Yet you use the word *love*. How
dare you? What can you possibly know of it? Yet I'll *allow*
you to know something—

"If you start with the fact that marriage is implausible to
begin with, here's a second fact of life. I married Vienna
because I know his limitations. I know what he is and

isn't capable of, as a human being, as a husband—certainly
that—and so I've whittled down my expectations. Whittled
and whittled. Until earlier tonight I married him. I'm lying
in bed with you, Peter, and I'll damn well admit to how desperate I've been in my life if I want to."

"Was it desperate all night with me so far, too?"

"The opposite. It was the first time I've felt truly happy in
five years."

"You love him or you don't love him?"

"I don't *expect* to love him."

"And now—what? You're stuck here in Churchill for you
don't know how long, is that it? Married to a criminal."

Kala thought this over a moment. She rubbed the sides of
her head, just as she had during her lecture. "When this last
plan went so badly awry," she said, "the one near Montreal, I
suggested to Vienna that it might be a portent. That it might
be time to change things. That we might go out to Vancouver. Or to the States—San Francisco. *Someplace*. Someplace,
what did it matter where, as long as he considered a different line of work. He said, 'You can't put portents in Radin
Heur's bank account.' He didn't speak to me for a week. Not
a goddamned word."

We didn't talk then, for what seemed an eternity. "I need
to think," I said. "But I'd like to think with you here, Kala.
Please stay."

Kala got up, walked over to my side of the bed, then saw
to it that I didn't think for some time. Later, when I woke
for the third time that night, it was still dark out. Kala was
sitting up next to me, reading *The Unclad Spirit*. The candle
on the bedside table next to Kala was burnt down nearly to

its hardened puddle of white wax. I don't think she noticed me open my eyes. She had the book slightly tilted to catch all possible candlelight. I saw her lips moving and she was tracing along the sentences with her finger, whispering a word now and then. But what I heard most clearly was "—the one who walks here."

## VIEW OF KALA MURIE

## AND ME ASLEEP TOGETHER

But for adultery the days soon seemed routine. It had happened overnight, adultery. And in a matter of weeks I knew what Driscoll Petchey meant when he asked, "Are you resourceful?" To put it bluntly, during the hours between my work in the darkroom and my time in bed with Kala, I often felt I was just killing time. As for Kala, it was as if I suddenly kept a diary in my head, each entry consisting of one sentence, "Kala Murie came to my room," then noting the exact time of evening or night. She in fact came to my room seven more times in September, eleven times in the first eighteen days of October.

I believed then, and still believe, that for a good two or three weeks Vienna was oblivious of Kala's visits, as she called them. Kala thought so, too. Some mornings I sat with Kala at breakfast in the dining room. Right out in public, because who'd think the worst of us? I worked for her husband—he'd invited me up to Churchill. To put it in a caption, onlookers might simply consider it *New Bride Keeping Polite Company*, and in that sense, adultery was camouflaged by normal goings-on. Yet I also knew a fuse had been lit.

Often at breakfast Kala risked stretching out her legs under the table, stockinged feet on my lap. The tablecloths in the Churchill Hotel were each oversized, as if they'd been bought secondhand from another hotel with larger tables. And maybe they were. She ordered the same thing most mornings, one scrambled egg, a piece of toast, jam, no butter, tea. Now and then she'd add a slice of orange, when Petchey remembered to import a bag of oranges up from Winnipeg. (I once thought of a caption, *Black Crow Fetching Orange Peel off the Snow*, an actual thing I saw near the hotel one day. But I didn't have a photograph of it.) On still other mornings I'd eat alone. So far, Vienna hadn't appeared for breakfast. Swain allowed him to prepare toast and tea in the kitchen and carry it up to the darkroom. Kala referred to this as "my husband's lonely candlelight breakfasts." People whom Vienna called "the other denizens of Churchill," meaning everyone other than Kala, me, and him, would drift into the dining room as early as 5:30 a.m., and Berthot, no matter how early, would be cooking. I learned that the chef—whom I'd yet to lay eyes on—took a nap in his room, number 30, between 2:00 and 4:00 p.m. "By that time of day, Berthot's so full of annoyances, you couldn't believe he'd be able to sleep peacefully," Swain said, "but he sleeps like a baby." At breakfast, Thomas Swain usually sat at the table nearest the kitchen, jotting down tasks for Samuel Brant, supply lists for Petchey's next flight to Winnipeg, and so on. Petchey also worked on commission for the Hudson's Bay Co. and for Reverend—or

*Father*—Painter. All through my time in Churchill, I was hard-pressed to figure out how Swain made ends meet, since, to my knowledge, the hotel had mostly vacant rooms. Petchey told me that Swain had sold the hotel he owned in Winnipeg at a handsome profit, then bought the Churchill Hotel. That was in 1920. Perhaps he didn't need to make money. Perhaps he simply enjoyed buying a hotel, living in it for a number of years, then moving on. As for Samuel Brant, he'd carry his breakfast from the kitchen through the lobby, plate of food in one hand, cup of black coffee in the other, fork and knife in a back pocket, set it all out on the check-in counter, and eat standing up.

I was supposed to join Vienna in the darkroom by 10:00 a.m. I was not to be late. I would tie on my apron. It was one of Berthot's old aprons. It had been offered through Swain, and I'd left a dollar in Berthot's mailbox. Anyway, Vienna and I stood side by side, developing the portraits. If he requested, I'd work with him at night, too, though it wasn't until mid-October that I first worked with him entirely through a night.

At about eleven o'clock one night—it might've been late September, or, at the latest, the first week in October—he said, "I miss listening to the radio."

He said it in a friendly way, inviting, it seemed to me, a response.

"Why not get a shortwave?" I said. "Petchey could get one."

"He brought me one last year, in November. It arrived damaged."

"Couldn't Samuel Brant fix it?"

"Not without parts."

"Why not send back a complaint, see if they'd send up a new radio?"

"I considered that. Another shortwave could arrive intact. Or it could arrive broken again. Or say it arrived intact and I heard some long-distance news I wish I hadn't."

I didn't for the life of me know whether or not Vienna was trying out his sense of humor on me. I glanced at him in the candlelight. He didn't look anything but serious.

"That's a risk a person takes listening to the radio, I guess."

"I've got to consider each decision carefully, don't I?"

"All I know is, I hear something I wish I hadn't heard almost every day, radio or no radio. So I'm not exactly sure what you meant by that, Mr. Linn."

"It's true, Duvett," he said, "you can't control where the truth comes from, can you? You open a letter, it might contain something you didn't ever want to know. Or you say to your wife, 'How did you sleep last night?'—her answer might be so peculiar, it makes you think you couldn't possibly have heard it from someone you've known for years, or at least heard it correctly. But you're too shaken to ask her to repeat it, because it might be exactly word for word the same answer. Or, say you tune in a station from—from London—and you might hear of the death of kings."

"Kings?"

"Never mind, I was just referring to Shakespeare."

"I had some of that in school."

Vienna remained silent for the next two hours or so. Silence loud as donkeys in a barn fire, as my mother said once,

when my father, mother, and I had a quarrel and sat not talking at the dinner table. And in the darkroom it was like that.
Like silence brayed in my ears. "—too stupid to leave the
barn, though." The Eskimo faces one by one floated up from
the solutions. The bins of developing fluid caught the
shadow of our hands now and then, like a bird flying low
over water. I hung each photograph to dry on the stretched
twine. The candles burnt down and were replaced. A cough.
A clearing of the throat. I went to the toilet. It was dark out
in the hallway. Vienna would move a candle down the length
of the table. By candlelight he'd enter a new Eskimo name in
the ledger.

Two months of adultery, two months of employment
under Vienna Linn, two months of meandering around
Churchill.

I often overheard the Eskimo language spoken, especially
when I went to the Hudson's Bay Co. store; a number of Eskimo worked there.

The weather had been like a crazy quilt: sleet, snow, hail
all in one morning some days. Or bright, glinting days followed by a storm off Hudson's Bay. And yet every day I tried
to get out for a walk and sometimes walked a considerable
time along the river, where I didn't see much of anything,
except ravens, a skittish Arctic fox now and then, drifts of
clouds, moving silhouettes of Eskimo people on the horizon.
I never went down to the flats. Really, there was no reason
for me to be invited. I had my curiosities, but no expectations. I hadn't made anything but nodding acquaintance with

any Eskimo or Indian people. But I did encounter Eskimo children by the river. We were friendly to each other. They taught me some complicated cat's-cradle configurations, using seal-gut string. Sometimes they tagged along behind me; I'd suddenly turn and see them imitating the way I walked, slightly stoop-shouldered, looking at the ground, as if searching for a lost item. They'd just laugh and run off.

I was at the river late one day, when Driscoll Petchey emerged from a shack about thirty or so meters away. In fact, it was the shack closest to the river. I happened to be looking in that direction. There was a young Eskimo woman standing just inside the shack doorway. What I recall most clearly was that she wore Petchey's fur hat. It may have been a gift. The door closed. Petchey took a few steps away from the shack, noticed me, and walked straight over. It was snowing across the river, but not snowing on our side—naturally, the snow has to end somewhere, and I'd been told that the river sometimes divided the weather that way. "See that snow over there?" Petchey said when he got right up next to me. "Reminds me of the time I was flying between here and Winnipeg and I ran into a storm that put me hard on the uplift. I mean, it was like a ten-mile-wide trampoline. It was an independent son-of-a-bitch storm seeking its altitude. It came right underneath my plane, and I got bounced around so badly, I was gasping for air, my friend."

"Did your life pass before your eyes, like they say it does?"

"No. But I did run through all my regrets, which took about ten seconds. The rest of the time I was scared out of my wits."

"Well, I've only flown once, but you're the best pilot I ever flew with."

Petchey laughed. "So, Peter, how's it with you these days?"

"Okay. Fine. I miss a few things in Halifax—not too many. But other than that—"

It was bitterly cold out, but I'd gotten outfitted at the Bay Co. store, good coat, fur-lined hat and boots. And there was something about the cold that required inward thoughts to distract you, which I liked. "Am I interrupting your thinking something through?" Petchey said. "I know you value your walks."

"Nothing at all like that."

"I just now in that shack built up some warm memories, and stepped right back out into this cold, eh? That's how life is up here. A person learns to adapt to quick changes."

"Yes, a person does. I agree with that."

We both stood looking over at the town of Churchill. "World-class skyline, eh?" Petchey said.

The buildings and houses were so scattered, you could see between them out over to Hudson's Bay. "They're putting lights atop some of the new tallest buildings in Winnipeg," he said. "So planes won't hit them. A radio tower was the first."

We stood close to each other, facing in opposite directions now. "I see you've got a lady friend up here," I said.

"Her name's Ruth. My other fiancée, Martha, lives in Winnipeg."

"You've got more than one fiancée?"

"Yes, I do, for the time being. Between you and me, in confidence."

"I didn't mean to pry."

"You asked. I answered."

"Anyway—"

"And who can predict? I might decide on behalf of my friend here in Churchill. Or she might decide against me. Harold Thompson, who runs the Bay Co. store—you know Harold a bit by now, eh? He likes you. Harold married a local girl, so to speak. It's four children later now for them."

"He's been very civil to me."

A funnel of snow spun wildly, almost zigzagging over a stretch of the river. We both turned to watch it run its course, thin out, then disappear. "Locals call that a 'snow snake,' " Petchey said. "By the by, how's relations with Mrs. Linn?"

"Beg your pardon?"

"I see you two at breakfast. She's always a bit standoffish toward me, which is her privilege. I was just wondering what she's like to talk with. I've seen you two talking at breakfast."

"Well, at breakfast she's not standoffish. But she likes to get back to her studies."

"Her ghosts, I hear."

"She doesn't think of it that way."

"You've conversed enough, then, to know how she thinks of it."

"I'm impressed she's a serious scholar on a number of subjects."

"And Vienna Linn? How are relations with him? You know, employer-employee. He strikes me as a taskmaster."

"I've learned a lot."

"You already knew a lot, Peter, from working at that Halifax newspaper."

"I've learned a lot more."

"Darkroom's close quarters, though, I bet."

"At times."

"But otherwise?"

"He pays me on time. He's paid me every Friday."

"I bet you feel you're earning it."

"Yes, I do."

"Things in the hotel have a familiar feel, then?"

"I'm comfortable. Thanks for asking after me."

"Okay. Good," he said. He squeezed my shoulder. "That's good." He started back toward town. I was staring out over the river. "Oh, oh, oh! Look who's coming!"

I turned to look. Racing full-throttle from between shacks was the widest-shouldered dog I'd ever seen. "Eskimo sled dog," Petchey said. "Usually they keep this one tied up. He's got a reputation."

"For what?"

"You're looking at it."

The dog was about twenty meters away. "We're just supposed to stand here, is that it?" I said.

"No, that's *not* it," Petchey said. "When a dog comes at you like this, bend over a little, hold out your hand palm up, and call for it. This one's got an Eskimo name, but there's not time to teach you to pronounce it right. Just say, 'Here, boy. Here, boy.' "

The dog stopped running, spun in a circle, crouched, growled, bit snow, working himself up. Then edged closer.

"What's his goddamn name, Driscoll?"

"In Eskimo it means, *I'll attack you.*"

"So if he lives up to his name, we're dead."

I bent down slightly and held out my hand. "Here, boy," I said. "Here, boy." Only ten meters away now, the dog snarled back his black gums, bared his teeth. Then he lay down on the ground, belly exposed, growling and whimpering. "Look at that," Petchey said. "I swear, that's never worked before. I just heard it might work, if conditions were right."

I patted the dog's belly. "Which conditions?"

"Conditions—if the dog was exactly the type to respond the way you wanted. Every other condition might lose you a hand. Or at least a finger."

The dog was playful now. When Petchey again started for town, the dog followed close behind, nipping at Petchey's boot heels, leaping up, snapping the air, running off and back, off and back. The dog kept up its antics the entire way to the hotel. At the hotel it sat on the porch.

Petchey was right, the darkroom was close quarters. As Vienna himself predicted on the day we first met, he most often preferred not to talk, or at least to control when a conversation stopped. However, on the subject of baptism, he got quite agitated. "Painter will get a hundred albums' worth out of me—but I need the money," Vienna said one late afternoon in the darkroom. "Then the church will promote him off to somewhere. He's got quite a scam going, if you ask me."

"He wouldn't call it that, I guess."

At which point I was pretty much resigned to hearing out Vienna's moralizing, sometimes upward of ten minutes of high outrage. And I would think of what Miss Houghton wrote, that "opposing forces of good and evil often reside in the same person." Because, if Kala was to be believed (I was believing her more each day), in the darkroom I was standing next to a man who'd performed murderous deeds. I had that almost constantly in mind. It held sway over my thinking. In fact, I once mentioned to Kala that her husband's hatred for Painter was unnerving. She took in this information calmly, poured a glass of Goldwasser, drank it slowly, as if the pace of drinking were part of the contemplation, set the glass on the bedside table, walked over, and embraced me. "My husband's a man who despises fraudulence," she said. "Yet he defines it. Which might make him hate it all the more. What's more, he's brilliant enough to understand the contradiction. I think he revels in it.

"I know who my husband is."

L ate on the night of October 22, we sat on my bed. I'd just put my nightshirt back on. Kala slipped on my frayed blue shirt. She'd brought a small package with her to the room. "Bet you think I forgot it's your birthday," she said.

"What's in that package, then?"

"I've got two presents for you."

She presented me with the package. I opened it and found a pair of gray woolen socks from the Hudson's Bay Co. store.

"I need these," I said. "Thank you."

She handed me a piece of paper. It had letters and numbers written on it: R31 L5 R19.

"It's the combination to my safe," she said. "It's a small safe. It's guess where?"

"In the hotel, I take it."

Kala got up from bed, walked to the stand that held the water pitcher and bowl. It also had a small, latched door. I had never had the curiosity or cause to open it. But now Kala opened it, and there was the safe. "Aren't you dying to know what's in it?" she said.

I sat on the floor next to her, in front of the safe. She worked the combination by heart. The safe clicked open. Inside was a bundle of papers secured by a length of twine. She handed the bundle to me. I took it to the bed. Kala stood by the window.

I untied the papers. There were various newspaper clippings. There were personal letters. Envelopes with British stamps and postmarks.

"What you have in your hands," Kala said, "is evidence of my husband's wrongdoing. His *crimes*."

I shuffled through the envelopes; they were addressed to Vienna Linn. "You kept his personal letters?"

"Some I took straight out of rubbish baskets in hotel rooms. Others he'd ask me to burn and I didn't. I suppose you might say he got careless out of trust in me. Though some he destroyed on his own."

"Why's this my birthday present?"

"Don't you give something intimate for birthdays?" she said. "Start with the clippings. Each one's about a so-called accident. The passenger train leaving Vancouver. The milk train on a night run to Regina. So on and so forth. Six in all, I believe. Those accidents so-called cover about five years' time. The five years I've been with Vienna. The letters are from Radin Heur. Not personally from Heur—I told you he's too smart for that. They're written by his loyal secretary.

"Set them side by side, the letters, the clippings, match up the dates, and it's like a jigsaw puzzle put together. The letters each begin with something like 'Mr. Heur tells me that when he was last in Canada'—and I highly doubt he ever set foot in Canada—'when he was last in Canada, he saw a wonderful sight, a milk train winding slowly through the snowy countryside. Oh, wouldn't it be terrible should a tragedy befall such a train. The toppled train cars. White milk poured out over the tracks.' Quite the frustrated poet, Mr. Heur. 'But if fate was benevolent, and a photographer happened by, even through pure luck, photographs of such an incident would be priceless to posterity, don't you imagine?'

"And then the die was cast. The *accident* suggested."

Kala looked out the window. "Peter," she said, "should anything happen to me, be a dear, will you, and send these letters and clippings to your newspaper down in Halifax, will you?"

"Happen to you?"

Kala sat on the bed, but still looked out the window. "Miss Houghton said the mark of a thoughtful person is that one is capable of the foretaste of regret."

"What's that mean?"

"It means that even though you're right in the present moment, you can imagine horribly regretting something you didn't attend to in life. You deeply feel regret in advance. It almost knocks the wind out of you. You suddenly become alert: 'Wake up. Wake up.' This thing is happening *now* . . . Like a punch or a slap. As a result, you correct your life accordingly, if at all possible. Do you understand?"

"You'd what with these clippings, then? Regret not putting Vienna Linn in jail?"

"I'd regret that I knew he'd committed such violent acts and I had nothing to prove them by. Should I die before my husband does, that is. Radin Heur's letters only suggest that accidents *could* occur. They *suggest* the photographs. They only prove that Radin Heur had—an imagination. They never out-and-out offer money. It wouldn't take Sherlock Holmes to make the connection, to connect up these letters and clippings. And even if Radin Heur or Vienna couldn't, finally, be punished in some way by the law, knowing that their reputations might be ruined, or anything, *anything* to make life miserable— That would keep me amused in the afterlife."

"Kala, do you actually believe there's an—"

"—*afterlife*? What does it matter what I believe? Time will prove the existence of an afterlife to me or to anyone, won't it, Peter? Won't it—because who cares if it really exists or not? I don't. Not really. I only care that I want it to so badly. That Miss Houghton wanted it to."

"I meant, nobody in that book of yours—"

"*The Unclad Spirit*. I *insist* that you call it by its proper name."

"—as far as I've understood, nobody in *The Unclad Spirit* announced ahead of time, 'Guess what, I intend to return in a spirit picture!' They didn't have any control over that, Kala."

"Still, they cross back over."

"Kala, are you afraid of Vienna? I'm asking straight out. Are you afraid of him?"

"Never afraid, no. I'm *aware* of him. I'm knowledgeable about him."

"As far as these clippings go, what do you want me to promise, exactly?"

"*Exactly*, I want you to promise that you'll set all these papers on some reporter's desk. And that you'll add the necessary explanations."

"I don't know that much."

"You know enough. You'll know more."

"All right. I promise."

"Simple as that?"

"For once, yes."

"Please don't promise just to end this conversation."

"I'm promising. And let's end it."

"Thank you."

Obviously I didn't have much foretaste of regret, because I said, "Why not materialize yourself, Kala. You know, if you should die, why not show up in a newspaper photograph, front page? I'll personally write the caption. How about, *Deceased Wife of Man Behind Train Wrecks Points a Finger of Guilt*—something like that? You could show up in the photograph. You could be floating there, just over his shoulder, pointing at him."

Wearing only my shirt, Kala slammed out of my room. Her clothes were left strewn on the chair and floor. I loved that sight, her clothes tossed about. But now it made me take five deep breaths.

———

The next day Kala did not come down for breakfast. I sat at the corner table. I had *The Unclad Spirit* set in front of me, next to my plate. I thought that if Kala came into the dining room, she might be pleased to see me reading it, perhaps let me apologize. But it was Vienna who sat down across from me. It was the first time I'd actually seen him walk into the dining room. As was his custom, he was dressed in his woolen suit and trousers, black shoes, "like a professor lost in the wilderness," as Petchey once described him.

He dipped a cloth napkin in the water pitcher and cleaned his glasses, then fit his glasses back on. "Dining alone," he said. "How nice." He then noticed the book. He picked it up. "I'll bring this to Kala," he said. "She's feeling quite ill this morning. Running a fever, I'm afraid. It's alarming. I'm sure having her book will comfort her, don't you think, Duvett?"

He drummed his fingers on the book's cover, and so it became an object of accusation.

"I'm sorry to hear she's ill," I said. "I saw Dr. Ott at breakfast a short while ago. In fact, he just left for the Bay Co. store."

"Yes, Dr. Ott, of course."

Vienna turned halfway from the table. "Take the day off work, Duvett," he said. "I'm not in need of you today. Take tomorrow off, too, please. And since it's my request, you'll still be paid the two days' wages. In order to keep things on the up-and-up, professional, you see. I'll expect you at 10:00 a.m., day after tomorrow, then."

Before I could respond, he walked into the lobby. He spoke with Thomas Swain a moment, went upstairs, came back down wearing his overcoat, hat, gloves, and left the hotel.

I did not see Kala at all that day. She did not come to my room that night, and I slept fitfully at best.

I did not see Kala the next day either, but she came to my room that night at about eleven o'clock. She set a bottle of Goldwasser on the table at the right side of the bed, which, over the weeks, had become the side she slept on. "Mr. Petchey now delivers my favorite bottles to me without me even having to ask," she said. "I've only one left, though." She lay back on the bed and closed her eyes a moment. "I've been half delirious all day." Her voice was raspy, her cheeks and forehead in a kind of fever hue, and otherwise she looked completely pale. She was wearing the black dress she wore for lectures.

"Why're you wearing that dress?" I said.

"I don't know, really. Sometimes—since I was a little girl—when I felt bad, I'd get dressed up."

"It's a bit morbid, don't you think?"

"No, I don't. I don't think of this dress that way at all."

"I'm sorry. Vienna—I saw him at breakfast—he did mention you were ill."

She pulled the nightclothes up to her shoulders. "May I have a glass of water?" she said. "I can't remember if it's starve a cold, feed a fever, or vice versa. This afternoon I was burning up."

I sat next to her on the bed, took her hands in mine. "I'm sorry about what I said. I've been sorry for two days," I said. "It was stupid of me. I apologize. I'm sorry."

She drank most of the glass of water I'd handed to her. Then she sipped from the bottle of Goldwasser. We didn't speak. Then she fell asleep, her head turned slightly to the left away from me. I took the bottle from her hand. Without undressing, I slid under the bedclothes.

There were two incidents that night.

First, at about 1:00 a.m., I would guess, I woke to the presence of five people in the room. They were more or less shadow-figures. Still, there was no mistaking them for anything other than four Eskimo children who were accompanied by Samuel Brant. Brant held a lit candle in a holder. Kala was sound asleep. Brant led the children to the window. One by one, they touched the glass. One child scraped at the frost with his fingernail.

There was a full moon. It appeared as if moonlight had been caught in the glass, saturating the frost, highlighting the frost's leaf shapes, curlicues, feathery swirls, etchings of various other wild shapes. The Eskimo shacks by the river didn't have windows. I could tell that the children were delighted. However, Brant had simply gone and opened my hotel room door. He was out and out trespassing on my privacy and obviously didn't care in the least. Since there must've been frost on the windows in the hotel's empty rooms, more than likely trespassing was the true reason for his visit. At one point he turned, held the candle out, looked at me and Kala in bed. (I closed my eyes.) He said a few words in the Eskimo language; Petchey had told me Brant was good at speaking it. I also heard him say, "Mrs. Linn," which made a few of the children giggle. Then Brant moved them out of the room. They ran off down the hallway. Brant stood at the end of the bed. "I charged the whole bunch a dollar to look at the pretty window," he said, obviously sensing I was awake. "But they got more than they bargained for, eh?" Brant shut the door hard behind him.

Kala stirred a little but didn't wake. Toward Brant I felt murderous, add humiliated and confused—no matter how clearly I'd been educated in Brant's temperament over the past weeks, I still could scarcely believe he'd walk in on us like that. I tried to think clearly. If I confronted him, he'd somehow use it to make things worse. I reached over to the bedside table, took up the bottle, and drank some Gold-wasser myself, then managed to fall back asleep.

Later in the night there came an altogether different incident.

I woke to a shuffling sound, but to whatever degree I'd come into consciousness, it was still in the slight haze of the Goldwasser. I woke, but my eyes remained closed, and what registered as if on the outside of my eyelids seemed like lightning. (The tourist brochure had mentioned "exotic winter lightning.") Perhaps two or three flashes at brief intervals, opaque as if they'd arrived through the moon-frozen window. Thinking he might have come back, I recall muttering an obscenity at Brant. Anyway, I then turned in the bed, falling into a deep sleep. And when I woke for good, I reached for my pocket watch and saw that it was 6:45. Kala was still asleep. I touched her forehead, then laid my palm flat against it. Not good, I thought, she's burning up. I woke her. "Kala," I said, "please let me get you back to your room. You should be in your room." In the hallway she leaned heavily against me, we slowly got to her room. I figured Vienna was in the darkroom—where else? I helped Kala lie on the bed, undressed her, but when I started to slip off the knitted sock from her right foot, she said, "No." I pulled the bedcovers up to her neck and she drifted right off.

That morning I was in the darkroom by ten o'clock. Not a word was exchanged between Vienna and me for two hours, during which time we developed a dozen portraits. I ate lunch alone. But as I was drinking tea, Vienna again approached my table. "It's room 25 today," he said, meaning that Swain had designated that room for portrait-taking. I don't know why he chose a different room each time, as the hotel was so empty, but he did. Anyway, I finished my tea and went up to room 25. Vienna was already there. I set up the backdrop cloth, chair, tripod camera. The first subject arrived at about 1:30. It was the woman at whose shack I'd seen Driscoll Petchey. She was wearing a well-worn parka, two shirts, leggings, and I could see the ends of long johns down over her boots. She had a very round face with dark red-brown skin. Her full name was Ruth Nipiiq. I knew this because I saw that Vienna had already written her name in the ledger. She came into the room, sat down in the chair, looked at me, and said, "You saw me with Driscoll."

"Yes, I did."

"He's taking Mary and Moses Nuqac down to Winnipeg. Mary Naniaqueeit, too. Mary needs doctors to take a picture of her insides."

"It's called X-rays."

"Mary needs those, yes. I'd let an Eskimo doctor reach inside me, but I wouldn't go to Winnipeg."

"She'll be fine."

"I don't know."

"Do you know when they're leaving?"

"Everyone will know—the plane makes a lot of noise when it flies off."

As it turned out, Ruth Nipiiq was the only one to have her portrait taken that day. Petchey had flown Painter up to Padlei so he could baptize several Eskimo families, then bring them to Churchill to be photographed. It was all worked out ahead of time. But for one reason or other, they refused to leave home. Petchey and Painter flew back and told Vienna and me this in the lobby of the hotel. "Painter will try with those people again," Driscoll said, "when I get back from Winnipeg."

"When exactly do you go down there?" Vienna said. "I need some materials."

"Day after tomorrow. Leaving at first light."

Ruth Nipiiq had her portrait taken, then Vienna and I repaired to the darkroom again. We had ten or so more portraits to develop, now including Ruth's. Suddenly he was in a pontificating mood. "I've noticed it's hard for you and Sam Brant to avoid exchanging hostilities," he said.

Working the print tongs, I said, "Every chance he gets, he doesn't avoid them."

"He was so inebriated at our wedding, they had to carry him out."

"Driscoll Petchey told me that."

"Even so, it's true."

"It's as if Brant holds a grudge against me. First—just for showing up and getting the job he wanted. Then I asked him to carry up my suitcase. He's the bellhop. It wasn't as if I'd asked him something you don't ask a bellhop."

"Bellhop's tasks are far down his list of priorities. Something I'm sure you've taken note of, Duvett. Even though he's paid for being a bellhop."

"I've never had a man hate me right off like that and not let up. The other morning I was in the dining room with Brant. I don't know how he made time to eat his eggs and toast, glaring at me full-time."

"Brant's hard to ignore. He drinks half the day long. The other half he's no doubt too drunk to know he's not drinking. That information, alas, comes from Thomas Swain, who finds Brant asleep in this or that empty room."

"When he's got to fix something, he sobers up, though."

"He's a fine mechanic. He's self-taught in motors. He keeps the hotel's generator running nicely. And Petchey pays him to keep the plane in good working order. He knows that plane like the back of his hand. Last summer, Brant built a windmill. It generated electricity. He built a windmill from the ground up. It's stored near the grain silos now."

"Talented at any number of things, Brant. I prefer to admire him from a distance."

"He often takes leaves-of-absence, you might say."

"You mean, sleeping it off in a hotel room?"

"No, I mean he goes downriver with Indian or Eskimo families. They get along famously."

"Mrs. Linn said that Brant reminds her—in looks—of one of the 'uninvited guests' in her book."

"She never mentioned that to me."

"Well, it was just in passing."

We developed a few more photographs without talking.

"You see, Duvett," Vienna finally said, "one result of living in so small a place as Churchill is that you see the same people so often. And that's predictable enough, isn't it. However, one unforeseen consequence has been that, now and then, Kala tries to—well, she probably can't help herself."

"Tries to what?"

"I'm referring now to what she said about Samuel Brant looking like somebody in a spirit photograph. It's not enough that Kala sees Brant every single day, or almost every day. She has to *complicate* his presence, as it were. By suggesting that Brant's died and come back to earthly form. I mean, she might not have said exactly that, but it's what she's possibly referring to, thinking Brant's the type to cause trouble in this life and then come back in a photograph and keep causing trouble."

"She's seen Petchey's likeness in her book, too."

"She never mentioned that to me," he said.

"Pity. Like life in Churchill's one big séance to her, eh?"

"Think of it however you wish."

"Maybe it helps pass the time is all. Mrs. Linn's a very imaginative woman, I think."

"Do you?"

"Yes."

Silence and more silence. "Well, before our time's done here, Duvett, we'll have Painter sitting at the hand of God, all these portraits."

"I need some air," I said. I left the darkroom. I started toward the stairs. On the second-floor landing I looked over and saw Kala in the library. She was at the desk, writing in one of her lecture notebooks. She had on her overcoat, a scarf around her neck. *The Unclad Spirit* was open on the table in front of her. That book moves through the hotel almost as much as any person, I thought. I was surprised to see that Kala wasn't completely bedridden. Just in the few minutes I observed, she both spilled ink from the inkwell and threw her pen across the room, slowly picking it up. While writing, it appeared that she pressed down hard on the pen. As if she was etching something into the paper.

I had a cup of tea in the lobby. Half an hour went by and I was again side by side with Vienna in the darkroom. Shortly after I stepped into the room, he said, "I've just now gone up to see how my wife is faring. And I found she'd taken her notes and correspondences into the library. I admonished her—scolded her, really, like a good husband. 'You must take care of yourself. You should be in bed.' But I let her be. I wonder if writing won't do her some good. I wonder if she slept well last night. Sleep, Dr. Ott said, helps most."

"Did he examine her yet?"

"So far, she absolutely refuses to let Ott touch her."

"Maybe she's seen a resemblance between Dr. Ott and someone in her book."

Saying that, I immediately felt my stomach knot up, at how I was making light of Kala's beliefs at her expense, just in order to keep up stupid banter with Vienna. It felt like a kind of betrayal.

"Yes, maybe I should insist that she see Ott," he said.

"I hear he's not much of a doctor. He's just the only doctor."

"He often suggests, if his patients are truly ill—down with something he's no expert at—that they go down to Winnipeg and check right into hospital. He's done so with Mary Naniaqueeit, as you might know. She's to get X-rays."

"I hope Mrs. Linn won't have to go there. Do you think she might?"

"To the ends of the earth, if need be, of course."

I hung Ruth Nipiiq's portrait up to dry.

"What, anyway, do you personally think of Mrs. Linn's scholarship?" Vienna said. I glanced at his face in profile. He seemed all seriousness. "That is, if you've thought of it at all."

"About Miss Houghton, you mean? Georgiana Houghton—"

"All of that, yes. Has she tried out any lectures or parts of lectures on you yet? I'd venture to guess she has. Perhaps in the lobby, or the dining room at breakfast, say."

"At breakfast once—maybe twice. Not a whole lecture. Parts."

"At breakfast. Or course."

"I admire her dedication to the subject."

"As for me—" Vienna moved to the corner and sat down on the wooden stool. "I'm afraid, in Kala's eyes, I'm a wretched unbeliever. I think the photographs—from a professional point of view, mind you—are all shams. Fakes, every last one. Every goddamn last one of them. Now, I realize there's detailed testimony to the contrary. That people have watched every step of the developing process and so forth. That, in such instances, there was no noticeable fakery in

technique—no sleight-of-hand. But what's sleight-of-hand
except successful deceit? I know the chemistry of it pretty
well, photography. Then, of course, there's the general notion
of any dead person—what's Houghton call it? *Materializ-
ing.* Let alone how laughable it is that they'd somehow have
the conscious ability to—to—'show up' in a photograph. To
*choose* to show up. Even if you subscribe to so-called divine
intervention—come now. It simply isn't possible. And you,
Duvett, knowing what you now know, hearing what you've
heard, perhaps having read some in Kala's book—would you
at this point call yourself a wretched unbeliever? About spirit
pictures, I mean."

"I hardly know anything about it."

"There's absolutely no backbone to that answer," he said,
highly irritated now.

"If I have to choose, then, I'd say 'wretched unbeliever.' "

"I'll keep it our little secret," Vienna said. "I won't mention it to Mrs. Linn."

I looked to see if there were any more portraits to develop. "It looks as if we're through for the day here, right?" I
said. I was desperate to get out of the room.

"Not quite," he said. "I've a few more to develop. And, if
you don't mind, let's indulge your impressive talents, Duvett."

"Talents for what?"

"Why, for captions. Captions, Mr. Duvett. I need captions
for these next three photographs—let's see, where have I put
the plates? Yes—" He reached up to a shelf, brought down
the plates. "Here they are."

"Are they portraits? Because you always just use the

name, date, the name of the person baptized—no captions."

"They're a different sort of picture. I've been *moonlighting*, you might say. I need a little extra money coming in, I'll be frank about it. Perhaps I can sell these three to an interested party. Here in Canada. Or London. Somewhere, I hope."

"Just the three, then?"

"And I promise I'll use whatever captions you come up with, and pay you in addition to your wages."

"Let's have a look."

I started to develop the first negative. "Captions aren't my strength," Vienna said, stepping back a way. "—the literary. Let's just refer to them as numbers one, two, and three, shall we?"

As I transferred the negative, developer dish to stop bath, I noticed that Vienna had now tucked himself to the corner of the darkroom, to the right of the door.

Photograph number one was of Kala and me in bed.

"You look stunned, Duvett. What's the problem—has it turned out all right? Can you see every little detail?"

I didn't answer. I stared down at the photograph: Kala and me asleep, the bedclothes turned down neatly, as if a house-keeper had simply worked around us.

"When my wife sleeps next to me," Vienna said, "she takes her clothes off. So you can imagine my surprise—"

Kala, wearing her black dress, lay with her head against my shoulder. The top three buttons of her dress were open. (I don't remember when this happened.) My right hand lay, gently it seemed, over her breast.

"As for a caption, may I suggest *Not Man and Wife?*" Vienna said. Trying, but mostly failing, to force a calmness into each word. "Or—we could foist a lie on some patron or other. Along the lines of *Man and Wife*, say."

"I think I won't develop a second one," I said.

I felt the barrel of Vienna's revolver against the side of my head.

"You'd actually sell this to someone, wouldn't you?" I said.

"Odd thing, Mrs. Linn wearing her dress as she sleeps. She *never* keeps her clothes on when she sleeps in the same bed as me."

"She says that's not too often. She says it wasn't ever often."

There was a long silence. Vienna sighed. "How much do you want to live, Duvett? How badly? I could easily use this revolver. I've used it against lesser remarks." He pulled back the hammer. "Put in the second negative."

"What's the point of it?"

"It's the work at hand."

He backed off a short way. I went to work. In the second photograph Kala had her mouth pressed to my ear. We both still appeared to be asleep.

Vienna stepped up close, then back against the wall. "That one," he said, "I'm afraid was tampered with a bit. I mean, I tried to remove your hand from under my wife's dress. But she stirred—and I *never* want to wake her, sleep comes to her with such difficulty. Sleep's been a rare—the rarest—commodity for my dear wife. Yet not as rare as it is for me. And she's been so ill of late."

Vienna lowered the revolver.

"Remarkable, isn't it? I work in a darkroom all night. I

fret about this and that. I mull things over. I work through my philosophical curiosities, this or that subject. I review my failures, with not a little torment—"

I bolted for the door, Vienna pushed me hard against the table, then struck my face with the barrel of the revolver a solid blow. Dazed a moment, I fell against the counter, then regained my balance.

"All the while"—he said, his voice raised. Then, in a more civil tone—"my greatest failure is taking place in a different room from mine in this very same hotel. I may not be sleeping with another man's wife, Duvett, but I indeed have something in common with you. When I do sleep, I sleep the sleep of the guilty."

"I didn't ask for this to happen, Mr. Linn."

He struck me a bit less of a blow, but still I reeled from it.

"Don't! Do not insult me. Don't suggest that my wife *pressed herself* on you. Backed you, innocent boy, into a corner. And don't otherwise insult my wife, that your charms were hypnotic."

"I have no suggestions at all."

I couldn't see the revolver. Vienna may have been holding it behind his back, or had set it down. It was as if my brain hurt. My eyes felt as if they were bleeding. I still leaned against the counter, just to keep standing.

"Mr. Duvett, now that we're permanently back on formal terms. Mr. Duvett, don't you think that I know my wife? I know my wife. I know that she's kept certain clippings. Certain letters from London."

"What are you getting at?"

He swept his arm across the table. Paraphernalia went flying in the near-dark, metal clattered to the floor. I think it was a pair of shears that ricocheted off my chest. Vienna was breathing hard. He seemed then to calm himself down a moment, leaned forward clutching the wooden stool. He pounded it with both fists. (He isn't holding the revolver, I thought.) "What I am *getting at*, Mr. Duvett, is that I now have the safe in my possession. I do not yet have the combination to the safe. But I intend to hire Samuel Brant to open it for me anyway. He's very good at such things."

There was so much tension in the room now that I broke a glass beaker in my hand without really realizing I'd even picked it up. My hand was split open; by candlelight I saw blood on the glass, on my sleeves, dripping into the stop bath.

"You'd better do something about that," Vienna said. "You better see if Ott needs to stitch up your hand. So it won't get infected. Or else you might have to go down to Winnipeg."

He left the darkroom. I swathed my hand in a towel taken from a stack of hotel towels we always kept for use in the darkroom.

When the bleeding stopped, I doused the wound in rubbing alcohol kept under the counter. Then I developed the third negative. In it Kala had turned her head away from me, but we held hands, and (I now remember this moment) I appear to be shading my closed eyes with my free hand. From this I had to figure that what I was reacting to was the vague shudder of light on my eyelids. Not "exotic winter lightning" at all, but the hand-held bulb flash of Vienna's camera.

———

It seemed unbearable to set foot out into the hotel just yet—and almost equally unbearable to stay in the dark-room another moment. I clipped the three photographs to the twine. I pulled over the stool, sat down on it, held the candle close, and looked at Kala and me a long time.

# VIEW OF KALA MURIE
## CUTTING IN ON GHOSTS

I admit that I read *The Unclad Spirit* on my own. Some mornings, Kala left it in my room. Miss Houghton wrote down some good stories about adultery.

On page 239 she says, "When I think back on all I've learned, I firmly believe that every spirit picture happened for an enlightened reason, God's logic, not ours, and not necessarily understandable at the time." That would be something Kala would want to discuss for hours. "Lucky for us," Kala said, "Miss Houghton had an inordinate interest in the drama of other people's lives. I think they liked to talk to her. They liked to send her letters. When she died, they say there were five hundred unanswered letters in her study."

I had my favorites, the one about Mr. Everett Ames, for example. Ames, who lived in Hay-on-Wye, Wales, had carried on an adulterous affair with Mrs. Bernard Sichel—Tess. The affair went on for eight years. Everett thought that his own wife, Mary Ames, had no knowledge of it. And six months later, when Mary died in 1880, Tess divorced her own husband, promptly marrying Everett. The marriage was "done in a flurry." The wedding portrait was taken by a Mr. Stephen Miles.

When Miles developed the photograph, there, standing behind Everett Ames, was his first wife, Mary, the uninvited guest. Claiming to be shocked by this, yet taking advantage of its incriminating nature ("in a very gossip-prone community"), Miles offered the photograph and negative to Everett Ames for 200 English pounds. He told Ames that if he had any doubts about the photograph's authenticity, he should be there in person when a second photograph from the same negative was developed. But Ames bought the photograph and negative right away.

About this situation, Miss Houghton wrote one of my favorite sentences in the whole book: "Now, what a person does with knowledge unpredictably gained either reveals one's most deeply informing dignity, or cowardice." (I was in bed with Kala when I first read that; it really got my thinker going. That was a favorite phrase of my mother's, to "get your thinker going." When the source or reason for something truly baffled or eluded my mother, she'd actually knuckle the top of her head like knocking on a door, say, "Knock, knock, knock, come on in and show yourself.") Whether inspired by dignity or cowardice, I don't know, but what Everett Ames did next was to invite a number of local newspapermen to his house. He related to them every sordid detail of his affair with the former Mrs. Sichel. As Miss Houghton describes it, this was a formal gathering. Ames served cookies and tea. The newspapermen sat in the living room, while Tess kept to the kitchen, listening in. Hearing Ames begin his confession, Tess went upstairs, came back down carrying a suitcase, walked out the front door, and never returned.

"Ames had the spirit photograph, expertly framed, displayed on the fireplace mantel, in a place honoring his shame, if you will.

"In fact, he'd removed from the mantel every evidence of good citizenship, family photographs, church citations, a caricature of him holding an enormous shovel, beneath which read, *Everett Ames, Councilman, Breaking Ground for New School.* The newspapermen wrote feverishly as Ames carried on for an hour or more. He ended by saying, 'I consider this spirit picture a sign from God. I therefore am, from this moment on, dedicating myself to the church, and will live in a constant state of repentance, and would gladly serve as a public spectacle, if it meant any chance of more merciful judgment at the Gates of Heaven.' The newspapers printed all of this."

However, one journalist—Donald Mangold—took it upon himself to look further into the matter. He tracked down Stephen Miles, who'd "fled to London." Over a number of whiskeys, Miles admitted that the photograph had been tampered with, the spirit picture was a fake. "When word of this got back to Mr. Everett Ames," wrote Miss Houghton, "it mattered to him not in the least. For even such deception had already served a higher purpose."

After staring at—I might say studying—the photographs of Kala and me in my bed for at least an hour, I left the darkroom and returned to my hotel room. Again I could only sleep in fits and starts. First thing the next morning, I got up from bed, shaved with a strop razor, dressed, and went downstairs. As I passed the check-in counter, I heard Thomas Swain say to Brant, "Take Mr. Linn's belongings to 310. He doesn't own much." When they noticed me standing there they fell silent. No greeting. I went into the dining room and sat down for breakfast. Swain came in; he was the morning's waiter. This wasn't unusual. It was always either he, a niece of Moses and Mary Nuqac's who was about fifteen years old, or, far less often, Mrs. Harkin, who doubled up work as bookkeeper at the Hudson's Bay Co. store.

"Toast and coffee," I said to Swain when he walked over to my table. I didn't look up at him.

"No bacon? No eggs?"

"Toast and coffee, thanks."

Swain shrugged, then delivered my order to Mr. Berthot in the kitchen. When Swain came back out, he took up his station behind the check-in counter, where, since I'd come to Churchill, I'd never seen anyone actually check in, except for me. Swain now played chess with himself. Petchey once asked him why he played alone like that, and Swain had answered, "You both win and lose, of course. But the odd thing is, if I beat my opponent—me—handily, I still feel pretty good about it."

In a few moments, Vienna walked in and, without invitation or protest on my part, sat down at my table. He set a bottle of Goldwasser between us. It was no later than 7:00 a.m. He unscrewed the top and drank from the bottle. "Mrs. Linn loves this stuff. Of course, you knew that, right?" he said. "As for me, I'm going to acquire a taste for it, right here and now, Duvett. Right while you're having breakfast."

Swain went back to the kitchen. He then brought out my breakfast. "One piece is slightly burnt," he said. "Berthot wants to own up to it." He turned toward Vienna. "Your room—it'll be 310. Sam's bringing your belongings over there as we speak."

"Very good," Vienna said, swigging from the bottle.

"Want coffee to wash that down?" Swain said.

"Each gulp will wash down the one before," Vienna said. "That's how it works. Thanks, anyway. Very thoughtful of you, Mr. Swain." Swain went back to his chess game.

"I'm going to detail out a plan," Vienna said. "And you're going to be a polite boy and listen."

"I've decided, if Kala is ill enough that she has to go to Winnipeg, I'm going with her," I said.

"Oh, I doubt she's ill as all that, Duvett. She had scarlet fever some years ago. It was much worse. She carried on."

"If she goes to Winnipeg, I'll accompany her."

"Perhaps I'll put that revolver to your head again, Duvett, and pull the trigger. Then *I'll* accompany my own wife to Winnipeg, should that be necessary."

"Threat after threat— You know what, though? I'm going to tell everyone in this hotel—Swain, Petchey, even Brant."

"Tell them what, exactly?"

"About Mrs. Linn's and my—behavior."

"Serving what purpose, do you think?"

"If everyone knows, they'll know you'll be fuming over it. And they probably already know you keep a revolver. Driscoll Petchey thinks you're some kind of criminal fugitive—"

"On the lam—"

"He's right."

"His famous intuition, Mr. Petchey's."

"Famous or not, he's right."

"Fugitive not from the *law*, Duvett, because the law has no idea yet about my part in that train wreck outside Montreal, for instance. Botched as it was. My wife knows of it. Mr. Radin Heur knows of it. And I'm sure by now Kala's told you of it, during one of your nighttime conversations. No, you see, I came to Churchill because I was a fugitive from Mr. Radin Heur. Not the law."

"Maybe I'll sit down with Swain and Petchey and show them the newspaper clippings. I'll say, 'Guess the real identity of who you've got in your hotel, here.' "

"Yet where are those clippings, Duvett? How will anyone believe you without evidence? No matter. Say what you want to whom you want. It'll all be futile. You'd only be preaching to the converted, because I've already *informed* Mr. Swain. Already *told* him about you and Mrs. Linn. Why do you think I've taken another room? I asked right out in public for another room. So of course Sam Brant knows, too. He's bringing my things to my new room, isn't he, Duvett?"

He took a drink of Goldwasser.

"In fact," he said, "it was Brant's suggestion that I take the photographs of you and my wife in bed that night. No, Mr. Duvett, you see, in effect all you'd accomplish is to make a small hotel seem smaller yet."

"I'll say you threatened my life."

"Say what you like." He sighed deeply, turned his entire body so that he was now looking directly into the lobby. "Just this morning I asked Samuel Brant to clean my revolver. To get it in tiptop shape. I made it clear that I was afraid you might attempt violence toward me, out of jealousy, of course. Get rid of the husband who's in the way. That in the throws of infatuation you might not be thinking as clearly as you might."

"This hotel's already so small, it's turned inside out."

"Anyway, Duvett—Kala won't be on the airplane because the airplane shall be having difficulties, I assure you. Severe mechanical difficulties. It's all arranged."

"Arranged—"

"You don't seem to have an appetite, Duvett." He reached out, picked up a piece of my toast, and took a bite. He dropped the toast onto the tablecloth. "Shall we repair to the darkroom, then? A more private place to talk about such private things." He drank more Goldwasser, stood up, wobbled a few seconds, caught his balance, then set out for the stairs.

I waited a few moments, then followed Vienna up. When I opened the door, he was sitting on the stool in front of the three photographs of Kala and me, which were still hung on the twine. "I think I'll keep these for my private collection," he said, slipping the photographs one by one into a satchel. Buckling the satchel, he leaned it against the wall near the door. Fumbling about, he found a box of matches, then lit three candles. "Sit on that side of the room," he said. "I'll sit here."

"Now—" he said. He took the revolver from under a stack of folded towels and set it on the counter. "—do you know what my morning reading's been?"

"No, I don't."

"Well, Samuel Brant opened the safe that my wife kept hidden from me all this time. It took him only a few minutes. And what an education in my own life's work I got, looking at what was in that safe. To see it all laid out like that. The letters. The clippings. And to think I sometimes worry my life's been a waste and a folly, Duvett."

"Kala doesn't know you have the safe, then?"

"You may not ask me questions, Duvett. You may only listen. You see, I'm under much duress, much strain. More than you possibly can imagine. Mr. Heur's capable of—"

"What's that have to do with Petchey's airplane?"

"It's all arranged. Samuel Brant will be getting the plane in proper working order, so to speak. In his own fashion, based on payment from me. The three Eskimo—and of course Petchey—will be on board. Nothing's foolproof, but I have confidence that when the plane departs early on the morning Petchey's to take the Eskimo folks down to Winnipeg, it won't be completely able to leave the ground. Or barely get off the ground. Damage, one hopes, will be impressive. It should be over in a matter of minutes. But a useful scene will be set. I'll be there to photograph it."

"Someone could get killed is what you're saying."

"If someone doesn't, I can perhaps lie to Mr. Heur and say someone did, which, to his tastes, makes a photograph more preferable. This photograph—or photographs—at worst, will reduce my debt and show good faith toward reducing it more. Later, I'll find a new place to work. I'm considering Europe. A European train here and there. It's my living."

"And why shouldn't I just tell Driscoll Petchey?"

He took up the revolver, pressing its barrel to my heart, and held it there.

"My wife's seductions, they've offered you a taste of the future, haven't they? You'll fail to apply your good conscience because of that, too. You want to be with her, don't

you? Unless I'm free to leave, how will that be entirely possible?" Vienna fell silent a moment. "If you're so worried
about the folks in that plane, Duvett, why not try prayer?
Maybe prayer will work. 'Now I lay me down to sleep, I pray
the Lord.' Well, you figure out what to ask God for. Try it,
Duvett—you're a wordsmith."

Vienna proceeded to blow out the candles, and when the
room was dark, he said, "After the accident, you'll help me
develop the photographs. Then I'll contact Radin Heur. And
then I'll follow with arrangements to leave this wretched
hellhole. And when my dear wife's recovered from her present illness, she'll look up and see you standing there, loyal at
her bedside. Kala despises me. I hardly need tell you that. Just
think of it: I get my money from Radin Heur—at least I can
enter civilization again, not worried one of his thugs will kill
me in the blink of an eye."

"I believe here and now you'd kill those people."

"Oh yes, Duvett, you most definitely should believe that."

"Brant might be a good mechanic, but he can't control
what happens to that plane."

"A challenge for him, granted."

"You're desperate enough about Radin Heur to risk add-
ing new murders to everything else?"

"Rest assured."

Carrying the revolver, Vienna now left the darkroom.
Standing at the door, I watched him walk toward the landing. He was holding the satchel as well. He stopped but
didn't turn around. "I've burned those letters and clippings,
Duvett," he said. He went down the stairs.

I waited a few moments, then went directly to Kala's
room. Dr. Ott was just leaving. "How is she?" I said.

"Quite badly off, I'm afraid," Ott said. "No visiting hours today, Peter. I must be firm about that. Or tonight, either. Her fever's down a degree, but she's suffering from a very stubborn infection of some sort. Minor delirium, I've seen much worse. There's been improvement. She's sleeping now. That's likely to help, sleep is."

Dr. Ott and I walked down to the lobby. He then put on his coat, hat, and gloves and left the hotel.

Less than an hour later I saw Dr. Ott taking tea with Driscoll Petchey in front of the fireplace. Ott had his black doctor's bag at his feet. I sat down in a corner chair, paging through a magazine, I don't even recall which. Their conversation faded in and out of my hearing. As I looked at Driscoll, I heard in my mind, word for word, Kala's astonishment that he looked almost exactly like one of the "uninvited guests" in *The Unclad Spirit*, then snapped out of it. I overheard a brief discussion about Kala's "condition" and would Ott be joining a poker game that night at Harold Thompson's house.

Ott then mentioned that he'd received an invitation to a conference in Winnipeg in the spring. "I'll fly you down," Petchey said.

"Did I ever mention, my brother plays piano during the cinema down there?" Ott said. "He gets me in free of charge."

In my hotel room on the night of October 18, I reflected on the fact that at best I'd become a person for whom confusion, if not outright cowardice, had replaced dignity.

And at worst I'd become a man who by dint of foreknowledge might become a murderer. If I did not act on behalf of Driscoll Petchey, or Mary and Moses Nuqac, or Mary Naniaqueeit, I therefore acted against them.

That night, I decided to warn Driscoll. I threw on my coat and set out for his room. I knocked, but there was no answer. I figured he might be with Ruth Nipiiq in her shack. I walked down to the flats. The wind off the river screamed in my ears. With every breath, air crackled in my nose. I'd failed to wear gloves, a mistake, even for a walk of a hundred meters in this cold. Hands in pockets, hunched into the wind, I knocked on Ruth's door. She called out, "What?" I opened the door. Ruth was lying under blankets, a quilt, and her overcoat, on a thin bed with a metal frame. Through the black grate of the potbelly stove I saw glowing coal. "Driscoll's for me," Ruth said—she thought I'd come to see her—"If you see him, don't tell him you came here, eh?" She turned, facing the wall, whose cracks were stuffed with newspaper. I shut the door behind me.

I went over to Harold Thompson's poker game at the Hudson's Bay Co. store. There were six players, none of whom had seen Driscoll. "If he's not here by now," Harold said, "I doubt he's coming."

I went back to the hotel. In a matter of hours, I could well have pounded on every door in Churchill. Instead, I lay down in my warm bed. Early enough in the morning, I thought, I'd get to the airplane. I would act on this and take the consequences.

I should have waited for Petchey in his room. I should have slept in the cockpit of the airplane.

---

In the pitch dark of my room, October 19, I'd been dreaming of Kala Murie. The qualities of this dream were in general harsh. We were quarreling. The words we spoke were brutal to no detectable purpose. Suddenly, through the wall of my room, we heard a scratchy phonograph playing a waltz. We got quickly dressed. Kala took me by the hand and led me next door. She knocked, the door all but floated open. Inside, many people from *The Unclad Spirit*, including "uninvited guests," were dancing in partners. For instance, I immediately recognized Edward and Emmeline Darling, and also Georgiana Houghton herself. Every last person in the room (except for me and Kala) wore a necklace made of metal parts, and now, when I think back on it, I realize the parts were from Petchey's airplane. Tachometer numbers, ribs of the wings, and so on—I'd dreamed the wreckage in advance.

Truth be told, I seldom remembered my dreams or, for that matter, credited them with any usefulness, really. But this one rendered things so vividly, I could not shake it. I know one thing: this dream's purpose was to tell me that I had become a man whose life had reached the low point of actually causing this exact dream.

In the dream, the moment she stepped into the room, Kala cut in on the Darlings, who'd appeared to be happily reunited. When Kala waltzed Edward over near the window, that's when I suddenly saw myself. I backed against the opposite wall, framed Edward Darling and Kala with my hands midair, and announced, "*View of Kala Murie Cutting In on*

*Ghosts.*" At which point all the guests, still dancing, turned to look at me, trying to understand what I'd just cried out, looks of pity on their faces.

And that's when I was startled awake by Sam Brant's pounding at my door. He shouted, "There's been a plane crash—somebody's probably dead!" Then Brant opened my door and said, "We need some help out there, Duvett. Get the hell out of bed!" He left my door open and ran down the hallway.

I threw on my clothes, boots, took my coat from the peg on the door, and went out into the hallway, put on the coat, and hurried downstairs. Nobody was in the lobby. On the porch I caught a slightly acrid smell: smoke, I thought—the wind was blowing in through the hotel's open front door.

I set out, rushing toward a scene much camouflaged by sleet. I could scarcely determine the outlines of people. Diffused light seemed to be bursting cloudily from moving oil lamps. And then, suddenly, I heard Brant's voice—I couldn't yet see him—"What have I done?" Then his voice choked up: "What have I done?" More or less blindly, I groped toward other voices, and then was amongst the dead and living, on the same level ground near the airstrip.

Immediately next I tripped over the body of Moses Nuqac. I fell directly on top of him. My face rammed into his face. I thought I'd broken his nose; that mine, too, was broken. I think I said, "Oh God, sorry. Sorry," as though all I had to do was help Moses up from the ground, brush his clothes off with my hand, and we'd go into the hotel and sit by the fire and have a whiskey. I pulled back, looked at his face a moment. His face was serene, sleet hitting it. His body was twisted, a leg peculiarly angled out. I stood up and shouted, "This man's dead, I think!" There was no reply.

The sleet let up slightly, or wind blew an open space in it, enough so that I could make out Kala Murie lying on the ground, the main body of the plane directly behind her. She was being attended to by Thomas Swain and Sam Brant. "I need some help here," I heard. First frantic logic told me that the voice must've been Brant's or Swain's, but actually, it was Vienna's. He'd set up his tripod camera and was sliding in a plate. "Hold this goddamn thing steady, will you, Duvett!" he said. His wife sprawled moaning not ten meters away and he was about to photograph her.

"Kala was on the plane!"—I wanted to kill him.

"Stay with the son-of-a-bitch you work for," Swain said. Torn-up envelopes like confetti swirling about. Packages spun along the ground. Two or three scattered fires hissed, doused by sleet.

"—son-of-a-bitch boss of yours taking pictures! We'll get her to the hotel."

When I next turned toward Vienna, he was lugging his camera over to where Moses Nuqac was. A touch more daylight—I saw that Mary Nuqac and Mary Naniaqueeit lay pretty much side by side, about fifteen or twenty meters from Moses. Mary's jaw looked jammed into a strange grimace.

"Duvett, get the hell out of the way, there's pretty good light now!" Vienna took a photograph.

Half stunned by the sight of it all (*half* was all I deserved;

I knew about it in advance), I then heard Driscoll Petchey groan in the cockpit. When I climbed up, I saw that part of the control panel had splintered into his chest. It was a grim sight. His jacket was torn open, his shirt soaked with blood. He was blubbering, spewing out words. His right eye was closed, already caking blood. It was cold in the cockpit.

"Where've people been?" he said. The engine was hissing. Driscoll then let out a sound that reminded me of a bagpipe's moan, not a musical note of any sort, exactly, more like his voice was being forced back down his throat. "I can't marry you today," he muttered. "Soon, though . . ."

"Driscoll," I said, "quiet now. Save your strength." But I knew he was nearly gone. Anyone could've seen that. Given the blood gurgling up in his voice, he had to be nearly gone. "Ruth, Martha, you decide—I can't decide." Stifled, drowning voice.

"You're finally going to marry Ruth or Martha, that's nice."

"Oh—" Petchey cried, "I'm going to sleep now. You decide for me, eh?"

"I'll do that. I'll talk to them both."

"All right."

"I'll just sit here a minute first."

But less than a minute passed before his eyes rolled back in his head. He loosed a small half-cry, half something I can't name, an unrepeatable utterance. I noticed that his hands were neatly folded, sideways to each other as if he were packing a snowball. I climbed down from the cockpit.

The fuel tank, flung twenty or so meters from the plane, exploded, sent metal flying. I flung myself to the ground.

When I got up, I looked at my hands and saw blood, but re-alized it was Driscoll's.

The wind shifted, envelopes flew right over me.

I recall an impulse to start gathering up the mail. Instead, I went back to the hotel. Room 3 had been turned into a hospital for Kala, the one survivor. Dr. Ott was in there with her. He had removed her clothing and was examining her. He had a stethoscope around his neck. Vienna came into the lobby. He set his camera upright in a corner. He was staring into the fireplace. Right then and there I wondered if he was displeased that Kala was still alive. Thomas Swain had set out three bottles of whiskey and a dozen or so glasses on the check-in counter. Now a number of men who worked at the Hudson's Bay Co. store set Mary Nuqac and Moses Nuqac and Mary Naniaqueeit, wrapped head to foot in blankets, on the lobby floor. Within ten minutes the lobby was filled with Eskimo people, quietly sobbing over the bod-ies, beside themselves with dignified, crazy-eyed grief. They carried the bodies from the hotel.

More men—I recognized a few from the Bay Company —carried in the body of Driscoll Petchey. They set him on the sofa opposite the one Vienna now sat on.

"Whom should we get hold of, do you think?" I heard Swain say to a few men. "Who're Petchey's loved ones?"

I stood outside room 3, looking in on Kala and Dr. Ott. Ott was listening to Kala's heart through the stethoscope. He'd turned the bedclothes down so that she was exposed from just below her breasts. The room was dimly lit. Ott felt along her ribs and she let out a painful gasp, opened her eyes, closed them right away. Following each aspect of the examination, Ott jotted something into a notebook. When he came out of the room, he looked ashen-faced and said, "Vienna's the husband. I should say this first to him—"

"Well, he's right there in the lobby," I said.

"I see that. Anyway, she's got three broken ribs, best I can tell, and by the look of things, her brain's no doubt severely disheveled, a concussion. Can't move her, not at all."

"How bad is it, though?"

"Hard to tell now. If there's no internal bleeding, and there's no sign of it yet—"

"You're saying she'll live."

"She'll live. Unless there's internal bleeding I can't stop."

"You'd better tell Vienna all this now."

"Peter, what the hell happened out there? I heard he was taking photographs. What kind of man would do that? His own wife— It was like a nightmare. People thrown all over like that."

"It *was* a nightmare."

"I better go talk to him now."

"Can I sit with her awhile?"

"I've given her a sedative. She won't completely know you're there."

"Probably for the best."

"Sit in a corner, then, and keep quiet. She'll sleep anyway, but if she wakes even for a minute, don't talk to her. Let her sleep." He shook his head in disbelief. "You're here—the husband's out there," he said.

"What you're thinking is none of your business."

"I suppose not."

Dr. Ott then went into the lobby and sat down next to

Vienna. Next to the wet tarpaulin in which Driscoll Petchey was wrapped stood Ruth Nipiiq. She wept, touching the tarpaulin with both hands.

I stepped into room 3. Kala's breathing was a bit labored, little raspy catches in her throat. She lay on her back, a position she never naturally slept in. Her face was partially swathed in thick bandages. The room smelled of antiseptic.

When Ott came back, he pulled up a chair and sat for a moment next to me. "Vienna said, 'I put her in harm's way.' Then he grabbed me and asked why I wasn't on the plane. As if I should've been attending to his wife."

"When was it decided that Kala needed medical care in Winnipeg?"

"Linn came to see me late last night. I told him I wasn't convinced she needed to go just yet. He persuaded me, I'm afraid. Naturally, a husband has the final say."

# ESQUIMAUX SOULS RISEN
# FROM AEROPLANE WRECK

"We don't have an official funeral home, like down in Halifax," Thomas Swain said to me.

Four men had placed Driscoll Petchey's body in the empty part of the woodshed in back of the hotel. Sleet had turned to snow.

I think it was about ten or eleven o'clock on the same morning of the plane wreck, when I knocked on Samuel Brant's door. Room 27. "Whoever that is, go away!" he said loudly, slurring.

I opened the door. Brant lay on the floor, staring at the ceiling.

"I know what happened and I know how it happened," I said. "I know everything, Sam. I know what the arrangements were. I know you did something to the plane."

"You going to bring the law down on me?"

"I might."

"I'm dead anyway; kill me here and now, because I'm going to jail my whole life, aren't I?" There were two empty whiskey bottles on the bed. "I never liked you, Duvett. Did you notice that?"

"It made no difference to me."

"I never liked you. I never liked Petchey and I'm not sorry he's dead. I'm sorry I killed him, though."

"What'd he ever do to you that was serious as that? How much did Vienna pay you?"

"You tell me, you know so much."

"How much, Sam?"

"How much he paid me is four hundred dollars, a lot of goddamned money, eh? I didn't think he had that kind of money, but he had it. He paid me it."

"So now you're four hundred dollars richer and Driscoll Petchey's dead. And those three Eskimo people are dead."

"I'm a good mechanic. I knew the plane would drop. I didn't think past that. I wasn't paid to think past that."

"And it all went wrong from there, didn't it? It went wrong. And Driscoll's dead. And—"

"Who in hell are you—God? You knew about it beforehand, or else how come you said you did?"

"You're right about that."

"Duvett, I know what kind of whore I am. Because I know what I did and why I did it. Four hundred dollars is why. Not a penny more, not a penny less, Duvett." He reached under the bed, rolled another bottle of whiskey toward him, opened it, took a long swig. "Because I saw you in bed with Kala Murie, and you think I don't know you might shoot Vienna Linn, to have her all to yourself? You think I don't know about things?"

"You're the stupidest person I've ever met."

He stared at me a moment. "I did it for four hundred dollars. *You*—you didn't warn Petchey. Both of us made a decision, didn't we? That makes us equal in my book, except you're stupider because you're a whore for no money. Plus which, you kept your mouth shut, so you yourself almost murdered your dear Kala there, didn't you? I didn't know she'd be on the plane."

"Would that have made any difference to you, Sam?"

"Not to me. She never gave me the time of day."

"Linn knew how to pick a revengeful little bastard, didn't he?"

"Oh—oh, I see you figured something out, I tried my charms on Kala Murie. Oh, yes I did, indeed I did, and she wouldn't give me the time of day. I could've been in bed with her."

"Sam, you're even stupider than I thought."

Now Brant managed to get up from the floor, wobbled toward the bed, stopped, pointed a finger at me, and said, "Why'd you keep your mouth shut?"—then fell backward onto the bed and blacked out.

I looked out his window. Snow blown around by wind. Yet I still could see that a number of Eskimo children were picking through the wreckage. Using a section of wing as a makeshift sled, one young boy, sitting upright, was being pushed along the ground by two others. Running alongside, barking and leaping, a sled dog snapped at ashes still drifting down.

That evening at about six o'clock the three men directly responsible for the airplane wreck sat at separate tables in the dining room, picking at their dinners. Arctic char, potatoes, canned beets. After a while Sam Brant could no longer bear the proximity. He took up his plate, carried it over to the check-in counter, and finished his meal there. Vienna sat two tables over with his back to me. When he was nearly through eating, Dr. Ott came in and said something to him. Vienna immediately got up from the table and accompanied Ott from the dining room. I almost said, "Is it about Kala?" but held my tongue.

I was in my room by 7:00 p.m. I lay on the bed sideways, curled up like a child. There was a knock on the door. I opened it, and there stood Vienna. "Ah, Duvett," he said. "You look distressed—what, the consequences of your actions are already at work on you? I suggest you come to the darkroom with me. I've something interesting to show you."

"I'm not going anywhere just now."

Vienna grabbed my wrist and yanked me forward. "You need to see this, Duvett, it might guarantee me getting out of your life."

I tore my sleeve pulling away from Vienna; but then I followed him up to the darkroom. Inside, he held an oil lamp close to a photograph he'd obviously just developed and hung on the twine. "You see there, Duvett," he said. "The smoky upward *smudging*—shall we call it that? *Smudging*. I do like the sound of it. *The Unclad Spirit* contains—if you read carefully—very nicely detailed instructions. Of course, Miss Houghton includes certain photographic processes in order to contrast such trickery to her so-called *true* spirit pictures, which claim to have no trickery about them whatsoever. I've been a close reader of that book, Duvett."

"What have you done here?"

"Look closely, how the smudging rises from both Moses Nuqac and his wife—yet *not*, you'll notice, from Mary Nani-aqueeit."

"I have no interest in this." I shoved Vienna; he nearly dropped the lamp.

"My dear Duvett," he said, in a grating, patient tone, "everyone's agitated after what's happened today. The tragedy. Everyone's on edge, aren't they? I nearly lost my wife. But if you could just keep a clear head and see your advantage here. Because what you have before you is my ticket to a new life—I might better say, a way to get back to my old life, with money in my pocket."

Vienna transferred his revolver from one suit coat pocket to the other, just to show it to me.

"This photograph I will present to Radin Heur," he said. "You see, Duvett, he has some very odd religious—*lean-ings*, Mr. Heur does. Perhaps my wife's mentioned this. He's something of a spiritualist, in that he gives considerable time and considerable thought to—which phrase of Miss Houghton's is Kala always quoting? Oh yes—to *truths beyond appearances*. He gives a great deal of money to groups claim-ing secret spiritual knowledge. I'm told he partakes of séances—weekly. Who could miss someone that much, to want them back like that? It's beyond me, Duvett.

"As for Mr. Heur, I don't know the names of such groups he supports, but I know he's a prominent figure among them. I think he can be persuaded that these smudgings are depictions of actual souls— Souls rising from these two *bap-tized* Eskimo bodies. I'll also inform him that the other is the body of Mary Naniaqueeit, who wasn't baptized."

"You expect Radin Heur to see this—"

"—as a sign of an almighty Christian God's fingerprint on earthly events? Yes, I do. I think he'll leap at the opportunity presented him by the photograph. Leaving it up to him how he'd present it to his own small circle of friends. It well could bring him all sorts of longed-for notoriety. He's already filthy rich. He doesn't need money. I've come to know Mr. Heur over the years—I believe he'll be pleased. Pleased, and pay handsomely for this good piece of work. Perhaps even well and above what I owe him."

"If you got that kind of money, you'd disappear somewhere?"

"That's my present thinking, yes. As I told you before the accident."

"*Accident*—"

"For Radin Heur's purposes, what matter the word I choose? The plane fell to the ground. The souls rose up."

"Good luck with it, then, because the sooner it happens, the better."

"For your purposes."

"Kala's and mine."

"Ah, Kala's and yours. How nice."

"Rot in hell."

Vienna held the lantern up near his face. "I'll need a caption," he said. "Make it provocative. Do your best work."

"Think something up yourself."

"Come now, Duvett. It's your chance to enter posterity."

"I don't care to enter it."

"Well, think it over. You see, now, I'm a good man, I haven't shot you through the heart yet, have I? I'll need to compose a letter to Mr. Heur, won't I? Provide him the proper information. To put this great discovery into clear perspective for him. I need to play to his deepest interests. The man does not suffer fools. It has to be worded delicately. I'll be giving Mr. Heur my whereabouts. I'll be putting myself directly at his mercy."

I left the darkroom. I spent the next few hours sitting next to Kala's bed. Under heavy sedation, she was sleeping. I'd placed *The Unclad Spirit* on her bedside table. I dozed off. When I woke, I adjusted my eyes to candlelight—though I had not lit a candle. There, in a chair on the other side of the bed, sat a man of about forty or forty-five years of age. Besides that, in the dim light I could scarcely make out his features; I could see that he kept worrying his hands through his hair, leaving splotches of flour on his head. Over his clothes he wore a spattered and flour-splotched apron. Given this, it came as no surprise when he said, "I'm Berthot—hotel's chef."

"You're getting flour in your hair, Mr. Berthot."

"Nothing new in that. The thing is, I felt so bad about Mrs. Linn, here, that I've been baking all night. Bread, mostly."

He seemed almost absentmindedly to slap his hands against his legs, and flour exploded up and disappeared. "I guess baking is how I deal with bad news," he said.

"All this time, we haven't met."

"Well, Mr. Duvett—"

"Peter."

"News of you arrives to the kitchen, of course."

"News."

"Look—it's you sitting here all night, not Mr. Linn."

We sat in silence, a good three or four minutes, at least.

"What do you think of my breads, anyway?" he finally said.

"I like them."

"Thank you."

He stood up from the chair. "If— That is, *when* she's feeling up to it, I'll bring something for Mrs. Linn. Dr. Ott permitting." He left the room.

I slept, woke—the candle had burnt out—slept. It was toward dawn that I thought up the caption *Esquimaux Souls Risen from Aeroplane Wreck*, antique French usage and all, which I hoped would be exotic enough to enhance things for Radin Heur. Hoping he'd send the money. I wrote the caption on a piece of Kala's stationery, climbed the stairs, and slid it under Vienna's door.

Four days later was Driscoll Petchey's funeral. It turned out he was to be buried in Churchill's cemetery. Nobody was able to locate any of his immediate or even distant family. On the way to the church I saw a man hacking at Driscoll's frozen grave plot with a pickax. Another man stood by with a shovel. Their breaths plumed out white into the cold air.

When I walked into the church and sat in the backmost pew, Painter had, I think, just begun his eulogy: "—a man caught up in evil circumstances is not necessarily evil," he said. "If you closely read the Scriptures, you come to believe that a man recognizing evil, who then embraces it, is not necessarily evil but perhaps only *weak*. But a man who *creates* evil, imposing it upon others, and the leavings of such are grief and sadness, *that* man should engage in ceaseless prayer for forgiveness."

It was the first time I'd been in Painter's church. In fact, I'd set eyes on him only once or twice, perhaps, in the Hudson's Bay Co. store, or as he stepped from his church. Never in the hotel. Granted, by any standards, Churchill was a small community, but Painter was often up at Padlei, Eskimo Point, other locales not even on the map. He almost exclusively socialized with his visiting missionaries, anyway. He and I had not so much as exchanged pleasantries, let alone had a conversation. I had received a note at the hotel in which Painter thanked me for assisting Vienna Linn in God's work.

Anyway, there were eight or ten Eskimo people scattered throughout the pews, along with at least twenty other townspeople.

Painter's opening words knotted my stomach, because I thought that he—a tall, bulky man, with a full head of silver hair, ruddy complexion, and big voice—had somehow found out about the cause of the plane wreck and was about to spew out anger and blame from the pulpit. It did not go that way at all. "But no one was evil here, in our recent tragedy," he said. "We have recently had, as you know, a visit from the esteemed Canadian authorities salaried and trained to investigate such unfortunate events. And they talked to many citizens of Churchill. And they left with the understanding that only sad fate violated life—indeed, stole lives from us. Sad fate was at work here. In the winds that pressed Driscoll

Petchey's airplane to the ground. It is a heart-wrenching entry into the ledger of our daily lives, the daily life of our
community. But, dear friends, the Lord, does He not, works
in mysterious ways. Life, death, joys, sorrows are each and all
aspects of God's eternal and compassionate logic. Perhaps it
is those very events that we cannot fully comprehend that
we feel most deeply . . ."

I left the church, glancing back once at Driscoll's casket
set on two sawhorses directly in front of the pulpit. Painter's
somber voice trailed me out: "But what have we here in
Churchill actually *experienced*? And what good can come of
it? And why do we feel so helpless in the face of tragedy?
Four good people perished on a bitter day, due to the failings
of a mere mechanical object, a fallible human invention
fallen from the sky."

I walked from the church to the hotel. After warming myself by the lobby fireplace, I went into Kala's room. When
I again sat by her bed, I didn't expect her to be awake. But
her discolored eyelids opened slightly and she whispered,
"Please read to me," nodding slightly toward *The Unclad Spirit*
on the bedside table.

"All right. Of course. Which part?"

"You choose, Peter."

I would have thought, at first sight of me or anyone, she'd
strain past her physical weakness and call out, "What's happened to me?" Or exclaim some incredulity, or let loose a
delirious cry of pain—but there was just the request that I
read to her.

I kissed her forehead, then her hands, pulled a chair close

to the bed, and sat. I began to read a chapter called "Mamma Extending Her Hand Toward Me," only because it happened to be where I opened the book. "Oh," Kala said weakly, "good. I know this is a good story, but I just now can't remember much of it. But I know it's good."

There was a corresponding spirit picture whose caption was identical to the chapter title. This story was about a woman named Jenny Macklin, of Wolverhampton, England. When her mother, Helen, died at age ninety, Jenny Macklin had a deathbed photograph taken. When the photographer, Mr. Joseph Harvill, developed the picture, he discovered the "milky countenance" of Helen standing over her own deathbed. Dressed in a "flowing gown," the standing Helen held out her hands imploringly. When Jenny saw the spirit photograph, she interpreted it to mean that her mother was asking Jenny to join her in the afterlife.

Hearing this, Mr. Harvill left the photograph in Jenny's hands, then ran off shouting, "No need to pay!" Worried that Jenny might take up her mother's pleas, Harvill began to call on Jenny every day.

His visits went on for two years. Jenny was a schoolteacher and went about her business, never spending more than a few minutes a day with Harvill. One day, when he came to visit, he found that Jenny was gone. Miss Houghton wrote: "He knew her house quite well by now. He was indeed chagrined to discover that Jenny had left behind everything but a few items of clothing, her diaries, and the spirit photograph. She'd departed Wolverhampton in the middle of a school year. Her disappearance was brought up in a town meeting, but not after."

A wince of pain on her face, Kala shifted slightly in the

bed, then whispered something. I leaned close. "What did you say?"

"Stupid, stupid Harvill—why couldn't he understand he was in love with her. Every morning for two years he went to see her. Why didn't anyone tell him? Why didn't they say, 'Propose marriage'?" Then, in a very few minutes, she was asleep.

In the following weeks Vienna seldom visited Kala in her recovery. The word she used to describe his visits was *furtive*.

"He comes in," she said, as I sat by her bed late one night in early November, "but I get the impression he's only here to see if I'm still in pain. One time I had a blinding head-ache. I asked him for a cold compress. He said, 'I'll get Dr. Ott—or Duvett—for that purpose.'"

"He must have found Ott. He didn't come get me."

"Of course he didn't. I know that. You'd have been here right away."

"Dr. Ott says your recovery's going well."

"I doubt him. Every waking minute I doubt him. But what else do I have to go on?"

"You have too much time to think, that's all."

"I close my eyes. I see Driscoll Petchey—he's standing there next to the plane, smiling. 'Well, Kala, let me help you on board.' I hear that over and over again, Peter. That little politeness. I see Mary. I see all of us, inside the plane. It spins down. Especially when the sedative wears off. The more pain, the clearer I seem to remember it. My fellow passengers."

"Let's talk about something else."

"I feel old—pain does that, doesn't it? I have a fear—it's a very precise fear—that someday I'll lose all memory except for pages of *The Unclad Spirit*—and I'll just sit in a corner, with a shawl around my shoulders, knitting needle dropped to the floor. And I'll be drooling, of course. Spittle at the corners of my mouth, and muttering—that, too. Muttering the only thing I can remember, page this or that. Page after page."

"You're just thirty-eight, Kala. You've got some years left before that happens."

"I think you want me to laugh. I've got to keep this pillow pressed to my ribs, in case I laugh."

"You're the most beautiful old maid I've ever slept with."

She laughed a little then; it fairly knotted her face in pain.

"Peter, it's these headaches. From the concussion, Ott says. The concussion's brought certain thoughts into my head, old age and such."

"Look, I've smuggled in a treat. Have to keep it a secret from Dr. Ott, promise?"

"Promise."

I produced a bottle of Goldwasser, opened it, poured barely a thimbleful into a glass. Kala sat more upright. I helped her get the pillows right. She sipped the Goldwasser, closed her eyes. "Heavenly," she said. "More, please."

"Not now, I'm afraid."

One night nearly a month after the plane wreck, Vienna sat right next to me as I ate dinner. Under the table he poked something into my ribs. Then he lifted his arm and displayed a butter knife.

"Left your trusty revolver in your room, Mr. Linn?"

"I don't have my revolver. I do have a question for you, however."

"Ask it and leave."

"Where would a man of modest means stay in Halifax?"

"Halifax?"

"Your home city, Duvett, remember?"

"Why Halifax?"

"Why not Halifax? It's got to be cheaper than living in, say, Montreal. My letter to Radin Heur can go out directly from Halifax. They've got a harbor there. We'll set up shop. We'll await an answer."

"*We'll*— Meaning?"

"Kala and I. Which means you'll follow along, tongue wagging, won't you, Duvett? The three of us. One happy couple. One unhappy couple."

"You've had a change of mind, then."

"As for long-term plans, no. No, I haven't. In fact, I can hardly wait to be rid of both of you. I'm sick to death of you both. But short term, I think it's best to stay in close proximity to Kala. I'm still her husband; on paper, at least."

"You can't mean you somehow feel responsible toward the wife you tried to murder."

I'd put it directly; he acknowledged the truth of what I'd said by not denying it.

"I feel *responsible*—heady word—to the *situation*. As I see it, Duvett, the situation calls for my staying close to Kala, should and when moneys arrive, to see things through, to erase the marriage, legally, I mean. To leave what money I see fit directly in Kala's hands. A bribe, you might call it, to divorce me, rather than attempt to gain half my earnings. She might be thinking like that, you see. Or you may already *know* what she's thinking. I'll need, in Halifax, to finalize things in my own fashion. Then I'll be gone."

"You seem sure Radin Heur will come through."

When Swain approached, asked Vienna if he wanted to eat dinner, Vienna said, "Sitting here I've no appetite." Swain went to his one-man chess game behind the counter. Vienna pushed back from the table. "I think Mr. Heur will be *mesmerized*. The money will follow. I'll be flush. Then you two lovebirds can fly off to wherever you goddamn see fit."

"And if the money doesn't arrive for a good long time? Or not at all?"

"Oh, I'll find work in Halifax. I always find work, you see."

"So I've heard."

"A decent, modestly priced accommodation, Duvett."

"The only one I know—it's called Haliburton House Inn, on Morris Street. I don't know the exact address. Morris Street on an envelope's enough. A letter would get there."

"Well, we've lived in London, you see. In European capitals. I think we'll manage quite well in Halifax, under great duress or no."

Late that night I found Vienna asleep facedown on the table, in the second-floor library. An empty bottle of Goldwasser was next to an ink bottle. A pen was on the floor. Twenty or more pieces of paper were crumpled up on the table. Under his left hand was the letter he wrote to Radin Heur. I lifted his hand and he woke. Coming alert straightaway, he said, "You don't have to steal it, Duvett." He held up the pages. "Here, read it. I'll expect you to return it shortly. I don't want your opinion. But, yes—read it. See how a professional goes about things."

He left the library.

I not only read the letter but hastily scribbled a copy to give to Kala for safekeeping. I have it in front of me now.

Mr. Radin Heur
28 Eccleston Place
London, England

Dear Mr. Heur,

Human agency is eager for compensation and acknowledgment, don't you think? And haven't yours and my affiliations above all been adventurous?

Just the other night I thought back on the wreckage of the train near the Canadian city of Calgary, photographs of which you called "splendid." It made me quite proud to know said photographs reside in your permanent collection. However, at the time I failed to provide in a letter the best details, for which I apologize.

Therefore, to make amends:

Arriving in Calgary by train on May 5, 1925, my now-wife Kala Murie and I took modest rooms at the Barrand Hotel. Through contacts I hired intermediaries, a Mr. Bronk and a Mr. Offet, for our purposes reputable, and yet, I admit, exceedingly unpleasant men. The schedule had it that the train with its cargo of sheep would pass over a wooden bridge about a mile west of Calgary at approximately 7 a.m. on May 15. I had made certain that the proprietor of the Barrand Hotel, as well as several most important of the staff, thought that I was in Calgary to continue my project of "photographing trains all across Canada," which, in its way, had some truth to it. I mentioned that I was working on assignment for the *Times* of London. Indeed, I noticed this made a very good impression. In fact, Mr. Gunnars, the proprietor himself, provided the train schedule for me. The following days and evenings were spent either in the hotel or at the train station; I took a number of photographs of station employees and waiting passengers. Mr. Bronk and Mr. Offet were, of course, in a separate hotel. We were not to be seen together.

The train was to be forty cars in length, not including locomotive and caboose. On the late evening of May 14, Bronk and Offet went out to the bridge with dynamite. That same evening Kala Murie and I dined at the hotel with Mr. Gunnars and his wife, good citizens. Later, Kala Murie met with a group of spiritualists. (You know of her interests.) There may have been a séance. Directly after cigars and cognac with Mr. Gunnars, I left a request with the front desk that I be woken at 5 a.m., not a moment later, and that I would take tea at 5:30 a.m. I find that, in hotels, fastidiousness of this sort, if one comports oneself with a certain impatient edginess, often brings results. In addition, I said that I expected my photographic equipment to be brought down to the lobby by 5:45. A motor cab was to be ready. I hired it through the hotel. The driver would take me out to the bridge. As I put it to Mr. Gunnars at dinner, "A train crossing a bridge would be particularly desirable."

Indeed, the driver, a Mr. Belenkey, delivered me at the bridge at 6:15. "A bridge as ordered," he said, actually doffing his cap. I asked that he return in two hours' time. He protested, saying he would stay for no fee, that he was himself interested in photography. But I insisted that he leave. I was quite surly about it. Yet I also said, "I need the time to take pictures of the surroundings. Rock formations and so forth. You see, Mr. Belenkey, an artist prefers to work alone." I then offered to pay him for the time in between leaving and picking me up again. He accepted.

The train, alas, was thirty-five minutes late. Mr. Offet, crouching well hidden, counted the cars through binoculars as it rounded into view; he later told me the number of cars was forty-four. As the middle or nearly middle car achieved the bridge, Mr. Bronk plunged the detonator. The explosives had been so expertly set, there was hardly any evidence of an explosion, really. I think, yes, it was the nineteenth or twentieth car shattered apart, snapping from its predecessor, the front cars continuing on for a moment, as if a blow struck a body had not yet registered in the brain. Then came the sound of the locomotive braking. The screech of iron wheels on track echoed like a giant bird of prey. The bridge scaffolding collapsed, a train car tumbled into the gorge, followed at intervals by sheep, some of whose legs were pointing upward, all made for a rare photograph indeed, I know you agree. I did not have to feign excitement, because the sight was far more astonishing than I had imagined it would be, and I imagined it would be quite astonishing.

When the driver Belenkey returned, naturally he was flabbergasted at the sight of the train wreckage, quite beside himself. He hurried us back to Calgary and immediately contacted the authorities. Naturally, I deposited a photograph—not in the least incriminating—with the police. I said that it was the only one successfully developed; they appreciated whatever witness it provided.

By the way, Mr. Heur, your secretary later informed me that you titled one of those photographs *Engineers Running Toward a Shattered Bridge*, which I consider to be a most brilliant caption.

All photographs from the arrangements in Calgary brought from you the handsome sum of £5,000 without delay.

But, Mr. Heur, so much for success. Where you naturally might conceive of me as failing was with the incident outside Montreal last year. The milk train. It was indeed, in the strict sense of final execution of plans, a failure, although my planning and intent were, as always, scrupulously applied. But allow me to ask: In the course of such endeavors—and we have worked together eight times to date—that is, in the long run, Mr. Heur, might not a single failure seem only part of the whole? Might you see it some other way than the one bad apple poisoning the barrel? For I remember with great pride the letter from your secretary, taken, I presume, from your dictation, dated November 9, 1925 (I keep close records), stating: "In their dark elegance, your photographs capture human drama at its highest pitch." Mr. Heur, you are indeed a poet as well. Again in letters from your offices I was to later understand that the photographs of the sheep tumbling through the air were to prove of particular notoriety and satisfaction to you. For which knowledge I was grateful.

You can imagine, then, in turn, with what severe degree of consternation I met news of your dissatisfaction with my failure to provide photographs of the milk train wreckage near Montreal. Indeed, there was no wreckage at all, such was the result of the ineptness of poorly chosen intermediaries, for which I hold myself entirely responsible. It all has upset and troubled me greatly. I wrote you directly about my failure, did I not? I did not keep it from you. And then arrived at my hotel in Montreal your finely dressed employee, who deposited with me a newspaper clipping. Said clipping reported the death of a Mr. Narayan. Well, Mr. Heur, given the circumstances and some knowledge of your expectations in such matters, naturally I could only assume that Mr. Narayan had failed *you*. Most certainly, I read between the lines. To even put me in the same category as this man was painful, a blow to my integrity.

And of course your emissary put the fear of God in me. And in our hotel room it was Kala Murie's life I feared for, far more than my own.

Mr. Heur, I owe you the sum of £3,000. Though it can hardly amount to a splinter in the vast forest of your wealth, still, that sum is indeed owed. That is a fact. No matter that I paid in Montreal a Mr. Konwicki and a Mr. Mitchell the sum of $250 to assist in technical matters, dynamite and such, promising them the same amount over if their work was successfully completed. No matter that I had our living expenses. The job was indeed botched, and according to necessarily unwritten agreement (all cables destroyed, one assumes), I am to return in full the money advanced. Presently, Mr. Heur, I do not have such funds. I have been living within decidedly modest means, doing what I suppose might be called the most dignified work available, in the desperately remote locale of Churchill, Manitoba, in the northern reaches of Canada. I have been making portraits of recently baptized Eskimo people for the Jesuits. I do not disparage the religious nature of this work, be assured. I only wish to indicate that if I began to tell you how removed from civilization my present life is, you would probably forward to me, as a mercy, a street map of London. You would need the best man from the Explorers Club, there, to further explain such a place where I now live and breathe, though at times it seems barely.

This exile, of course, is not directly of your design per se, only indirectly, as I continually remind myself of the fate of Mr. Narayan, you understand. However, allow me now to describe our great good fortune, yours and mine.

On October 19 the opportunity presented itself for me to take a number of photographs of the wreckage of a small airplane, piloted by a man named Driscoll Petchey. He was loath to set out in rough weather that morning but, honor-bound under church employment, did so anyway. On board was my very own dear wife, Kala Murie, who wished to travel to Winnipeg to be examined in hospital for a pernicious illness. The local physician had suggested that she *eventually* go. I had no knowledge in advance of her middle-of-the-night decision. I had been sleeping in a separate room in order to leave her the utmost restfulness. As for boarding the plane, in her fever she no doubt acted impulsively. The other three passengers—in addition to the pilot—were of the Eskimo race. Of those, two had been baptized—the third, an elderly woman, had not.

As a result of the accident, Kala Murie has, in body and mind, been terribly damaged, and I beg you to consider, amongst many things, the costs of her recovery, in relation to your present disposition toward me.

As for newspapers, Mr. Heur, which naturally use such terms as *acts of terrorism* when referring to political sabotage, said term cannot possibly embrace the complexities of how, between patron and artist, an end justifies a means. Here in Churchill, having the sudden opportunity of a plane fallen to earth, I made photographs of it. A packet of said photographs is herein enclosed.

However, the one photograph I most wish for you to see is not in the present packet.

My assistant, a Mr. Peter Duvett, formerly of Halifax, Nova Scotia, at my request has authored the caption for the absent photograph: *Esquimaux Souls Risen from Aeroplane Wreck*. In this photograph one sees the three Eskimo sprawled on the ground, their bodies oddly bent. Yet, Mr. Heur, the true astonishment is this:

Rising from only the two baptized Eskimo are, what with professional verification will no doubt prove out, their human souls.

It is a quite staggering sight.

Naturally, these souls should cast great doubt on their own authenticity, because *who before has ever seen this phenomenon*? Yet I personally have no doubt, for the simple reason that I developed the negative myself. I, who would be capable of manipulating a negative to almost any chosen result, did, in this instance, indeed not do so.

You will of course wish to see this photograph, I imagine, as quickly as possible. I implore you to at least send an expert to verify its authenticity.

Those in your circles with the desire, but not yet the evidence, to more completely believe will now allow themselves to believe. This photograph shall alter their lives.

And all unbelievers shall secretly envy you. For they live in a world in which nothing is true.

Therefore, Mr. Heur, I openly tell you where I shall

soon be living in Halifax, Nova Scotia, Canada, and
rely on the dignity of your restraint and your intellectual and spiritual embrace of possibility, and implore
you to contact me at:

> Haliburton House Inn
> Morris Street
> Halifax, Nova Scotia
> CANADA

where, in my wife's good company, if her present recovery keeps to hopeful pace and weather-in-travel
reasonably allows, I shall hope to arrive by January 10,
1927.

I shall never forget that I was hired by you to cre-
ate a train incident and photograph it. I failed. I am in
your debt. I am offering to share my recent good fortune to establish once again your confidence in me
and my work. I pray you agree that we deserve to
continue to sustain each other's natural affinities and
private exhilarations, let alone zealously maintain our
need to lavish against conformity.

> In friendship—
> your humble employee,
> Vienna Linn

Then, on January 1, 1927, we left for Halifax, we three.
The Muskeg express train, Churchill-Winnipeg-Halifax.

There was a postal window at the Halifax train station.
First thing off the train, Vienna posted the packet containing

the letter and photographs. "Given the weather, this might not get out for a week or more," the clerk said. He was surly, as if he'd been cooped up in the train station days on end. He weighed the packet, told Vienna the cost; Vienna paid. The clerk tossed the packet into a bin.

In front of the Halifax station we managed to arrange for a horse-drawn carriage. It had just pulled up. Our driver was in a foul temper. "Carriages, a few automobile taxis, can still get around in this mess," he said. "Birney Cars are all shut down, though. Where are you going?"

"The Haliburton House Inn," I said. "Morris Street."

He looked us over. "It'll be twice the normal rate," he said, "take it or leave it. Or risk the icy streets with your luggage, eh?"

"We'll take it," I said.

I assisted Kala up and she settled on the far side of the seat. Vienna climbed up next to her. I sat next to the driver. The driver handed Kala a blanket. When she unfolded it across her lap, roasted chestnuts fell out. One remained on the blanket, though. The driver spun around, plucked it from Kala's lap, shrugged, and said, "Sorry—looks like there's just one left." The horse snorted, started forward without much news from the reins. (That's a phrase my father, who drove a phaeton, one of those old-fashioned four-wheel horse-drawn carriages in London, often used: "I really gave my horse news from the reins today, stubborn old brute.") "They finished the Birney tracks across the Common, links Cogswell and Quinpool Road and Windsor Streets. Birneys are damn near trying to put me out of business."

"Good luck," Vienna said.

"Haliburton House is on a steep hill," the driver said. "I'll get you close as I can. Help with lugging bags uphill's another dollar, but I'm willing."

"We'll manage," Vienna said.

"That's what a fellow said yesterday, and he just about slid into Halifax Harbor. Like his suitcase was a toboggan, I mean to tell you."

"Thank you," Vienna said, "we've heard quite enough."

"Just making conversation," the driver said, chewing on the chestnut, "though I'm not paid for it."

Kala pulled the blanket tight around her. "No matter," she said. "It feels good to be off that train and out in the air. It's my first day without much pain to speak of."

For the first week I either kept to my room or walked the streets hours at a time. I ate dinner an hour earlier than Kala and Vienna, who were keeping up man-and-wife appearances for Mrs. Sorrel, the proprietor. Then, at about 7:00 a.m. on January 15, Kala knocked on the door of my room in the annex. When I opened it, Kala said, "I'd much prefer falling in bed with you, Peter, but I'm not quite feeling up to it yet. It felt nice this morning, just being able to bend down and put on my own shoes, hardly an ounce of pain."

"Can we at least have breakfast together?"

"I'm afraid Vienna might be there, too. His habits have changed a little. He's eating breakfast in public."

"I don't care if he's there or not."

When we got to the dining room, Mrs. Sorrel was serving Vienna toast, sausage, and eggs. "Oh, Mrs. Linn, Mr. Duvett," she said. "Here's your husband, Mrs. Linn—come sit."

We walked over to Vienna's table. Kala had not thought to hang up her coat. She folded it and set it on the fourth chair, then sat down next to Vienna, who continued reading last evening's newspaper. I sat down across from Kala. From behind the front page he said, "Out for a walk bright and early, dear? That's a good sign. Soon life will be back to normal."

"Life was never normal," Kala said. "How dare you suggest our life was ever *normal* in the least."

"It was just a turn of phrase," Vienna said. "I meant about your—concussion. Your bruises. Your ability to put on your shoes, as you did this morning."

Kala tore the newspaper from Vienna's hands. This opened up my view of the dining room. Mrs. Sorrel stepped from the kitchen. She saw the dustup, turned right around, and went back through the kitchen door on its back swing. Freddy Sorrel, whom I'd met our first day there, came in and sat down at a corner table. He looked pleased to see Kala's temper. He didn't turn away.

"Your turn of phrase turns my stomach," she said.

Mrs. Sorrel opened the door, hesitated, saw that things might have settled down a bit, so she brought before-breakfast orange slices over to Kala and me. "Look at that endless snow," she said. "I'm afraid we'll see Eskimo any minute on the streets of Halifax, if this keeps up. You didn't have any Eskimo stowed away on your train come in from the north, now, did you?"

"No, you're safe there, Mrs. Sorrel," I said. "Check our rooms if you like."

"Of course," Mrs. Sorrel said, lowering her voice an octave, sharing a confidence, "Eskimo would be welcome in my establishment. Anyone who pays in Canadian dollars is welcome."

"We're all in agreement, then," Vienna said. "We've no Eskimo with us. Though they'd have been welcome."

"I'll bring tea," Mrs. Sorrel said. She left for the kitchen.

"I imagine she wouldn't recognize an Eskimo if one sat on her lap in a Birney Car," Kala said.

Mrs. Sorrel returned and served tea.

"Mr. Duvett—your assistant—tells me you're a professional photographer, Mr. Linn," she said.

"Mrs. Sorrel, that's quite true," Vienna said. "Indeed, I'm here in Halifax for quite special private engagements, you see. I'll need a darkroom. Do you by chance have a spare room—nothing fancy, mind you. Nothing elaborate. Just four walls and a sturdy table, and Mr. Duvett can set things up nicely."

"We're quite cluttered as it is," Mrs. Sorrel said.

"Naturally," Vienna said, setting down an orange rind, "there would be a financial arrangement."

"You've just given me an idea," Mrs. Sorrel said, touching a finger to her forehead. "I've two pantries off the kitchen. For storage; I suppose I only need one. A pantry might serve your purpose. Yes, I think it might do. Why not go inspect it, if you wish. Both are of equal size, really."

Vienna stood up from the table, with its white tablecloth, and went into the kitchen. He was gone only a few moments. When he returned, he said, "The pantries are quite large. It'll be fine. Thank you."

"Shall we discuss—at some point," Mrs. Sorrel said.

"Would ten dollars a month suit you?" Vienna said.

"Nicely."

Vienna took a ten-dollar bill from his suit coat pocket and handed it to her. "A month's payment, then."

"You might not wish to carry so much money around with you, Mr. Linn. Your not being from Halifax, you might not recognize our local riffraff. Oh yes, we've got our unsavory sorts. Why, they leap right out of an alley at you!"

"So we've settled, then, haven't we?" Vienna said.

Mrs. Sorrel looked at me. "I'll ask that you do the cleaning and setting up between breakfast and lunch," she said. "That's usually a quiet time. Off-season, of course, it's quiet most of the time anyway. There's just you three in residence now"—Freddy left the dining room—"and of course my son, Freddy. I live here, too. It's not always easy, a son living under the same roof as his mother, not at his age, anyway. Especially since he works for me. Anyway, business does pick up summers."

"We may be gone by then," Kala said.

"Oh, I hope not," Mrs. Sorrel said. "As Peter knows, Halifax can offer a good life. You did say you left Halifax but came back home, didn't you, Peter?"

"I left and came back, yes."

Mrs. Sorrel touched her finger to her forehead. "My goodness, Mr. Linn, you've given me another brainstorm. Might you consider taking my portrait? And a portrait of Freddy as well?"

"Let's add it free of charge to our arrangement," Vienna said, bowing at the waist. "We'll get the darkroom set up first, of course. In the meantime, put some thought into where you'd like your portrait taken."

"Oh, in the sitting room," Mrs. Sorrel said.

"The sitting room. Fine."

"Well, things have started out nicely, haven't they?" Mrs. Sorrel said. She returned to the kitchen.

I spent the next three days unpacking Vienna's photographic equipment. He'd arranged to have the packing crates, which were loaded at the Churchill station and carried in the baggage cars Churchill-Winnipeg, then Winnipeg-Halifax, finally delivered to the Haliburton House Inn. He wrote the costs of all this in his ledger. I scrubbed down the pantry, then set up the darkroom. Vienna continued my modest salary. It was my sole income. I hadn't the resources to go out and find other work. Besides, I wanted to stay near Kala. I could suffer Vienna for that. It was finally as if we all three wanted to keep close proximity, each for their own reasons. The whole effect, the *atmosphere*, seemed to me to sometimes correspond to Miss Houghton's idea: *There is another world, but it's in this one.* On certain days and nights, Halifax at large just seemed blocked out. The Haliburton House Inn, for better or worse—often worse—contained world enough.

Right at the beginning of February I said to Kala, "Why not move into my room?"

She was in my bathtub. She'd bought a fragrant bath soap and was slightly annoyed that I wouldn't leave her alone to luxuriate. "Mrs. Sorrel's got a reputation to uphold, Peter. We have to take things slowly, dear."

"It's a degradation is what I feel."

"What is, Peter?"

"Drawing pay from your husband."

"Go back to the newspaper, then." She looked pensive. "I know. I know, but his money's tainted because I'm his wife and you're in love with me. Come smell my skin, Peter."

I sat on the rim of the bathtub, leaned down, and smelled Kala's shoulder. "It's lemon, in case you didn't recognize it," she said.

"Does Vienna like the smell of lemons?" It was an unforeseen moment; I suddenly was struck by a storm of jealousy, a touch of rage.

"Look at you," she said. "At such moments, why must you make the wrong choice. You could just slide in here with me. There's room. If you'd want to, you'd fit. Instead, you throw a little tantrum."

I think that sometimes if you want something badly enough, you turn away from it. I left the warm, steamed-up bathroom and stood by the window, the coldest possible place.

"Vienna sleeps on the loveseat," Kala said. In the bathroom mirror I saw her gently rubbing her shoulders, chest, back with a washcloth. I turned to look out the window. "He curls up pitifully. Quite the gentleman, letting me have the bed, don't you think? I can scarcely stand it a night longer, Peter, not coming to see you. I've found a doctor, on Mrs. Sorrel's recommendation, and if he tells me that my ribs are healed and so forth, then let's have our reunion. Really, I'm moving about with very little pain now." Kala hummed a tune. I had no idea which. "Half my married life, Vienna's curled up on a sofa, chair, whatever furniture's other than the bed," she then said. "It's as if he's expecting to end up in a cramped coffin, practicing for it. You know, I keep having this dream—where I simply stand up, point my finger at the door, and say to Vienna, 'You're excused!' Like a school-teacher."

When at breakfast Kala had burst out with "Look at us!" it had caused an odd sensation, as if I'd stepped out of my body a moment, stood against the opposite wall, and diag-nosed my situation. And concluded that if I called the reason I continued to throw in my lot with these people *my love of Kala*, it wouldn't entirely suffice, even if I added *my fear of Vienna*. Then later, as I lay on my bed, I put it to myself sim-ply (far too simply, I'm sure): *You've stumbled into this fast-moving river, flailing, so what choice do you have but to dread and wonder, but also not give up hope on what will happen next?*

Now, any sane man might have said to Kala, "Let's just get out of here—now." Or, not wanting the encumbrances of love—or afraid of it—he might not even have bothered to pack his suitcase, just fled the Haliburton House Inn on his own, disappeared into Canada.

It would have been easy to do, really. I could have taken a Birney to the train station, boarded a train. To borrow a phrase from Miss Houghton again, I could've "disengaged from this life." And engaged into another life right away. However, to my mind, the larger unknown world seemed less a plausible choice than even the constant nervous feeling of impending treachery I felt in Vienna's presence. Dramatic sounding or no, it's what I felt.

That is to say, my confined world at least held possibilities, ones I could taste and feel and talk with. When finally I slept next to Kala again, I dreamed of Kala. When I woke next to her, she seemed a continuation of my dream of her. Past all that, yes, my fear of Vienna—what he was capable of—puppeteered my behavior, so to speak. I took care of menial tasks for him, just to keep a level of civility. I kept everything in the darkroom—blower brushes, glass beakers, developing trays, shears—neat and clean and in their own place. I faithfully attended to my employment. To bide my time. To stay close. Though maybe I was too easily persuaded by his revolver threats, still, they did persuade me. I still believed he might kill me. He had killed many people.

Then there was this. On page 411 of *The Unclad Spirit,* Miss Houghton wrote:

I am firmly of the belief that people are divided into two categories: those who act and those who are acted upon. And sometimes, circumstances are so desperate, compelling, or unavoidable that a person simply must change course. That person must set aside all hesitation and dependency, fling himself into the maelstrom, to *act on behalf of a truth forged by private communion with his own heart.* There are many a person I have met and worked with who simply deride themselves into taking some action. They experience the foretaste of regret; that is a realization that the moment has arrived, and that if they continue to act on contrivances instead of urgencies, they will eventually crumble inwardly, in a fashion akin to a house subservient to gravity, a house collapsed in on itself, floor by floor, until the entire edifice is in a useless heap.

When I'd first read that—months earlier—I thought, Maybe this Miss Houghton should just stick to spirit pictures and stop trying to find such philosophical ways of describing people's foibles and cowardice and natural flaws using such preachy language. Yet sitting on my bed, late at night on the day Kala had come back to the Haliburton House Inn and told me the doctor had given her a "clean bill of health," waiting for her, I read the passage again and felt defined by Miss Houghton's words. I felt *acted upon*—by love and fear in equal measure.

Whatever was to be Vienna's scheme with *Esquimaux Souls Risen from Aeroplane Wreck*, I vowed that, in the meantime, I wouldn't let the Haliburton House Inn swallow me up like Jonah's whale, the way the Churchill Hotel almost had. I promised myself that no matter the weather, I'd walk, walk for miles, breathe new air, try to think clear thoughts. On February 3—I remember the date because it was my mother's birthday and I went to visit her grave—I walked in bitter cold a good half day. I stopped twice for tea, once in a little five-table restaurant, next at the new Lord Nelson Hotel. Otherwise I walked and walked.

I only had wanted to distract myself from the present. But what happened that day was that the past came down brutally hard. I remembered too much.

I'd set out down Morris Street at about 10:00 a.m. I walked to Water Street, turned left along the harbor. I walked past the Dominion Coal Co. dock, which had huddled gulls on it. DeWolf's, Black & Flynn's, and then along Pier 1, Pier 2, Pier 3, Pier 4, Pier 5, biting sea wind all along the H.M. Dockyard, and finally I walked on out to the rocky beach at the Narrows.

I looked out over the water to Tufts Cove, then back to the beach again. At almost this exact spot, the *Herald*'s photographer Roy Polito had taken the photograph *People Watching a Resuscitation*, which had appeared on the front page, July 17, 1926.

It was at this beach that I had been permanently apprised of adultery.

# PEOPLE, AGHAST,
## WATCHING A RESUSCITATION

My father, Gerard, was ten years old when his family moved from France to England. "That's when we added a *t*," he told me, "and subtracted the French pronunciation of our name. Life in a new country was difficult enough. We wanted to fit in. It was our decision; there were plenty of French people in London who chose to do otherwise. Your grandparents set money aside and hired a tutor to teach us English. We tried erasing our accents. They thought it best." Having met in school and grown up less than half a block apart, my parents were married in London, both at age nineteen. My mother's name was Martha. They took a small flat two blocks away from Gerard's parents.

I was born on October 22, 1898. Peter Gerard Duvett.

At age eighteen I moved into my own flat. My grandparents were already gone. Then, in 1923—April 22 to be exact—in a "freak accident" (as the obituary had it), the horse-drawn cab my father operated around London overturned; the horse, gone berserk, had kicked backward to where my father had already been thrown to the street, and he was killed.

My mother kept the details of the accident from me for nearly two months; I don't know why, exactly. It's also true I didn't ask. One day my mother knocked on the door of my flat. The moment she stepped inside, she said, "I'm going to join my sister in Canada. Do you want to come along?" Politely like that.

And I immediately said, "Yes, all right. Yes." Just as politely.

The night before we left shipboard for Halifax, we ate together in a restaurant, a rare occurrence. "One thing I wish I could forget," my mother said, "was that the cab company took the customer's refund out of our insurance settlement. Salt to the wound, I'd say. I hope, dear, you don't mind terribly that I bring up the subject." I just reached out and held her hands in mine a moment. The waiter served our dinner. "Such vivid memories help credit my leaving England. I see one of those carriages and I nearly faint."

"No need to credit leaving on my behalf," I said. "I'm excited about going."

"Anyway—there'd been three passengers that morning. A mum, dad, six-year-old daughter. They'd mentioned she was six. When the horse went haywire, they said it looked as if a bee had stung up under its blinder. They managed to leap off. Oh, they each maybe had a fright and a scrape, nothing much. Their tour had scarcely begun. Your father tried to rein in the horse, they said.

"I'd warned him against that horse. It was not to be

trusted. It wasn't a seasoned horse. What's more, it didn't accept apples, and what sort doesn't? I held an apple out, so maybe I put it in bad temper, who's to say? My fault, maybe. My fault, I'm sure. I was standing by the carriage. Your father up in the driver's seat looked handsome in his waistcoat.

"It was a slow hour passengerwise. You remember, Peter, how I often brought breakfast to your father, don't you? Just a biscuit and steaming tea all in a cloth-covered basket. He preferred just that. Anyway, I held the apple up close to the horse's mouth; it swung its head and knocked me flat down. But by the time the family had stepped around in sight of us, I was already up dusting myself off. Had they seen, I'm certain they would have never climbed aboard.

"Now at least Gerard had work. The father helped the mother—up you go. Then up you go to the child. I waved goodbye, winked, cocked my hip like a wench, but only so Gerard could see. Waved goodbye still holding the basket, and off your father went. Clip-clop around the corner. And then definitely came the bad luck."

My aunt's name was Esther Markham. Markham was my mother's maiden name. Aunt Esther had already lived in Halifax for five years. She'd gotten married and divorced all in her second year in Halifax and, as my mother put it, was "moneywise set up for life. Impolite to inquire of details, unless Esther brings up the matter, which she no doubt will." My aunt and mother had arranged our passage through letters.

At the time of my father's death, I'd been apprenticing in darkroom technique at Bowdin's Photography. I worked for the owner, Terrence Bowdin, mostly developing wedding photographs. It was barely a living, but he'd recently given me hours behind the sales counter, so I began to see a future there. Terrence Bowdin was completely fair, he paid me the wages he actually could afford to pay me, we got along. When I told him I was leaving, he gave me my Christmas bonus five months in advance.

My mother and I arrived in Halifax on August 30, 1924. My aunt met us at Customs. I hadn't seen her in nearly six years and had all but forgotten the physical likeness she shared with my mother. My aunt was thirteen months the elder. They both had coal-black, unruly hair; "The only way to fashion our hair," my mother said, "was to wear hats." As young girls, my mother and aunt combed each other's hair exactly one hundred strokes a night. "And it scarcely helped at all." They were each about five feet five inches tall, slim, and, as my father said, "had small frames but tough as trees." He said this right after we'd lost to my aunt and mother at tug-of-war. Tug-of-war, it seems to me, was a game that in my family was more an inevitability than an enjoyment, though we did have laughs at it. My father always brought the tug-of-war rope along on picnics. Sooner or later, no matter how hot a day, he'd say, "Let's have a little show of strength, shall we?" He used that sentence to mimic British upper-class speech. Every once in a while, in a word here, a word there, a lilt or odd phrasing, I'd detect in my father's voice my grandparents' native French.

My mother and aunt had dark brown eyes. One time, when my mother was rubbing salve into the skin below her eyes, she said, "The shape of Esther's and my eyes comes from Mongolia. It's our exotic trait. Family rumor has it that my great-grandfather traveled to Mongolia, a merchant of some sort or other. And he came back with a Mongolian bride. One doesn't ever learn if she was a legal bride or not, or ever became one."

It took us about three hours to clear Customs. We were near to dead exhausted. I hardly remember getting from the dock to my aunt's house at 43 Robie Street, near Citadel Park. I think I nodded off in the automobile cab my aunt had hired, "a little show of wealth," my mother said later, "but a nice convenience on a rainy night after traveling so far." In front of her house my aunt paid the driver. We stood next to our steamer trunk—we'd come all that way with just the one trunk—and stared at the house in the dusky, rainy light. It was a one-story wooden house, dark green, with black shutters and slate-gray shingles on the roof. I saw an attic light was on. Once we stepped inside the house, my aunt said, "Peter, the attic is yours. A young bachelor should have his privacy. Look at you, handsome as can be. So much of Gerard, plainly, though you're a head taller. Strong, lovely man, your father, I loved him. I wish he could be here. Well—Peter, the attic's yours. And Marti"—it was her nickname for my mother—"I've put you in the guest room, dear."

"Can't thank you enough, Esther," my mother said. "You paid for the cab, but rest assured, you haven't adopted waifs here. Not charity cases. A little time to get on our feet—"

"I'm beside myself with happiness you're here, Marti. Let's put on some tea, shall we."

Within a few moments, my mother was asleep, head down on the kitchen table. Shipboard for eleven days, I had pretty much eaten only bread, not out of poverty—we had some money from the sale of my mother's apartment—but from merciless seasickness, which had emptied me out. Somehow, I didn't feel hungry, though, only displaced, light-headed, so tired that I couldn't muster enough strength to open the steamer trunk and find a nightshirt. I fairly crawled up the attic stairs. Lying on the two-poster with my clothes on, I took in the room a moment before drifting off. There were two small windows, a throw rug, a bed, of course, a bu-reau, a nightstand. The floor had been painted a light gray, knotholes included. A melancholy struck—to be starting this new life without my father. Or, it might be said, starting it because of him. Then I fell asleep.

Sometime in the night I woke to my mother's and aunt's voices. The kitchen was directly below. They may have al-ready been talking for hours, for all I knew. "Marti," my aunt was saying, "you'll have to beat the pavement. Now, there's an American phrase for you, isn't it?" They both laughed a moment. "But you'll find work, I'm certain of it." I was so worn out, I only allowed in the simplest thought: Are they getting on? And then: Will we all get on?

As it happened, a month later my mother and I found employment on the same day at the same place, the Halifax *Herald* newspaper. My mother was hired in the business of-fice. She did basic accounting. But also she earned an extra amount each week proofreading obituaries. "What a fine introduction to Canada," she said one evening at dinner, "getting to know all of these dead people, where I've scarcely otherwise made a friend. Present company excepted, of course." She worked at proofreading late into the night at the kitchen table.

I'd been hired in the darkroom. Developing photographs

was the one thing I could call a profession. I was in the newspaper's darkroom ten, sometimes twelve hours a day. It was in the basement. I had to wear a sweater, over which I wore a chemist's smock. My direct boss was named Stewart Bishop. I was instructed to call him "Mr. Bishop." He was fifty-three, roughly six feet tall, with a handlebar mustache flecked with gray, thinning gray hair combed straight back on a long face, deep-set blue eyes—his eyes, in my opinion, allowed some warmth, even affection, but otherwise he struck me as aloof, even cold. I hardly saw him at the newspaper. He only came into the photography section to run through the day's schedule: which photographs needed to be done right away, which could wait and until when. One urgency replacing another, et cetera. Mainly I worked alone. Sometimes, though, I had a working partner, an elderly man named Jarvis Moore. He was not much for conversation, Jarvis, except on technical matters; he was polite enough to make any small advice and instruction sound like an off-handed remark—"By the way."

Life went on predictably enough for three or four months; long days at the *Herald*. My aunt, mother, and I always had Sunday dinner together. Like a children's song based on routine: sip of soup, a little talk, sip of soup, early to bed.

Yet all along my mother had been carrying out a secret courtship. Because one Sunday late in February of 1925, she brought Mr. Bishop home for dinner. I could not have been more surprised by this, or judged it more harshly to myself. Formal introductions were made, even to me. "Peter," my mother said, "this is Mr. Bishop, from the newspaper, as you may know." She placed Mr. Bishop's hat and coat on the coatstand in the front hallway.

"Nice to see you in broad daylight," Mr. Bishop said to me. "Well, just past broad daylight, I suppose. It's what, seven o'clock?"

"Yes," my aunt said. "Seven on the button. And welcome, Mr. Bishop. Sit down. My sister's told us nothing about you. Let's have a chat before dinner. We're having scrod and potatoes. Even if we'd known you were coming, we'd have had the same."

"Please, it's Stewart," Mr. Bishop said.

Then Mr. Stewart Bishop was in our lives. In fact, he came to dinner every night that following week. Some nights I was there, some nights at work. It was as if my mother was accelerating a courtship and wanted us to witness it. That first Sunday dinner, my aunt allowed me to serve her and my mother first, as was the custom in our house. My mother or aunt would cook, I'd serve. But the very next night, Monday, my aunt insisted on serving, and served Mr. Bishop first, sliding two pieces of roast chicken onto his plate with great deference. (In the dozens of times we'd eaten roast chicken together, I never once placed anything but one piece on a plate at a time.) Taking notice of this, my mother registered a curious expression, more resignation than surprise, I thought, but still some surprise, too. Mr. Bishop was the first to be served every night I was there for dinner; I'm sure it was true of the nights I wasn't there, too. On Saturday evening of that same week, he lit his pipe at table. Usually, he waited until after dinner, repaired to the living room, sat in the rocking chair, lit his pipe, and said,

"Fine dinner. Fine dinner." As though he were the head of our household—it made me cringe. My mother and aunt seemed charmed by it, each in her own fashion, even though I knew them not to suffer fools, men or women. To me, Bishop was, to use my father's words, "the original bloody fool."

Anyway, on that Saturday night Bishop said to me in the living room, "A bit sloppy, your work in the darkroom this week, Peter, eh?"

"How do you mean?" I said.

"The photograph which was supposed to be on the front page Sunday—the kite-flying competition? Smudged work, Peter, and our chief photographer, Mr. Knowlson, you know his temperament, was not pleased, let me tell you. Not pleased one bit. I thought I'd warn you in case he rakes you over the coals."

"He and I get along well."

"Till now." He tamped in new tobacco. "As you know, we allow for a five-dollar bonus for a front-page photograph, and Mr. Knowlson is out that five dollars and asked me to dock your salary accordingly and transfer it to him. Which won't entirely make amends, but will help soothe his nerves, eh? I was thinking of saying, 'Now, Knowlson, you took a photograph worthy of the front page, was going to be *on* the front page—so here, just take five dollars out of the till.' But then I realized that might humiliate Knowlson, if word got out the newspaper paid him, no matter that his photograph didn't appear. So taking care of it in private will do the trick, Peter. Don't you agree? Knowlson's been with the paper many years."

"I thought the photograph looked fine."

"Mr. Knowlson didn't give it his final stamp of approval, so that's that."

"I guess I'll have to live on five dollars less."

"Smudged—not up to Knowlson's high standards. He gets to make that determination."

"I judged it differently."

"Obviously you misjudged is what I'm telling you." He smoked his pipe a moment. "How old are you, Peter?"

"Twenty-seven."

"When I was sixteen—*sixteen*, mind you, I was out on my own. But then again, I suppose it's nice to be taken care of by two women, eh? Dinner on the table. Dishes cleared."

My mother's secret life came boldly out in the open that week. But what I couldn't foresee was how my aunt, over the next few months, herself fell in love with Mr. Bishop. I got my first inkling of it when my mother announced her and Mr. Bishop's engagement.

It was on the last Sunday in May 1925. We were eating peach cobbler when Mr. Bishop tapped his spoon against his water glass and said, "Ahem." He stood up, wiped a fleck of peach cobbler crust from his mustache with his napkin, and said, "Martha, you have something to tell your family?"

My mother inhaled deeply, as if bursting to the surface of a childhood swimming hole—she suddenly had a young girl's expression. "Yes, yes," she said, blushing. "We're to be married. Late June, which is coming up quickly now, isn't it? We'll set the exact date this week, won't we, Stewart?"

My aunt stood up from the table, walked into the kitchen, a smile nailed to her face. She stood where only I could see her through the doorway, her back to me. She took a knife from the rack, picked up a pear from a wooden bowl, sliced it into four pieces. She began to eat the pear, and when the last piece was still in her mouth, she called out, "Congratulations—both of you!" then spit some pear into the sink. Then she bent over the sink, put her mouth to the spigot, turned the faucet, and drank. Standing upright, she then rubbed water on her face, turned off the faucet, dried her face with a dish towel, turned, and saw me looking at her.

"What's that again, Esther?" my mother said. "We could hardly hear you."

My aunt didn't answer. And I thought, Something is very wrong here.

The wedding in fact took place not in late June but on June 15. It was held in my aunt's living room. It was a sunny day, with a nice breeze up from the harbor, a little salt in the air. My aunt had placed four vases full of white lilies around the house. The wedding had been set for one o'clock. The man hired to officiate, a Reverend Brackage, arrived at about noon. I never learned his actual religious affiliation. My mother held to none in particular, though she'd been raised an Anglican.

There were about twenty-five or thirty people in attendance. Most were employees of the *Herald*. Everyone was nicely dressed, summer finery. My aunt was meeting most of them for the first time.

My aunt's best silverware was neatly laid out next to china plates and a three-tiered wedding cake. I'd hoped she wouldn't, but my mother in fact did wear her original wedding dress, the one in which she'd married my father. I'd asked her to buy a new one. "My love for your father hasn't gone in the least," she said to me in the kitchen. "And that's exactly why—privately—I'm wearing this dress. It's like wearing a precious memory. It'll be yours and my little secret. Besides, I asked Stewart if he minded terribly, and he said he minded a little. He can be generous that way."

"I hate him. You know that, don't you? I can hardly stand to breathe the same air as he."

"It's only natural you should. But don't hate me for this marriage."

"I don't."

Rev. Brackage gave his little talk, which was followed by "You may now kiss the bride," but I was in the kitchen by that time, making sure there was enough lemonade for the half dozen children in the house. But I did hear, "You may now kiss the bride," and, despite my inclinations, stood in the kitchen doorway and looked on.

My mother did not kiss Mr. Bishop. She had something more urgent to attend to. That very instant, she made a beeline toward my aunt, who stood at the back of the tightly gathered crowd. As onlookers stepped aside and my mother approached, my aunt's mouth fell open as if she were saying, "Oh!" and held a look of disbelief in advance. My mother stepped directly up to my aunt and slapped her—I mean a dull *thwack!*—stunning my aunt. My aunt quickly drew her hand to her cheek, as if searching for a bruise. My mother had provided her guests with a permanent memory, all right, which most weddings probably don't. Quite a spectacle.

I would guess that it wasn't more than three minutes be-

fore the house was empty of people, with the exception of
myself, my aunt, my mother, Mr. Bishop, Rev. Brackage, and
several children who ran around slapping each other's faces
gently in a game, until their parents gathered them up and
got them out. My mother handed Rev. Brackage an envelope full of money; he said, "Thank you and good luck," and
hurried from the house. Mr. Bishop retreated to my mother's
bedroom and lay down on the bed, his hands pressed over his
eyes as if holding a cold compress. I followed him in.

"What in hell just happened?" I said, closing the door.

Mr. Bishop could not bother—or maybe wasn't capable
of it at the moment—sitting up or even looking at me.
"Don't be a dunce," he said, an unnaturally exaggerated
space between each word. "You've got eyes in your head,
don't you, Peter? Well then, open them as wide as you can
and try to see something, for goddamn Christ's sake, you little goddamn mamma's boy!"

I left him there.

After they were married, my mother and Mr. Bishop
lived in Mr. Bishop's house on Connaught Street. I
found a one-room apartment on Water Street.

I continued to have dinner with my aunt every Sunday
night, much to my mother's chagrin and disapproval. In turn,
I had dinner with my mother and Mr. Bishop every Saturday
night. I was forbidden to mention the name of either sister
in the other's presence. It was painful.

I had been courting, for a few months, a woman named
Caryn James, who worked in the *Herald*'s advertising depart-

ment. Now and again we slept together. She was a few years younger than I, with short-cut black hair. She liked me very much, I liked her very much, as we both kept saying to each other. One night, sitting in a middle row of a theater, I whispered, "Can you spend the night?" She said, "I've been looking forward to seeing this picture. I want to pay it proper attention. Please be quiet." She moved two seats over. After the picture we went to The Carieton Hotel for tea. We knew things between us were over. "Don't be angry, Peter," she said. "You have to try out people, don't you? Some fit, some don't."

The weeks went by, I worked steadily at the *Herald*. I got better acquainted with the photographers, typesetters, a few reporters. I developed photographs of their weddings, their children's birthdays. I did that on my own time for free. It made me feel part of the newspaper family in a small way.

Mr. Bishop came in quite often to berate my work. The predictability of it was something of a joke around the newspaper, but never to Mr. Bishop's face. The subject came up now and then in conversations I had with a fellow named Paul Amundson, a Norwegian typesetter. He'd lived in Canada since he was fifteen. When Paul had a few drinks, he'd crank up his Norwegian accent (his parents had spoken only Norwegian) and do an imitation of Mr. Bishop berating me: "Ya, ya, ya, ya know, Paytor," a thick Norwegian accent like that. "That photograph you develop, ya? It's a failure, ya?" And all of us would fall apart laughing.

Then one Sunday—August 3, 1926—I went into the

newspaper's darkroom earlier than usual, maybe 5:00 a.m. It wasn't unusual for me to go in on a Sunday, just not so early. The night before, of course, I'd had dinner with my mother and Mr. Bishop. It had been like opening a door and walking into a storm cloud. They'd been quarreling, I'm certain of it. During dinner the conversation at best was stilted, as if none of us had ever met before and had been thrown together at a train's dining car table. My mother picked at her meal. Mr. Bishop stood up from the table in the middle of dinner and walked out the door without a word. My mother and I chatted amiably awhile. About this and that. "Did you read, a bookmobile—a bus converted to have shelves full of books. It's a library that'll drive around Halifax every day. It's just been launched like a new ship at Government House. They actually broke a champagne bottle against it," my mother said. "I hope it comes down our street. I need to do some reading, I think." As she spoke, she'd been biting her lip, wringing her hands, her voice full of forced cheerfulness.

She got up and walked into her and Mr. Bishop's bedroom, returning with a small book or what at first looked like a book. But then I saw it was marked DIARY on the front cover. "I meant to give this to you earlier," she said, handing me the diary. She then wept hard a few moments, but didn't look away. When she'd gained her composure a bit, she said, "It's from the first year of Gerard's and my marriage. Read it if you wish. You'll find few trials and tribulations. My writing's a disaster—my handwriting, I mean. But the value is in the memory, of course. I do still miss your father by the minute, you know. Some wise novelist or other said, 'Life makes its offerings and you choose to embrace them or not.' And I chose to embrace Mr. Bishop—what's the way the vows put it? 'For better or worse.' "

When I said goodbye to my mother and stepped onto the porch, I slipped the diary into my raincoat pocket. It had been raining so often in Halifax that I always took my raincoat wherever I went. I then noticed Mr. Bishop leaning against the side of the house, furiously smoking his pipe. I couldn't help think of a miniature smokestack. Something of a cartoon there, I thought. He knew that I was looking at him, but he stared at the ground. "Good night, Mr. Bishop," I said. He went around behind the house.

Then Sunday, August 3, I was in the darkroom. Work was backed up. Some political dignitaries were visiting Halifax and there were a few dozen photographs of them to develop. Mr. Knowlson might choose one for the front page. I'd been in the darkroom less than an hour, I'm sure, when there was a pounding on the door. "Peter! Peter!" I recognized the voice as Gordy Larkin's. "Hold on, Gordy," I shouted back. "Give me a minute in here!" "We don't *have* a minute!" she shouted back.

I dropped what I was doing, slipped out the door so as not to expose any film, and there was Gordy, looking both panicky and excited. Gordy Larkin was the first woman reporter on full-time staff in the *Herald*'s history. She was so agitated now, she had to sit down. "I saw your raincoat on the table there, eh?" she said. "Why here so early, Peter?"

"You don't seem to have time for small talk, Gordy. What's up?"

Gordy was about twenty-five, tall, with a beautiful, sharp-featured face, dark brown eyes, dark brown hair fashionably

cut, though I didn't know what fashion to call it. She was
very smart. I thought that she was smart from the get-go.
And newspaper reporting seemed to suit her perfectly. She
once matter-of-factly said to me in the cafeteria, "I'm not
ashamed of my journalistic ambitions, you know." I never
forgot how she said that in front of the assistant photography
editor, Michael Katzenberg, and a number of other men eating lunch. She also told me that she eventually wanted to
move to Montreal, work at a newspaper in that city, then
go on to a newspaper in New York and, finally, London.
She asked me a lot of questions about London. She had endless curiosity and couldn't seem to get enough information
about life there. She had the order of her cities worked out
already. Gordy was very pretty and bluntly fended off any
flirtations; from me she basically wanted facts about London.

"Peter," Gordy said, "there's been a drowning at the Narrows. It was just dumb luck I happened by, the middle of the
night like that. I was on my way home from arguing with—
never mind. Never mind all that. This drowning, it's as sad as
can be. But what's done is done, and don't think badly of me
if I see it as a boost for my career, okay? I'm angling for a
promotion to Features, right?"

"What're you asking, here, Gordy?"

"I happened upon this drowned person about 4:00. I
called the police right away, and I'd already got Roy Polito
out of bed—oops. Anyway, Roy lives two blocks from the
Narrows. He's down there setting up his camera. Will you
right away develop what pictures Roy takes?"

"Sure, okay," I said. "Jesus, settle down a little, will you?"

"A drowning—seeing, you know, seeing her body like
that. How can I settle down?"

"Her?"

"Most definitely it's a woman." Gordy started for the door, stopped, turned around, and said, "Will you come with me? It's creepy—I mean, Roy'll be there and I know you've got a lot of work here, but go down to the Narrows with me, eh?"

"Okay." No hesitation on my part. "Okay, let's go." She walked over to the chair, picked up my raincoat, and tossed it to me.

By the time we reached the Narrows, a small crowd of people, eight or ten, stood near the body. A doctor—or medical person of some sort—had been called. He was leaning over the body. Gordy moved closer, I lagged back. Roy Polito was moving his camera for a better angle. I couldn't actually see the drowned woman; through the crowd I glimpsed only her feet sticking out from under a tarpaulin. Then I heard the doctor say, "It's too late. She's been gone awhile, I think. I can't get her breathing again, that's for sure." Two policemen stepped up and pulled the tarpaulin over her face. Gordy had gotten up quite close.

The crowd thinned out, a few stragglers stayed behind, but everyone else walked slowly up from the Narrows to the street. Three policemen remained standing by the body, each staring out over the water, smoking a cigarette, as if thinking private thoughts. Still, Gordy walked right up to one and said, "Is there any identification?"

The policemen ignored her. "I'm from the *Herald*," she said, and displayed her reporter's identification. "I've got my photographer here. I'd like a photograph for the paper, please."

The policeman who looked to be the oldest of the three

flicked his cigarette off Polito's camera and said to him, "I saw you just take one."

"He needs—" Gordy said. She cleared her throat. "We need to have the tarp rolled back. If possible—"

I felt Gordy was going too far. The policeman she was talking to looked as if he wanted to punch her in the face. I turned my back on this scene. But I could still hear everything. "You have exactly one minute to take things in," he said, "then I'll personally see that you leave."

"Fine," Gordy said. "Will you turn the tarp back, please?"

"I will not do that voluntarily, no," he said. "No, I won't. Big opportunity, eh? Think a minute if you were the husband, or, or, or—or the daughter of this poor woman. How'd you like her picture plastered on the front page?"

"I'll turn it back," Gordy said. "One picture's all we need."

I turned slightly, enough to see the policemen conferring only by looking at one another, calibrating, it seemed to me, obligation in relation to their disgust with Gordy. Silently, they each walked from the body in different directions, until they were ten or so meters away. I looked back up toward the street. But I heard Gordy pull back the tarpaulin and let out a little gasp. I heard Polito slide in a plate. "Okay—got it," Polito said. I heard Gordy move the tarpaulin again. "We're done here," Gordy said, loud enough for the policemen to hear, but they didn't bother to even turn around. They just wanted Gordy out of there. Gordy, Polito, and I walked back to the *Herald*. Outside the darkroom, Gordy handed me the two plates. "Thanks much, Peter," she said. "I'm going upstairs to write things up."

"I'll get to this right away, then," I said.

I think that even before I started to develop the photo-graph I had in mind the caption, *People, Aghast, Watching a Resuscitation*—I mean, for the first photograph I'd seen Polito take, when the doctor was still leaning over the woman. So I developed that plate and it came out well, and I hung it up to dry. I wrote out the caption and clipped the piece of pa-per to the photograph.

Then I began to develop the second plate.

There, floating in the developer dish, was a woman dressed in her overcoat. You could almost feel the weight of the harbor-soaked coat. Her hair was smoothed back, soak-ing dark, too. Her eyes were closed. Her legs were swaddled tightly in the tarpaulin, giving the impression of a tailless mermaid. The tarp was pulled down only to her stomach.

My mind had registered the details but not the truth: *slowly—it can't be true.* The woman lying under the tarpaulin at the Narrows was my mother.

Suddenly it was too late for five deep breaths. It was too late for What-am-I-doing-here. I attempted to make it out of the darkroom, reeled dizzily into the corner, where I vio-lently retched. I needed air. Opening the door, I saw Jarvis Moore. "Jarvis—" was all I could manage. I sat down on the floor.

"Peter—Jesus, look at you," Jarvis said. "What's wrong?"

"I got sick in there, Jarvis. I need to get home." I sat on the floor.

"All right, yes, you go home." He reached out to help me get up, but I pushed him away.

"I'm going, I'm going—"

As I left the room, I vaguely heard Jarvis say, "Want me to finish up in there?"

I didn't leave the building, though. I went upstairs, entered the first office I came to, and dialed the police. When the police operator answered, I said, "My name is Peter Duvett. I—"

"Where are you, Mr. Duvett?"

"I develop photographs at the *Herald*. That's where I am. I'm there now. I just developed a photograph of—"

"Of what? Calm down, please, if you can."

"Of *whom*? Of whom."

"All right, then. Of whom?"

"The woman they found at the Narrows this morning. Her name—the police said they didn't have any identification yet. But her name is Martha Duvett."


The evening's *Herald* had *People Watching a Resuscitation* on the front page.

The next day a police inquiry took place. I sat in my mother's living room, along with Mr. Bishop and my aunt. My aunt sat on the opposite end of the sofa from me. Mr. Bishop stood behind my aunt. The police went over certain details. "Where were you at such and such a time" and "When did you last see the deceased?"—with that question I burst into tears, not being able to help it, really. I didn't feel twenty-seven, I didn't feel any age at all. A moment later I all but shouted, "My mother loved to walk by the wharf— down to the Narrows. That was a favorite place of hers to walk. She *enjoyed* it there. You should know that."

The man in charge was named Inspector Lennart, and he just nodded and wrote that down.

I cannot fully recall all that transpired that day. I can hardly recall, except in the most general sense, my mother's funeral, held five days later. In fact, during the following weeks I seemed to be choking on anger and blame. When I was a boy, whenever I got truly angry at someone, my mother advised that I write that person a letter. That I write everything I felt with utter and uncompromised honesty, and invent the bluntest language possible without cursing. "Don't hold back in the slightest," she'd say, "and write it over and over again as many times as it takes. And then tear it up and throw it away. Because a letter like that actually *never sent* can do the letter writer a world of good."

About a month after my mother's death (I hadn't set eyes since the funeral on Mr. Bishop or my aunt, except once, when I happened to pass by a restaurant in which they sat at a windowside table), I sat up an entire night writing a letter addressed to Inspector Lennart. I described the wedding. The slap. How it was clear that my mother had tried with that slap to stop Mr. Bishop's adultery with my aunt (which I think had already started, in fact), and how I knew for certain that every time he told my mother he was working late, he'd met my aunt at the Lord Nelson Hotel, at least for tea. I knew this because the brother of a typesetter at the *Herald* was a bellhop there and he told me. I connected everything up for Inspector Lennart. I wrote about my last dinner with my mother, all of it. All of it, and I suppose I was trying to directly blame Mr. Bishop and my aunt for my mother's death, accusing them. I wrote: "In my opinion, Mr. Bishop was capable of pushing my mother into the harbor. She did not know how to swim."

I sent the letter.

A week later, Inspector Lennart knocked on my apartment door. He did not want to come in. He wanted to say just one thing. "That letter you sent, Mr. Duvett, it's gone into the file," he said. "Of course, all papers related to your mother's death go into a file. And I'm sorry about her death, Duvett. But it's officially been declared a suicide—you know that. I'm sorry for you in that, the son. But it's officially declared. It's closed." He reached out and gripped both my shoulders. "That letter—the truth is, should Mr. Bishop or Esther Markham turn up dead, your letter's incriminating evidence against you. See my point? Think that over. Think how things come around and come around. We have your letter on file, eh? We have to keep everything on file."

He offered a stiff grin, then, to my surprise, reached into his back pocket, took out my letter, and tore it to shreds.

That was a low point. That was a real debasement and humiliation. And how, then, could comprehension of what Inspector Lennart had all but pounded into my head, his warning, have inspired me to write a second letter? The second letter included how my aunt had cut up the pear into four pieces—I got very detailed. This second letter and the eight that followed must've struck Inspector Lennart as the grief-filled ravings of a madman. (Who knows what kinds of letters he reads on his job?) Anyway, I wrote a letter per day for nine days. And within a week of posting each one, I received an official *Receipt of Property* from the police department, nothing more.

My aunt and Mr. Bishop boarded a train for Vancouver. I learned this from a card Bishop sent. It arrived the day after they had left. I stayed working at the *Herald* until I saw Vienna Linn's advertisement, and immediately posted my letter.

I was desperate to get out. Naturally I thought, being a city boy, the north has more breathing room. And then I ended up mostly in a hotel.

# PORTRAIT OF
# A DANGEROUS MAN

Freddy Sorrel sat for his portrait directly after breakfast on February 11. He insisted that he be photographed sitting at a table in the dining room. He was quite dressed up. "This is my church suit," he said, "which I've never worn to church, because I don't go." He'd just washed his hair. It was combed straight back. You could see the comb tracks. After I set up Vienna's camera and the cloth backdrop, I stood off to the side. Sliding in a plate, Vienna said, "All right, Freddy, how about a smile?"

Freddy stood up, walked over to Vienna, stood directly in front of him, poked Vienna's chest with his forefinger. "You ask me that again," Freddy said, "I'll poison your food. Except I'll wait. I'll bide my time. You ask me to smile, you might as well not ever eat in this room again." He sat back down in the chair.

"Ah, you see yourself as a dangerous character," Vienna said. "I'll try to capture that." Vienna focused the camera.

"You know, Freddy, it's a normal thing, asking someone sitting for a portrait to smile. But you absolutely don't have to, of course."

"You ever see the portraits of the Canadian Most Wanted?" Freddy said. He couldn't seem to find a comfortable position to settle into. "They don't smile in theirs."

Vienna stood upright, waiting for Freddy to stop fidgeting. "I suppose if I were one of the Most Wanted, I'd tend not to smile, either."

"Well, it'd have to be a photograph from *before* they were a Most Wanted, wouldn't it? I mean, once they were a Most Wanted, they wouldn't wander in to sit for a portrait, would they? It's just in their nature not to smile, is what," Freddy said, pleased with his observations.

"I see," Vienna said.

"This goddamn chair's got one leg shorter than the other," Freddy said. He stood up, sat down again.

"Freddy, get any expression on your face you choose."

"You're looking at it."

"Fine," Vienna said. "That's an expression, all right. It certainly is."

"It's my WANTED poster expression, I call it. I've practiced it in mirrors."

"I see."

"I've had a few run-ins with the authorities. Brushes with the law."

"Have you now?"

"Yes, I have."

"You know, the minute I saw you, I thought that there was something unusual in your bearing."

"A good judge of character, eh?" Freddy said.

"You might say that."

"I just *did* say that."

"Hold that expression. I'll take the photograph."

Freddy forced an even more nasty-looking downward grimace, his eyes squinted half-closed, his face tilted as if he'd gotten a sudden twinge of pain in his neck.

"Impressive," Vienna said. "Very impressive— Now hold still."

Vienna took the photograph. He slid out the plate, handed it to me, slid in a second plate.

"I suppose you won't privilege us with exactly which kinds of brushes with the law you're talking about?" Vienna said.

Instead of answering, Freddy looked at me. "Haven't I seen you in Halifax before, Duvett?" he said. "I think I've seen you."

"I worked at the *Herald*," I said. "Up till last September."

"I used to deliver scones my mother made over to the *Herald*."

"I've eaten some of those. That must have been where you saw me."

"Don't you have a house? Why're you living here, Duvett? You scrounging off this married couple or something?"

"I'm paying my own room and board, just like anyone else. And I don't like your questions."

"I'm prepared for a second picture," Vienna said.

Freddy got his favorite look on his face again. Vienna took the photograph. Freddy stood up, yawned loudly. Vienna left the room. Freddy leaned against the wall. "Your boss there's an intellectual son-of-a-bitch, isn't he?" Freddy said. "I know the type. I've served dinner to that type. They look down on me, like they don't think I can even recite the alphabet or something. We get professors from Dalhousie University in here. I always feel like reciting the alphabet to them before throwing down a menu. From listening in, I can tell they live inside their heads, just like your boss Vienna Linn. I mean, I say, 'What would you like to order?' and they answer, 'Could you perhaps strike a different tone with us, young man.' Then I say, 'That answer's not on the menu this evening,' and they say, 'Well then, may we talk to the proprietor?' and I say back, 'That'd be my mother, and she's indisposed at the moment. In fact, she's upstairs with a favorite guest'—wink, wink, wink."

"Mr. Linn is intelligent," I said. "You're right about that."

"I'll give him my permission to sell my portrait to the police, when they need a likeness for a WANTED poster."

"How will you earn that poster, if you don't mind me asking?"

"I haven't figured it out as of yet. It'll be something memorable."

"I bet it will."

"Maybe I'll poison Mr. Linn there."

"Poison him. Flee the city. That'd work. I'll see to it your portrait gets to the police."

"You'd do that for me?"

"Yes, I would."

"I know a Sergeant Maitlin with the police," Freddy said. "He comes here with his family for dinner."

"Sergeant Maitlin. Okay. I'll contact him when the time is right."

Vienna had gone to get Mrs. Sorrel for her sitting. When

they came into the dining room, Freddy left without a word.

"How about the same chair as your son?" Vienna said.

"I much prefer the sitting room," Mrs. Sorrel said. "But all right. I wouldn't want you to have to move all this equipment and such." She sat at the table. She folded her hands together, took a deep breath, let it out in short sighs, then looked at the camera. As Vienna made his adjustments, Mrs. Sorrel said, "I imagine Freddy offered up some of his criminal daydreams. It's what he's apt to do with a captive new audience like yourselves. You really must ignore his criminal daydreams, such as they are. He's an only child. His father was gone by the time he was five. Gone for good, and good riddance, but that's when—right after—Freddy began to have imaginary friends. These imaginary friends were each and every one a policeman."

"Was that here in Halifax?" I said.

"He was born and raised here, yes."

"Sorry to interrupt—" I said.

"—policemen. Then, of course, there's all that nonsense about WANTED posters. I suppose he mentioned that."

"He did mention it," I said.

"He has boxes full of his own designs—I shouldn't be saying this, but, Mr. Linn, you seem like a man of the world. Worldly; and the fact is, my Freddy offers himself up to the police at least once a week."

"For what reason?" I said.

"Fascinating," Vienna said. He was now ready to take the picture, but also, I could see, genuinely interested in what Mrs. Sorrel was saying. "Yes, I'm equally as curious for what reason your son 'gives himself up,' as you put it, Mrs. Sorrel," Vienna said.

"Well," Mrs. Sorrel said, "he sees a crime in the newspaper—*unsolved*—he walks right in, says, 'I did it.' That sort of thing."

"His moment in the sun, is that it, Mrs. Sorrel?" Vienna said.

"He's a resourceful one, my Freddy. One time, two years ago, he was to deliver some scones to the police station, one of my best customers—they have a steady order. Freddy for some reason decided to throw my scones in the harbor, and he did that. He tossed them to the seagulls. And then he continued on to the police station, and when he got there, he confessed—quite dramatically, I'm told—to throwing scones into the harbor. A Sergeant Maitlin there, who's familiar with my son, to say the least, said, 'Well, Freddy, go back and tell your mother what you did, and then ask her please to bake a new batch; you bring those on down to us and make amends.' Said result was that it put Freddy in such a foul mood, being talked to like a child, he wasn't fit to even wash dishes that night, let alone wait tables. The next day the newspaper said that dozens and dozens of seagulls had washed up on shore. The police never made the connection, but I certainly did. Sergeant Maitlin never figured out just how close he was to becoming, possibly at best, deathly ill. Now, I'm sure to most people down by the harbor that day, it was just a nice picture, a nice young man feeding the gulls, but to a mother with a son like Freddy— let's put it this way—his turns of mind are simply not like yours and mine. They simply aren't."

"That's good to know," Vienna said. His patience with all Mrs. Sorrel's talk now seemed narrowed down to the thinnest-lipped smile, and he actually waved his hand in the air, as if brushing away a fly. "Well, fine then, Mrs. Sorrel, you do have an interesting son in Freddy. But don't you agree, Mrs. Sorrel, sometimes a person hears too much to take in all at once? Don't you think that's possible?"

"Oh, I see—" Mrs. Sorrel said. "Absolutely. You're absolutely correct, Mr. Linn. Too much to take in all at once. Because, look how I've gone on! And here you are, a famous portraitist and your time is precious. All my motherly woes. Perhaps I was just, in my own way, warning you about Freddy's nature. His basic nature. All I ever ask of him, really, is to get the plates full of food and bring them out to the table. Or to use enough soap on the dishes and keep the rinse hot enough."

"And I thank you for the good information," Vienna said. "Now smile, please."

*Mother of the Man in Wanted Poster*, I couldn't help but thinking as I looked at Mrs. Sorrel.

"Very nice," Vienna said, sliding out the plate and handing it to me. "Let's do just one more, shall we?"

However tedious and edgy Freddy Sorrel's ramblings, however long-winded Mrs. Sorrel, they'd given Vienna an idea, offered him an unforeseen opportunity. A few days after he'd taken their portraits, he told Kala and me about it. As was now to be our custom, we'd sat down to dinner that evening at 7:00 p.m. at the windowside table. The table was always set for four. Kala would sit down next to me, Vienna across from her. Then Mrs. Sorrel would stop by and remove the fourth place setting.

Now—this took place on February 15. I recall the date, because I'd finally developed Freddy's and Mrs. Sorrel's portraits and marked down the dates in the ledger. They were the first photographs I'd developed since I'd set up the cramped, stifling, but adequate darkroom.

"I've come up with work here in Halifax," Vienna said.

"Oh?" Kala said. "And what work is that?"

"I was quite bold about it, really," Vienna said just after dinner. "I went right over to the police station. There I introduced myself to Sergeant Maitlin. You recall the name, I'm sure, Duvett. Freddy's contact in the police, you might say." He sipped his tea a moment. "I told Sergeant Maitlin that my wife and I were new to the city. I said we were set up in the Haliburton House Inn. I told him of what I'd overheard at dinner one night."

"Which was, pray tell?" Kala said. It disturbed me how interested she was, drawn in, listening like a child to a story.

"Well, I said I'd overheard the waiter. I said I believed he was the son of the proprietor. That I'd overheard this waiter named Freddy telling someone he was going to rob a bank! He seemed quite conspiratorial about it, I said. Naturally, Sergeant Maitlin nearly choked laughing on his sandwich.

"I looked insulted and said I'd come there acting on good faith, that there was no need to mock me, and so on. I started for the door. But good Sergeant Maitlin stopped me, apologized—still laughing, mind you—then sat me down and corroborated Mrs. Sorrel's tales of woe about Freddy's—"

"Criminal daydreams," I said.

"That's correct," Vienna said. "We continued talking, good Sergeant Maitlin and myself. We talked about the local radio shows. It seems the sergeant and I share a fondness for the radio. I told him that I intended to buy a radio and put it in the darkroom. One subject led to another. And *then*— what a moment earlier would never have occurred to me suddenly became obvious. I suggested that he sit for a portrait. More talk followed, and in a matter of an hour or so, I was employed."

"One portrait hardly—" Kala said.

"—I'm to take all the official police portraits," Vienna said. "Of each and every policeman, you see. Top rank to bottom, every last one, at the expense of the city of Halifax. I stopped by the station again today, and my good friend Sergeant Maitlin gave me final approval."

"I must say, you've outdone yourself this time," Kala said, damning with faint praise. Her expression was pinched.

"Thank you," Vienna said. "A rare compliment."

"Perhaps testing fate a bit, though," she said. "All those fellows coming by, with their trained curiosities. Their police curiosities."

"It's good to be employed," Vienna said. "A person should use the skills God gave, 'no matter how suspect or closed-minded the world at large.' I suppose you know who said that, don't you? Your Miss Houghton. From one of your own lectures, dear."

"She was referring to skills put to a higher purpose," Kala said. She hadn't yet touched her tea.

"My low purpose," Vienna said, "is to pay room and board."

"You never do anything with just one purpose in mind," Kala said. "When and where does this new employment begin?"

"Right here, in the estimable Haliburton House Inn. And it begins tomorrow, in fact. Much needed plates provided by—guess where, Duvett? The very newspaper you once worked for. All arranged by Sergeant Maitlin. He can pull strings in Halifax, that's clear."

"Have you told Mrs. Sorrel about your newfound fortune?" Kala said.

"She's quite impressed. Thrilled, really. Except of course for how the policemen might give her son the jitters."

Vienna stood up from the table. "I'm off to a pub—if they call it that here. That's what I'm off to, no matter what they call it. Meeting Sergeant Maitlin and some of his colleagues." He went upstairs. Kala and I stayed at the table. When he returned, he wore his coat, gloves, galoshes. Kala and I watched through the window as he set out down Morris Street.

"Will you be up late, do you think?" Kala said.

"If you will."

"Have a fire going, will you? The few steps between here and the annex will be bitter cold. In two hours, then?"

"How long do you think Vienna will be out?"

"What does it matter, really? At this point."

Kala went upstairs.

I retired to the sitting room. In a few minutes Vienna came in again. He saw me and said, "Forgot something." He made his way back upstairs. I wondered if he and Kala would exchange words. He was gone just a few moments. Instead of leaving, though, he sat down in a chair across from me. He was holding his leather satchel. "I'm going to say two things, and I suggest you memorize them," he said. "I don't give a damn if you mumble them in your sleep when you're in bed with my wife. Where, I presume, since she's feeling so much on the mend, you'll be later tonight.

"*Two things*, Duvett. One, Kala has very little money of her own. Very little. And it's my latest intention to definitely *not* provide her with a single penny, once I sell Radin Heur the photograph. You might ask why this change of heart. Because as far as I'm concerned, she's now more married to you than to me. I was hoping she'd get sick and tired of you—the novelty of it. But apparently she hasn't.

"Why not urge her to drum up some work. Perhaps locate some of her spiritualists. There's bound to be some here in Halifax. A lecture here and there might help. For some years now, she's been something of a kept woman. Why not encourage her—practice being a husband that way.

"You may keep working for me. I'm paying you to have to see me every day, Duvett. You do good work. Competent. But do you know the saying 'No good deed goes unpunished'? You do good work, but you have to work in the same room with me. I hope that's punishment to you.

"Know this, Duvett: I think the most murderous thoughts about you every single minute."

"What's the second thing? You said there were two things."

"During my get-acquainted time at the pub tonight, I intend to mention my personal wounds, my forbearance, as concerns my wife. In fact"—he held up the satchel—"I have the photographs of you and Kala right here. I'll produce these when the timing is just right, a few drinks under our belts, you see. I intend to speak openly about what the situation is here, in the Haliburton House Inn. I will own up to it all, and say that as soon as I'm able to save enough money, I'll leave Halifax. So, Duvett, when you finally meet Sergeant Maitlin, you will know that *he* knows. I'll say I'm a man capable of a great deal of discipline, able to withstand a great deal of humiliation. But it will be understood that every man has his limits.

"The Halifax Police Department, thanks to Maitlin, has hired me to take portraits, earn money, leave Halifax. Allowing me a dignified way to avoid committing a crime of passion. He'll make the connections, I'm sure."

"You think you've got it all worked out, then."

"I'm a student of people, Duvett. I make it my business to study people. I studied Kala before marrying her. I've studied you. I sized up Sergeant Maitlin right away. Yes, I think things might work out nicely."

Vienna left the Haliburton House Inn. I knew anger had bested him, because against every ounce of fastidiousness and force of habit he relied on, Vienna left the front door open. Snow gusted right into the sitting room.

That night Kala came to my room about eleven o'clock. As she had requested, I'd got the fire built up. She set *The Unclad Spirit* and a bottle of Goldwasser on the bedside table. She opened the bottle. She blew out the candle. Within a minute she'd undressed and drawn me to the bed.

"It's been some long while, hasn't it?" she said.

"Let me get out of these clothes."

And then I got undressed and slid under the bedclothes beside her. We made love, and Kala did not return to her room. However, in the middle of the night, she woke up, sat with a lit candle at the desk, and wrote on page after page of stationery. I had woken, too, and watched her writing. She never once looked over at me. *The Unclad Spirit* was open on the desk; she traced a finger along a sentence, another sentence, another, wrote something, turned a page, read, wrote more. I fell back asleep. When I woke at 6:00 a.m., Kala was not in the room. She didn't appear at breakfast. After I'd eaten a muffin in the dining room and was about to go for a walk, maybe get tea at the Lord Nelson, I saw Freddy and Vienna talking in the sitting room. I stood by the coat pegs. Vienna was showing Freddy his portrait. As I started out the door, I heard Freddy say, "I officially approve of this for my WANTED poster," no trace of irony or humor in his voice at all. Just said it matter-of-factly, as if, now that the right photograph existed, a crime had to follow.

I looked over. They both stood up and shook hands. I opened the door just as Vienna said, "Anyone who sees this will know right away you're a dangerous man."

# VIEW OF KALA MURIE
# DRINKING CHINESE COFFEE

Almost daily throughout the rest of February and on into the beginning of March, Vienna made individual portraits of the Halifax police. Once word got around, even some retired officers made appointments, too. He kept a separate ledger. Names, dates, ranks. Some pictures were botched in the taking, or in the developing, and an officer was asked to return for a second sitting.

Sergeant Maitlin, however, was the first to have his photograph taken. He came to the Haliburton House Inn on February 16.

He set his overcoat on the wall peg in the hallway, then combed his hair in the small mirror by the front door. He wasn't wearing his day-to-day, but some sort of dress uniform. He was, I'd guess, in his mid-forties, with a wide mouth and tobacco-stained teeth, a neatly trimmed red beard, thick red hair fastidiously combed. He had the florid complexion my mother called a "pub crawler's," as if a bit flushed from drink. Like a nearly six-foot-tall pickle barrel, or by any other measure a large man, his bulk all but distracted you from his rather fine, delicate nose. As he sat for his portrait, he said, "When I was coming of age, I took boxing lessons and got into fisticuffs whenever I could; you just looked at me the wrong way—and lots of ways were wrong—I'd throw the first punch. No doubt I was trying to alter the shape of this nose, see."

His portrait was done quickly, no fanfare at all, little small talk, though he did further say, "I worked my way up from being a lowlife pissant ruffian on the street to a policeman in less than ten years, made sergeant in another five."

He seemed friendly and admirable enough, given just the brief time I saw him at the Haliburton House Inn that morning. He'd come in at 9:00 a.m. After his sitting, he took tea, then left by 9:45. Three other policemen had pictures taken that day.

And in his own methodical way, Vienna continued to cultivate his friendship with Maitlin. One week, for instance, they met at a pub three nights in a row. At dinner, Vienna enjoyed relating to Kala and me their conversations, in a way that implied he was being privileged secrets about the criminal element in Halifax. His stories were mildly entertaining, "all grist for the mill," he said, "all useful information."

Most days the portrait work was over by 11:00 a.m.; Vienna and I developed them in the darkroom after lunch, which we ate separately.

The second day of working with the police, Vienna bought a large brown Grundig-Majestic radio and put it in the darkroom. He loved to listen to CHNS, which was broadcast from the Carieton Hotel. He listened to radio auctions, bridge games, *Rakwana Tea Time*, featuring the Rakwana Revelers, for the family circle. He most enjoyed the evening comedy show *His Gang*, starring S. L. (Roxy) Rothafel and his sidekick, Frank Moulan. Any and all such programs, really, including *Live from Your Very Own House*, supposedly true-to-life dramas about things that the host, Robert Conlon, claimed happen to the "common man" all across Canada. On occasion, Vienna was also able to tune in WHAF, broadcast from New York City, or WGY from Schenectady, New York—U.S. programming went on later into the night than in the Canadian Maritimes. Generally, he kept the radio turned low. He wanted me to concentrate on the photographs. Bad weather interferences caused voices or music to drift in and out, static, static, static, which didn't bother me, really. I got used to it. Though sometimes it sounded like a mouse scratching inside a wall. Or what a person hears, perhaps, when he begins to lose his mind.

Yet there was another endeavor which kept Vienna in the darkroom much of the night as well. He was making duplicates of all his most self-incriminating photographs. There were, by my rough count, some one hundred plates. They'd been sent by train in two separate trunks. Vienna kept them under lock and key.

On nights when Kala wasn't in my bed, I often helped Vienna develop these plates.

And it was on one such night, I think March 3 or 4, as we worked in the darkroom, that he said, "No word yet from Mr. Heur."

"You must have doubts now."

"I have no doubt he'll respond. What manner of response, now, there's the catch."

"Afraid you might not wake up one morning?"

"Oh, I know all about instilling that fear in a man—or woman—don't I, Duvett?"

"It's an expertise of yours, I'd say."

"I'd say it was."

"Well, there's the weather—mail's slow all across Canada, I'm told, let alone from overseas."

"He'll respond. He always responds."

"If you say so."

"Duvett, do you know what I'm accomplishing here, with these negatives? I'll tell you. Should Mr. Heur not send his verificationist—" Vienna now seemed to be staring into the fixer dish a moment or two. "Revenge is in the Bible, you know. The Bible's rampant with it. Why do you suppose Kala kept the clippings, the letters? I know why and you know why. To turn me in someday. She absolutely cannot bear the thought she's spent all these years with me. How can she find some use in it?—see me rot in prison, is one way.

"But I've taken a cue from my wife. I've seen the intelligence in preparing ahead. And that's why I'm making duplicates here. My life's work on record. I intend to package them up and put them in safekeeping in the bank. IN CASE OF UNTIMELY DEATH instructions will be included—the photographs will go directly to Sergeant Maitlin. All the details: Radin Heur's part in every incident, and so forth."

"I'm to take it, then—yes—you are worried he might kill you."

"It's six of one, half dozen of the other. I'll be either rich or dead."

We then developed five photographs depicting the wrecking of a milk train, Vancouver, British Columbia, 1923.

And there, in the darkroom, I got quite lost in these photographs, I admit. It is a mesmerizing sight, a train wreck in progress. If you saw this photograph on someone's wall, I imagine you'd feel a shock of emotion first—get drawn in——and only later ask, *Who would have a photograph like this in their house?* In one photograph of the Vancouver wreck, the caboose was just tilting off a bridge, while the rest of the cars—each one aslant—reached from the bridge to the bottom of a gulley.

It didn't escape Vienna's notice how I took just the extra moment to stare at it. "That caboose fell on top of the other cars. The engineer crawled right out. He was possibly fifty meters in the air. He just sat there the longest time. I found out his name and sent him a copy of the very photograph you're now looking at, Duvett. It was sent anonymously, of course."

At dinner on March 5 Kala announced, "I've found my own employment." Mrs. Sorrel had just cleared the dishes.

Vienna immediately left the table.

"He never could stand it, really, when I earned even a pittance. It subtracted something from him. I once made $200 for three lectures, and he was inconsolable. He insisted that he take it and divvy me out small amounts, like a child's allowance. I felt like breaking into the piggy bank. He used to make me keep a ledger of all my expenses—everything. Toilet articles, socks, a cup of hot cocoa in a hotel restaurant."

"What work did you find?" I said.

"You see, Peter, Mrs. Sorrel introduced me to a Mrs. Durrematt, an avowed spiritualist. One day last week, when I said I'd been out for a walk, I'd truly *been* out for a walk, but also had stopped by Mrs. Durrematt's for tea. In her comfortable—very comfortable—living room, she asked, 'Are you by chance the same Kala Murie whom my cousin Edna saw lecture on spirit photographs less than two years ago in Montreal?' 'Why, yes, yes.' And the long and short of it is, Mrs. Durrematt has, here in Halifax, what she calls her 'secret ladies' club.' She presides. And then came more tea and cookies. And then she said, 'Would you lecture to my group?' I asked about a fee. 'One hundred dollars.' More than generous, more than generous, I said. I then took a chance and said, 'Can it be opened to the public?' And a smile crossed her face. She said, 'I've always wanted this very opportunity. If even one person—just one—other than those in my club, should attend, it would make my husband realize that our beliefs and interests are perhaps shared more widely. Of course, he thinks we're all daft anyway, but I don't care one single bit.' So it was done, all agreed upon, with a big embrace and kiss upon the cheek, Peter. And the announcement's to appear in the *Herald*."

Indeed, on page 11 in the March 12 edition was a brief article whose heading ran, EXPERT TO LECTURE ON SPIRIT PHOTOGRAPHS. The article read as follows:

Mrs. Kala Linn (professional name, Kala Murie), wife of the highly regarded portraitist, Vienna Linn, formerly of Montreal, London, Copenhagen, will lecture on the phenomenon of spirit photography at Hages Auxiliary Hall, 8 p.m., April 9. Mrs. Linn is scholar-advocate of the writings of the late 19th-century spiritualist, Georgiana Houghton.

"It promises to be a memorable evening," the sponsor, Mrs. Hans Durrematt, said. Admission will be charged.

Gordy Larkin, *Herald* reporter

When I read the article, I thought, Gordy still hasn't made it up to Features.

The evening the article appeared, Kala and I got back from Springs All-Purpose store, where I'd bought her two pairs of socks, at about 5:00 p.m. Stepping out of the wrenching cold, we'd set our boots and gloves by the fireplace in the sitting room, sat down next to each other on the sofa, still wearing our coats, scarves, hats. "Tonight," she said, "I'll be wearing a pair of socks you just bought me. But you may slip them off. I suddenly feel bold about it. Bold is as bold does, you see, and you've changed me, Peter. Because lately, I've actually thought it possible to sleep with my socks off. Which I haven't since I was—oh, I'd say age ten." She said all this with great good cheer, laughing at herself.

"You don't want to change too fast now."

She laughed again.

"Someone should photograph the occasion," I said. It just flew out. I'd told her, of course, about Vienna's photographs of us in bed, in the Churchill Hotel.

But Kala played along. "Yes. Freddy, I suppose. He's the sort to tiptoe in and take that picture, isn't he?"

"The way I've seen him gawk at you, Kala, my guess is you've already been in one or two of his criminal day-dreams."

"Jealous, are we?"

What I thought then, I kept to myself. I thought, Buying those socks, my paying for them, was my first act as a husband. Besides what happened in bed so far, I meant. It was a small thing, really, asking the clerk, "How much for the socks?" and then paying. Kala could just as easily have paid. She had *that* much money. She had her money out and ready, in fact. When I paid, she simply said, "Why, thank you, Peter," then picked out two pairs for me, costing almost exactly the same amount.

We sat near the fire a moment. Kala then stood up and said, "Peter, Vienna received a letter from Radin Heur."

"When?"

"Several days ago. I was going to mention it, but didn't. I thought it best to wait. No good reason, really. Only that I didn't want it to ruin how nicely our nights were going."

"What did the letter say?"

"I'll bring it up at dinner."

Before I could protest, Kala went upstairs to her room.

Then, at dinner that night, March 12, she hounded Vienna into reading the verificationist David Harp's letter to me.

In bed at 4:00 a.m., Kala asleep beside me, the world for a few moments seemed in perfect order. But then I felt a jolt of unease.

Eventually I got out of bed. As I poured water, I nicked the glass with the pitcher; Kala sat bolt upright. "Oh, Peter, I'm happy it's you," she said.

Kala then told me her dream of sitting among all the wreckage of the plane. When she asked did I think it possible that Vienna had purposely attempted to murder her, I dissembled. "You're right, he is capable of such a thing. But I don't believe that's what happened."

"I'm afraid you're wrong," Kala said.

"Maybe so."

"No, it has to be true. The day before the airplane wreck, Ott had told me earlier in the day that I was recovering nicely. He said he was still cautious, of course. Said I needed to let him know the slightest change in my condition as I noticed it. All the same, he seemed confident—his exact words were 'In a month you'll be fit as a fiddle.' I remember it, because I'd suddenly got some humor back and said, 'Secondhand fiddle, you mean.' It was a small thing, but I remember it.

"But late that night Dr. Ott came back. I was awake, and he said he'd had second thoughts. Better safe than sorry— and that Vienna *insisted* that I go to Winnipeg to see a specialist. Ott said that Vienna's insistence brought him to his senses. He now agreed that I should go—and that Driscoll Petchey was to leave first thing in the morning."

"And you think he arranged for you to be on the airplane simply because he knew about us?"

"*Simply?* How can you use that word? It might have been a *simple* fact, Peter. But it wreaked havoc in Vienna's mind, didn't it?"

"Why didn't he just murder me, then?"

"The opportunity with the plane must've come up sooner. He's an opportunist, my husband, if nothing else."

And here again I might have had the foretaste of regret, cried out, "Before I let you say another word—" but I didn't. I didn't tell her what I knew.

"Peter, try to understand, probably I've known this all along. But it hadn't come clearly until the dream. In *fact*, though, I've been dishonest with you, my dearest, dearest Peter. And I deeply regret it."

"Dishonest in what way?"

"—in *fact*, I had thought it true. Before the dream, I thought Vienna had tried to kill me. He'd given me murderous looks—but it wasn't that. It was something else. He must have known—he's not a stupid man—how deeply I'd begun to love you. He simply *knew* how desperately sad I'd been. How could he not see I felt *trapped*? He looked at me when we exchanged wedding vows and must have seen it even then. *He had to have seen it.* After all, he had those thick lenses of his on."

"Why did you wait to tell me?"

"I don't know, exactly. Probably I had to wait until I felt you loved me. That I could count on you."

"Of course you—"

"Because in my lecture, I'm going to address *Esquimaux Souls Risen from Aeroplane Wreck*, and how Vienna tried to murder me. I'm going to accuse him right in public. Right in Hages Auxiliary Hall. Of course, I have no concrete evidence, do I? If only I had someone who actually *knew* he'd tried to kill me. I've racked my brains—it could only have been Samuel Brant, couldn't it, whom Vienna got to tamper with the airplane. He was the mechanic on hire. Petchey said Sam Brant knew that plane inside out. No, it couldn't have been an accident, Peter. It *wasn't* an accident."

I sat on the edge of the bed. "You don't think me mad, do you, Peter?" Kala said.

"Of course I don't."

"I hardly want you to leave me out of your sight."

"I feel likewise."

"I'm going to send out an invitation list to my lecture. Every policeman Vienna photographs will be on it. Including Sergeant Maitlin. Probably no policeman will attend— but the invitation can't give away my big surprise, can it? It can only mention spirit photographs."

"Why not accuse Vienna to his face?"

"I can scarcely look at his face."

"You're right, it might put him over the edge, some way or another."

"No, I'll do it in public. No matter who attends, I'll have said it. I'm going to contact the same newspaper reporter who wrote the announcement. Her name is Gordy Larkin."

"I knew her at the *Herald*."

"Miss Larkin came in for dinner one night—you'd already gone back to the annex. While she was eating, Freddy asked her to go out for a cup of Chinese coffee with him. It seems that Freddy frequents a restaurant owned by Chinese, and likes their coffee."

"What is Chinese coffee, anyway?"

"I don't know, exactly. But Mrs. Sorrel and I had quite a chat about it. What's worrisome to Mrs. Sorrel is that Freddy enjoys the company of Chinese. She obviously thinks there's a secret ingredient in their coffee that makes it *Chinese coffee* somehow. She thinks the coffee might harm Freddy. She's warned him against it."

"What did Gordy Larkin say when Freddy asked her to go have Chinese coffee?"

"She stood up, paid in full, but left right away. Freddy pouted off into the kitchen, as you'd expect. Mrs. Sorrel said, 'That young woman has common sense. She's the sort I dream about as a daughter-in-law. Of course, in that same dream my son isn't Freddy.' Without knowing it, that's how Mrs. Sorrel recommended Miss Larkin's character."

"She's got ambitions, Kala. That's part of her character."

"I don't care about that. I only want her to be at my lecture. I'm going to try to reach her tomorrow."

"There's no way I can talk you out of including the plane wreck in your lecture?"

"None whatsoever."

"Then I'll be there, front and center."

"I'd like you to get back in bed with me now, all right?"

"Yes."

We embraced, then kissed a good long time, and that seemed to be enough.

When Kala finally fell asleep, I got up and ran a bath. As I soaked in the bathtub, there was a knock on the door—my life over the past five months contained too many knocks on my door at night.

Unless it was Kala, it never was good news.

"Who is it—at this hour?" Kala said.

I heard Freddy's voice: "Just back from my Chinese friends. I brought you something."

"It's a bit late for visiting, don't you think, Freddy?"

"I brought you something."

"Did you bring it for Peter as well? This is his room, you know."

"Do what you want with it," Freddy said.

"Please leave it outside the door, thank you."

"Sure thing," Freddy said. "Sure thing, because you might not be wearing much, eh?"

"You should go now, Freddy."

"I left something out here, then."

Stepping from the bath, I opened the bathroom door a crack. I watched as Kala cautiously opened the door. She bent down, then carried in a tray with a mug on it. Kala set the tray on the bed, sat beside it, held the mug under her nose, shivered a moment, then took a sip. She took three more sips, seemed to enjoy whatever Freddy had brought.

"That was Freddy, wasn't it?" I said.

"You know it was, Peter."

"What's that he brought you?"

"Chinese coffee, I'm fairly certain."

I wrapped the towel around me but didn't open the door. "And you drank it, just like that?"

"That's right. And you spied on me, didn't you?"

"He might have poisoned it."

"Freddy and I exchange smiles every day, Peter. Why would he poison my gift of Chinese coffee? You can't bear the thought of him offering me a gift and me accepting it, that's all. You should taste it, Chinese coffee. I can tell you now, it's another way to get your heart to beat fast."

When I stepped from the bathroom, Kala patted the pillow next to her and said, "Come sit by me." She set the tray and cup on the bedside table. I sat next to her. She leaned over and kissed me.

"Kiss me back," she said, and I did. "That bath soap doesn't suit you. I should have a talk with Mrs. Sorrel about replacing it."

"Oh, of course," I said. " 'Look, here, Mrs. Sorrel, I prefer a different soap in Mr. Duvett's bath, please.' That'd go over well."

"It doesn't matter about the soap, because two people can't please each other perfectly, can they? Oh, perhaps at certain moments. Certain intimacies. But otherwise—"

When I was in the bathroom she'd lit the candle, but now she blew it out again. Light from the fireplace, diffused light from the gas lamp across Morris Street. Letting the towel drop away, I got under the bedclothes. Kala said, "Did you ever wonder, when you first learned that Radin Heur had actually threatened my husband's life—in Montreal—how that actually came about?"

I suddenly felt cold, got up, went back into the bathroom, put on a nightshirt and robe. I opened up the bureau's top drawer, took out a new pair of socks, and put them on. I added another log to the fire, used the bellows, and when the fire built up fully enough, I sat in the chair. "Naturally, I wondered about it," I said. "My guess is that Radin Heur hired rough trade, and maybe one of them paid you a visit. Or else Radin Heur sent Vienna a letter that clearly spelled things out. But then again, Vienna seems to thrive on threats, doesn't he? He gets them and he dishes them out."

"I can remember *exactly*," Kala said. "We were in that hotel in Montreal, you see. I already knew the train wreck had been botched. Vienna was pacing the room. It was likely to drive me insane, his pacing. Crazed—he was *crazed*. Then came a knock at the door.

"Vienna pacing—he refused to answer the door. He only shifted his pacing farther away from the door. He said, 'At this hour, who could that be?' It was about ten o'clock at night. So I answered the door myself. And there stood a nicely dressed man. Exquisitely dressed, and he bowed, courtly. Said, 'Terribly, terribly sorry to disturb you.' British accent.

"Polite, but he got right to the point, standing there, not invited in. He said he was employed by 'Mr. Radin Heur of London,' and that he'd traveled a very very long way, was exhausted, but had wanted to act without further delay. He said he'd come to collect a reasonable portion of the advance on payment. 'You know what for,' he said. 'For the artistic photographs of a certain train. Which, in Mr. Heur's understanding, will not be forthcoming.'

" 'And just what amount does Mr. Heur consider reasonable?' Vienna says. I knew he was holding the revolver behind his back, and it made me terribly nervous. Almost sick from nerves.

"And this courteous man—nameless—says, 'In fact, 90 percent. With—generous on the part of Mr. Heur, if you don't mind me saying—the other 10 percent he's subtracting for expenses incurred.'

" 'Well, we simply don't have that much on hand,' Vienna says. We had quite a bit, but not 90 percent. We knew we'd need every dollar to travel and live on.

" 'And when, sir, might you have it, then?' Mr. Nameless says.

"And when Vienna doesn't answer, Mr. Nameless says, 'You must have it a week from today. A week from this minute'—he takes out his pocket watch and says, 'Ten-twenty,' or close to it. 'Is that clear, Mr. Linn?'

"My husband says, 'Please inform Mr. Heur—' but Mr. Nameless interrupts: 'Mr. Heur's been informed of all the information he needs be informed of. Which is why I'm standing here, mate.'

" 'In your educated opinion,' my husband says, 'is there no room for compromise?'

"To which Mr. Nameless says, 'My employer doesn't traffic in that.' Mr. Nameless snaps open his satchel, plucks out a single piece of paper—a newspaper clipping, actually. He sets it on the bed. 'I'm in room 17,' and he backs up, never once taking his eyes off Vienna. Backs right up out of our room and shuts the door.

"Of course, I immediately looked at the clipping. Its heading was TWO FOREIGNERS FOUND DEAD. The article said the police suspected a murder-suicide. And Vienna and I knew right away that it was nothing of the sort. And that both men were hired by Vienna, had botched a train wreck in India, or something like that, and were done in by one of Mr. Heur's thugs in India."

Kala came over and sat on the arm of the chair. "That clipping—very, very rapidly—inspired us to leave that hotel within the hour. We went to a rooming house, the dingiest,

most repulsive place I'd ever stayed in. From there, arrangements to get out of Montreal were made."

"How and why Churchill, though?"

"More of my husband's contacts. He has no friends. He
has contacts. I recall him saying '—under cover of the
church,' but it wasn't really so mysterious, now, was it? It
wasn't some espionage drama, was it? It was only a job someone knew about. And Vienna snapped it right up. Into the
godforsaken north, as poor Mr. Petchey liked to say."

Kala rose from the bed and sat on the arm of the cush-
ioned chair. We sat close but didn't touch. The warmth of
the fire at our backs, crazy flickering shadows on the
wall. "Even on my wedding night," Kala said, "when you and
I— I expected one of Radin Heur's well-dressed thugs to
burst in."

K ala stayed the remainder of the night with me. But she
was out of the room by 6:00 a.m., and I went next door
for breakfast an hour later. When I stepped into the main
building, there stood Sergeant Maitlin. He was hanging up
his coat, obviously having just arrived.

"Ah, Duvett," he said. "The assistant."

"Good morning, Sergeant."

"I decided to get a second portrait made," he said.
"Breakfast first, though."

I hung up my own coat, then followed Maitlin into the
dining room. Freddy was waiting tables. Vienna Linn sat at
the table in the corner farthest from the streetside window. I
sat at the windowside table. Maitlin sat at Vienna's table.

"Freddy, my boy," Maitlin called out, as Freddy, who was

unshaven, his clothes disheveled, reached into his pocket for a pack of cigarettes. "This cold just about froze my drain-pipes——" He tapped his chest with his fist. "Pour some spirits into my orange juice this morning, will you? And it's hush-hush about it when you next drop by the station. Hurry up now, my drainpipes are near frozen."

Freddy went into the kitchen, came right back out carry-ing a glass of orange juice. He set it on the table in front of Maitlin.

"Hey, Freddy, you sleep in those clothes?" Maitlin said.

"Not last night," Freddy said. "The night before."

Maitlin downed the orange juice in one swallow.

"I've seen you wield a mop," he said to Freddy. "You ever need a job, Fred, come down to the station, we'll hand you a mop. Bring some of your mother's scones. And don't dunk them in the harbor first, eh?"

"I'll come down to the station, all right," Freddy said, in a tone as if he was talking through his teeth. "But I won't come in on my own steam."

"Oh, I get it," Maitlin said, winking at Vienna. "We'll have to cast a dragnet."

"Far and wide, yes sir," Freddy said.

"If you have a change of heart, Freddy, the mop is wait-ing," Maitlin said. It made Freddy wince. "Mopping will al-low law enforcement to keep an eye on you. Now, how about some toast and eggs."

"The same for me," Vienna said.

Freddy looked at me. "I'll have a muffin and coffee is all," I said. Freddy went back to the kitchen.

But it was Mrs. Sorrel who delivered my breakfast, then Maitlin's and Vienna's.

"Where's our original waiter?" Maitlin said.

"My son's gone for Chinese coffee at the Chinese restaurant," Mrs. Sorrel said. "He knows the Chinese owner. The family lives over the restaurant. Freddy stops in at all hours. He even knows a few words in Chinese."

"What words are those?" Maitlin said.

"He knows the word for coffee, for instance," she said.

Maitlin practically fell off his chair from laughing. Catching his breath, he said, "I've had it investigated once or twice, that restaurant. It's the only place in Halifax that serves Chinese coffee." He laughed hard again.

"The joke's on me, surely," Mrs. Sorrel said. "All I really know is, ever since it opened, Freddy's gone there. Real Chinese run it, you know."

"As I said, I've been there."

"Did you drink the coffee?" Mrs. Sorrel said.

"Not on your life," Maitlin said.

"Of course not, an officer on duty."

"Chinese-prepared coffee running through Freddy's veins," Maitlin said. "Now, that no doubt explains something about your boy, don't you think?"

"What exactly do you think it explains?" Mrs. Sorrel said. "In your judgment."

"I don't know. Something. If you like, I'll look under 'Chinese coffee' in our files, see if I can get a hint. Our files are in good order."

"That won't be necessary," Mrs. Sorrel said. "While it might explain something, it can't, you'll agree, explain everything. A son like Freddy, a mother needs everything explained, because what's left out is most frightening."

"I just don't know what to say, then," Maitlin said.

Finally, when Maitlin and Vienna, talking all the while, had finished eating, they walked over to my table. Vienna handed me three negative plates. "Three police portraits here," he said. "Sergeant Maitlin is interested in the development process. He's never seen it done. I allowed that he might go in with you this morning, Duvett. To see how you manage things."

I didn't protest, but didn't show any enthusiasm, either. "Sounds as if you already said okay to it," I said.

"Explain it step by step, please," Vienna said.

Sergeant Maitlin accompanied me through the kitchen, into the darkroom pantry. I lit three candles, began working without comment, other than to name things: "Print tongs, developer dish, fixer dish," and so on.

"Doesn't seem as if you enjoy your work much," he said.

"I enjoy parts of it."

"That's good to know. That's good to know."

"I'll enjoy it when it's over for the day, for instance."

"Then what'll you do the rest of the day? Oh look, there's Officer Battan—David Battan. Mr. Linn really caught a good likeness, didn't he? But you wouldn't know from this photograph that Battan's got a boisterous sense of humor, now, would you? He looks so dead serious here." I hung Officer Battan's portrait up to dry, then entered *David Battan* in the ledger. "Of course, a photograph can't reveal everything. No one should expect it to, should they?"

Maitlin was close, directly to my right. I slid a new negative into the developer dish. "How's it working out?" he said.

"We'll see, won't we?"

"I meant—with Mrs. Linn."

Suddenly I realized the radio was emitting thin static—Vienna quite often was absentminded this way; I reached up and switched it off.

"Duvett, I asked how it's working out with Mrs. Linn. I mean, how do you *work* it, exactly? Remember, I've heard every possible kind of marriage story at the station. I had a husband and wife shoot at each other at a church social. 'Oh, oh, oh, I don't know *what* we could've been thinking, Officer!' You can't surprise me. Nothing new under the sun, and all that. Adultery, and so on and so forth."

"In what capacity are you inquiring, officer of the law or friend of Vienna's?"

"Let me think now—"

"Because both capacities have something in common."

"Which is?"

"Which is, both are none of your goddamn business."

"I see your point. Wait—go ahead, finish up this photograph." When I hung the second photograph up to dry, Maitlin inspected it, said, "Morning, Officer R. K. Hickleson," saluting. I wrote *R. K. Hickleson* in the ledger. "I see your point, Duvett, man to man. But you don't see *my* point, because I haven't got to it yet."

"Get to it, then, and then get out, and tell Mr. Linn anything about my hospitality you want."

"Vienna Linn showed me those photographs of you and Mrs. Linn. From that hotel room up in Churchill, Manitoba. No hired detective could've done better, I must say. I told Linn as much, too. Anyway, Duvett, the photographs—to my taste—were very stimulating. Though, if it were up to me, if I owned them, I'd take my trusty scissors and cut you right out and leave the rest. Though the hand over her breast is a nice spot of action, eh?"

As I started in with the third negative, I said, "You want copies of those photographs, I take it."

"That's what I'm saying."

"I don't have copies."

"The negatives must be somewhere."

"Why not ask your newfound friend, Vienna Linn. You're good buddies now, aren't you?"

"Oh yes, indeed we are. We've had heart-to-hearts."

"A friend in high places he has in you, right?"

Maitlin was silent a moment. I let the negative float in the stop bath. I leaned against the wall. "She's a handsome woman, Mrs. Linn," Maitlin said. "Obviously you agree, Duvett, risking life and limb as you are. Linn's told me he's capable of violence toward you, for violating his marriage and such. I've no reason to doubt him. I know—with professional scrutiny—when not to doubt such a thing."

"I don't doubt him, either."

I completed developing the third photograph; it came out all right. Maitlin looked at it. "That's Officer Chet Cole," he said. I wrote *Chet Cole* in the ledger. "Cole's a very decent fellow, unless he catches you trying to clobber a store clerk for ten dollars in the cash register."

I hung up the photograph.

"Here and now, Duvett, I'm going to offer you fifty dollars Canadian. Hard-earned, I might say. That is, fifty dollars each. Which adds up to $150 for the three photographs of you and Mrs. Linn intimate in that hotel room bed, no questions asked, no secrets told. No, wait; I'll add another hundred dollars. There goes *all* my fun. That hundred more than accounts for what those in the criminal element like to call 'hush money.' "

I turned to face him in the candlelit dark. "My answer is, go to hell."

Maitlin opened the door slightly. "Shut your eyes, boys, here comes the light!" he said to the portraits on the twine. He opened the door the rest of the way. "You don't want to sell me the photographs, fine, Duvett. I suppose I can always approach Mrs. Linn to help me out. I hesitate to discuss this sort of thing with a woman, though—even the one in the photographs, eh? Does she even know about them? As for my asking Vienna directly, why ruin a new friendship talking about a business transaction?" He went into the kitchen, leaving the pantry door open.

# THE VERIFICATIONIST

## DAVID HARP

The verificationist, David Harp, arrived on the liner *Winifredian*, at about 4:00 p.m. on March 18. Kala had spoken with Mrs. Sorrel, who prepared room 19 for Harp, at the opposite end of the hallway from Vienna's room. Harp cleared customs without a hitch. Vienna then escorted him to the Haliburton House Inn. Mrs. Sorrel, Freddy, Kala, and I met him as he stepped through the door at about 7:00 p.m.. He'd traveled with two small suitcases and a steamer trunk, which I later saw was full of chemicals and equipment.

Harp was about thirty. His voice was memorable. When he extended his hand, said, "David Harp," it was like hearing a baritone horn, almost comical. But as introductions were completed and Harp removed his gray overcoat, conversation quickly fell into casual banter and his voice, oddly enough, became comforting. Still, it was at the lowest octave I'd ever heard in a voice. He struck me as quite talkative.

"Lovely to be here," he said to Mrs. Sorrel. There was at first an altogether nice manner about him.

Kala didn't join us for dinner. After Harp had unpacked, had a bath, changed clothes, he joined Vienna and me in the sitting room. More small talk. Then we sat down for dinner.

"My wife, Kala, isn't feeling well, I'm afraid," Vienna said. "She sends her apologies."

"Not at all," Harp said, a polite-seeming man who looked directly at you when talking.

He was about six feet tall, with thick sandy brown hair. In the careless cut of his clothes, stubble of beard on his cheeks and chin, he had a slightly unkempt air about him. He had a neatly trimmed mustache, though. And impeccable table manners. He had highly educated speech, the baritone enunciation of each word, the way he constructed a thought, as if there was exactly the same interval between words and sentences—more as if he were reading aloud, rather than merely talking. He had ruddy skin, dry—perhaps from the sea air— flaking at his thick sideburns. (Later, he mentioned a "bad re- action" to shipboard soap. It required ointment provided by Mrs. Sorrel.) He had a broad, open smile, which squinted up his eyes. He said, "Yes, yes," before he laughed at someone's comment. What made him laugh at table was Freddy Sorrel, our waiter for the evening. We'd each ordered a steak, pota- toes, mushroom sauce on the side, and we shared a bottle of wine. When Freddy set down our plates, he gave Harp one of his long-practiced threatening stares. No reason in partic- ular. Well, that didn't take long, I thought.

"Why, Freddy," Harp said, in that congenial voice, "that's

the very look my wife's lapdog gives me when I've forgotten to air him."

"Is that right?" Freddy said.

"Well, not exactly," Harp said. "But close enough. Mean little bugger, that dog. I don't miss him a lick."

"I bet you miss licking your wife, though," Freddy said. He picked up the wine bottle and filled Harp's glass, though Harp hadn't emptied it yet.

Harp half stood up, thought twice about it, sat down. He cut a piece of steak and ate it. Looking at Vienna, Harp said, "A man must pick his battles wisely, don't you think, Mr. Linn?"

"I do indeed," Vienna said.

Freddy stalked off to the kitchen.

"Tell us, Mr. Harp," Vienna said, "how long have you been with the British Museum?"

"Nearly seven years," Harp said. "Mr. Heur helped get me the position."

"And Mr. Heur, how long in his employ?"

"We can talk business after dinner, if you'd like," Harp said, glancing at me. "Over cognac, a cigar, perhaps?"

"Let's begin now, if you don't mind," Vienna said. "Duvett, here, is privy to—"

"He's seen the photograph in question, then?" Harp said.

"He saw the actual *taking* of it," Vienna said.

"The unfortunate—"

"—plane wreck, yes," I said.

"I'd like to begin my work as soon as possible," Harp said. "Though not tonight. I'm tired, you see. My concentration would be lacking. Besides, I've got to set up a small laboratory, as it were. Where's your darkroom?"

"Through those doors," Vienna said, pointing toward the kitchen.

"Adequate for my needs, I'm sure," Harp said.

"I hope so."

"Under lock and key?"

"No, in fact."

"I see," Harp said. "I won't mention that to Mr. Heur."

"Much appreciated," Vienna said.

"Prickly about details, Mr. Heur," Harp said.

"A decisive man," Vienna said.

"Nothing if not that," Harp said.

"He requires of his employees—"

"—absolute and complete fealty," Harp said.

"Does not suffer fools," Vienna said.

"Now and then I've had the unsettling feeling," Harp said, "that Mr. Heur would like to dedicate a year of his precious time to carrying out, in the most severe fashion imaginable, *revenges*. Grudges long held, from wounds and slights suffered as long ago as his childhood, incidents in which he lost out."

"That squares with my sense of him," Vienna said.

"It seems we're already talking business," Harp said.

"The business of what happens when things concerning Mr. Heur go badly."

"Precisely," Harp said.

As I listened, I felt that I was hearing, to some extent, a foreign language, one that only *sounded* like English, but whose deeper, terrifying meanings could only be alluded to, not uttered directly. I wanted to throttle them both. Scream, "Just say it! If the photograph's a fake, Radin Heur will murder us!"

We went on with our meal, very civilized, Vienna and Harp chatting about London, photography, this and that. When we finished eating, Vienna said, "Mr. Harp, I hope your first night here is restful. Breakfast at seven?"

"Seven it is," Harp said. They shook hands and Vienna went upstairs.

"Mr. Duvett," Harp said, "might you spare me a few moments?"

"All right." We went into the sitting room. Harp lit a cigar, leaned back on the sofa. I sat in the rocking chair.

"Peter—all right if I call you that?"

"Fine."

"Peter, were you actually present when the photograph was developed?"

"I was not."

"But you've seen it."

"Once."

Vienna came back downstairs, saw us, sat down on the sofa next to Harp. "My wife's asleep," he said. "It's lonely when a man's wife falls asleep and he's awake. Am I interrupting?"

"Your assistant and I were just discussing the photograph," Harp said.

"What's been said so far?"

"I was *about* to say, we'll know soon enough if it's authentic," Harp said.

"I could take that as an insult," Vienna said.

"You could take the color of my shirt as an insult, for all I care, Mr. Linn. Let me speak frankly. No more polite conversation at table. I've traveled a long way. And every minute of that travel, Mr. Linn, I knew your photograph was a fake. From your first mention of it—in your idiotic, self-congratulatory letter, which struck me as all but trembling with fear. But of course, it *was* offering Mr. Heur something he's deadly serious about.

"It is Mr. Heur—listen to me well, gentlemen. It is *Mr. Heur*, not I, who believes in the possibility of 'souls' and other apparitions evidenced in photographic art. I personally don't believe in any sort of life after death. If anything, I'm an atheist. In the museum, I work in the technical realm. I work with chemicals and light. I tell my curators, 'Go ahead, buy this,' or, 'This is a preposterous fraud.' They're intent on building the world's finest collection. That's all fine and good. But as for me, I go to work and come home and I don't mention the word *photograph* in my house.

"I've always supported my family with my technical skills. Then my wife fell ill. The nature of her illness is a private matter. I have my meager museum salary, true. But it takes a small fortune to keep my wife in doctors.

"Now, Mr. Heur hires men to cause catastrophes, does he not? His house has walls full of the results. Your photographs are on those walls, Mr. Linn. We're all men here. We can speak directly, can we not? Do you not think I know who you are, Mr. Linn, and what you do for a living?"

"Your tale of woe means nothing—just do your job," Vienna said. "The rest is of no concern to me."

"Oh, that's where you're quite wrong, Mr. Linn. That's where you're entirely wrong. My 'job,' as you put it, is not to work for Mr. Heur. Not even to please him. My *job*, gentlemen, is to keep my wife alive.

"I'm tired." He rubbed his eyes and face. "But I'll say this: Mr. Radin Heur has to be one of the sickest, most degenerate human beings on the earth. And through your *association* with him, the kind of service you supply, you, Mr. Linn, are sick and degenerate. Even sitting here speaking with you makes me feel sick and degenerate.

"What's more, what I'm about to offer will make me feel worse yet.

"Because, gentlemen, no matter what I find tomorrow— and I'm certain I'll find your photograph to be a sham—I'm willing to report to Mr. Heur that it's authentic.

"And before I send my report off to Mr. Heur, you and I, Mr. Linn, will come to an agreement."

"The nature of this agreement?" Vienna said.

"Half," Harp said.

"Half of what sum?" Vienna said. "Knowing Mr. Heur as well as you do."

"Should the photograph—what? *Esquimaux Souls Risen from Aeroplane Wreck*"—Harp snickered at the title—"be verified as authentic, it would elevate Mr. Heur's status even more amongst his inner circle of believers. His coterie. His séance practitioners.

"And you simply have no idea from what walks of life these people come. You simply have no idea how prominent many of them are. What public figures.

"If I were you, I'd ask for £20,000."

"No one has that kind of money to spare," I said.

"Mr. Heur could spare it weekly and it wouldn't even be gossip at the bank—a bank, by the way, in which Mr. Heur has part ownership," Harp said.

"What's £20,000 in Canadian currency, I wonder," Vienna said, betraying not a little excitement.

"I'm not a banker, Mr. Linn," Harp said. "I verify photographs."

David Harp stood up and yawned, looked at me and said, "Well, assistant Duvett, you've got yourself quite an earful of pertinent information, haven't you? Are you good for keeping your mouth shut?"

But he didn't wait for my reply. "Well," he said, "I've had this long journey, you see." He reached into his trouser pocket, took out his room key, and went up the stairs.

Vienna Linn and I sat in stunned silence for at least five minutes. Then he went to the coat pegs, donned his coat, hat, scarf, and galoshes, and left the inn. On his way, no doubt, to meet his police cronies.

I knocked on Kala's door and opened it. She was sitting up in bed. She looked quite pale. "It's just a small recurrence of some sort," she said. "Nothing, really. A small recurrence."

I sat in the chair in the corner. "I missed you at dinner," I said.

"Tell me your impressions of our Mr. Harp," she said.

After I'd told Kala all that had transpired downstairs, she insisted on spending the night in my annex room. In the middle of the night, we were both awake. It was snowing out. Kala was paging through *The Unclad Spirit*, taking notes in preparation for her lecture. She'd been coughing slightly. "Peter," she said, "listen to this. It's where Miss Houghton feels humiliated while giving a lecture. Hounded out of the lecture hall, actually."

"Is that where the man screamed, 'This business be all deception!'?"

"Yes, and later that same night, the missing *X*'s."

"The story with the dunce cap?"

"Yes, but first comes Miss Houghton's hurt feelings, remember?" Kala brought the candle closer on the night table. She slanted the book to get the best light, then read:

This evening, the world was thrown into grim relief. I should say! My lecture attempted to take to task a derogatory article in *The Journal of British Photography* railing against spirit photography, but my lecture was met by howls of derision and mockery, even violent accusations of Devil-mongering. No previous incidents have been worse. I noticed, off to my right nearly in the shadows, several believers, but they did not dare come forth, frightened as they must have been by the general atmosphere, and yet I fully hoped and expected to see them at my hotel room later in the evening, and was not in that disappointed. There were three ladies, Mrs. Rose, Mrs. Galvin, Mrs. Mellen. We sat downstairs in a side room well away from the lobby. Tea was served. I addressed each and every question, responded to each and every doubt; all in all we made up a sisterhood of cordiality. "But tell us, then," Mrs. Galvin said, "of the experience that most astounded you. Because, surely, even you can be astounded, couldn't you, by what, in *Faith and Spirit*—

we each get that magazine privately delivered—you called 'the sheer strangeness of some of the Lord's messages'?"

"Why, yes, I am constantly astounded," I replied. Then I told about the missing X's.

The story of the missing X's concerned a boy, aged ten, named Butler Pond. He lived near Oxford. The "pinkie" finger on his right hand had a thick scar running its length; what's more, the finger jutted out at roughly a 45-degree angle, all caused when a teacher named Jack Blithy struck Pond with a wooden ruler, when Pond (then age nine) had smarted off to him. Blithy said he'd only meant to slap Pond's hand with the ruler, but it sliced the finger and Pond cried out in pain. Instead of immediately allowing Pond to go see a doctor, or the school nurse, Blithy made him sit on a stool in the corner of the room, wearing a dunce cap. In half an hour or so, he made Pond, still wearing the dunce cap, write the alphabet fifty times on the blackboard, using cursive lettering. Pond was left-handed, so he still could write. But he was so distraught, in so much pain, he forgot the letter X. It was as if it had been plucked from his memory. Seeing that he'd left out the letter X, a few children snickered, which drew Blithy's attention to the blackboard. Blithy saw the absence of the letter X as mocking his authority. He instructed Pond to stay after class and write the letter X one hundred times on the blackboard, which Pond did.

It turned out that Pond's father, Alvin Pond, was a notorious drunk and grudge holder, a widower, a chimney sweep by trade, but when Butler came home and showed Alvin his damaged finger, Alvin simply hurried his son to the doctor. Yet, almost a year later, bingeing, stumbling pub to pub, Alvin Pond finally went at midday to the school. He called Blithy outside and shot him three times in the chest. The police tracked Alvin Pond down, found him hiding in a sawmill. When he refused to surrender, the police went in after him, a skirmish took place, a revolver was fired, and Pond fell into the stream that powered the sawmill.

The police photographer, Jason Haywood, took the official photograph of Blithy lying on the ground in front of the school, and of Alvin Pond, whom the police had dragged up to ground next to the sawmill.

When Haywood developed the photograph of Alvin Pond, however, he discovered a strange sight. The smoke-draped figure of Blithy stood above Alvin Pond at a blackboard, holding a long pointer. The blackboard was festooned, in wildly haphazard constellations, with dozens of the letter $X$.

"Every time I read that story," Kala said, "I can't sleep afterward."

"Which part keeps you awake the most?" I said, just trying to make conversation.

"The whole thing, Peter. The whole thing. That poor boy, Butler. The letter $X$. The whole thing."

"How's your lecture coming along?"

"All right. I'm working diligently."

"Are you afraid of howls of—what was it?"

"Derision and mockery. No, not really. As long as there're a few like-minded people attending, I'll get by."

Kala poured and drank a glass of Goldwasser; I drank one, too, just to keep up.

"Do you know what I wish for most?" she said.

"To marry me as soon as possible."

"What you just said, by the way, was not a proposal of marriage. It was the answer to a question. I just wanted to make that clear."

"The minute you're officially a free woman, Kala, I'll propose. I do have something of the gentleman left in me."

"Fair enough—but in the meantime—" She set *The Unclad Spirit* on the table, turned, and pressed herself against me. "I wish for something to humanize me."

"I don't know what that means."

"Miss Houghton used the word. I suppose I mean it like she did—to have a total dedication to another person. She had total dedication to her daughter, Dahlia. She had total dedication to an idea, too, of course. To spirit photography. But she speaks in so heartfelt a way about her daughter. I want to feel those things, too."

"You can't toward me yet, I don't think."

"Not yet. There's still too much in the way. Give it time."

"What choice do I have except to wait?"

"None, really. Miss Houghton's phrase *grim relief*. The world thrown into grim relief. Don't you think that somewhat applies to our present situation, Peter?"

"Maybe David Harp will change things."

"If not entirely for the better, less for the worse."

"That's some improvement."

"Well, from what you've told me, Mr. Harp's struck a deal with the Devil, hasn't he?"

"Yes, he has."

"Mrs. Harp's a fortunate woman," Kala said. "To be loved that deeply."

"Now *you* sound jealous."

"I suppose I am jealous of her, to know that sort of love from a husband."

"You believe Harp, then, lock, stock, and barrel, about his sick wife?"

"Yes."

"I guess now you're going to ask what would humanize me most, in my opinion."

"Why shouldn't I ask?"

"The answer is to marry you."

"My friend from childhood, Larissa, would call that *romantical*."

Kala pulled away from me. She got up from the bed, drank two more glasses of Goldwasser in quick order, stood near the window, began nervously to draw stick figures on the foggy glass.

"*Will* you marry me?"

She wrote *Yes* on the window. "Once I'm a free woman—"

The next evening after dinner Kala and I were back in my room again. "I didn't see Vienna all day today," she said.

"He was sleeping off a drunk, from being out with Sergeant Maitlin and the boys till all hours. He was in the darkroom only a short while, then went out again. I don't know where."

"I went to the doctor today. I told you I had an appointment."

"Was it good news?"

"Fine—top to bottom, all strength returned."

"I've noticed."

"It seems to please you."

"It does."

"I still need my naps."

"Clean bill of health, then, except for getting tired?"

"Nothing permanently damaged. A very good report, Peter."

"I couldn't be happier."

I was sweeping out the fireplace grate and now put kindling, then two logs on. I lit the kindling and didn't have to use the bellows at all. The fire blazed up nicely.

"You know, Peter, I saw Miss Gordy Larkin today. She was across the street when I was walking back here. She didn't see me. How well did you know her?"

"A little."

"Intimately a little?"

"No."

"Intimately a lot?"

"No."

"I had a funny thought, seeing her today: that I knew little of your past. And that Miss Larkin might have been an intimate in your past. You simply hadn't told me. And I in turn didn't know how to ask. Just a woman on the street, Miss Larkin."

"I'll tell you anything you want to know."

"Any burning curiosities I might have?"

"Yes."

"Do you have any—toward me?"

"There's a few things I want to know, but don't dare ask yet."

"Afraid what you'll learn?"

"Afraid it'll spoil what I know and feel is all."

"About my life with Vienna, I suppose."

"Why you took up with him in the first place, for instance."

Kala stepped over to the fireplace. She had on the dark green sweater over a pale green blouse, ankle-length black skirt she'd worn at dinner. "Destitute is how I felt when I first met Vienna Linn," she said. "It wasn't as if he pulled me up by my bootstraps, though. No, he was closer to being down at my level back then. He wasn't yet involved with Radin Heur.

"We met in Vancouver. Vienna was photographing the Chinese out there. He'd venture into their enclaves, their shack villages and so forth. He'd take family portraits and try to sell them back to the families; no luck—they had a phrase, 'Pockets empty as bamboo'—no luck with that at all, though a few magazines bought a picture or two.

"I'd already discovered Miss Houghton and made a few dollars lecturing at a library, a private home here and there. Anyway, we met. In fact, the first time I laid eyes on Vienna, he was smashing an umbrella against the porch railing of a hotel. It was only drizzling out. The umbrella had obviously failed him, and he was doing it in. At the time it seemed funny. Looking back on it, well—

"I offered to share my umbrella, one of my few possessions. He refused my help, but we'd met.

"A conversation here, another, another. Whoever had the penny paid for the toast. Definitely, it wasn't a romantic courtship. We simply took up with each other. And Vienna sort of pulled me along with him; I felt more pulled than invited. But—certainly—we were now a *couple*. I viewed it that way, at least. Then we moved to Calgary, to a hotel there, and Vienna set up in the lobby. I walked around with a sandwich board. You know: PORTRAITS TAKEN—ONE DOLLAR. My portrait was on the sandwich board. I'd walk around the streets.

"It was in Calgary that he was first contacted by one of Mr. Heur's representatives. We lived in a shabby little hotel room, Peter. In that hotel room was where I first heard the name Radin Heur."

"Was it a train, that first time?"

"Actually, yes. But not there in Calgary. When this *representative* of Mr. Heur's saw Vienna's photographs from Vancouver, the Chinese, he hired Vienna to sabotage a train carrying Chinese railroad workers. It had all the exotic elements Mr. Heur most sought, you see. We didn't understand much of that at first. And I certainly was not privy to the details of his being hired. In fact, when Vienna went back to Vancouver, I stayed behind at the hotel in Calgary. Vienna was gone nearly two months. When he came back, he had more money than we'd ever dared dream about."

"You might've been a widow before even getting married."

"It might have gone badly in Vancouver, yes. But it didn't. When I asked for details, Vienna would only call it a *success*. I'm sure the Chinese railroad workers and their families had other words for it. Vienna had been handsomely paid, but now he worked for Radin Heur." Kala hesitated a moment, began to speak, thought better of it.

"What is it?"

"As far as bed is concerned—" she said.

"I think I've heard enough."

"I haven't *said* enough, though. As far as bed is concerned, I've been dutiful. A wife can be dutiful but absent in her mind *during*. I remained dutiful; he was my *fiancé*, after all. Yet I knew he'd become a man involved with quite terrible things. He'd go off for a week, two weeks, a month at a time. More or less, I was kept in the dark. At first I was able to see it all as separate from myself. As Miss Houghton says, 'I delved deeper and deeper into spiritual possibilities.' All the while, I was sleeping next to a man causing terrible pain in the world."

"Drink making him, what—*timid* every night?"

"Not every. Often enough to make it a surprise when it didn't. I read my book. I waited in the hotels. That is definitely who I was—partly. My loyalty was my good deed."

"And no good deed goes unpunished," I said.

"Yes. That's it exactly. The plane wreck was my punishment. For my loyalty to Vienna all those years. And—yes, *yes*. For going to your bed on my wedding night."

I could not agree, but didn't say so.


Kala fell asleep on the bed; I fell asleep in the chair.
       About 7:00 a.m. David Harp knocked on the door. "Sorry to disturb you and Mrs.—" he said. "I'm setting up now. I could use your help, Duvett."

"Give me a little time, I'll be over."

"Fifteen minutes would be good."

I turned and looked at Kala, wide awake now. "It didn't take him very long to learn what's what, did it? 'You and Mrs.—' He had to say *that*."

I washed up, got dressed, and went next door and into the darkroom. I saw that Harp had already got his chemicals and equipment in place. "This is a pathetic little dungeon," he said. "But it's what's here so let's get to it. In the main, I need you to take down all these photographs of policemen. And get this other stuff and whatnot out of my way. I've still got more to unpack, and I need the elbowroom. I'd like to get right at it. I'm getting a cup of tea, then."

When I finished making more room for Harp, I called him back in. "Those police blokes," he said, "they look right at the camera, don't they? They've seen a bit of life, haven't they? They don't look away from life, do they?"

I don't think Harp expected any answers, and I didn't offer one. "Anyway, thanks for the help in here, Duvett. You understand, don't you, about my need to carry out my specialty in absolute privacy? Mr. Linn's given me the negative. I've got my own box of tricks I work with." He kicked the side of the black steamer trunk. It was double padlocked. "I've got the keys around my neck like a Catholic's cross." He tapped at his chest. "Now, if you'll excuse me."

I left the darkroom. Harp shut the door behind me.

In the dining room sat Kala and Vienna at the same table. To me, it was at best a peculiar sight. I never expected to see it. Freddy had just served them muffins and tea. I stood in the entranceway. Vienna looked at me and said, *"Man and Wife Meet for Breakfast."*

"Just sit down, please, Peter," Kala said. She was wearing the same clothes she'd worn to my room the night before. Her hair had been hastily combed. She looked all nerves. Vienna, on the other hand, was clean-shaven, neatly tucked, and prim. He sipped his tea. He said, "Well, it's a fine, fine morning—so far, it looks as if Freddy hasn't poisoned my food, so what more could a man want?" Kala looked distressed at his good spirits. "I slept a solid two hours last night—miracles never cease," he said. "And how did you sleep last night, Duvett?"

"Not well."

"Worried about Judgment Day, were you?" He took a bite of muffin. "Mr. Harp's in the darkroom as we speak."

I looked at Kala. "It's not really Judgment Day, though, is it?" she said. "Because last night Peter told me of Mr. Harp's remarkable offer."

"No room for secrets in the Haliburton House Inn, is there?" Vienna said.

"The point *is*, Vienna," Kala said, driving the blunt end of her spoon into the tablecloth with a force that seemed to surprise her, "Mr. Harp is following through on his commissioned task. In order to fill out his report, a report which will say that the photograph is authentic. He's just going through the motions. Acting the professional."

"Ah, finally something we all three can agree on!" Vienna said. "The photograph's a fake and Mr. Harp will report it isn't."

Freddy stepped from the kitchen, walked to the front door, and started to leave. His coat was not buttoned. He had no scarf or gloves. "Drop us a postcard now and then!" Vienna shouted at Freddy. "Don't be a stranger!"

Kala stood up. "I'm going to visit Mrs. Durrematt," she said to me.

"And I'm into the darkroom," Vienna said. "To watch an expert at work."

"He won't let you watch," I said.

"If he's to get half of what Mr. Heur pays, then I'm half his employer. I'll insist he let me watch."

Vienna went into the kitchen. Kala and I reached across the table and held hands. "For all these years," she said, "I've lived with a man more comfortable to be around when he's in a bad mood than a good one. You can see how confusing that might be."

"You have a nice visit with Mrs. Durrematt," I said.

Early in the evening I took another long walk. I had no appetite, didn't want to eat dinner at all, just wanted to walk. To clear my head; but as usual, it got more cluttered. The weather had gone from snow to sleet to, finally, cold rain in a few hours. It had iced up here and there. I went down by the harbor for a while. Then I decided on the Black Horse, a pub on Water Street. The place was crowded. Squinting, getting accustomed to the light, I finally noticed Vienna Linn, Sergeant Maitlin, and a few other policemen in uniform at a far table. They were talking and laughing, a bottle of whiskey and glasses on their table. They didn't notice me. I stood at the far right corner of the bar. When I looked across to the other end, there stood Freddy. He looked already to be in his cups. Glassy-eyed, he was talking to himself, or at least the man and woman to his right were ignoring him. The barkeep said something to Freddy, who shook his head, then threw back a shot of whiskey. Freddy pushed off from the bar, combed his hair, returned the comb to his back pocket, walked over to Vienna's table. He sat right down, insinuating himself into their company. Maitlin had to squeeze into a tight spot against the wall. One policeman (I think it was Chet Cole) cuffed the top of Freddy's head, slapped him on the back with mock camaraderie, or so it appeared. Freddy looked confused one minute, pleased the next, but then, suddenly, Maitlin shoved Freddy, who fell to the floor. The men at the table all laughed loudly. Freddy said, "Hey, what—?" He got up and stomped out of the Black Horse.

I had just one shot of whiskey. When I left the Black Horse, I walked a block or two, and reaching an alley, I noticed some movement off to my left. I stopped, backed up a few steps, stood at the corner of a storefront peering down the alley. I saw Freddy halfway down the alley. He wielded a knife, held it at arm's length, performing awkward stretching jabs as if he held a fencing foil. He looked ridiculous and lethal at the same time. He had to be very drunk, talking to his shadow on the brick wall. Some threat or other, I couldn't hear, exactly, just took in the tone of it. Then I did catch a few sentences: "You think I wouldn't dare do that? I'd do that in a minute." Jab. Jab. Jab with the knife, and he'd swipe the knife at his own shadow. "More tea, Freddy. More tea, Freddy, my boy!" He actually struck the wall with the knife then. There was a friction spark. He backed up a bit, put the knife in his pocket, stepped forward, leaned his head against the wall, unzipped, and pissed down the wall.

I hurried on. I thought, Freddy could have been threatening any person at all who had ever come to the Haliburton House Inn for dinner. Me, Vienna, Maitlin, any customer at all.

## VIEW OF KALA MURIE
## ADVISING ENDLESS PRAYER

In my annex room an hour before her lecture, Kala had a bad case of nerves. "Laughingstock," she said, pinning up her hair in front of my mirror.

"I highly doubt it," I said.

"Hand me that bottle, will you, Peter?"

I took a bottle of Goldwasser from the table and set it on the bureau. "Probably it's not a good idea to—"

"—not, not, not what? Drink too much beforehand? Of course not. I'm not stupid. I only need to take the edge off, you see."

"Do you have your lecture memorized?"

She poured a small glass of Goldwasser and drank it. "I think so, yes. But I've also got it written out."

I was wearing a brown tweed jacket, white shirt, brown trousers, black socks, brown shoes, all purchased for the occasion, $26 head to foot at Springs All-Purpose. Kala wore the same black dress she always wore at lectures, cameo pin at her neck.

"Vienna threatened to attend my lecture," she said.

"Along with?"

"Along with whoever else attends, Peter. How should I know?"

"I only meant, will he come with Sergeant Maitlin? You wanted Maitlin to be there."

"He was the first one I invited."

"You look very nice."

"But do I look serious?"

"Just right for the occasion."

We bundled up and walked to Hages Auxiliary Hall. Standing at the back for a moment, Kala said, "The word *dilapidated* comes to mind." The hall was drafty, there were cracks like an enormous map of a river system on one faded, peeling wall. The steam radiators produced dungeon clanks. There was a pigeon in the rafters. Slat chairs were lined up in wavering rows. An old man was hand-swabbing pigeon droppings from the last row of chairs with a wet rag, a bucket of sudsy water alongside. Inside the hall you could hear Birney Cars rattling past. A threadbare Canadian flag hung on the wall behind the wooden podium. There was a school chalkboard to the left of the podium as you faced it. "I didn't request a chalkboard," Kala said.

A few people drifted past us and found seats. Kala took a deep breath, walked up to the podium. I sat in the front row, six chairs in from the center aisle on the right. As Kala squared her lecture pages on the podium, a woman, roughly age thirty, with dark brown hair combed high on a long face, tall, slim, with a determined gait and dressed in an expensive-looking overcoat, walked up to Kala.

"Good evening, Mrs. Linn," she said.

"Good evening," Kala said.

"I'm Mrs. Trundle—my husband, Mr. Trundle, owns this hall. He's your host tonight in that sense. I'm sorry to say, however, I can't stay for your lecture. I'm here, actually, to tell you that my husband is suffering a cough and fever. Neuralgia, I'm afraid. He can scarcely get out of bed, poor dear. He sends his apologies. He wishes you all good luck and attendance."

"Thank you," Kala said. "It was kind of Mr. Trundle to allow the use of this hall. I do hope he's feeling much better soon."

"Your modest fee, I'm told, will be delivered to the Haliburton House Inn by Mrs. Durrematt, a friend of my husband's."

"Not of yours, too?"

"I'm afraid not, actually."

"Oh dear."

"I'll bring my husband your best wishes, then." Mrs. Trundle furrowed her brow, debating, it seemed, whether or not to say anything more. "You see, Mrs. Linn—and I know the notice said Murie, but— Well, word has it it's Mrs. Linn. You see, what your subject is tonight I think is pure gobbledygook. Utter nonsense. A waste of time, *completely*. Folly at best; at worst, it raises the hopes of the bereaved. I don't know why my husband opened the hall to you. I opposed his sponsorship. I'd have willed neuralgia on him, in order that he not be able to be seen here tonight, as he'd intended."

"If you have an opinion, Mrs. Trundle, don't hold back on my account," Kala said, staring daggers.

Mrs. Trundle hugged herself, said, "Brrrr, it's cold in here, isn't it? But it'll have to do, I'm afraid. Perhaps a *brief* lecture is best for everyone's health." She turned and walked down the aisle and out of Hages Auxiliary Hall.

Kala looked at me. "Did you hear all that?" she said.

"Looks like your worst enemy just left. That's a good thing."

Kala studied her pages. I surveyed the room. In the right-hand section of chairs, in an aisle seat halfway to the front, sat a quite elderly woman. She was bundled in a frayed overcoat. She reached into her coat pocket, took out a newspaper page, ran her finger down a column, cleared her throat loudly, and said, "Miss Murie, if you please!"

Kala looked up from the podium. "Yes?"

The woman now had a brief coughing fit. "It says here," she said, holding up the newspaper page, "you'll begin at seven. I hope so. My children expect me back by 8:30, nine o'clock at the latest. Up to then, they'll keep my dinner warm."

"Perhaps you should have had dinner beforehand," Kala said.

"Oh, we aren't getting along, now, are we?" the woman said.

Kala smiled tightly, perused her lecture notes again. By seven o'clock there were eleven people in the audience, counting myself, and including what appeared to be an entire family: mother, father, son, two daughters. They filled the front row, left of the aisle, and each held a Bible. I thought they might be trouble. But in fact they cast warm, encouraging looks at Kala. "Hello, Miss Murie," the mother said.

"Hello," Kala said. "Thank you for being here tonight."

"We've lost a son," the mother said, "just three weeks ago. We're using up our savings, having traveled here from Advocate Harbor on the Bay of Fundy, Miss Murie. We intend to have our portraits taken—individually, and family portraits as well, and in various combinations of two and three of us, as many as we can afford. We're quite hopeful Teddy—Theodore, that is—that Theodore might have the strength and be blessed by the will of God and appear in one of our portraits. We've heard about your work. We know of all the uninvited guests. But Teddy—he'd most certainly be an *invited* guest, wouldn't he? Invited guests are possible, too, aren't they?"

"Indeed they are," Kala said.

"Theodore was nine," the older daughter said.

"Nine. I see," Kala said.

"Nine and a half," the younger daughter, herself no more than five, said.

"What I'll speak about tonight, however," Kala said, weighing her words carefully, "it's more to the point of how some people find it necessary to *fake* a spirit picture, actually."

"Well," said the father, "you have to recognize the Devil in order to deepen your devotion to angels."

"And whatever you speak about tonight, Miss Murie," the mother said, "we'll take to heart."

"Thank you again," Kala said.

"Might you have a few moments afterward to speak with us?" the mother said.

"Of course," Kala said.

As I watched Kala study her pages yet again, I thought, So this is what it's been like for her. This is where scholarship, beliefs, meditations, all of those nighttime readings of *The Unclad Spirit* are employed. This is where she, as Miss Houghton said of one of her own lectures, "attempts to do good."

Kala looked out at the audience. She introduced herself, thanked Mrs. Durrematt, "who unfortunately slipped on the ice, sprained an ankle, and is bedridden," gave a brief biography of Georgiana Houghton, held up her copy of *The Unclad Spirit* for all to see. She took a sip of water from the glass provided.

Then began her lecture.

"On October 19, 1926, I was almost murdered by my husband, Vienna Linn. Mr. Linn is now standing at the back of this very hall."

When I turned to look at the back of the hall, I saw that twenty or so people now sat in the chairs, and seven uniformed police officers leaned against the wall. Sergeant Maitlin stood next to Vienna Linn. Vienna still had his overcoat on, Maitlin held his.

When Kala said, "I was almost murdered by my husband," three people moved up to the front row.

Whatever else people had expected to hear, it couldn't have been this. They'd come out into the cold night. No one left.

"I *shall* come around to spirit photographs," Kala said. "Please stay with me here. It *will* connect up."

She took another sip of water. "We were, my husband and I, living in Churchill, Manitoba—I must say, a rather forbidding place in the north. Terribly cold already in October, snow had fallen days on end."

I now noticed that Gordy Larkin had come in and sat at the far end of the second row to my right. She looked very pretty, altogether much the same as when I'd last seen her, the day I'd given notice at the *Herald* and she'd said, "Good luck, wherever you're going. It's not London, is it?" I caught Gordy's eye, she seemed almost stunned to see me. But she smiled, shrugged, held out her hands palms up, mouthing something to the effect of, Why are you here? I could only smile back, then return my attention to Kala.

Kala's strategy in her lecture struck me as brilliant and effective. People seemed to follow along: maybe if you hear "murder," that becomes the subject, and that keeps you in your seat. I don't know. Anyway, she plaited together the beliefs of Georgiana Houghton with a description of the plane wreck and its aftermath, including her physical pain in recovery.

Ten or so minutes into the lecture, she defined for the audience the term *uninvited guest*. She read the definition twice. "As for the airplane wreck," she then said, "instead of me coming back in the photograph my husband took of it, I *lived*. I survived. The good Lord invited me to stay on this earth a while longer, as you can plainly see."

The family in the front row applauded, parents and children alike.

Kala then proceeded to unleash against fraudulent spirit photographs, lingering on the subject for a good fifteen minutes. "If I had been murdered in the airplane wreck *planned by my husband*, Vienna Linn, who is standing at the back of the hall— *Had* I reached that unfortunate end, I would have liked to come back in the photograph my husband calls *Esquimaux Souls Risen from Aeroplane Wreck.*" Kala now described the photograph in detail. In fact, she did find the chalkboard useful. Because she took up a piece of chalk, made a crude drawing of the plane and stick bodies lying about. She circled one. "This," she said, pointing to it, "was me. It was where I fell, after I was flung from the airplane fatally tampered with under orders, I'm sure, from my husband, Vienna Linn—there!" She pointed at Vienna.

No small thing, to stand up in public like that, point the finger of guilt again and again, meanwhile, through the general subject of the lecture, attempting to heed a "higher calling." As I again surveyed the room, I saw a number of very confused looks, some interested looks, and Gordy Larkin flipping fast the pages of her small notebook, trying to get down Kala's every word. As for the policemen at the back wall, many were young men; they no doubt were just being polite in attending, as a favor to Vienna Linn, who'd taken their portrait and then had received an invitation to his wife's lecture. A few seemed to take cues from their sergeant: they laughed quietly amongst themselves or with Maitlin.

"Why do I present you with all this information?" Kala said. "Why tell of my woes—me, a perfect stranger to you— why? Why tell of this photograph of the plane wreck, onto which my husband cynically and maliciously imposed the images of the so-called *souls* of those two poor Eskimo people, husband and wife? Because, as my new friends here tonight, sitting in the front row, said, 'You have to recognize the Devil in order to deepen your devotion to angels.' "

No small thing, to accuse your husband of four murders and one attempted murder, in public like that, derisive, snickering policemen staring at you. No small thing at all. However, looking behind me again, I now noticed that Maitlin had sat down in the back row. Immediately the rest of the policemen followed suit. Vienna had remained standing.

Somewhat ceremoniously, Kala now took a drink of water, set down the glass on the podium, and said, "Though Miss Houghton took great care in describing fraudulent spirit photographs, she loathed them. She loathed those who foisted them on a vulnerable public. She called these insolent inventions *spirit models.*" Kala's voice was tense with indignation.

No small thing, to end your marriage once and for all in public like that.

"I have marked the pages in *The Unclad Spirit*"—she held up the book again for all to see—"wherein Miss Houghton judiciously uncovers these hoaxes. In clear language illustrating her deep knowledge of the photographic process, she describes the complex technical procedures and methods by which these spirit modelers plied their trade. She herself interviewed several of them in person. She recorded their shameless, bragging confessions. In addition, she acquired testimonies given in courts of law.

"You see, money from bereaved families hoping to again see a dear departed loved one was paid to such sham artists. The hearts of innocent people were broken.

"There are the real spirit pictures. There are the fake ones. And so it is in this life, my friends.

"And as for spirit photography, all I ask is that you keep an open mind."

She looked directly at Sergeant Maitlin when she said that.

Kala stepped back from the podium and gave a little bow. Only the family in the front row—and I—applauded.

By my watch, the lecture had taken one hour and six minutes.

"Well then, thank you," Kala said. At which point Vienna Linn shouted, "I'm going to the Lord Nelson Hotel for a drink. Anyone who cares to hear other than the ravings of a madwoman, please join me!" He was the first to leave Hages Auxiliary Hall.

Gordy Larkin rushed up and had a few moments with Kala, then walked over to me. "Peter," she said, kissing me on the cheek, "where've you been and what the hell are you doing with this crackpot?"

"She's a scholar on the subject, Gordy."

"Oh, a scholar. I see."

"You see what?"

"She's a bedmate is what you mean."

"I meant she's a scholar, is what I meant."

"Look at you! Red as a beet. You're sleeping with this crackpot, aren't you? My goodness; well, I won't put *that* in my article, no sir." Gordy patted both my arms just below the shoulders, as if I were a small boy getting fitted for a new suit. "Gee, maybe I lost out on something when you asked me to dinner that time."

"Maybe so."

"Well, I've got to go file this story, Peter. Look me up at work, eh?"

"Sure, Gordy, I will."

She held up her notebook. "This'll run tomorrow," she said. "Not front page, but still."

"Gordy, are you going to write about the plane wreck? Because—let me tell you something. I was there. I saw it happen. Every single word of it was true."

"Uh-huh."

"True as I'm standing here."

"A plane wreck in Churchill—the *sticks*. And when—last year? Oh, that'd be of real interest to my daily readers, now, wouldn't it?"

"WIFE ACCUSES HUSBAND OF MURDER would be."

"I believe I'll come up with my own heading, thanks."

"SPIRIT PHOTOGRAPH AS EVIDENCE OF MURDER ATTEMPT."

"Thanks, but no thanks. She didn't even produce the photograph in question, Peter. Where was this damning evidence, anyway?"

"Gordy, I'm telling you—"

"I've got to go file."

"This story could get you up to Features."

"Ghosts, goblins, Eskimo souls floating around would get me sacked, is what."

"Gordy, that man you saw, Vienna Linn. He's killed dozens of people." I could only have sounded crazy to her.

Gordy scrunched up her face, shook her head rapidly

back and forth a moment, then stared at the floor. "Peter," she said, "I always liked you. I'd heard you had some sort of mental breakdown or something, after your mother— I don't know if that's true or not. I hope not. But you've obviously—fallen in with some sort of cuckoo clock, my friend. I don't know what all else has happened to you, but you seem to be in some serious trouble"— she pointed to the side of her head—"are you, Peter? Can I help?"

"Just go file your story, Gordy."

"Here I go," she said. "Look me up."

Gordy hurried out.

I walked the streets. I walked down to the harbor, then back to the Haliburton House Inn. As I stepped into the main building, I saw that the family who'd sat in the front row at Hages Auxiliary Hall were all in the sitting room with Kala. They were drinking tea. Kala glanced at me, smiled, then continued speaking with the family. I stepped to the coat pegs and eavesdropped. "—as for the return of your son in a family portrait," she said, "ceaseless prayer to that end, my dears. Ceaseless prayer."

Kala came to my room just past midnight. "After that nice family left the inn, I was tempted to drop by the Lord Nelson Hotel to see if anyone had taken Vienna up on his offer," Kala said. "Just to peek in. But I finally thought better of it."

Kala sat on the bed, lifted off her dress, then her underthings, and got under the bedclothes.

"The way I saw it," I said, standing at the end of the bed, "you addressed a good part of your lecture directly to Sergeant Maitlin. As if you wanted him to get right up and arrest Vienna then and there. Slap handcuffs on your husband, cart him off to jail."

"That would've been beyond my wildest dreams."

"I don't know whether Maitlin was convinced. But once he sat down, he looked as if he was thinking hard."

"What *good*? What good does all my talk do?"

"You seemed to bring some comfort to that family in the front row."

She blew out the candle. "I'd bet you that every last one of those policemen in attendance joined Vienna for a drink or two," she said. "At the hotel."

"Know what? I saw Maitlin walk off in a direction away from the Lord Nelson."

"Did you?"

"Yes, I did."

I took off my clothes and got under the bedclothes next to Kala. "I don't know what I thought of your lecture, Kala," I said. "Except it was brave. And I'm glad it's over."

She wrapped her legs around my legs, pressed herself against me, spoke directly into my ear. "There's something I need to tell you, but it can wait." Then, when we'd finished making love, she said, "Now it can't wait."

I sat up against the headboard. "What can't wait?"

"You'll be the third to know, Peter Duvett. I'm—as they say. As they say—" Kala now edged over, drew me to her, then lay on top of me, and, in little louder than a whisper, said, "I'm with child. As they say. Naturally, I was the first to

suspect it. I was fairly certain. Then the doctor, Dr. Thur-
bon—the same one I'd seen earlier—he was the next to
know. You're the third."

"You're all right, then. I mean—"

"Oh yes. Yes. Fully recovered. Nothing broken inside.
More than fully recovered, wouldn't you say?"

"Are you pleased? I'm pleased. Are you?"

"It's what was supposed to have happened. I'm deeply
pleased."

We lay there not talking. Just breathing. The sound of the
fire crackling in the grate, sudden rain blown against the
window, my watch ticking. Finally, Kala said, "Vienna will
have to be told."

"He'll have to, yes."

"But he won't be fourth, Peter. Mrs. Sorrel, I think."

"Poor Mrs. Sorrel, she might be aghast: what's been going
on at night, in her inn."

"Oh, don't kid yourself, she's been alert to things, no
wool pulled over her eyes, believe me. One morning, when I
stepped out of your room, she was standing in the hallway
holding a dust mop."

"Housekeeper's day off?"

"I don't know. But there she was."

"You never told me."

"I should have. I'm sorry."

"What a look she must have had."

"It *was* quite a look. But then she looked away."

Kala then fell into an uncontrollable laughter; she pulled
the bedclothes up to her neck, rolled over facing away from
me, pressed her face into the pillow. She laughed into the

pillow a good full minute. "I'm glad you're so happy about this," I said.

"Cold tea," she said, coming up for air, then pressing her face back to the pillow again, laughing even harder.

"I don't understand—cold tea?"

Kala got up from the bed, laughing almost to the point of tears, and walked to the chair by the fireplace, wrapped herself in the quilt that was folded on the arm of the chair. "I'm sorry," she said. "Our child— Of course, that's first and foremost on my mind, Peter. Of course. Such happy news. And at my age—what a blessing. But—" She laughed more, turning toward the window, then toward me. "Yet I was just now thinking back to a lecture I gave in Vancouver. Perhaps five years ago. I think five, yes. It was about Miss Houghton, of course. A sparse crowd, but a good audience, and when the lecture was done, up stepped a rather haggard-looking woman, fifty, possibly older. Her name will come back to me—oh yes, Ebertat. A Mrs. Ebertat, about fifty and with a Canadian dollar bill sewn to her feathered hat. She threw a cup of cold tea at me, Peter. Cold tea! And she cried out, 'Hearing such nonsense has put me over the edge!' She'd brought some sort of family photograph with her, but she tore it up right in front of me. It had been one of my more successful lectures; in fact, the next day a discussion in a private home was organized. Followed by a séance—from which I begged off."

"That's a good clear memory, all right. But, Kala, why's it so funny to you. Sorry to be so dense here. I just don't—"

"No, it's not you, Peter. It's me. It's that she said, 'Put me over the edge.' " She looked quite serious now.

"And?"

Kala stood up and walked to the bed, sat down next to me, stood up again, walked to the fireplace. Facing the fire, she said, "It was nervous laughter. When Vienna learns of this child, Peter. When he hears this news—*whenever* he hears it. It's likely to put him over the edge. And I'm quite afraid of what, then, will happen next."

Near to 3:00 a.m.—we'd been talking all along, Kala in the chair, me in the bed—there was a knock at the door.

"My God, why even *have* a door?" she said. "At this hour—"

The voice through the door: "It's Harp."

"It's as if we've eloped and Daddy's tracked us down," Kala said. She got up and slid on a nightshirt. I hurriedly got dressed, just trousers and shirt, and went to the door. Kala sat down in the chair. I opened the door and Harp pushed past me, walked to the window, looked at Kala, and said, "Canadians, I suppose, have ideas about arrangements out of wedlock; that's it, isn't it?"

"And Londoners don't?" Kala said. "Come now, Mr. Harp, squeamish over the blunter facts of life, are we? Shall we find a blindfold for you to wear, after you've barged in on us, Mr. Harp?"

"I'm here on business that can't wait," Harp said.

"Get on with it, then," Kala said.

"I've completed my work in the darkroom. What I have to say to you, I'll say also to Mr. Linn later on. I saw him

stumble in—quite indisposed." He reached into his overcoat
pocket and pulled out two sheets of Haliburton House Inn
stationery. "What you see in front of you," he said, "are two
letters."

At which instant Vienna Linn opened the door and liter-
ally stumbled onto the bed. Kala stepped over to the fireplace. Still dressed in his overcoat, scarf, boots, and hat,
reeking of liquor and cigar smoke, Vienna crawled under the
bedclothes. "Please continue, Mr. Harp," he said. "I'm at repose now. Please go on."

Harp looked from face to face, looked out the window a
moment, then said, "What you see here"—holding a letter in
each hand—"are two letters. Letters saying exact opposite
things, but each addressed to the same person, that being my
employer, Mr. Radin Heur."

Harp now stepped close to the fire and read by its light:
"Dear Mr. Heur, I am writing about the photograph in
question."

Harp stopped reading, stretched his arms wide, and said,
"No need to read them through. In my left hand here I hold
a letter stating with absolute certainty that the photograph is
authentic, never seen anything like it. And in my right hand
I hold a letter stating—how did I put it?" He looked at the
letter. "Oh yes, I state that the photograph is a purposely malicious fraud. I later use the word *insulting.*"

"Coffee, coffee, coffee!" Vienna bellowed. "—all of this
calls for sober thought!"

Kala took her clothes into the bathroom, shut the door,
and got dressed. In a few minutes we all were in the main
building of the Haliburton House Inn. Kala went into the

kitchen to percolate coffee; Harp, Vienna, and I went into the sitting room. Vienna, scowling, eyes half closed, lay down, boots on the sofa. Kala came to the sitting room, said, "Peter, it's all on a tray. Bring it in, will you?" The tray held four cups of coffee and a container of sugar and a spoon. I set it on the table between the sofa and the chair Harp sat on. I'd never known Kala to drink coffee, except Freddy's Chinese coffee. But she drank it now.

"This is an important moment," Vienna said, sitting up straight now. "Fates being sealed, et cetera." He drank some coffee. "—requires sober thoughts."

We were all silent a moment; then Harp said, "Well, which letter do I send?"

"The burden of choice," Vienna said, "is now lifted from you, Mr. Harp. The choice is mine. Mine, because if I choose the one that says the photograph's authentic, we may well get the money. And my life may be saved. My *life*. So, then, Mr. Harp, do your job as verificationist—verify the photograph as authentic."

"And in return?" Harp said.

"*If* compensation from Mr. Heur arrives—"

"I have all confidence," Harp said.

"*If*—then you'll be paid exactly half of what I'm paid. Are we agreed, Mr. Harp?"

"Fully agreed."

"It's done, then."

"Because, you understand, of course," Harp said, "I'm still at liberty to send the other letter. I'll still have it in my possession. Or, because I'm his employee of long-standing, once I'm back in London, I can always walk into Mr. Heur's office and refute—absolutely deny—any old thing I wish to refute and deny."

"Mr. Harp," Vienna said, drinking more coffee, "I want you very much to send the letter verifying the photograph as authentic. I'm asking you, please, to do so." Vienna finished his cup of coffee.

"Then that I will," Harp said. "That I will."

Vienna stood up. "Harp, I admire your business savvy. But I must ask that I put the letter in the post myself, with my own two hands. I trust you don't mind."

"I'll escort you," Harp said.

"Breakfast at seven, then?" Vienna said. "Followed by a brisk walk to the post office together."

Harp and Vienna actually shook hands on the deal, Kala stared into her coffee. Harp went up to his room. Vienna said, "Kala dear, five policemen joined me at the Lord Nelson last night. We had any number of laughs at your expense, I'm afraid. But they were grateful for a night's entertainment and asked me to tell you that. Very busy men, they don't get out much." He walked unsteadily up the stairs.

From my window the next morning at 8:45, Kala and I watched Vienna and Harp set out side by side down Morris Street. Harp handed Vienna the letter, which he slid into his coat pocket.

Gordy's article ran in that evening's *Herald* on page 7:

HAGES AUXILIARY HALL LECTURE DEEMED "ODD"
Last evening's lecture at Hages Auxiliary Hall on the subject of spirit photography might best be considered

a jigsaw puzzle that was missing a few pieces; the general design suggested was interesting enough, but our lecturer, Kala Murie (Mrs. Vienna Linn), for all her confident assertions, seemed to expect too much sympathy for what one audience member called "odd beliefs." Briefly, followers of spirit photography believe that a so-called uninvited guest—that is, a person not actually seen at a wedding or funeral—later appears in spirit form in the photograph taken of that event. Murie referred often and was beholden to the writings of Georgiana Houghton, a 19th-century eccentric philosopher.

"Georgiana Houghton," Murie said after her lecture, "is one of our greatest unsung religious thinkers. I believe, as she did, that true spirit photographs are acts of God."

It turns out, Murie had only recently arrived in Halifax from the northern reaches: exactly, Churchill, Manitoba. Some audience members may have suspected cabin fever as the cause of the impolite air of outrageous marriage complaint throughout her lecture, which seemed ultimately to draw attention away from the main subject of spirit pictures. When this reporter suggested that Murie's northern isolation may have done her a disservice, sharpening her reliance on Miss Houghton's elusive philosophies, Murie replied, "Her philosophies are by no means elusive. Besides which, I've lectured on this subject all across Canada, long before I ever set foot in Churchill."

Last evening's event was sponsored by Hages Auxiliary Hall, Mr. Garrison Trundle, owner, and the Spiritual Sisters of Water Street, Mrs. Hans Durrematt, chairwoman. This reporter learned a good deal about what is commonly termed "spirit pictures" and commends Murie for her scholarship.

Gordy Larkin
*Herald* Reporter

On March 27—David Harp received a wire stating that Radin Heur would be purchasing *Esquimaux Souls Risen from Aeroplane Wreck*; it was referred to only as "the photograph you so enthusiastically wanted me to own." In response, Vienna packed up *Esquimaux Souls Risen from Aeroplane Wreck*, and that evening it left for London aboard the steamer *Parnassus*. David Harp wired Radin Heur's office: "Photograph en route."

On March 28, £20,000 Canadian was deposited by wire transfer to the account of Vienna Linn, in the Bank of Nova Scotia. That night at about 8:15, just as we'd finished our dinner, Vienna took a message, delivered by private messenger, from his suit coat pocket and read it. Present at the table were David Harp, Vienna, Kala, and I. Vienna read:

Dear Vienna Linn,

    A deposit in the amount of £20,000 has been made in your name. Your account number is #3345. A bank book will be provided at your nearest convenience, at which time proper identification will need to be provided. Should you have a change of address (Haliburton House Inn), please notify our offices.

Welcome to the Bank of Nova Scotia.

Sincerely,

Duncan Lambek, President

"Remarkable," Harp said. "Truly remarkable, Mr. Heur sent the money, yet with the photograph sight unseen."

"Shows how much he trusts your professional judgment," Vienna said.

"I'm the bloke's got to stand next to him admiring it on his wall," Harp said. "There in London, keeping my nasty secret to myself."

"Ten thousand pounds for your discomfort, Mr. Harp," Vienna said.

"A man could do worse," Harp said

"Ten thousand pounds," Kala said. "At least enough for new socks." She looked slightly ill a moment, drank some water, said, "You'll have to excuse me. I need to lie down on your bed, Peter." She left for the annex.

"She goes where there's comfort," Vienna said. "Many people do."

Now Freddy Sorrel came in to clear the dishes. We hadn't yet seen Freddy that evening. He was a sight. Both his eyes were blackened, the right side of his face and his right hand along the knuckles were bruised. There was a considerable zigzag gash on the back of his left hand. When he stepped up to our table, he touched his face. "Last night at knives," he said. "During a pub crawl, as the English might call it. It happened outside the same place frequented by you, Mr. Linn, and Sergeant Maitlin, eh?"

"The Black Horse?" Vienna said.

"The very same," Freddy said.

"You should have that hand looked at," Vienna said.

"I looked at it all morning," Freddy said. "I emptied half a bottle of Mrs. Linn's favorite liqueur on it to kill off infection, drank the other half for the same reason. A home remedy, you might call it. It's nothing, really. All in a night's work." He picked up Harp's plate, then mine.

"It looks like the other man's night's work," Harp said.

"Leave it alone," I said to Harp.

"Well," said Freddy, "let's just say the other one's crawled to church to thank his maker he's alive."

"We'd like a pot of tea, Freddy. Thanks."

I had the immediate image of Freddy jabbing at Vienna in the alley, both their shadows dancing on the wall. Freddy mocking and shouting at Vienna, "We'd like some tea, Freddy. Tea, Freddy. Get us some tea!" like a talking parrot's voice.

"Pot of tea, is it?" Freddy said, looking at Harp and fairly spitting out his words in a mock British accent. Freddy picked up Vienna's and Kala's plates and walked into the kitchen.

"I had a look at Freddy's room the other day," Vienna said.

"He invite you in for Bible studies?" Harp said.

"I just happened by," Vienna said. "What decorates his walls is interesting."

"Probably not to me," I said.

"What's on the walls, then?" Harp said.

"Facsimiles—sketched-out copies of police WANTED posters, done, no doubt, in Freddy's hand. Variations on a theme, you might say. The theme of Freddy Sorrel as a dangerous man. So many different self-portraits; it's remarkable, really, how a man can see himself in so many different likenesses. Some with mustaches. One wearing thick eyeglasses, definitely *my* eyeglasses exactly. There's no other pair he could have meant. A very good drawing of them. In these posters he's wanted for various crimes. Big bold lettering. One said, DARING DAYLIGHT ROBBERY."

Freddy brought tea, cups, sugar. "Anything else?" he said.

"Daring daylight waiter," Harp said.

Freddy seemed shaken by the comment, humiliated by Harp's exact enunciation. "Need anything else?" he said.

"No, we're fine here, Freddy," Vienna said.

"Pick up after yourselves, then. I'm off to the cinema," Freddy said. "It's the first talkie in Halifax." He went into the hallway, took his overcoat from the peg. Through the window we saw him put his overcoat on and set out down Morris Street.

"I wonder if they'll let him into the cinema, looking the way he looks," Harp said.

He poured tea for everyone.

"Oh, how very civil, Mr. Harp," Vienna said. "The three of us at tea. Two newly rich men—then there's one rich man's assistant."

Harp could see trouble coming, got us onto a different line. "I seem to recall you mentioning Europe, Mr. Linn. Is that your next destination?"

"Loose ends here to tie up first," Vienna said. "But yes, with this kind of money Europe is quite possible. Fine hotel to fine hotel for a while."

"Back to London, maybe," I said.

"Get to the goddamn point, Duvett!" Vienna said.

"Sign divorce papers—leave Halifax," I said.

"Gentlemen," Harp said, "congratulations and good luck to us all." He left the table.

After Harp left the room, I said, "I'd personally walk you to the ship. I'd take the photograph myself: you standing next to the ship's captain. I'd develop it myself. I'd give it to the *Herald: Police Portraitist Departs on European Tour.*"

"I do like the sound of that, Duvett. You have a small talent with captions, if nothing else."

"I'll study up on the shipping page for you. You can pick your day."

"Not yet. Not yet. I've a few small errands to run, a few items need clearing up before I leave Halifax. I've even got half a dozen more policemen to photograph. Unlike you, Duvett, I approach the smallest task with a sense of decorum. Everything in due time—and then, as if a magician's cape was swept over the Haliburton House Inn, Vienna Linn will be up in a puff of smoke. Just *gone*. And my wife, Kala, will only be able to post her regretful, forlorn, perfumed love letters, hoping to catch me at one fine European hotel or other. Poor dear, how frustrating for her."

"I'll persuade her not to set pen to paper. Not to be frustrated."

"Do try, Duvett. There's enough suffering already, don't you agree?" He sipped the last of his tea. "Let's see, then, what's for tomorrow? Oh yes. First thing in the morning, I'll

show my identification at the bank. Prove my name, my
Canadian citizenship, all of that. I'm considering giving you
a dollar per week raise, Duvett—until I leave Halifax. That
should help pay for some of Kala's very expensive habits. The
Goldwasser alone sets me back quite a sum. She earned,
what, all of twenty-five dollars for her failed lecture the
other night."

"Actually, she got one hundred dollars. And I'm told—
Kala told *me*, her doctor recommends she stop drinking that
stuff. Entirely stop."

"I trust there's a better reason than the fear of stumbling
down the stairs and hurting herself."

I found myself clutching a table leg with each hand. "If
she fell down the stairs," I said, "our child might be injured.
Then we couldn't forgive ourselves, could we?"

Vienna took off his eyeglasses. He dipped his napkin in
the water pitcher, then cleaned both lenses. He put his glasses
on again. "You realize, Mr. Duvett," he said, "your child may
well be half-orphaned before it's even born." He pushed
slightly back from the table. He pointed a finger at me, pre-
tended to shoot his revolver.

I stood up before Vienna did. "Kala's waiting," I said.


When I opened my room door, I saw that Kala had
been sitting on the chair in the dark. "It's a cold rain
out now," she said.

I closed the door and knelt down in front of her. I took
her hands in mine. "I was laughing to myself just now," she
said. "I haven't even built a fire. I'm sorry."

"Laughing about what, in the dark here?"

"An aside. An aside, written by Miss Houghton. An after-thought, really. She'd been writing about a particular spirit photograph, its effect on a particular family, and she went off on a little tangent."

"Something funny to her, I bet."

"Probably not. Probably it was quite terrifying to her. Yet it's made me laugh."

Kala drew my hand to her neck, then allowed me to un-button only the top button of her dress. "What the tangent was, Peter—well, let me try to recite it by heart: 'When I pass into the next world, what I much look forward to, and hope will happen, is eavesdropping in on my dearest friends; I want to hear, in their private conversations, a certain candor as it applies to me. And listening in, I should hope to hear all manner of unsettling discourse: malicious gossip, venomous hearsay, conjecture, lovingly harsh judgment, rumor of amo-rous misconduct, any and all—: oh, that posthumously I might provide my friends with such entertainment! It would therefore provide me with the same. I, who would walk among them, my invisible ear-horn held to my ear. How pleased I would be, should my dearest friend, Ella Welch, say, "Bless her heart, but dear departed Georgiana was not every moment wholesome!" But what truly terrifies me no end, what would so sadly disappoint and cause no limit of cha-grin, would that what I ascertained in my eavesdropping be nothing but *exactly what each dearest said to me in person when I was alive*, had said to me at table or on a lovely walk on a country road. If ill sorry fate had altitude, this would stand at the topmost. To discover, alas, that my friends were thus so transparent, dullards so lacking toward me in fecklessness, whose true emotional coloring was the dull flat gray of a windless sea off England. Please, Lord, let my friends after my death cast upon me poetic admonitions, boldly and honestly settle scores I never knew even existed to be settled; I don't care to hear only what I already know of myself.' "

"You recited that very well," I said. "And I can see why it'd make you laugh."

"Tell me."

"It's back to what you called *humanizing*. Because it's a human failing, to want people to talk about you, even to say bad things, as long as they're talking about you. She's so honest about it, it's funny, in a way."

"She doesn't want her friendships to end. She just wants them spiced up."

"I never had many friends. I was never that worried about it. But I knew it was true."

"You just need one, really. I think one suffices, if they can keep a secret. When I was a girl, I had a friend, Larissa, and I'd make things up left and right, just to tell her, just to have secrets for her to keep. We were twelve. Girls at twelve, you have no idea; they can be monsters. But Larissa wasn't. We weren't to each other. I like thinking about that. Shallow bitches, some of the others, but not Larissa."

"Your Vancouver childhood, of course."

"Yes, and perhaps Larissa still lives there. I've thought of her lately. Thoughts, very specific thoughts about her have flown into my head. Actually, such thoughts started in Churchill. When I was hardly able to turn to my right or left without crying out. I don't know why, but I thought of Larissa. It eased the pain. She was such a good judge of character. Even then, even at age twelve. She had poise—not at all intimidated by all the usual sneers and rebuffs and cat-scratching and such. My own mother noticed it to the point that whenever I'd get sullen and confused—suffered some slight or other—she'd say, 'How might Larissa think about this?' And it seldom failed to help. Larissa just had a—*lack of betrayal*. That's it, really. Lack of betrayal, and, oh, how heavenly that was.

"I think about all that, Peter, and I think that what was enviable about Larissa, most of all, was that she had a natural dignity. If she received a wound, she'd say, 'Stupid, stupid person, nothing better to do!' First off, she'd admit to the hurt. Then she'd judge the one who'd hurt her. Then she'd immediately get on with life.

"And do you know what else I thought, sitting here, waiting for you? That Larissa would approve of you."

"I gratefully accept the compliment."

Kala unbuttoned her dress and slipped out of it. I was about to attend to the kindling and matches, to take things in the usual order, but she took me by the hand and we stood by the bed, where she undressed me. To then have waited, even the moment it would have taken to pull back the bedclothes, would have been "time turned to anguish."

Later, we slept, and when we woke together in the middle of the night, I said, "I told Vienna about our child."

In a moment or two Kala said, "I'm somehow very calm. But be a dear, will you, and lock the door?"


"Merciful Lord—Mr. Harp's been killed!"

It was about eight o'clock in the morning, March 29. Kala and I had just walked the short way from the annex and come in out of the rain and were hanging up our coats, about to go in for breakfast. At this point, Vienna be damned, whether he saw us come in together or not. Or if Harp did. Or Mrs. Sorrel, or Freddy, or anyone.

"Merciful Lord! Merciful Lord!"

At the top of the stairs, Mrs. Sorrel fell to her knees. "I'll pray. Yes, I'll pray." I don't believe she knew that we were watching her yet. " . . . not, please" was all I then heard. I went halfway up the stairs. "Please, God, let it not have been my son Freddy."

"Go on up, Peter," Kala said. "Have a look at what she's seen. Harp may only have fainted or is dead drunk. He may not actually be—"

I continued up the stairs. And as I stepped around Mrs. Sorrel, she looked up at me and said, "Freddy's at the market for potatoes."

Harp's door was open. He lay on the left side of the bed. I moved closer and saw that he was wearing only his nightshirt. I pressed closed his eyelids. It appeared that he'd been shot through the heart, or near the heart. The bed looked otherwise as if it hadn't been slept in. I was slightly in a panic: Think now, think now: *Verificationist No Longer Able to Help His Wife*, as if a caption could actually organize the starkest of truths. Harp's nightshirt was soaked in blood. On the floor, in a place suggesting that it may have fallen from Harp's outstretched right hand, was a revolver. It looked similar to Vienna Linn's revolver. I could easily have been mistaken, though. I didn't know revolvers, and I'd seen Vienna's only in the half-light of the darkroom.

I shut Harp's door, leaned against it, looking down the hallway.

*View of Mrs. Sorrel Huddling into the Corner of the Landing;*
*View of Mrs. Sorrel Clutching Kala Murie's Legs; View of Kala*
*Murie Leaning Over, Stroking the Top of Mrs. Sorrel's Head; View*
*of Kala Murie Helping Mrs. Sorrel Down the Stairs; View of Mrs.*
*Sorrel Ringing Up the Police; View of Mrs. Sorrel Nearly Fainting*
*in the Sitting Room; View of Mrs. Sorrel Refusing Tea from Kala*
*Murie; View of Police and Men from the Coroner's Office Moving*
*up the Stairs.*

Describing a wake she'd attended in 1883, Miss Houghton said, "It was a day of great distress, cringing hearts,
bewildered souls." That seemed right for March 29, 1927,
Haliburton House Inn, Halifax, Nova Scotia, too. Kala had
found Vienna drunk, muttering, lying on the floor of the
pantry darkroom, radio playing static. I walked around Halifax much of the morning. Kala, she told me later, fell into an
exhausting despair and slept in her room, waking so vio-
lently from a dream she couldn't remember that she'd almost
been thrown from the bed. All the while, the police were attending to the scene of the crime. Finally, David Harp's body
was taken to the morgue. Then, at about 3:00 p.m., Kala, Vienna, and I seemed almost dumbstruck to each have wan-
dered into the kitchen at the same time. First, Kala prepared
a cup of tea, then went back to her room. Next, Vienna prepared a cup of tea and returned to the darkroom. I drank my
cup of tea sitting in the kitchen, then went to the annex. No
one had said a word; neither Kala nor I had screamed the
one surest truth at Vienna: *Just as you had with Samuel Brant*
*in Churchill, you hired Freddy Sorrel to act on your behalf. The*

*money will entirely be yours now!* No, we'd gone about preparing tea like somnambulists.

About 6:00 p.m. Sergeant Maitlin gathered Kala, Vienna,
Mrs. Sorrel, and me together in the sitting room, where he
introduced us to a Inspector Destouches. (I was relieved that
it was not Inspector Lennart.) "He's been with the Halifax
police for eight years now," Maitlin said. "A very able man."

Destouches looked all business. He was about forty-five,
with sandy brown hair, a broom-straw goatee. He was a
somewhat small man, tautly built, wore a tweed suit coat, had
an overall buttoned-up look, precise of movement. When we
all sat down, he lined up three pencils in a row on the table,
then sharpened each one with a jackknife as we watched.
The shavings fell into the ashtray. No one spoke for a good
two or three minutes. Finally, Destouches, without looking
up, said, "Mrs. Sorrel, whose fine establishment I pass by
every day on my way to work, has given me a list of people
living here, including her own name. There's just five altogether, isn't that right, Mrs. Sorrel?"

"Yes, that's right," Mrs. Sorrel said.

"And four out of five are present, correct?"

"My son, Freddy, is living here. But he's not here this
minute."

"So noted, Mrs. Sorrel," Destouches said. "Now, I'll be
talking with you each, individually, of course. Sergeant
Maitlin will be in attendance as much as time allows. Police
stenographer, Mrs. Raymond—due shortly—will be present
as well."

As if on cue, Mrs. Raymond opened the front door, hung
up her overcoat, slipped off her rain galoshes, put on a pair of

shoes which she'd taken from a small carrying bag. She was, I'd guess, fifty, quite tall, with a narrow face and salt-and-pepper hair. She smiled and went immediately into the dining room.

"There's no need to speak to Mrs. Raymond directly," Destouches said. "Mrs. Sorrel, I'm afraid the dining room is closed to the public."

"I understand," Mrs. Sorrel said. "I'll put a notice up on the front door."

"Go ahead and serve your present guests as usual, though not in the dining room," Destouches said.

"And you and Mrs. Raymond?"

"If you might bring us a little dinner," Destouches said. "Well then. I'm not going to pick straws." He looked at his list. "Mr. Linn—Vienna Linn. I'll speak with you first."

Vienna went into the dining room.

"The rest of you, I must ask that you remain on the premises until I speak with you," Destouches said. "I'm not officially declaring house arrest but close to it. Don't step out even for a breath of fresh air, eh?"

"My room is in the annex next door," I said.

"You can go exactly that distance, then," Destouches said, annoyed. "Understood?"

"Yes," I said.

I went to the annex. By my watch it was 8:20 when Mrs. Sorrel knocked on my door and said, "Peter, you're being asked for."

In the dining room Maitlin sat two tables away from Detective Destouches and Mrs. Raymond. Mrs. Raymond had a cup of tea in front of her. Her notebook and pencils were set out neatly. The left side page of her notebook was filled with shorthand. At the top of the right-hand page, in regular lettering, it said PETER DUVETT, the time and date, followed by: *Interview by Insp. Mark Destouches.*

"Please sit," Destouches said.

I sat directly across from him, which was next to Mrs. Raymond.

"Mr. Duvett—it's Peter, isn't it?"

"Peter Duvett, yes."

"Duvett, I'm obligated to say, you do not sit in a place of safety. What we call this situation is a 'suspicious death.' We're presently sorting out evidence. We've got people thinking it through. This is a preliminary interview, Duvett. To get background information. Mrs. Raymond will write down our every word. Understood?"

"Yes."

"Now, Mr. Duvett"—Mrs. Raymond was writing—"when did you last see David Harp?"

"I can tell you almost to the minute. About 8:00 or 8:15 this morning."

Destouches looked at Mrs Raymond, who showed little expression. "I meant *alive*, Mr. Duvett."

"Last night at dinner."

"Have a hearty appetite, did he?"

"What?"

"Was Mr. Harp of good appetite?"

"He ate dinner. Then he went to his room, I think."

"Mr. Linn said, present at dinner were himself, you, David Harp, and Mrs. Linn. Mrs. Linn was feeling indisposed, so she left the table. After dinner, you, Mr. Linn, and David Harp remained at table. Is that your recollection?"

"Yes."

"Mr. Linn said business was discussed."

"Business, yes."

"My understanding is that you are merely Mr. Linn's darkroom assistant. Yet you were privy to this discussion nonetheless. Is that correct?"

"Yes."

"Mr. Harp, my sources tell me, worked for the British Museum. We have official notice of this. Now, Mr. Linn has described for me what 'business' was discussed at dinner last night. Tell me in your own words, please."

"Here is what I have to say. Vienna Linn murdered David Harp. If he didn't do it himself, he hired someone. He's done this exact thing before. He did it in Churchill, Manitoba. I was there. He did it there, and now he's done it here in Halifax."

"Mrs. Raymond, did you get all of that down?" Destouches said.

Mrs. Raymond read back my words.

"Thank you," Destouches said. "Now please add a note that Mr. Duvett refused to answer my question as to what exact business was discussed last night at dinner," Destouches said. "Duvett—someone's got a world of trouble here, Duvett. You know what? It's probably not you. Don't look so nervous, Duvett. You're nearly green. You going to throw up, Duvett? You going to be sick?"

"I don't think so. No."

"All right, Duvett. I'll get back to the discussion of the so-called business arrangement later, once your brain cools down some, eh?" Destouches consulted his notes. "By the way, I'm apprised of the lecture given by Mrs. Linn the other night at Hages Auxiliary Hall. I've already spoken to Miss Gordy Larkin, a newspaper reporter who took notes. I've read her notes. It's all pretty far-fetched religious nonsense, in the main. But my job is not to judge what people believe, Duvett, but what their beliefs make them do. You get a belief on this hand, you get a behavior on the other. I connect them up. That's my job. A man says, 'Oh, I think this man shouldn't live.' So he kills him. I connect that up.

"Let me try to ask you a simpleton's question, then, Duvett. Maybe you can answer it. Maybe we can start over again. And don't give me your sorry notions about who murdered whom, based on whom you're in bed with every other night and want eventually to be in bed with *every* night, or based on anything else. Just answer my questions, all right? This is a preliminary interview. I'll come talk with you every day for the rest of your goddamn life if I want to, you stupid lame. You aren't on some big adventure?" Destouches half-stood, then whacked me across the side of my head with his notebook. "You understand?"

I stood, raised a fist to strike Destouches, sat down. I looked at Mrs. Raymond, who seemed only to expect my answer. "Yes," I said.

"What did you see when you walked into David Harp's room?"

"He was lying on the bed. There was blood all over his nightshirt. There was a revolver on the floor. Somebody had shot him."

"Possibly."

"I know what I saw."

"No, you don't. You only know how to describe what

you saw. Mr. David Harp may have shot himself. For instance."

I looked out to the hallway and saw Mrs. Sorrel embrace Kala. Mrs. Sorrel wept and spoke loudly, "Poor man, he paid for a week in advance. And who's to tell his family?"

"Maitlin," Destouches said, "please ask them to go somewhere else."

"Should I tell them we've already contacted Harp's wife?" Maitlin said.

"That'd be fine," Destouches said.

Sergeant Maitlin walked over to Mrs. Sorrel and Kala and gestured for them to go into the sitting room, out of Destouches's earshot.

In a few minutes Mrs. Sorrel brought in a bowl of stew for Maitlin, Destouches, Mrs. Raymond.

"Thank you," Destouches said. "Mr. Duvett here can eat later."

After she left the dining room, Destouches looked at Maitlin, winked an eye. "Off the record," he said, "just because she's served us stew doesn't mean she didn't murder David Harp."

Maitlin ate a spoonful of stew, then plucked up a carrot separately. "Stew's very good, though," he said.

Destouches looked at me and sighed. "Years of doing these interviews— The long way around the park, it might seem to you, eh? Everybody, *everybody* has fears, Duvett. You sit here and look at me and think, Fuck you, my life's as sweet as yours, you son-of-a-bitch, eh? Don't accuse *me*. Don't try and take my life away, *finding me out*."

"I didn't kill David Harp," I said.

"Note how sensitive he is, the slightest provocation," Destouches said directly to Maitlin.

"I'd like to shove my badge down his throat," Maitlin said, then went back to eating his stew.

"Sergeant Maitlin," Destouches said, "considering the obvious hostilities between you and Mr. Duvett here."

"Right," Maitlin said. He stood up. "I'll be at the station if you need me." He left the inn.

"I'm tired, Duvett," Destouches said. "You know why? I've just had a very long, detailed conversation with Mr. Linn. Detailed conversations worry me, you know why? Because I worry that if my mind gets foggy during—tired, run-down—I might be persuaded by non-truths in abundance, Duvett. Non-truths in abundance. Non-truths tend to abundantly gather, trying to form a truth. Intelligent intellectuals like Mr. Linn, it's my experience that when they sit in front of a detective, they truly believe the detective's like everyone else they talk to. They think that saying something in nicely formed sentences is the same as telling the truth. God Almighty, Mrs. Raymond, how many more years do I have to put up with this?"

I shifted in my chair.

"Comfortable there, Duvett?"

"Comfortable enough," I said.

I now looked over and saw Gordy Larkin staring in through the window. She's been assigned to look into the murder of David Harp, I thought. Gordy came into the Haliburton House Inn, spoke briefly with Mrs. Sorrel, who quickly sent Gordy away. She stopped in front of the window again, tilted her head slightly, and smiled, shrugged, then left.

Destouches checked his notes. "Getting back to the business arrangement you were privy to, Duvett," he said. "Whatever the details, Mr. Linn said that he and David Harp were—I quote—*equal partners*. Police inquiry to London, then the Bank of Nova Scotia, shows the sum of twenty thousand pounds deposited in Mr. Linn's name. Equal partners would mean that David Harp was owed ten thousand pounds—whatever that is in Canadian. Does my math square with what you were privy to, Duvett?"

"Yes."

"Yet as of this minute, the full twenty thousand remains in Mr. Linn's account. Was there a written contract, this *equal partnership*, to your knowledge, Duvett?"

"There definitely wasn't."

"Partnership dissolved," Destouches said to Mrs. Raymond.

Destouches ate some of his stew, Mrs. Raymond ate some of hers. "I'm tired," Destouches said. "The complications of life wear me out, Duvett. For instance, did you know Mr. Vienna Linn has offered to pay liner passage for David Harp's widow and her two children to come to Halifax, retrieve David Harp's body, and go back to London?"

"Generous of him," I said.

"I thought so," Destouches said. "However, paying the family's passage doesn't mean he didn't murder Harp. Sympathetic gestures—we find in police work—sometimes send up a warning flag, eh?"

"You're a cynic, Detective Destouches."

"Oh yes, indeedy. In fact, every day I struggle to work my way *up* to cynicism, this job being what it is. Human nature being what it is." Destouches studied my face a moment. "Anything in this business arrangement for you?"

"Not a penny."

"So you got to listen in and hear what you weren't getting, eh?"

"The photograph Kala Murie lectured about—it was of a murder scene, Inspector Destouches." I instinctively flinched, but Destouches didn't try to strike me again. "Mr. Harp was arranging payment for *that*. It's blood money. I didn't *want* any of it."

"You're a saint, Duvett. A real saint. I'm sitting having stew with a real saint, Mrs. Raymond."

Mrs. Raymond didn't write that down.

"Duvett," Destouches said, "here's the part where I let you establish an alibi. Saint establishes alibi, Mrs. Raymond. The coroner's report isn't complete yet. But give or take, they say David Harp died from a single gunshot wound to the heart about 2:00 a.m., possibly as late as 4:00 a.m. Now, Mrs. Sorrel was tending to"—he checked his notes—"an elderly sick aunt. Asleep on the aunt's sofa. That checked out. She wasn't on the premises here. She came back at about 6:00 a.m. She'd been left a note—instructions in Mr. Harp's hand to call him down for breakfast at 7:00 a.m. However, once back here, she herself sat down a moment in the sitting room and dozed off, and got to Harp's room late, according to her, 'just after eight.' That's about when you heard her crying out, 'Harp's dead,' et cetera. So now, Duvett, routine question, eh? Between the hours of 2:00 and 4:00 this morning, you were?"

"In my room."

"That'd be room 28, the annex, correct?"

"Correct."

"Embarrassing, eh, but if I was to ask Mrs. Linn where she was, 2:00 to 4:00 a.m., might she say room 28?"

"If she didn't, she'd be lying."

"Good for you, Duvett. Good for you. What's that French fencing word, Mrs. Raymond?"

"*Touché*," Mrs. Raymond said.

"Didn't have to leave the inn to have a night on the town, eh?" Destouches said. "Well, I'll have to ask Mrs. Linn to corroborate anyway, I suppose."

"I suppose so."

"My own colleague, Sergeant Maitlin, witnessed Mr. Linn sprawled head down on a table at the Black Horse between 2:00 and 3:00 a.m., then sobering up a little with coffee at the police station, sleeping it off on a cot till 5:30 a.m., then dropped off at the Haliburton House Inn directly. Pending a change in the coroner's report, Mr. Linn was not on the premises at the time of the murder."

"He *arranges* such things. He never dirties his hands."

"You talk like a dime novel, Duvett. I'm laughing at the way you talk, ha, ha, ha, 'dirties his hands.' You talk like an American gangster—those gangster radio dramas, eh? Would you agree, Mrs. Raymond?"

Mrs. Raymond rolled her eyes, looked impatient.

"Let me do a little human arithmetic out loud a minute," Destouches said. "Bear with me; all the way through school I had to add and subtract out loud, funny thing." He counted on his fingers like a schoolboy. "Unless I'm sadly mistaken, if we subtract you, Mrs. Linn, Mr. Linn, Mrs. Sorrel—five take away four. That equals *one*. That leads me to the question: What were your relations with Freddy Sorrel?"

"He served me breakfast and dinner."

"Spend any time with him outside these premises?"

"Just the other night, I saw him pissing against a wall. I was out for a walk."

"Hardly a prearranged meeting, eh?"

"Hardly."

"Any knowledge of how he was predisposed toward the deceased, then?"

"From the little I saw, they despised each other."

"Did you ever witness David Harp threaten Freddy, or vice versa?"

"No. Though, almost everything Freddy said sounded like a threat."

"So I've heard. So I've heard. He has a personal style, Freddy does, doesn't he? Word has it, Freddy Sorrel once asked for a job as a police artist. You know, give him some basic physical traits, nose, mouth, hair, et cetera, he said he'd come up with a likeness. What I heard, the duty sergeant just paid Freddy for his mother's scones and threw him out on his can."

Destouches folded closed his notebook. "Mrs. Raymond, I need a few minutes alone now with Mr. Duvett, please."

Mrs. Raymond carried her notepad into the sitting room.

"The thing of it is," Destouches said, "David Harp took a single bullet in the heart. Quite a close-up operation. And now what we have is a British citizen murdered on Canadian soil. This has complications. This causes headaches. It makes headlines. It ups the ante all around.

"Now, Mr. Harp arrives in Halifax to do business with Mr. Linn. Something goes wrong. Harp is dead. One, two, three— I will connect it all up. Life's little secrets, eh, Du-vett?"

"Vienna Linn hired someone to murder David Harp. I already connected it up for you. It's not anybody's little secret."

"I'm tired, and I've still got Mrs. Linn to talk with."

"There're lots of empty beds in this place. I'm sure Mrs. Sorrel wouldn't mind you taking a nap on one."

Destouches stood up. "This was *preliminary*. Don't take a vacation, Duvett. We have a man at the train station, for instance. That's the trouble with trains, eh? They leave Halifax."

"I'm free to go, then?"

"For now."

Destouches went to speak with Mrs. Raymond. I went back to my room, waited for Kala's interview to be over.

Freddy Sorrel had gone missing for over two weeks. During that time, Inspector Destouches had instructed Kala, Vienna, and me to keep to a 9:00 p.m. curfew. "Until we get things sorted out," he said. "Plus which, there's this cat-and-mouse with Freddy Sorrel."

In my annex room late on the night of April 2, I sat in the chair, Kala on the bed. "I've been taking closer and closer notice of Vienna," she said. "Just out of the corner of my eye, and from what I've gathered from Mrs. Sorrel. And even in rare passing conversations with Vienna himself. And I've come to the conclusion, Vienna's suffering a plague spot."

"What's that?"

"It's—it's a *decline*," Kala said, touching the side of her head. "Late this afternoon, when I got back from my walk, I had the strangest conversation with him."

"How's that?"

"He came to my room and seemed—resigned."

"Resigned to what? Being found out by the police?"

"In part, perhaps. He quoted, of all people, Miss Houghton. To the effect of: 'I who have worked for the world's benefit am now treated with scorn.' "

"Feeling sorry for himself?"

"Delusionary—'worked for the world's benefit.' But then he said, 'It's all my doing. My fault. I've led a life sacrificed to money. I could have been known as an artist!' "

"The money's gone to his head."

"Something's gone to his head, Peter. Do you know what he did then? He recited a comedy routine. From one of his radio programs. He just went on and on. He obviously knew it by heart. Much of the humor just went by me, I admit. But it was as if he were auditioning, that he was going to march right down the street to a radio station and try out as an actor."

"Was it *His Gang*, with Roxy Rothafel?"

"I think so, yes."

"Because that one's pretty good. Some of the others aren't."

"You and Vienna, listening to radio comedies together in the darkroom, how nice."

"I didn't say it was nice. I just said some programs were better than others."

Kala fiddled with the scalloped border of the bedsheet a moment, then said, "Vienna said, 'Now the money's come, now that I'm a rich man, I sleep even less. I've got only an hour or two left a night *not* to sleep. The furies that loneliness imposes on the mind even at its clearest repose—' My God, Peter, he's quoting Miss Houghton! 'If you are fated to be alone, fine, do good work born of loneliness, then.' That's right from *The Unclad Spirit*. I believe that my husband's the only person capable of making that blessed book nauseating, quoting from it like that."

"Maybe he's doing it on purpose."

"There's more."

"What—"

"Do you know what Mrs. Sorrel showed me? Yesterday she showed me the registry. You know, where people sign in. Now, have you found any reason to sign in, since the first day we arrived here, I mean?"

"Of course not."

"Of course not, because a person signs in only when they first arrive. But since David Harp's death, Vienna's signed in every day. Go see for yourself. What's more, he's whittling away at his name. In order of occurrence, he first signed *Vienna Linn*—his complete name, right? But after that, he signed *V. Linn*. That was followed by *V.L.* And—go look—just yesterday, he signed just the letter *L*."

"He's disappearing." It was a wishful-thinking joke that didn't go over.

"You know what else he told me? That he's going to start to give away the money. He's not giving me a goddamn penny, that's been obvious for some time. But giving it *away*—that lunacy comes from his suffering a plague spot."

"Give the money to whom?"

"I asked him that, and he said, 'Police functions.' He named a few. The Police Benevolent Fund, or some such thing. For the wives and families of policemen killed in the line of duty. He named the Police Benevolent Fund, a hospital charity organized by the police, two or three others. If I didn't know better, it'd seem like a striving for redemption."

"He's trying to stay friendly with the police is all. More *delusion*. Wouldn't you say?"

"He already returned every penny he was paid to take the police portraits."

"Who told you that?"

"Sergeant Maitlin, in person."

"Well, he hardly needs that money now, does he?"

"That's true, but still—"

"How long did he stay in your room?"

"About an hour. I was fully dressed and sat in the chair the entire time. Oh, and how dramatically slumped and profoundly exhausted Vienna looked, too. The weight of the world; as if poor David Harp was the straw that broke the camel's back, one too many men and women dead by his hand. The ghastly man I'm married to. I'm the one who needs redemption most, for this marriage."

"I won't pity you, Kala."

"But you do love me, don't you? I have to know this."

"I do love you, yes."

"It's quite laughable, isn't it, my husband suddenly thinking he has the burdens of Job."

"I'd like to lie down next to you now."

"Not quite yet. The room's still a little too warm. Open the window a bit, will you, darling?"

I propped open the window with an ink bottle.

"I trust—if it's a girl," Kala said, "that you'd approve of the name Georgiana."

As it happened, three or four nights earlier I'd stood outside the darkroom and heard Vienna imitating Roxy Rothafel, the radio personality.

Roxy Rothafel's voice could be excited, slightly loony, hysterical, somber. Roxy often referred to his moods in terms of musical instruments, as if he—Roxy—was a one-man orchestra forever playing "the music of my life" for his fans. He revealed all sorts of personal anecdotes, making his listeners at least think they were getting real notices about a real life. "Gee, sunshine and breezy, the weather makes me feel giddy as a piccolo," he'd say. "Just saw my girl, Sally, who makes me feel like the entire brass section out on a lark in the park." Or: "My Sally's down with the grippe today, makes me feel like a cello alone on the deck of a ferry in the rain." Things like that.

When I'd put my ear to the door, I'd heard Vienna in the midst of imitating Roxy, except that he was combining a number of routines. Not only that, but he had replaced "Sally"—Roxy's girlfriend or wife, he never let on which—with "Kala." I was dumbfounded and mesmerized at once. Not only at what griefs and laments Vienna unleashed, but at the sheer fact of him being more animated than I'd ever seen or heard him. "Today my Kala was blue, blue as the deep blue sea," he half-sang, "and I feel like a bassoon up to its neck in French wine, all choked up and tears of sadness sliding down my long face," then, scarcely drawing breath, "Oh, oh, oh, my Kala's gone for a walk and hasn't come back when she said she would, and I feel like the roof of the timpani torn through by a beautiful bird shot from the sky," and "Now, today, my Kala only paid me glancing attention, and I feel like the third-chair violinist, some street thug poured cold porridge through the sound hole of my violin when I wasn't looking."

But it was Kala herself who discovered what work Vienna was doing in the darkroom those weeks. On the night of April 9 she came to my room at about 3:00 a.m., woke me up, and said, "Peter, you must come see this. Wake up, Peter. Now."

I got dressed and followed Kala next door. I waited at the bottom of the stairs while Kala made sure that Vienna was still in the darkroom. We then proceeded upstairs and into Vienna's room. Kala lit a candle. "Life's taken an unusual turn for my poor husband," she said. She then raised the candle, moving it along the wall to the left of Vienna's bed. "Eskimo and police confabulations," she said.

"Sssshhh, just let me look."

Tacked in rows were copies of the police portraits. And in each one was an uninvited guest. "Recognize them?" Kala said. It sounded as if she was near to crying.

"Of course I do," I said. "Here, behind Sergeant Maitlin—I don't remember how to pronounce her name. Naniaqueeit."

"Mary."

"And there's Moses Nuqac. And there's Mary Nuqac."

"Last one on the left, Driscoll Petchey, floating above that policeman's face, Peter. As you can see, my husband's labored long hours at this."

"He's done it skillfully, too."

"I wish each and every one of those people would have come back on their own. Made themselves *seen*."

Given the depth of feeling I heard in her voice, all I managed to say was "Well, that would be a lot to ask."

I couldn't take my eyes off these photographs. Some of the Eskimo faces were from the baptismal portraits Vienna had made. Others were from photographs taken at the site of the plane wreck. The faces or bodies floated pale at different angles to the policemen's shoulders and heads. "Manifold in their present phase of spirit manifestation," as Miss Houghton wrote.

"Peter, do you notice the way these poor Eskimo people seem to be whispering into the policemen's ears? The way they seem to be confiding. You know what Miss Houghton calls the appearance of actual conversation in a spirit photograph?"

"I'm afraid I don't recall."

"*Confabulating*. She calls it *confabulating*. Now, that's a word that seems somewhat stuck in another century, doesn't it? To me it does. It's an antique word. It's a nice word, though. I've always liked it."

Kala studied the photographs a few moments.

"Did you read Miss Houghton's glossary definition of a *haunting* as I asked you to?" she said.

"I did read it. 'Never leaves a person peace of mind.'"

"*That's* what's happened to my husband."

"That—what? He can't get the Eskimo faces out of his mind? Or Petchey's face, either. Any of them. All of them, from the train wrecks, too?"

"Precisely."

"You're saying he's created spirit photographs to haunt himself."

"Yes."

"My guess is, then, he's gone nearly over the edge."

Then, at about 6:00 p.m. on April 15, I stepped into the dining room of the Haliburton House Inn to find Mrs. Sorrel sobbing at a table. I sat down next to her. "They've found my son, Freddy," she said. "He was living in squalor, they said. Living in squalor in a rooming house over in Dartmouth. They should have found him earlier—his picture in the newspaper was a good likeness, so they should have found him earlier. Had they found him earlier, he wouldn't've had time to live in squalor, would he?"

"That's true. Should I get you some tea?"

"Please."

I brought in tea and lemon for Mrs. Sorrel. "Where's everyone?" she said.

"I don't know."

"They might've seen me sitting here crying like a baby and got frightened off. Crying frightens off some people, you know."

"I believe Kala will be in for dinner soon. I haven't seen Vienna Linn much at all."

"Freddy had just a mattress in his rooming house."

"I'm sorry to hear that."

"Somebody talked him into the bad deed, Peter. He didn't do it on his own. Not entirely."

"I believe that."

"They told me Freddy called up Mrs. Raymond, the stenographer, and gave her a full confession yesterday. Telephoned her right at home. Imagine that. He asked her to write it down in advance. The police said that was a first. Leave it to my Freddy to come up with something new like that. And now he's signed the confession in person."

"This is very difficult news for you."

"I'm closing the dining room tonight. I'm just not up to it."

"Anyone would understand that."

"He—Freddy—was difficult from birth. I think he's the reason his father left me. A difficult man, plus a difficult son, adds up, doesn't it?"

"Sounds as if it did, Mrs. Sorrel. Have some tea."

"That's a good idea. I will."

She sipped her tea a moment.

"Mrs. Elroy, Freddy's landlady at the squalid hovel in Dartmouth where they found him, she has nerve," Mrs. Sorrel said. "The minute she heard Freddy was arrested, she took the ferry directly over and informed me he was a week behind on his rent."

"I hope you tossed her right out."

"What's owed is owed, and he's my son."

# THE HAUNTING OF L.

We looked at the registry. April 16, 1927. No one had signed in.

"Does this mean Vienna's here or not?" I said, half joking, but Kala was not amused.

We'd gone into the dining room at 7:00 a.m. Serving us breakfast, Mrs. Sorrel looked haggard. "Didn't sleep a wink," she said. "As you might well imagine. I saw Freddy in jail last night. Today's newspaper's to have his picture front page again. Miss Gordy Larkin's been around already this morning. I sent her away, but she'll of course be back. It's her job to be back, isn't it?"

"Have you seen Mr. Linn?" Kala said. She and I had had a nearly sleepless night together as well.

"I'd think he'd be in the darkroom, wouldn't you?" Mrs. Sorrel said.

"Possibly," Kala said.

"Starting around 3:00 this morning, I made muffins."

"We'd love some," Kala said.

Mrs. Sorrel went into the kitchen. "Go look, please," Kala said. "See if he's there."

I walked past Mrs. Sorrel at her oven, into the darkroom, shutting the door behind me. I lit two candles. I didn't expect Vienna to be there and he wasn't. The radio was on. I turned it off. Hanging in a row along the stretched twine were more sham spirit pictures. Vienna had been hard at work. Some of the photographs were less accomplished than others. Several had bodies or faces of people obviously killed in train wrecks years ago floating above the faces of Halifax policemen. And there were more depicting Moses and Mary Nuqac, Driscoll Petchey, Mary Naniaqueeit. Vienna had tried his hand at a few captions. A note attached to one read: *Officer Caleb Brice Receives a Guest*—the guest being Mary Nuqac. That particular photograph was off-kilter. It had watery undulations mixed with smudges down the left side and at the bottom. Though it was not without a certain eeriness all the same. But, technically, it was a failure. In fact, I thought that the most successful one depicted Driscoll Petchey, bright-eyed, very much alive, an almost comically grisly sneer on his face.

Anyway, there was Driscoll's face, neck, and barely the top of his shoulders, tilted to the right at about a 45-degree angle, like a macabre carnival balloon that had followed Officer Brice to the Haliburton House Inn. I suddenly remembered Driscoll had said to Vienna, "I'm an authentic type." I needed some air.

I was about to leave the darkroom when I saw an envelope marked *P. Duvett* (he was whittling away at me as well, I thought) nailed to the door. I immediately read the contents:

Duvett,

I'll be found out, but I've in one way or another always been found out, just never caught up with so inevitably as I soon will be, through the agency of Freddy Sorrel's inevitably turning evidence against me. He *will*, I guarantee it, turn evidence against me.

Over a whiskey Maitlin shrugged off any hint of my complicity in the matter, but I've learned even in our brief acquaintance that he is a thorough man, police work assures his meaning in life, his serious police work. Maitlin will eventually look past Freddy's ravings to find that Freddy was my hireling.

I'm just now musing, what a remarkable day, wasn't it, when the money actually arrived from Mr. Heur? It is quite easy to imagine *Esquimaux Souls Risen from Aeroplane Wreck* as being the brightest star in his constellation! He may well ask for an audience with the Archbishop of Canterbury! He will ask for an audience with God!

Duvett, here is the most ruinous thing I can offer, which I'm certain you will find consistent not only with my nature but with what—through your cuckoldry—you have brought on yourself: I give you and Kala my blessing. I bless your child.

As my wedding gift I suggest a collaboration, Duvett. A way to honor my life. And by doing so, privately give you the opportunity to appease your guilt at the sin you've committed. Obviously I am not one for moral instruction. Besides, it is too late for redemption, and redemption, mind you, is quite unwanted by me, anyway. I am, as Kala's beloved Miss Houghton would fully agree, already "haunted." You cannot begin to imagine, Duvett, what demons occupy my mind, and they each and every one have a mortal's name. Those many faces float in front of my eyes day and night. They lay siege.

But understand, Duvett, I may be considered evil—an evil man—(and certainly Kala truly must consider me this) not because I was somehow born that way, but because I did not refuse evil's unusual rewards. The power over people's lives? Hardly. The money from Radin Heur? Again, hardly. No: it was that I was afforded the opportunity by Radin Heur to follow my discovered passion. Look in *The Unclad Spirit*, page 444. Houghton writes of a man put up to public ridicule because of his belief in the communications possible in séances. He was a man who sponsored séances. (I consider séances utter nonsense, but nonetheless . . .) Miss Houghton calls the local magistrate who sentenced this man to a short stay in prison *evil*. "This man was no criminal. He had no association with evil of any sort. Now, of course, there are men who would be criminals simply because evil represents their moral system, their philosophy, and that they would pursue their calling just as fanatically as others would pursue the good."

The latter defines me perfectly, Duvett. I pursued

my calling, just as Kala, when she is most pure in intention, pursues good.

(As if there is good in this life—)

Therefore, Kala's and my union will be made permanent by this connection, a connection of opposites, and there simply is nothing you can do about it.

Perhaps in time, and tutored by Kala in her own fashion, you will be able to comprehend at least part of what I've told you here. I do not expect you to be able to completely understand it, Duvett, you being of limited imagination. You will, I predict, forever be in the employ of someone else's imagination—terrible fate—but do try to put that employment to good use.

This very night at 3:00 a.m. I stood outside the door of your room, where you lay in bed with my wife. My beautiful wife—no longer my wife. The door of a man with a talent for captions, if nothing else.

And standing outside your door, I was carrying a revolver and had intentions. But then another plan replaced that one.

That is how it has gone for years now, new plans suddenly replacing old plans. I'm quite used to it.

Therefore, Duvett, I offer this information:

Near the corner of Barrington and Prince Streets there is the site of the new store called Eatons. Birney Car #138 heads south along that route. It is the only Birney in Halifax painted white, and written in bold black letters above the windows is SLOW DOWN— SAVE A LIFE. Below the windows is written: CITY

STREETS MAKE POOR SPEEDWAYS—DRIVE WITH
CARE—PREVENT ACCIDENTS. How the city of
Halifax takes care of its citizens! Yet there is so often in
spring much fog in the early morning, the orange Birney Cars are much easier to see, whereas this white
one, I wonder . . .

Either on the first run of the morning of April 27,
or possibly April 28, I shall be on car #138. Arrangements will be made. You are now apprised. My camera
is in the darkroom.

Perhaps you recall Mr. Heur's address: 28 Eccleston
Place/London, England.

L.

P.S. You might try and contact Roxy Rothafel to deliver my eulogy at my pauper's funeral.

I stuffed the letter in my pocket and went back to the
breakfast table, sat down, shrugged, said to Kala, "He's not
there." I saw that Mrs. Sorrel had set out a basket of muffins.

"It took a long time to discover that, didn't it?"

"There were new photographs he'd developed. I was
looking at them."

"What sort of photographs?"

"Photographs of the same sort."

The evening *Herald* carried the headline LOCAL MAN
CONFESSES TO MURDER OF BRITISH CITIZEN;
Freddy's picture was front page center. The article was writ-

ten by Gordy Larkin, now obviously promoted to Features. Harp was described as "a family man visiting Halifax on business who, according to Inspector Destouches of the Halifax police, was here to see the sights and procure the services of Mr. Vienna Linn, an expert portraitist, on behalf of a client in London. Mr. Linn has of late taken the official portraits of our Halifax police officers and generously given to the Police Benevolent Fund and other charities." Each paragraph contained a fact, but the truth was entirely bypassed.

Mrs. Sorrel was not in the Haliburton House Inn to serve dinner. She was visiting Freddy in jail. Kala prepared steaks and potatoes. We sat for dinner together at seven o'clock.

"No word from Vienna, then?" she said.

"I haven't seen him."

"Maybe the police have him."

"We'd know of it, don't you think?"

"Peter, we do agree, don't we— I mean, we're in complete agreement, aren't we: Vienna simply did not want to share the money with David Harp. He hired Freddy. Freddy was hired."

"We're in agreement."

Kala ate in silence a few moments, then said, "I'd like to live in London."

"London?"

"Where you were raised. And I want you to walk with me and tell me everything you remember of when you were raised there. Promise me you'll do that."

"I promise. Did you like London when you lived there?"

"I lived there for two months and seldom left the hotel. I sat in parks."

"I have no employment. How can we afford to travel? To get set up?"

"I've taken steps in that direction."

"What sort of steps?"

"I was hoping to tell you later."

"Tell me now. Please."

"I'd prefer to tell you later."

"Kala—"

"I have no money, you see. Back to being destitute."

"What *steps*?"

"You're to be my husband and I can tell you anything and you'll forgive me?"

"To my mind, you've done nothing that needs forgiving. What steps?"

Kala shifted her chair back from the table a short way. She stared at her hands, fingers locked together on her lap. "I sold Sergeant Maitlin the photographs of you and me in bed together. In the Churchill Hotel. Maitlin approached me, told me he'd seen them, that Vienna kept them in the darkroom. Vienna had shown them to Maitlin. Apparently to demonstrate what a sane man he was, not to have strangled you and me both, despite being so humiliated.

"Please don't make me go into details here, Peter. Suffice it to say, I've sold the photographs to Maitlin. He can't share them, because what kind of policeman would own such things—and he signed a letter of receipt. I made him. It was my one guarantee he'd keep them private." Kala didn't look at me at all. "He paid a good amount."

"How much?"

"Two hundred fifty dollars. It's enough to begin at a hotel at least."

"I can't say I'm pleased."

"Don't look upon me with kindness or pity, *either* one."

"I'm just taking in what you've told me, is all."

"I've done a low thing—for practical reasons. To help with our passage to England, I've included you in a low thing."

I wanted to scream, I knew about the plane wreck in advance and did nothing about it! Or I might have settled for a lesser confession: Vienna destroyed the newspaper clippings, the letters! Or I could have shown her the letter Vienna left for me in the darkroom. But at this moment, what possible good could come from any of it?

"I've taken the radio from the darkroom," I said, "and brought it to the annex."

"Do you think we can get London on it? I'd like to hear our future home."

"Let's just lie in bed and listen to whatever's allowed us to hear. It's unpredictable, what channels will come in and what channels won't. There're better radios Vienna could've bought."

Kala took my hands in hers. "I've done a low thing, Peter. I'm sorry."

"We'll listen to the radio and try not to think."

I fought off a cold and slight fever in bed all the next day. That morning Kala had set me up with a water pitcher, compress, bottle of Goldwasser, then gone in for breakfast. "I haven't touched a drop," she said. "Proud of me?" Every few hours I'd go next door, boil a saucepan of water, set the pan on a trivet on a table, tent a towel over my head, and breathe the steam, clearing my throat and chest and nose. Late in the morning Kala looked in on me. When sick I prefer to be left alone, and told her as much. "Well, I just learned something about you for the future, didn't I?" she said.

"It's just a cold, I think."

"How will I know if it gets worse if I leave you alone?"

"You'll see me lying facedown out on Morris Street."

"Fair enough. I'll look on the sidewalk every now and then."

Kala left the room. All day she was off somewhere, reading in her room, doing who knows what. Mid-afternoon she told me she'd met a new tenant, a Mr. Andrew Kline, from Toronto. "He told Mrs. Sorrel he had bought, sight unseen through his lawyers, the Biograph Cinema. 'It'll be playing nothing but talkies from now on,' he said. And that he's staying at the Haliburton House Inn just until he can find a house to buy."

"How does he seem?"

"Nice enough. Pleasant."

"Which room is he in?"

"Next door to Vienna's—formerly."

"Good for Mrs. Sorrel, to have some money coming in."

"Legal fees for Freddy. Maybe she has a little savings."

"Did you find out when the trial begins?"

"Wednesday, next week. You and I might be asked to

testify. Mrs. Sorrel told me that. We'd each be a 'character witness,' it's called."

"We don't want to do that, Kala. We want to leave Canada."

"It's illegal, Peter. Not to testify if asked."

"They won't call us back from London, I bet. Can we study the shipping page? Let's get the next possible steamer out."

"I was going to sit Mrs. Sorrel down and tell her I'm divorcing Vienna. Tell her only as much as necessary. Ask if you and I might be married in the Haliburton House Inn. That may allow her to feel our untoward behavior right under her eyes is sanctioned, finally. That she can be the witness, and we'll get a clergyman to marry us and put things right, and we'd like to stay friends. But then it came to me, if Vienna's left Halifax—say he's *fled*, Peter—he can't sign divorce papers. So the divorce can't be legal, anyway. So I spared Mrs. Sorrel the news. She's got enough on her mind."

"You're right, of course. But how can we be married, then?"

"After a while, the marriage can be annulled," Kala said. "It's called an annulment. It's just dissolved."

"That's second best, I suppose."

"Comes to the same good end, though, doesn't it?"

"Freddy's situation's broken Mrs. Sorrel right in half," I said. "Anybody can see that."

"The trial will be hell on her."

"She's alone in it. Can we spare anything for her?"

"I've rifled through Vienna's things," Kala said. "I've come up with $30. And how about some of what Maitlin paid me, too?"

"Let's give some of that to Mrs. Sorrel. Put our guilt to good use, as Miss Houghton said."

"You're right, she did say that, didn't she. In Chapter 19, I believe. Yes, I'm sure of it. Nineteen."

In the morning I felt neither better nor worse. I got dressed, went next door. I went into the darkroom, took up Vienna's tripod camera and two plates, and left the Haliburton House Inn for the corner of Barrington and Prince Streets. Fog was thick, light swirled near the street-lamp globes, I could hear gulls but couldn't see them. I set up the camera. It wasn't more than ten or twelve minutes before I heard the Birney Car. When it ran directly past, I saw the driver. He was looking straight ahead. He applied the brakes, the Birney rattled to a stop. As best I could tell, there were four passengers, two women seated and Vienna Linn, who stood staring out the rear window. He simply nodded at me, as if to say, I knew you'd be here. Standing next to Vienna, also looking at me, was Sergeant Maitlin. The Birney continued on without incident. I was startled as if from a trance by a voice: "How much do you charge?"

Shafts of sunlight came slantwise through the thinning fog. I was standing there, out on Barrington Street, like a vendor. "Didn't mean to startle you, eh." I saw it was one of the policemen who'd come in for a portrait. I didn't recall his name. He wasn't one whom Vienna had included in a sham spirit photograph, I knew that much. "You're the assistant, aren't you?" he said. "Have you been moonlighting all night out here?" He did the laughing for both of us. "A little extra income's always needed, eh?"

"No, I haven't been out here very long," I said.

"What's your fee, then?"

"Five dollars."

"That's steep, on my salary."

"Okay, two dollars."

"Where do you want me to stand?"

"I'll need a dollar in advance. You can pay me the rest when I deliver the portrait."

"Okay." He handed me a dollar bill.

"How about with Eatons behind you?"

The young policeman looked behind him, made sure Eatons Department Store would appear over his left shoulder (I suddenly envisioned Mary Nuqac's face floating there, had to blink it away), turned back, fixed a courteous smile on his face. "Ready," he said. I took the picture. "Bring it down to the station, then," he said. We shook hands. He reached into his pocket, took out two tickets. "Police Benevolent Fund dance," he said. "It's tonight, the new Lord Nelson ballroom. It's a charity."

"I'm not much for dancing."

"Take them for free. Nobody'll make you dance. There'll be food and drink. And it's a good time for a good cause. You're working hard out here, early in the morning. Plying your trade—same as me. I see you moping in the corner tonight, I'll let you dance with my wife. One dance only, mind you." He winked, turned around, and walked down Prince Street.

"A dance," Kala said. "How nice."

I'd set the tickets on my bureau, and when Kala knocked and let herself in, she saw them first thing.

"I was out getting some air and I ran into one of the policemen who'd had his portrait taken. We got to talking."

"Out for a walk, Peter? None too smart, what with your health, was it? Did you have breakfast?"

"No, can we have it together?"

"I'll have to cook again, no doubt. Mrs. Sorrel's at the jail. I saw her leaving. She apologized, poor thing. She said she's been spit and jeered at on the street."

"Simple eggs and toast would be much appreciated."

"I can manage that. What time is the dance, by the way?"

"Eight o'clock."

"The opportunity to dance with all those men in uniform— To dance with everyone but my husband. Who could pass it up?"

"I don't find that funny."

"I didn't intend it to be."

"I'll take you to the dance."

"I can buy my own ticket, you know."

"These were free."

"How nice."

"It's at the new Lord Nelson Hotel."

"A dance amidst all this grimness."

"It's for a good cause."

Next door, Kala went into the kitchen and prepared toast

and eggs, set our breakfast on the windowside table. "I've got the shipping page here," she said, setting it down between us. "The S.S. *Haverford* leaves in two days, the *Saturnia* in a week. Then, in nine days, the *Oscar*—it's Scandinavian. I inquired—there's passage available on all of them, Peter. Our finances would allow third-class steerage, possibly second. But I'm told we'd be comfortable. It's a ten-day crossing, give or take, depending on the weather."

"If you want to go to London, then I want that, too."

"Getting married by a ship's captain, that's romantical."

"Married, well . . ."

"You're right. No divorce yet, is there? No annulment yet—"

"Something might work out."

"Yes, a little optimism might be in order. I'll picture myself as a new bride, no matter when it happens. How's that? All I allow myself, really, is to be optimistic one time a day."

"Now *I've* learned something about you for the future, too."

"—optimistic once a day. Better than not at all."

"As for the dance, Kala, you may be disappointed. I'm flat-footed."

"I took lessons as a young lady. I learned steps by heart. I was very good. I'll teach you."

"All right."

"Yes, just sign my dance card and wait in line."


The Lord Nelson's lobby had an enormous chandelier, large sofas and chairs in various configurations, a magazine stand next to the registration counter. The caged doors of the electric lift opened, passengers stepped out, others stepped in, the doors closed, solicitous bellhops were everywhere. Just outside the ballroom, two policemen sat at a table and sold tickets. At either end of the table was a wooden box like a ballot box; each had a piece of paper taped to it: DONATIONS. Kala and I showed our tickets and went in. Things were lively. The rafter beams were festooned with white, black, and red crepe paper banners. There was a ten-piece band on the elevated bandstand, the musicians and bandleader wore tuxedos. They were playing a tune I thought I'd heard on the radio, the trombone was featured. Couples were on the dance floor. The singer, a man in his thirties who had a pudgy face and slicked-back hair, bent over the microphone on its stand like a dance partner and half-sang, half-shouted, "Swing, swing, swing!"

Young women and girls were sitting on wooden slat chairs along the walls; young men, many of them sullen or bewildered-looking in their church suits, huddled in groups, punching each other's shoulders or staring at the floor, talking amongst themselves. The policemen were all in uniform; there must've been over a hundred.

Kala was wearing a dark red dress, with a pattern of big black flowers on it, a black velvet vest, black shoes. She had on the cameo necklace, too. She'd braided her hair up in back. She looked beautiful. I wore my same tweed suit, shoes polished for the occasion.

"Don't be nervous," she whispered. "But there's Sergeant Maitlin over by the refreshments. Don't let him ruin our good time, all right?" Kala led me out onto the dance floor. I felt that I was stumbling about, but she held me close and we danced to a slow tune, which was fine with both of us. "This is nice," she said. The music stopped, but the band picked right up with another romantically slow tune. "You know, Peter, here in Halifax, I doubt women ask men to dance," she said, and walked right up to a policeman, no wife in sight, said something to him, and he immediately obliged. I stood close to a group of five or six sullen boys and watched. The boys watched Kala, too, made lewd remarks, knowing I was listening.

Kala was a good dancer. She moved gracefully. I watched as she chose policeman after policeman, seven, eight dances' worth. Finally, she walked over to me. "All that's over and done with now," she said. "I feel as if I just made up for those years with my husband. Danceless years, I mean. I whispered something nice to each of the officers. I could tell it was appreciated."

"Can we dance together now, or should we go home, or should just I go home?"

"Jealous boy—"

"You did warn me, didn't you?"

"It's a benevolent cause. I felt benevolent is all."

It was another of the slower tunes. The singer showed dramatic reverence for the lyrics, leaned forward as if singing privately to a particular couple close to the bandstand. The couple stopped to listen, holding each other, swaying. The dance floor was crowded, Kala and I danced near the wide doorway. Over her shoulder I could see into the lobby. Near the electric lifts I saw two men standing close to each other. They appeared to be in a heated discussion of some sort. Finally, I saw that it was Vienna Linn and Sergeant Maitlin.

Maitlin then shoved Vienna in the chest; Vienna reeled backward, slamming up against the wall between the two lifts. Vienna then pushed past Maitlin and walked toward the front door of the hotel. It was the last I saw of him that night.

Noticing my attentions were elsewhere, Kala said, "Peter dear, you should be staring into my eyes. Like in the cinema."

"I'm sorry."

"They don't teach you that when you take lessons. It should come naturally."

She was smiling warmly, having a good time. She closed her eyes and pressed herself against me. I stepped back slightly. We stopped dancing. "Don't worry, Peter," she said. "You can't damage me, dancing like this. You can't harm anything." We embraced, danced awkwardly a moment. With a discreet motion she situated my right hand flat on her belly. And then we continued on like the other couples.

We left the Lord Nelson Hotel around midnight; a little after, maybe. In my room we made love right away. We did not even make it to the bed. We were in the overstuffed chair in front of the fireplace. When we finally did lie in bed together, it was nearly 3:00 a.m. "I saw Vienna tonight," Kala said. "Just a fleeting glimpse. It wasn't my imagination. Definitely not. It was Vienna."

We lay there not talking; by diminishing firelight, I saw the flung shapes of our clothes strewn on the floor. That sight caused me no small exhilaration.

"Why would he show up there?" Kala said.

"He provided a large donation, didn't he? He gave a lot

of money to the police charity, didn't he? He gave the
money, that's the good deed. No doubt he saw us dancing
together—that's the punishment."

"He saw the *three* of us dancing together." Kala drew my
hand to her belly. I kissed both of her hands, kissed her belly;
she turned and I held her as we faced the same direction, toward the fireplace. "I should take my own advice," she said.
"Possibly ceaseless prayer will make him finally leave Halifax."

She slept; I didn't.

B efore dawn I left Kala in bed, took Vienna's camera from
the darkroom, and returned to Prince and Barrington.
The fog was even thicker than on the previous morning.
There was a damp chill in the air. I set up the camera. I
hoped that yesterday's officer was not punctual on his morning rounds. The streets were empty, at least as far as I could
see. I slid in the plate.

I heard Birney Car #138 before I saw it. But now it
rounded the corner, and at one point seemed to disappear in
a thicket of fog, then emerge again, its lights diffused. It was
about thirty meters away now. There was sparking along the
overhead wire and the track. If Vienna was to be believed, he
was about to shut himself of this life. I stood there, my legs
splayed slightly wider apart than the tripod's.

Birney Car #138 was beautiful in its own way, I thought,
and then my heart felt as if it exploded as the Birney did.

Contained as the explosion was, even muffled, it seemed,
by fog, still it threw me backward to the pavement. Glass

flew, metal screeched, and the Birney slowed, friction sparks under the wheels. The Birney stopped almost directly in front of me. I saw the driver slumped over the wheel. He had managed to brake the car, then blacked out, or was dead—I hoped not that. I saw an elderly woman step out, dazed, clutching her raincoat. Her forehead was bleeding a little. She didn't look terribly wounded, but she wobbled, then sat right down on the pavement. I lifted the camera into the Birney.

There were no other passengers besides Vienna. He had obviously sat near the explosives. He lay face up in the aisle, his face scorched on one side. His expression of severe annoyance I'd seen so often, that even in death it only looked familiar. His trouser leg and greatcoat were torn open. There wasn't in fact much blood to be seen. I noticed that the frame of his eyeglasses was somehow stuck in the roof, dangling, the lenses blown out.

There, in the aisle of broken glass, shreds of clothing, twisted metal seats, cold air sifting in, I set up the camera. I took the first photograph.

The driver's side door had been flung open; now a man rushed aboard to help the driver. As he leaned over the driver, I saw his mouth move. He then turned toward me. I realized that my ears were ringing. He had a contorted look of disgust, as he shouted words I could scarcely make out: *What are you doing? I need your help here!* The driver suddenly jerked upward, then fell again to the wheel.

I looked out through a broken window. On the pavement I saw yesterday's police officer running toward the elderly woman, who sat on the pavement. An ambulance pulled up;

even before it stopped, its front doors opened like wings with red crosses on them.

Two ambulance crew, dressed in white uniforms, rushed into the Birney and appeared to almost pry the driver from the wheel. They carried him out, laid him on a stretcher, and lifted him inside the ambulance. The siren pulsed in and out of my hearing as I observed one of the crew assisting the injured woman passenger to the ambulance's front seat. Finally, the ambulance moved off, navigating around a twisted bus seat in the middle of the street. The policeman stared after the ambulance.

I slid in a new plate. I took a second, then a third photograph. Alone with Vienna on the Birney Car, I took my time.

When I stepped from the Birney, the ringing in my ears gave way a bit. I met the policeman's eye. We looked at each other, like friends sharing the strangest possible moment. Maybe he thought, *Here we are again, out this early—and look at this!* I turned away from the wreckage. I heard a man's voice: "Are you from the *Herald*?"

Stunned by disbelief in the sitting room of the Haliburton House Inn at about six o'clock that evening, Kala sat with Mrs. Sorrel, the evening edition of the *Herald* on the table in front of them. The headline was:

ONE DEAD IN EXPLOSION ON BIRNEY #138
DRIVER AND ELDERLY WOMAN INJURED
Cause of accident as yet unknown

At 9:00 a.m. that morning I'd stood outside the *Herald* building and arranged with Gordy Larkin to have her deliver the photograph to Jarvis Moore.

Gordy was obliging, for which I was grateful. Early afternoon we met in the lobby of the Lord Nelson Hotel. She handed me $50. "Here's what you got paid," she said. "Look, they used your caption, too." She showed me a copy of the front page. Under the photograph it read, *Police Portraitist, Vienna Linn, Victim of Birney #138 Explosion.* I thought, What more can a caption tell of the truth?

"Thanks, Gordy," I said, putting the money in my pocket. "And thanks for having them not credit the photograph to me. It'll be our little secret, okay?"

"Fine with me," Gordy said.

"I won't forget what you did for me today."

"You said you might be going to London. Maybe you can buy me lunch there one day."

"Wouldn't that be something?"

"Horrible thing, that Birney Car. At least the driver lived, did you hear?"

"I'm glad to know that."

"I was thinking: Maybe your great love isn't completely nuts after all. If her husband did himself in, could be his mind wasn't right all along, eh? Maybe he did some of the things she said he'd done." She shrugged her shoulders. "Either way, Peter, I still think you fell in with dubious folks, my old friend. Dubious folks."

Except for bellhops, and a man selling candy and magazines, the lobby was empty of people. She leaned forward to kiss me goodbye, thought better of it, and we merely shook hands. She started to walk from the lobby, reached the big glass doors, stopped, turned around. "See you in London, then," she said.

Gordy walked back out to the street. I sat on a leather sofa in the lobby a good two hours, I think—until a bellhop said, "Sir, are you staying with us?" I went back to the Haliburton House Inn.

# VIEW OF KALA MURIE
## TAKING THE SEA AIR

It is May 25, 1927. I began writing this thirteen days ago, the evening Kala and I sailed aboard the Scandinavian-American liner *Oscar*, which will deliver us to London. The first ten days we had some weather. Tonight the sea is calm, the smokestack smoke meanders off, the upper deck lights of the liner slant out and reflect off the black water. The most recent word is that we are still four hours out of England.

If someone had taken ten thousand photographs of everything that has happened to Kala and me since September 1926, I could provide captions—but attempting to render it all, *that*, I'm afraid, is quite different! I'd write five, ten, even fifteen pages in notebooks I purchased at Springs All-Purpose, then stare out to sea. I'd get up from the table in the ship's library, walk on deck along the railing, study the seabirds, or get half hypnotized by the patterns of waves, glint of sun, or storm clouds building up. An hour or so drifted by. I'd go back into the library. I'd see the stewards hurrying past the door. I'd hear the clink of silverware and plates being set out in the dining room. Still, the pages accumulate.

There's been the almost constant cries of gulls—a sea passage is never without that, I suppose. I've worked through a dozen or more pencils. I admit I filched the pencils from Mrs. Sorrel's tiny office at the Haliburton House Inn. (Much cheaper than pen and ink, which you can purchase on board ship!) In these pages I may have unwittingly copied Walter Manning's style of writing in *The Strange Life of Mrs. J. Doyle*, a book I left in the sitting room at the Haliburton House Inn. I like to think that Mrs. Sorrel might one day enjoy reading it.

Our first week at sea Kala suffered "morning sickness" ("All day, really," she said), and I felt seasick now and then, though not nearly as badly as when I'd first traveled to Canada. We'd been settled into our modest third-class steerage only a night when Kala sought out the ship's captain, P. Grommyk, and asked him to perform our wedding ceremony. He agreed to it. My understanding is that unless there's a fugitive from the law making the request, it's simply the captain's duty. Grommyk seemed in a jovial mood, told us that on one London–New York passage a woman's jewelry was stolen from her first-class room. A few days later, Captain Grommyk was officiating at a wedding. Unbeknownst to the groom, over the past few days his fiancée had befriended the woman whose jewelry had been stolen and asked her to be the legal witness at the ceremony. When the groom took a wedding ring from his pocket and began to slide it on his bride's finger, her new friend cried out,

"Thief!" The groom spent the remainder of the journey in the brig. I complimented Grommyk on his story, then asked, "What happened to the bride?"

"I didn't care to know," Grommyk said. "Then, a year later, surprisingly, I welcomed both women onto my ship again. The witness was with her old husband, the bride with a different husband than the thief. Life is interesting."

"Captain Grommyk," Kala then said, "we've both been a little under the weather. We'd like to wait until we're feeling better to be married."

"Yes," Grommyk said, "that's best for everyone."

Back in our room Kala said, "We don't have wedding rings, Peter."

"I doubt they're required. Let's buy them in London."

"First thing, though. It has to be right away, promise?"

"Of course." I held Kala's hands in mine. "Where's your—"

"The ring Vienna gave me? I pawned it in Halifax. It wasn't exactly a big sacrifice, Peter. I just walked into the pawnshop on Water Street, said, 'How much for this ring?' The owner told me a sum. I said fine. It was the simplest transaction I'd had in a long, long time."

Kala then got into bed and stayed there until dinner.

I don't understand how all these birds get so far out to sea. There've been birds the entire length of our passage. I don't mean just seagulls—other kinds, too. Some of the children aboard ship toss them pieces of bread. The birds set up a loud squabble on deck or just off ship.

For the past three days Kala has enjoyed sitting in a deck chair, reading *The Unclad Spirit*, working on her lectures, talking with me, or simply looking at the sea and sky. Me, on the other hand, I've been writing. Writing, writing as if to beat the Devil. Kala sleeps hours in the deck chair. She's two or three times mentioned her concern at how the English spiritualists might receive her lectures. Once she mentioned a fear that Radin Heur might attend one. "There's little we can do about that," I said. "If a lecture's publicly offered."

Captain Grommyk wrote up the papers and married us in his stateroom at 8:00 p.m. on May 23. Kala and I dressed nicely for the occasion. The ceremony took only a minute or two. When Captain Grommyk said, "You may kiss the bride," Kala and I kissed, Grommyk said, "Very nice," then signed the papers. Grommyk's personal steward, a man named Olafson, who'd served as a witness, signed the papers, too, then opened a bottle of champagne that was kept on ice in a wooden bucket. Grommyk's toast was simple: "To the bride and groom." He was formal but his voice betrayed some emotion, which pleased us. Kala took the slightest sip; I drank my glass straight down, then finished her glass, too.

I need to mention here that we had packed but one steamer trunk. We'd arranged with Mrs. Sorrel to ship a few additional things off to us, once we had a London address. "I'll keep you up to date about Freddy, if that's all right," she said. It was a tearful departure from the Haliburton House Inn, a departure, though, without regret. To say the least.

In fact, other than clothes, a photograph of my mother, my father, and me standing together in London when I was ten, I'd brought with me only Vienna's tripod camera. Though it carried with it certain obvious, terrible associations, still, it was a finely made, expensive camera. I was thinking exactly in such practical terms when, at the Haliburton House Inn, I wrapped the camera in a blanket, securing it with twine.

I'd brought the camera to Captain Grommyk's stateroom. After champagne, I quickly instructed Olafson how, in a rudimentary way, to take a photograph. I calibrated the distance and focus; the background would be Grommyk's desk with its exquisite globe, glass inkwell, ship's clock, polished cigar box—framed painting of his wife on the wall.

Kala and I stood in front of the desk. Olafson said, predictably, "Smile," then took our wedding picture.

"Very good, very good," Grommyk said. "Well then, things to attend to. Ever busy, ever busy." He politely ushered us out. I carried the camera along.

Kala and I stood at the railing awhile. We were bundled up now in overcoats. Kala had on two pairs of socks. White and darker birds flew across the horizon, tinged with the last of sunset. "Just follow us," Kala said, "you'll get to London." She giggled. "My oh my, Peter. No liquor all these days now—and the one small sip of champagne's gone to my head, I'm afraid. I'm speaking to seabirds!"

"You've liked seeing them, haven't you?"

"Very much."

"Maybe let's go down to our room now. What do you think?"

Kala kept looking out to sea.

"Captain Grommyk had a beautiful desk, did you notice?"

"I did notice it."

"I'd like to write a lecture at one like it someday."

Kala locked her arm in mine and we walked down to our room. Inside, we fell on the bed, laughing. Suddenly Kala said, "*New Bride Being Optimistic.*"

"I'm glad for that," I said.

For the next few hours the sea provided a convenient rocking motion for our wedding night.

When I later woke with a start, it was pitch dark in our room. I fumbled for my pocket watch, found it alongside my crumpled trousers, saw it was 4:30 a.m. What with the bed and steamer trunk, there was scarcely room for Kala and me, let alone for someone's presence not to be felt, even in the dark. Still, I said, "Kala?"

I'd woken violently, because I'd dreamed Vienna had appeared in our wedding photograph.

I checked the camera, the negative plate was gone. I threw on my clothes and hurried on deck. It was a cold, clear night, a number of pale stars, the slightest hint of dawn on the horizon. I stopped at the top of the iron stairs. Looking to my right, I didn't see anyone. When I turned to my left, there was Kala, leaning forward, one arm outstretched, the other clutching the railing. I quickly walked to her side. Immediately she turned and held on to me, as if for dear life. Her entire body convulsed with her taking a deep, sobbing breath. "We're both up here in the cold, Peter," she managed to say. "Did we want to be assured of the same thing?"

"Yes, we did," I said.

Over her shoulder I saw the negative plate eddy a moment, then disappear beneath the black water.